Crime Frontiers

By Crime Frontiers

Author's note

The characters and criminal events in this book are fictitious, and any resemblance to any event or actual person, living or dead is purely coincidental.

Dedication

Thank you to everyone who helped me in my life – whether you knew it or not.

CONTENTS

1. Playing with Monsters` 1

2. Crime Frontiers 11

3. Sandra's special little secret 15

4. Thorns and tumbling petals 22

5. The lengths that a piece of elastic will go to 26

6. New Horizons 30

7. Cellmates 34

8. it's not easy being a psychopath! 38

9. This one 59

10 Tales of "Trish-trash" Trisha 64

11. Chief Inspector Miles Rupert 86

12. Glittering horizons 93

13. A matter moral-indigestion 108

14. Fingertips across the ocean 113

15. Trying to get rid of a cold by sneezing it over someone else! 123

16. Rupert goes to school 127

17. The callings 138

18. Unrequited acquaintances 142

19. There's a bright-green elephant in the room 153

20. Better the angels you hardly know, than the devils who you think you do 162

21. A collection of motives 169

22. Nice one Harry! 175

23. Preparations 181

24. Obtaining the bait 185

25 Trisha goes to war 189

26. Planting the bait 198

27. The presentation 204

28. Guns and mirrors 214

29. Playing it by numbers 219

30. Slave Labour 229

31. Pinning courage down 244

32. Keeping track 247

33. Negotiation 253

34. "A Quiet Moment" 258

35. "Nice to meet, you!" 269

36. The Catacomb 277

37. Dangerous empathies 294

Final chapter. When (and beyond) 312

Other works by the author 323

Chapter 1
Playing with Monsters

From the Crime Frontiers hand book:

'According to the given circumstances, anyone can be big enough to be a bully! But the real measurement is ;will you be big enough to stop yourself from becoming one.(because apparently, size does really matter).'

According to my (laptop) Thesaurus, there are two definitions for a Monster. The first is "a fiend" the second is "an ogre." However, since the animated film versions of 'Shrek' appeared, it has of course, become very difficult to associate the name ogre with … very … nasty things! So, the definitions of a fiend are perhaps more applicable, and they are as follows: *an evil person, a brute, a beast, a cruel person, a wicked person or a wrongdoer!*

On the other hand, to the inspired mind and grubby heart of a criminal, the term "wrongdoer" can often seem a relative term. What may be seen as a minor wrong to one victim (or offender), may be felt as a major offence to another – indeed to the offender, it might even appear as a major moral right! As for the meaning of, moral, then we could spend the rest of the book, and many others, "moralizing" about such definitions, but we won't!

Instead, we will turn to an alternative meaning of 'wrong,' which for the purposes of this story (and by more than a mere coincidence) also embodies the essence of a moral wrong or crime; and its meaning is defined as a … *mistake!*

So returning to the definition of a monster, well then, obviously, a monster is a person who makes monstrous-mistakes! However, being who they are, it is in the uncaring nature of all monsters to randomly allot the destructive consequences of their monstrous-mistakes, to a wide variety of places and people! Unfortunately, human nature being what it is, specifically, allots that the majority of all this post-crime carnage, ends up on the doorsteps of the families, friends and neighbours of the various victims, of the various monsters!

On a more personal level, unless you (dear reader) have had experience of it, it can be difficult to either quantify or qualify the pervasive-cost of receiving such post-crime "parcels of purgatory!" Never the less, if you can imagine yourself waking up every day, and having to sign for a (monster) parcel of 2*crap* … then rest assured, you'll be on the way to qualifying the quality of crime! Now if you can further imagine what you'd feel like, if you also found that you had little choice, but to pay for the postage as well … then rest assured, you'll be even more qualified to quantify the cost! As for the cost to the direct victims of the murders, rapes, physical and sexual abuses, and other numerous daily crimes … well let's not open that package just yet!

Mind you! If a relative or friend, etc., of a victim, were somehow to slip into the prison cell of the monster who committed the crime (presuming the monster had been caught of course), then many (though not all) may well end up behaving like "monsters" themselves! And let's face it, who amongst us could (wholeheartedly) criticize them for behaving so?

After all, if you, dear reader, held such a (revenge? justice?) opportunity, in your quivering hands, would there be any other place or thing, that you would prefer to be or be doing … apart from the obvious that is?

The obvious "other" place of course, would be to be somehow "conjured" back to the crime scene itself – just before the crime was to be committed, and the "doing" would be to prevent the crime from happening at all, or at least trying to prevent it!

But, we are getting ahead of ourselves! Besides, real monsters are never born bad (nobody is), and although the incurably idealistic amongst us may well insist, "That we are all in our own way born *perfect!*" it is equally (and sadly) the case … that no one ever remains so! However, let us not bother with such fairy-tale-fantasies of revenge or last minute rescues, for as pleasurable as they

may be, they are only playing with the idea of facing up to a monster!
So, let us go to a real playground – and play with a real monster instead!

Of course it may be more dramatically exciting to ignore our young monster innocent years completely, and go straight onto his crimes. However, that would be editing, Steven, in the same way as he edits the value of other peoples' lives. So perhaps the most convenient, and certainly the safest (bland?) time for a short tour Steven's world, is probably when it and he were mere youngsters.

It is Steven's first day at his new school. It is playtime and 12-year-old Steven is standing friendless; like a leafless tree in the corner of playground. In an attempt to draw some much-needed courage, the young Steven briefly daydreams. He daydreams about leaving a wake of whispering wonderment, as he sweeps through a paparazzi packed and admiring cheering crowd, then takes a seat in his private balcony box at his, already Oscar nominated film premiere!

With the admiring crowd, swarming paparazzi (and of course his astonishingly beautiful girlfriend!) still inside the young Steven's head, he crosses the school playground, and then saunters up to a circle of friendly boys and girls, who in turn are talking and laughing together.

The young Steven doesn't want to be left outside the circle; instead, he wants to be in the centre of the circle, commanding attention and admiration! However, to Steven, the centre of attention also means a yawning, dark hole of ridicule – into which his lack of social skills may drag him into, at any given blunder! Unfortunately, young Steven is too inexperienced to understand that he cannot only find happiness in the centre of the circle; he could also find it in being part of the circle itself. In being part of the circle, the nasty hole in the centre can be full-filled!

It wasn't so much that Steven acted slightly strange, it had more to do with him just standing there, doing and saying nothing, even when some of the (nicer) boys and girls smiled at him!

Of course if Steven had of realized the mutual benefits of so-called, "small talk," he would have made some initial attempt at thawing the fast-forming social-ice-barrier, that he felt was rapidly freezing him out! For instance, he could have shared something that he had liked or had noticed. Unfortunately, the young Steven is too inexperienced to realize that the more you share with others, the more likely it is that others will want to share with you. He was also too inexperienced to note, that some of the other members of the group were like himself, awkwardly quiet.

However, Steven was no quitter, and so after standing there for five or so minutes, he bravely decided to try to break the ice – or at least thaw it a bit - by doing his "party piece!"

Since he was around six years old, Steven had found out that he could roughly mimic other people's voices. Although in truth he wasn't a natural smiles from his parents and friends.

Having picked his target, (the most talkative boy of the group), Steven launched into his impersonation, by repeating word for word what the boy had just said. It was a fair imitation, and his efforts gained quite a few smiles and grins from within the group. However, the boy Steven had just mimicked was far from pleased; he thought that Steven was trying to make fun of him!

'What do you think you're doing?' the boy demanded, none too politely!

Immediately all smiles within the group disappeared, and Steven began to blush profusely (as he felt himself being irresistibly drawn towards … the hole!).

'I'm sorry,' Steven started to apologize, 'I was just trying to …?'

'He was trying to sound like you,' one of the other children interjected.

To Steve's confusion, the boy Steven had tried to imitate stepped up, stared him down and demanded, 'Who do you think you are? What's your name anyway?'

'Steven,' Steven replied as he felt "the hole," not only rapidly deepening but in a curious way become more inviting!

'Well Steven!' the boy snarled, 'You don't sound like me! What do you want to sound like me for anyway, don't you have any personality of your own?' then stepping back, he pointed to Steven and laughed to the other children, then shouted out, 'Look everyone, he doesn't have any personality … he's a *nobody!*' Then turning to his audience as if he had just had a brain wave, he shouted out, 'Look everybody here's Steven Nobody!'

At that moment, to Steven, it felt that most if not all the group had instantly burst out with laughter! Steven meanwhile stood and said nothing, whilst vainly hoping that it would all die down and soon be forgotten. It was of course not forgotten, what is more, Steven was nicknamed "Nobody" by his school peers for the rest of his school days!

To make matters worse, the boy who originally nick-named him, went on to achieve success in both school athletics and in his academic exams – whilst Steven went onto develop his deep streak of jealousy, for anyone who achieved … success!

Back in the playground the highly embarrassed (and angry) Steven, was glad to see rain starting to fall and the teacher calling a premature end to playtime! Even at that late stage, it might have helped Steven to join the group if he had commented on the rain, so that the other children could have sheltered under his social-umbrella! However, even though the young Steven had thought of actually saying: *"Fuck this for a playtime, it's getting too much!"* he just didn't want to make such an unguarded offer. But then again, it may not have made the slightest bit of difference!

Regardless of the past, time flies, and we also need no longer dwell in interesting but safe places! Since his childhood, Steven has gradually created a complete and utter world of his own. Complete, in the sense, that he believes and feels that the emotional demands of others are an unnecessary intrusion to his world, and therefore are an "invasion" upon his world! And utter, in the sense, that he has become utterly mad, sad and …very… very, bad!

In Steven's world, there had been an increasing, but never the less self-attracting, conflict, between the "outer world" and "his world!" In the outer world, he has developed a ruthless crusade to save his daily life from invasion, by the pious demands of the bland (or the bland demands of the pious)! Whilst in contrast, in his world, Steven had nurtured an acute jealousy of anyone who has achieved prominence and success! Moreover, for the latter part of Steven's recent adult life, the moral-gravity of both worlds have been tugging at each other with an alarming and dangerously accelerating rate! Which all means, that it will not be very long, before both worlds become very … messy! It is a situation that would have both appalled and surprised his parents (had they still been alive), never the less, like Steven, we need not spend any more time with his parents.

It is now twenty years after the playground incident, and the now 32 year old Steven, stands friendless and umbrella-less, under a tree that is drip-drop-dripping with rain, in an (almost) deserted park.

In an attempt to draw in some much needed cowardliness (for by this time Steven is aware; that such a motivation is a key part of what he is about to attempt), Steven briefly thinks about how it could all change. He fantasies about leaving a wake of whispering wonderment; as he is swept through a horrified, jeering crowd, towards the security of his private courtroom dock, at his media studded premiere appearance, at the Central Criminal Courts of the world renowned, Old Bailey! Not that he wants to be caught, but if he is, then at least his achievements should bear the symbols, of … success!

Meanwhile, back in the almost deserted park, the lone woman, who is hurriedly walking toward the park gate, seems to be nervous as she draws near to Steven. It wasn't so much that Steven, looked strange, it was more that he just stood there, doing and saying nothing, even when she briefly smiled at him.

If … Steven had just smiled or maybe waved back, or just mockingly shrugged his shoulders at the rain that fell on the both of them, the woman would have probably smiled with him, and both would have gone on their ways; comforted by their shared moment of mutual helplessness. Sadly, however, Steven did not offer any such social umbrella, to either woman or himself.

Now, as Steven quickly moved out from beneath the tree, the plainly nervous woman quickened her pace even more! Maybe if, even at that late stage, Steven had noticed that the woman was wearing a navy-blue woollen jumper, he might have asked himself, "Who chose it and why?" However, sadly Steven did not ask such a question.

In fact, if Steven had asked such a question, he would have been partaking in a, Crime Frontier's exercise, called "The M.E. exercise."

M.E. is shorthand for Motivational Empathy, a Crime Frontier's recommended exercise, to encourage a real-time change of motivation, from potential offending into not offending. The exercise can be very useful because the "tools" of the exercise (i.e. the clothing, belongs or lifestyle of the intended victim) are there at the very time that the potential offender is either; in a real-time crime situation or fantasizing about one!).

Even as he moved out even further, maybe, if Steven had noticed that the now, plainly fearful woman, was wearing a matching sky-blue woolly hat and scarf, he might have asked himself, "Were they a birthday present from someone, or perhaps she bought it herself to look nice, and feel warm and protected, or even uplifted against the chill autumn wind?"

Maybe, if Steven had of wondered about such questions, he would have then gone on to wonder, "Who were the others in her life, were they good or bad people, warm or cold people?" But, Steven hardly noticed the woman's scarf, hat or jumper, and sadly, he didn't wonder about her friends, or her life.

In fact, Steven hardly noticed the woman at all; not the real woman, the full-length woman, with her hopes, her fears, her plans, her friends, her strengths, her vulnerabilities, her sadness's and of course her gladness's!

For if he had of reflected about these things, he might have also recognized many of his own hopes, fears, strengths and vulnerabilities – being mirrored back at himself! In such a last minute reflection, Steven might well have discovered some, empathy, for both the woman and himself, and even a mutual respect! However, the chasm between right and wrong is full of might-bees, and sadly, Steven did not ask such questions about the real woman, let alone about himself. All Steven visualized, as he rushed towards the now, terrified screaming woman, and was yet another reflection of his distorted self!

As with many victims of many such attacks, Ruth, the woman who Steven attacked did, in part, become a version of her attacker! After being attacked, Ruth also sank into an emotional-quagmire, of fear, self-doubt, self-delusion and paranoia, from which no sky-blue scarf could pull her.

Indeed, to those that knew her, Ruth seemed to be another person altogether. Although Ruth's family and friends did try their very best to, "Pull her out of it!" the Ruth of old became more and more, swallowed up! Yet in an attempt to protect her family and friends from being drawn into her deepening quagmire, Ruth began to desperately, shun her family and friends!

Ruth became a loner, and even her children could not help her – nor could she help them! At 9 years old, Reginald, Ruth's oldest child, became confused, angry and frightened about her, himself and the world!

Neither Ruth nor Reginald recovered from the pervasive effects of Steven's attack! Even at Reginald's school Open Day, he and Ruth just stood beside a small friendly crowd of parents, who were talking about things like: 'The old school seeming to be smaller!' and about how someone else's child had, "Done their very best!"

Nevertheless, neither Ruth nor Reginald joined in any of the "small talk," instead the two of them just stood beside each other, in the corner of playground, like a pair of leafless-trees, in an ever spreading leafless, forest!

As it happened, Steven had not paid much, detailed, attention to much of what had happened in the park that day, mainly because he was unusually drunk! Not that being drunk and violent was a totally new experience for Steven. However, he would not totally blame the "demon drink!"

As far as he was concerned (which was not that far), he would say that alcohol, just made him act more, reckless, than usual. Others may argue that, having a hair-trigger temper was one thing, but it was another matter entirely, when he knowingly put the safety-catch of sobriety, into the insolent position of "*fuck off!*"

However, even though the opinion of "others" had little influence on Steven's attitudes, the fact that he became careless and sloppy, when drunk, did cause him to give up drinking alcohol, some six months after the attack on Ruth.

What is more, his abstinence may go some way to explaining how, when it came to his Steven's first murder, he was not only stone cold sober, but he would be able to recall the whole incident, in detail, for many years to come.

Except that is, as far as Steven was concerned, the so-called "murder" of Mary and her "stupid dog" had been in fact, a clear case of self-defence!

He had been quite, innocently, walking through a lesser used part of Hampstead Heath on that summer filled afternoon. Suddenly and without any provocation on Steven's part, a young Alsatian dog, in spite of still being held by its lead, had started trying to attack Steven's ankles.

With his back to a ditch, Steven had tried to "shoo!" the hound away, but that only seemed to encourage it to attack even more! In the meantime, instead of pulling the hound back by its lead, the dog's owner, Mary, just shouted at it to stop!

Attempting to restrain himself, and the dog's attack, Steven tried using his right foot to forcefully, push, rather than kick, the "stupid" animal away. It was then that the dog bit Steven on his left ankle; and so severe was the bite, that it drew blood!

Then, to Steven's outraged disbelief, instead of trying to apologies for her dog's attack, the Mary woman not only verbally attacked Steven, but she also struck him across the face, with the other end of the dog lead – for kicking her dog!

The unwarranted attack was a far too much for Steven's sense of fair play. Therefore, in a fit of moral rage, he forcefully lashed out at the woman and the dog!

Steven's punches knocked "Wolfe" the dog unconscious immediately – but the floored Mary was only dazed! However, as confused as she was, Mary had already managed to pull her mobile phone out from the side pocket of her, olive green and white striped, jacket – and was clearly about to call the police!

It took Steven about three quarters of a second to realise, that he would be the one who would be, painted, as the "wrongdoer!" It took another three seconds to realise that he, the woman and the dog, were the only ones in that particular wooded area of the heath!

It then took another, surprisingly, long five minutes, to garrotte both of his assailants to death, using the dog's lead to do so – a task hampered by the fact that; whilst Steven was feverishly trying to strangle the struggling Mary, the dead weight of poor unconscious "Wolfe," was still "loyally" attached to the other end of his leash!

In truth and in spite of the distressing experience of being attacked by the woman (and her dog) Steven did feel remorseful about killing them! He therefore (even though he feared that he still might be suddenly discovered) took the time, to reverently place the dead dog onto the dead woman's chest. It was a gesture, Steven judged, that both the woman and her dog would have appreciated!

After making sure that the woman and the dog looked comparatively respectful, Steven then left the scene. He left the heath as quickly and unobtrusively as possible, taking the woman's gloves and the dog's lead with him. Steven took the items in order to avoid leaving any of his fingerprints or DNA. Although, as far the latter was concerned, Steven would be shocked to discover many years later (from the then Detective Sergeant, later to become,

Chief Inspector Miles Rupert), that his efforts at destroying all of the evidence had been flawed, by the "dogged" pursuit of a future cold-case forensics team! However, as it turned out, when he did eventually discover the flaw, Steven was far more consumed with achieving success – in his personal quest – to break the Crime Frontier's Code of Anonymity!

Chapter 2
CRIME FRONTIERS

It started from a joke, then it became serious, and now it is the law!

In essence, the law states: A Crime Frontiers Advisor-negotiator, working for the Crime Frontiers confidential Crime Advice-line, will never be successfully prosecuted (in any criminal or civil court), for refusing to divulge any information about any past or intended crime, which has been revealed during a confidential advice-line session.

To put the law into some perspective: the general aim of the Crime Frontiers website is to supply: "A free source of open information, for anyone who wishes to learn the real truth about a crime (as opposed to a fantasized version), so that he or she will be persuaded not to commit that crime."

However, Crime Frontiers also runs a free, confidential crime-line phone-in (the Crime Frontier's Advice-line). The help-line is for anyone who wishes to speak openly, and anonymously, about any crime that he or she has already committed – or is thinking about committing! It's somewhat similar to "Victim Support" except that it's for the victimizers!

On the reasoning behind offering anonymity to any potential criminal phoning the Crime Frontiers chat-line (no matter what their past or intended crimes), David Bell, the founder of Crime Frontiers, answer was:

"Whether you are offering or thinking of taking up such an offer, of anonymity for callers, refusing such an opportunity, is like refusing a condemned criminal a "last wish!" before he or she has committed their crime!'

Although Bell was the creator of the Crime Frontiers advice line itself could not fully work without its guaranteed, anonymity for all callers. The worldwide introduction of the mobile phone, particularly (though not necessarily) unregistered ones, was of great help too! Never the less, the controversial, Crime Frontiers Statuary Rights to Anonymity Bill, became law in England only after its founder David Bell, overcame a sometimes near manic legal and social opposition! As to the many arguments, both for and against having a Crime Frontier's style advice service for criminals (and or their concerned families, friends or neighbours etc.), well ... I'll leave that to your imagination and judgments ... dear reader!

Never the less, when asked how it was, that he even hoped to gain legal protection for the Crime Frontier's Code of Anonymity, David Bell quoted in a written reply, two of his favourite principles on conflict and success.

Bell's quote on conflict was, "Sometimes, the most fitting thing that can be slotted in between, an immovable obstacle and an unstoppable force, just happens to be a question mark!"

On the subject of success, Bell's answer was: " Charity may help you onto the foot of the ladder to success, and competition may well get you to the top, but sooner or later, we will need the willing hands of mutual-benefit; to move the dammed ladder to where we really need it!

P.S. Hope you enjoy the view!

David Bell.

However, probably the best (or at least the most poetically just) way to get a feeling for the Crime Frontiers chat-line; is in the way that Bell described its initial creation. Being a pursuer of poetic justice, Bell (unfortunately but again predictably) describes it in a partly poetical format.

The calling

He sits; he sits in a chair and stares, like a desperate man

risking all that he cares. He stares out beyond his bedroom window,
watching the lights of the town twinkle and glow, The lights seem to call him.
As to what they call him for ... he already knows. He sits as if in a waiting
chair; it's almost as if he's not quite all there, like an off-stage actor waiting for
his entrance cue, hoping his well-rehearsed lines will feel dramatic and new,
in a play he has already written – but others will improvise! Now his

audiences seem to call him. As to what they will call him . . . he already knows!

Bell then goes on to explain, 'The sitting man is not real person, but just a drawing of a man, I saw on a page in an old book, many years ago. The book was written long before the introduction of mobile phones or the internet. I think the book was about a real murderer. I was very young, and he was the first murderer I had "met," so to speak. Before that, I thought that murderers were like goblins, dragons or monsters . . . not really real! It was the sort of meeting that I would not forget!

On that page of the book, some joker had drawn a speech bubble coming out of the sitting man's mouth. In the bubble, the wag had written:

"Will I get a longer prison sentence if I commit murder on the Sabbath?"

Bell then continues: Maybe the man is still sitting there, waiting in between the yellowing pages, in some dusty-shelved bookshop. Of course, now that I am of a wiser age, I think I now know what he is really waiting for.

If I found that book now, I would photocopy the page and slip the new page in, as a sort of . . .latecomer! However, before doing so, I would draw a mobile phone; one of those that is a combined earpiece, the earpiece would already be connected into his ear. Coming directly out of the earpiece, I would draw a very large speech bubble, and inside the bubble, I would write:

'Hello you have reached Crime Frontiers; this is a confidential advice line for anyone who wishes to talk about any crime.'

Bell then goes onto to explain; What and why the sitting man would do next is open to debate, and would certainly require even more inserted pages. For example, it would not be easy being a Crime Frontiers Advisor-negotiator at times; knowing that you could prevent a crime by disclosing the villain's dastardly plot, but self-committing yourself not to do so; in the143 hope that the shared common risk, will lead to a shared common sense! But then again, what villain will risk all, by sharing a stage with someone who is not prepared to share some of the risk? Or to put it another way, what villain would share the stage with some who is prepared to share that risk?

Yours hopefully, David Bell.

Just over two years after its initial creation, the legally protected 'Crime Frontiers' confidential chat-line, along with its less confidential, open web site, went online. The chat-line offered a one to one service for those wanting a more personal contact, as well as a more, accessible service, for the considerable number of habitual criminals who have reading difficulties. Bell took the first call himself, the caller wanted to know; if she could be arrested for not telling the police, that her boyfriend had burgled her parent's flat!

However, (dearest reader) let us not bother with such details for now! Instead, let us leave Bell and his reasoning, and go to the larger theatre of this story. Though we will have to hurry, for the stage is set and the all the players are already back stage, calmly waiting or pacing to and fro, what is more, the audience is already . . . hushed!

"Quickly now … me thinks I hear the curtain rising, but there is still just time . . . to slip a late-comer in!"

Now the villain and hero are entering (the hero stage right – the villain stage left) and … Oh! Bye the way (dear reader), please make sure that your mobile phone is continually turned on, throughout this particular performance tonight!

Chapter 3

SANDRA'S SPECIAL LITTLE SECRET.

The time and place are cold. It is mid-winter in the USA. So far, Crime Frontiers has yet to be created in England, let alone introduced to America. Never the less, a future Advisor-Negotiator of the Crime Frontiers advice line, and one of the leading characters in this story, is about to embark on an important and personal "negotiation" of her own!

Sandra Lott, aged 22, is about to negotiate with her father. Having failed to gain his unconditional love as his daughter (and she really did try very hard!) she is about to "negotiate" for his unconditional surrender!

The specific place is the prison visitors' room, in the high-security-lifers' wing, the prison is situated Utah. Whenever the prison guards leave the outer doors of the visitor's entrance open, particularly on a cold day, the plasticized-glass partitions separating the prisoners from their visitors, would mist over, at face level, on the convict's side.

As his two visitors began to approach his booth, Danny Lott began to vigorously, wipe the condensation away, so that he would be able to see his two daughters, as clearly, as if there were no barriers between them and himself at all! When little three year old Debby Lott, saw what appeared to her to be, her daddy enthusiastically waving to her, Debby waved back as energetically as only three year olds do! At three ("and a little piece") years old, Debby was of course too young to appreciate the term, "Natural life" or even "Prison." As far as Debby's understanding went; her daddy was living in "A sort of very big cot . . . for grown-ups, who misbehave!"

Even so, and although she was glad to see her daddy, Debby did not really like the prison itself. After greeting her father as best as she could, through the barrier that separated her from the only parent she had left in the world, Debby became quiet. Never the less, Danny managed to fill up the next five minutes, by asking Debby about her time at her friend's recent birthday party.

Once Debby had finished her story of her adventures, Danny then asked Sandra, Debby's older sister, about everyone's health and wellbeing. However, after a short while, Debby stood up on her bright orange, plastic, visitor's chair; looked at her daddy and then balancing forwards, she proudly began to trace with her forefinger, the letter *F* that was already scratched into the plastic glass.

At 22, Sandra, Danny's only other daughter, understood the term "Natural life" only too clearly, and by the time Debby's finger had reached the letter K of the scratched graffiti, Sandra took her little sister's finger and gave it a kiss!

'Why don't you go to Uncle John and Aunt Betsy, out in the waiting room next door, that way you can continue your game in your new lettering book, and I'll see you all very soon?' Sandra suggested.

For a moment, Debby looked uncertainly at her daddy, and then at her big sister, then she suddenly shouted and waved, 'Goodbye!' As she skipped away, Debby also gave an unabashed 'Goodbye!' to several surprised and amused incoming visitors, and a cheery wave to the watchful yet smiling guards. Then, as Debby swept through the open doors, she turned, and with a smiley, double-armed, goodbye wave to everyone; she disappeared as suddenly as a butterfly from a hospice ward!

To some of those left behind, on both sides of the visiting booths, the departure of Debby did indeed leave behind a feeling of saddened gratitude. Particularly for some of the lifers, who would in turn go back to their "cot," to count the seamless years until their own final release! To others, the departure of Debby merely allowed the numbing-dogma of prison existence, to make its legally prescribed return! For one or two others, who judged Debby's care-free attitude to be a blasphemous contempt, for the moral retribution of prison, her overdue exit came as a righteous blessing (presuming of course, that butterflies are capable of blasphemy!).

Meanwhile, back inside the visiting booth, Sandra sat and smiled rather stiffly at her father. However, as she moved forwards and spoke, her smile disappeared altogether.

'Uncle John and Aunt Betsy said, "That although they are still very angry at you, for killing mummy, they will still bring us up to visit you."

Danny immediately nodded his head in genuine gratitude for Aunt Betsy and Uncle John (not only for bringing his two daughters up to the prison – but also for volunteering to bring his virtually, parentless, daughters up!). He then opened his mouth to speak, but Sandra carried on in a matter of fact voice.

'But I told them it was, cool, because after today; we won't be visiting you again anyway … ever!'

Sandra then placed her hand flat onto the plastic screen; almost as if she were trying to close her father's half-open mouth, then she continued to speak, 'But you really don't need to look so worried Daddy!' at that point Sandra took her hand away and moved even closer to the partition. 'Because even though we won't ever be seeing each other again, we shall have a new … special little secret … that will keep us together for always!' With that said, Sandra dropped her hand altogether and leaned further forwards, then with a humourlessness smile she added, 'Just like, and perhaps even more than our, other, special little secret has kept us together, for all these years!'

As Sandra uttered the phrase "Special little secret," Danny Lott's memories were rapidly and irresistibly drawn into a vortex of similarly themed recollections; until they were flushed out amidst the memory of himself "fondling" Sandra, as a so called "Birthday present!" for her sixth birthday!

Sandra's sixth birthday had not been the first time that Danny Lott had sexually abused his daughter, nor was it the last. Never the less, we (dear reader) have no need to delve into the numbers or the descriptions of his actions, for like the abuses themselves, they have no worthwhile purpose!

However, by now, Danny's focus had been pulled back into the present by Sandra's next movements! Leaning forwards yet again, until her lips were almost brushing the barrier between her and the only parent she had left in the world, she spoke in an almost whisper.

'And our new special secret is, Daddy. That I know that you didn't really kill mummy! I know you didn't really kill her – because I did!'

At first, Danny Lott frowned, as if he thought that he had somehow misheard Sandra's half-whispered words. Never the less, and without waiting for a reply, Sandra continued, but now even her stiff smile had completely disappeared. The enormous change in Sandra's appearance was so startling, that Danny began to draw back from the barrier! Moreover, as he sat staring at his sneering daughter, he could feel his scalp and face suddenly grow cold; as blood rushed from his head in a futile bid, to anesthetize his brain from an unpredictable realisation – and horror!

However, Sandra had planned for this moment for many months, and she was not going to let her victim bleed-out, at least not until she had had, her last dregs of pleasure! As she saw her father's face pale, Sandra sat back, and although it was still more of a sneer, she managed a smile. For a while, Sandra patiently waited, until her father's face and composure regained some colour and focus. Then, as Danny started to speak, Sandra leaned forwards again and continued, in a low but distinct whisper.

'It was me, that stabbed her not you, you pathetic idiot! You were too drunk to do it anyway – even if you had of wanted to! I stabbed her when I came down and found you both laying there, in your usual parental, drunken comas, on the couch!'

By now, Danny sat limp and still opened mouthed as the onslaught continued. Only Sandra moved, as she again, inched closer to the barrier.

'It was me, not you that went to the kitchen and fetched the carving knife, you stupid idiot, and it was me that stabbed her! Do you know …' Sandra gleefully explained, whilst giving out a short noise that was somewhere in between a grunt and a laugh, '…she didn't even cry out when the knife went in! So I kept on stabbing her, just like she kept letting you stick, that, (at that point Sandra glanced down to Danny's groin, hidden beneath the shelf of the visiting cubical) into me, and pretending … she didn't really know! But I knew she knew!'

For a brief moment and in spite of what he had just been told by his daughter, when Sandra spontaneously slumped, gleefully, back into her chair, Danny Lott was suddenly reminded of her at one of their annual "Birthday Happy Meals." On all of her pre-teens birthdays, he had dutifully treated Sandra and her young friends, to a birthday-meal out!

However, as confused as he was, Danny was never the less instantly willing to poor out a cascade of righteous, even outraged, pleading for his wife's innocence; for as far as he knew, no one had any knowledge of the abuse of his daughter, except for himself – and Sandra of course!

Yet, the sudden sight of Sandra leaping violently forwards from her chair, instantly made Danny so fearful that she would smash through the barrier itself, that it silenced him! It also choked off his intended plea for his wife's innocence! To Danny's (partial) relief, Sandra again stopped millimetres away from the barrier, but as she continued to speak, she was snarling as much as she was sneering!

'When I knew for sure she was dead,' Sandra half whispered, 'I pulled you off of her, and wrapped your hand around the knife – it felt so good to do that – wrapping your hand around the knife! It was even better than stabbing you – which I had wanted to do in the first place! After that, . . .' Sandra explained, whilst miming innocence, '. . . I ran out screaming, until my screams brought the neighbours in.'

Sandra then seemed to relax completely as she leaned back and concluded, 'You should have seen the horror on their faces when they saw me covered in her blood – they thought I was the one that had been stabbed!' She then continued, relaxed but smug, 'I knew you wouldn't be able to remember when you eventually woke of course. You never could remember anything, when you got that drunk – everyone knew that! That's what gave me the idea in the first place! And after that, the hardest part was having to wait, for the right time!'

By now, Danny Lott's face had stopped tingling, and apart from his feet, which felt strangely hot, he just felt cold all over! Then Sandra slowly leaned forwards yet again, until her lips were once again almost brushing the barrier as she stated, 'But please don't worry, Daddy, because I will never admit to anyone, ever, that you really are innocent of that crime anyway!'

Then smiling once more, she added, 'So you see there's been no real need to worry at all! For now we both have an even, bigger, special, little secret that will bind us together for always . . . Daddy!'

Danny, still open mouthed, stared at his daughter as if she were some sort of stranger (which, in so many disrespects, she had become, both before and since her sixth birthday). It was the same disrespect that also prevented Danny from unconditionally loving her (after all, when all is said and done – it's not so easy to unconditionally love a stranger!).

However, Sandra was not in the mood to be dumbly, stared at! As she leaned forward, she continued with an ominous tone in her voice, 'And as for our other, special little secret . . . you don't have to worry about that, because I won't be telling the police or anybody about that either!' then she looked him up and down and added, 'I figure it is best kept between us, for now! Besides, as I understand it,' she said raising her voice, 'they don't take too kindly to that type of crime in here!'

When Danny did not even attempt to respond, Sandra leaned back slightly but lowered her voice again, 'So . . .I think it will be best if we both keep our secrets. . . just between us! Besides, if you tell anyone about what I've said, I'll just tell them that I was only telling you that, I wished I'd done it, not that I did!' then looking deep into her father eyes, Sandra "asked", 'So I think it's best that we agree, to keep our special little secrets very secret, don't you agree, Daddy?'

Having finished her "negotiation," Sandra rose from the bright orange visitor's chair, and then looked down into her father's face. For a briefest of moments, a shimmer of sadness rose up from the dark depths of her pupils, then just as quickly, it disappeared! Whether her sadness had been, snuffed out, by feelings of satisfied revenge or un-requited grief, was hard for even Sandra to tell!

Never the less, looking down at the letters crudely scratched into the plastic barrier, Sandra then leaned gently forwards and placed her own forefinger on the "F" then, very deliberately, she drew her finger along the letters of young Debby's unfinished word game.

Finally, after Sandra had traced out the *"Fuck"* she traced along the letters of the remaining word *"You!"* However, when she reached the, dot, of the exclamation mark, she emphasized it with a savage twist of her finger! She then twisted her upper body around, as if trying to read the words from the perspective of her father, and then she plainly stated, in her normal voice, 'It's such a shame you always saw everything, from the wrong way around!'

As she stood upright, and for a flicker of a moment, Sandra once again looked inwardly sad, as she stated, 'I just guess we were both … unlucky … daddy!'

As she finally turned to leave, Sandra casually added, 'By the way if you are expecting a "Father's Day!" card from me this year … then if I were you … I wouldn't hold your foul breath!'

By the time, Danny Lott had closed his mouth, Sandra had gone, and the condensation had returned to the plasticized glass partition, but by now, he saw no reason to wipe it away!

Chapter 4
THORNS AND TUMBLING PETALS

As soon as Sandra was outside of the prison, after the visit to her father, she gave a long sigh, and then she smiled to herself. It was a genuine relaxed smile, which did not diminish even as she looked up at the cold blanket of snow-filled clouds. Walking hurriedly to the waiting car, she got into the rear passenger seat alongside Debby, and gave her little sister a squirmy kiss and a big hug. Then securing her own and Debby's seat belt, they both opened Debby's wordbook and together they began to fill it in.

As the four of them left the prison behind, the atmosphere in the car was sombre rather than tense. However, when Debby asked why there were so many people in the prison, and Aunt Betsy replied, 'Well, Sugar, there are lots of high and mighty reasons why people commit crimes, Honey-pie! But when you pile all those high and mighty reasons up, against just a little ol' piece of common sense, then they don't mount up to a hill o' burnt-beans!' Then Aunt Betsy lifted her right leg, poked out her tongue and blew a short, but very loud, raspberry, and at that moment, everyone laughed out aloud, and began to relax a lot more!

On the long journey back home, Uncle John did the driving and Aunty Betsy gave her opinions (interlaced with occasional questions) on every subject from the weather prospects, to prison reform, and the correct way to pluck a chicken! Aunt Betsy and Uncle John were not usually so talkative; but it was a lengthy drive home, and the conversations helped to keep Uncle John from becoming too transfixed, by the long inter-state highways.

It was not long however, before Debby fell asleep in the back of the car, and Sandra began re-running the whole prison visit, detail by detail, through her mind. In truth, Sandra knew that what she had told, the police, about that dreadful day; was word for word – the truth! It was all true; including how she had sauntered into the cluttered, beer smelling, television room and beheld the horrendous scene before her. Just as it was also true, of how she then almost swooned with shock - as she saw her blood soaked dead mother's body, sandwiched, in between the crushing weight of her drunken comatose father, and the blood-drenched cushions of the floral patterned couch! It was all to the very last word, the total truth!

Just as it was also true, of how she had desperately pulled, slithered, and then finally hauled her unconscious father off her mother, and onto the blood-soaked floor. Furthermore, it was also true, that she then desperately hugged her mother's pitiful dead body, to her own, whilst pleading with her to, "Please come back Mom – please!"

It was all, totally, true!

This meant, of course, that what Sandra had just told her father, in the prison visitors' room: that it was she, and not him, who had stabbed her mother to death – was an absolute and total . . . lie!

It was all a total lie!

As for the lie itself? It was a lie that Sandra had shaped, honed and rehearsed over and over and over again, since the very first moment that she had thought of it! Ironically, that moment, had been during the church service for her mother's funeral! The lie; the lie had come to Sandra during the sermon, to which the priest had dedicated to the family (or to what was left of it!). The priest had been saying something about, "The blind leading the blind," when the lie's glimmering shape first formed within the depths of Sandra's mind.

However as the shimmering possibilities of the lie quickly grew and grew in clarity, so did Sandra's rising excitement! Suddenly, Sandra found that the feeling was so intense; that she had to use all of her will and self-discipline, to stop herself from uncontrollably giggling – out aloud! As the priest solemnly preached on, Sandra had to bow her head, deeper and deeper into her already trembling shoulders; knowing that without doubt, the merest 'gig…' of a giggle,' would streak along every arched-buttress and every arched-eyebrow, within that mourner filled church – and then detonate off every unforgiving wall!

For what seemed like a living purgatory, Sandra bit down her lower lip … until it bled! Then abruptly, it all got too much! All at once, and before she could do anything more to prevent it, Sandra found herself sobbing, bleeding and laughing, into the hot depths of her black, silk, handkerchief! Yet such was the blistering bliss, of such a "just" lie (so desperately snatched from the pyres of her grief), that in the end, Sandra hardly cared a dam, who saw her – or what they thought!

Even when she was finally outside, and in the cooling fresh air, Sandra still could not push the lie out of her mind! As the fellow mourners respectfully stepped forwards, to give their condolences, her mind was racing through the ways of getting her father to, somehow, believe the lie: that *she* had killed her mother, and that *he* was innocent, and wrongfully imprisoned – for *life!*

In truth, as much as she had often both loathed and loved her parents, and herself, Sandra would never have murdered either of them! From a young age Sandra knew; that the deliberate taking of someone's life, would be a far greater wrong, than even abuse of her own life by her father, (although there had been times when things had felt so bad, that such a drastic decision had come down to being a very-close-call; especially as Sandra became older!).

Never the less, as Sandra laid her head on her pillow that night, after her mother's funeral, she snuggled up to the lie for comfort! It would not replace the cruel absence of her mother or a fatherly love, but she had gotten used to latter from an early age – whatever love was? Of course, it would also mean that she would have to tell a lie; she would not only have to tell a lie, she would have to tell a massive lie, and that could be a big thorn in her side! For Sandra was not only against telling lies, she was also not that good at telling them!

However, the more she thought about it, then the more her sleep bound mind began to wrap itself around, the pristine plausibility of the lie, and its alluring reward! By the time she had finally closed her fluttering eyelids, the lie had begun to shine and bedazzle; then like an avenging angel - rising triumphantly from the shards of her shattered life - the lie at last became

Sandra's, uppermost . . . *desire!*

Now, many months later, and having finally planted the lie in her father's mind, Sandra eased back into the worn leather, rear seat of Uncle John and Aunt Betsy's car. As the car sped, far, far, away from the prison, Sandra began to feel the soporific warmth of dream-bearing sleep, seep into her limbs and thoughts. Moving with care, so as not to disturb the loudly snoring Debby, Sandra nestled into her corner of the rear seats and began to let all her worries, about truth and lies, blend together. Even so, as she huddle further down into her corner, she tried one more time to hold onto her thoughts. For Sandra knew that her father, who had genuinely testified that he could not remember, "A single damn thing!" about that fatal afternoon, was at least in that respect, almost certainly telling the truth!

Then, finally, Sandra let go of any decisions, as all of her doubts and fears fell from her mind, like frost-tipped petals tumbling from a hibernating rose, and leaving only one central truth! Moreover, that truth meant; that unless her father did somehow remember, then he would never really know, if it should be himself or his abused "deranged" daughter, who should be in prison for the brutal murder of his wife and her mother! However, if he did not remember, then the lie . . . would become his own special little "cellmate" for the rest of his un-natural, life!

Chapter 5
The lengths that a piece of elastic will go to

Of course, not all Crime Frontier's Advisor-Negotiators had such an unusual a childhood as Sandra! What is more, even if the crime-chat-line would have prevented Sandra's father from abusing her, it is of course a moot point. For a start, as mentioned, Crime Frontiers had not yet been created in England at that time, let alone in the USA, so neither Sandra nor her father knew of it. Never the less, Crime Frontiers eventual establishment in England, and its sometimes contentious view, of occasionally, employing Advisor-Negotiators who were also ex-offenders, was not only to play a massive part in Sandra's life, but in the lives of other too.

London, England

Andy Jones, a London born and bred man, was a street-wise and a basically, good-hearted, 30 year old. He had two convictions for TDA (taking and driving away) in his mid-teens. However, being street-wise, he had seen the writing on the wall, and had led a lawful life since.

As it happens, Andy was also a non-gambler. However, if you had of offered him good betting odds, on whether he would become a Crime Frontiers Advisor-Negotiator, he would have bet; his home, his market stall pitch and his winter over-coat, that there was, "No bleeding chance of that 'appening in a month of Bank 'oliday Sundays!"

Never the less, chance, by its very nature, never goes around, without at least one pack of Jokers, up all of its many sleeves!

However as we catch up to Andy, he is in the "The Feathers," his local pub, and he is passing the time with three of his friends.

'You know all you compulsive gamblers should carry an elastic band around wiv yer!' Andy stated to his long-time friend, Almost. Andy then unwrapped the elastic band from around the, rarely used, bunch of cocktail sticks from the bar. He then stretched the band to its very limit, and then aimed it, as if to fire it at the brass bell behind the bar – but he only let one end of band go! Smiling mischievously at Almost, Andy dangled the now limp elastic band in front of Almost's frowning face, and then unceremoniously let the limp band drop, into Almost's nearly empty beer glass, whilst stating.

'So you'll always be able to accurately measure yer future potential ... me 'ol mate!'

Andy, Tom, Sparkles and Almost, were at the bar of The Feathers, talking about Almost's gambling problem. Almost, who was a likeable giant of a man, had gotten his nickname by having once won over eight grand on the horses on a Monday afternoon! He then, almost, held onto it for a whole week; before he lost the lot back by the following Saturday night – and the only thing he managed to buy, was a very expensive leather coat that, almost, fitted him!

In truth, Andy was doing most of the talking and continued to do so, 'You see you lot, 'ave gotta' learn, me ol' mate, that yer never gonna be able to bribe, reality! But then again Almost, me ol' mate, you also gotta see, that trying to get rid of a bad habit; is like trying to get away wiv' picking yer own pocket . . . wiv' a pair of bleeding boxing gloves on!'

In response to Almost's look, Andy continued, 'Which means you gotta' stop pussy footing around, and take the pussy footing gloves off! So you can get a real grip on the situation! Which in your case means, accepting the fact that a Dingbat like your good self, can't do anything without a bit of outside 'elp? Outside that is, of that sealed collection box, you call yer brain!' With that said, Andy finished his pint of beer whilst Almost, in unison with Tom and Sparkles, nodded their solemn agreement.

'Which means,' Andy continued, placing his empty glass on the bar, 'Yer gotta' use a distraction – just as if yer really was picking someone's pocket! Except in your case, you're going to 'ave to put the distraction in your own 'ead!'

Seeing that Almost had so far followed his logic, Andy pressed his luck and followed through, 'In other words you need a challenging 'obby or sumink!

And let's face it, Almost, it ain't gonna' take a lot to challenge you, is it?'

Reaching into his hip pocket, Andy then took out a medium sized roll of money and removed a twenty-pound note. He then folded the note, with a "flourish," and then put the twenty pound note into Almost's shirt pocket, and then asked Almost to, 'Try picking it back out again – but without catching yourself doing it!'

After six and a half attempts, Almost, finally gave up!

'Ok! Sunshine, let's try this!' Andy reassuringly suggested. He then took the twenty-pound note out from Almost's shirt pocket, and then stuffed it into his own back pocket. Andy then took a clean napkin from the bar, folded the napkin, with a "flourish," put the napkin into Almost's top pocket, and then told Almost to try and pick the napkin out instead!

At Almost's first very reluctant attempt to "pick" the napkin out, the twenty-pound note (which Andy had palmed and surreptitiously 'flourished' into the folds of the napkin) came out also! The twenty-pound note then proceeded to glide, with a more or less conceited air, down towards the bar room floor!

Andy then bent down; picked up the twenty-pound note; opened Almost's hand, took the napkin out from it, put the twenty-pound note in, then he closed Almost's open hand and mouth, and announced with another flourish, 'See, you've just picked your own pocket without realising it . . . because you were distracted!'

Almost, looked down at the twenty-pound note in his hand; then he looked at the elastic band, limply lying at the bottom of his nearly empty beer glass, and then looking at his three companions, he paused, and asked, 'Right! Anyway, talking of bleeding boxing, who won the big fight last night?'

The three companions looked at each other and then back at Almost.

'I just don't bleeding well believe you!' Sparkles said with sheer astonishment!

'Simpson in the ninth!' piped up Sid the barman, whilst clearing the empty classes from the bar, 'But . . .'

'What!' exclaimed Almost, as his wide mouth broke into an even wider grin, 'Simpson! I bet fifty quid on him at 2/1 with Ladbrokes!' Then without a "How's yer father?" and before anyone could even reply, "Very well thank you!" the delighted Almost ran out through the bar room door!

'What's up with that Ding-bat?' asked Sid, whilst refilling Andy's empty pint glass, 'He saw the whole fight here on "Sport Live" last night … and he moaned for the rest of the night about how he had backed Thompson, not Simpson! Whose round is this?'

'It was bleeding Almost's round, that's whose round it was!' replied Tom, then turning to Andy, he added, 'And he's still got your twenty pound note!'

'I know that you Pillock!' Andy replied as the three remaining companions looked at each other, 'What a bleeding loser!'

As Sid served the remaining companions their drinks, Tom turned to Andy and suggested, 'You know sumink Andy, you'd make a bleeding good ferapist or sumink. You should join those Crime Frontiers lot, they're always advertising for people. You know … where they 'elp people to give up crime and all that bollocks! It made sense what you said to Almost, even if he is too fick to understand it.'

Andy slowly downed a good quarter of his fresh pint, before smiling and replying, 'You know Tom, you don't say much mate, but when you do, I've got to admit … that it's an absolute load of bollocks!' Andy then downed some more of his pint and added, 'Besides the only pist I'm interested in being, is, well pist, and that ain't bleeding likely to 'appen waiting for you to buy a round in, is it?'

Tom shrugged his shoulders and went back to his own drink – but not before he and Sid (the barman) had passed a mischievously conniving look between them. Unbeknown to Andy; events were soon to take place that would establish that Tom's opinion about Andy's "ferapy" skills, would prove to be a sounder bet, than any of Almost's betting predictions would ever turn out to be!

Chapter 6
NEW HORIZONS

Five years after the final visit to their father in the prison, Sandra and Debby were visiting the JFK Air Terminal, and were watching a live traditional English seaside "Punch and Judy" puppet show.

The puppet booth and setting were situated in a corner of a busy public concourse. The puppet show itself was a part of a travelling exhibition touring the USA, and had been organized by the British Tourist Authority. The BTA had even managed to create a "Traditional English" seaside setting; including a seafood stall (including fresh jellied eels!) and a candyfloss seller, all of whom plied their ware alongside a traditional Punch and Judy puppet show. The staged settings prudently did not however include; a wind machine (set to gale force 9), nor did it assault the audience with a deluge of freezing cold salt water – apparently, neither the BTA'S budget, nor the airport's health authority, would stretch that far.

Even though she was over 8 years old by now, Debby was never the less, gripping onto Sandra's arm with a mixture of fear and excitement. They and the rest of the audience were watching, with trepidation, the traditional hand puppet, crocodile, as it (in keeping with the many generations of crocodiles before it) slowly, but … ever so …slowly… crept up behind the unsuspecting Mr. Plod, the traditional puppet policeman! From the enthralled and transfixed audience, and in keeping with the many generations of audiences before them, the cries and shouts of dire warnings surged forth in an ever-rising crescendo.

Cries and shouts of, 'Watch out!'

'There's a crocodile!'

'It's behind you!'

All these warnings rang across the echo enhancing causeway, along with the slightly more muted but equally traditional shouts of, 'Hooray!'

'Hooray for the crocodile!'

Then when Mr. Plod, the puppet policeman turned to the audience and asked, 'A crocodile you say! I can't see any crocodile! Where is it?' the audience to every child, man and woman screamed out!

"It's behind you!

On being told that the crocodile was behind him, Mr. Plod the policeman, in time old fashion, slowly . . .but ever . . . so slowly . . . turned around – but not before the crocodile had managed to smoothly curve around behind Mr. Plod!

Then, just as the many generations of children and adults had done before them, Debby and Sandra started to fervently shout, scream and point at the crocodile, as it crept even closer ... and closer . . . with its mouth opening wider and wider, towards the hapless Mr. Plod!

'It's behind you! It's behind you! It's behind you!' the by now almost hysterical audience screamed louder and louder, as both the crocodile and Mr. Plod turned around faster, and faster, and faster! Whilst Mr. Plod kept asking,

'Where is it? Where is it? Where is it?'

By the time Mr. Plod had asked the audience, 'Where . . .is . . .it?' for the umpteenth time, the crocodile was not only directly behind him but above him too – with his jaws wide open! Then, yet once again, the hapless Mr. Plod asked, the now completely hysterical audience, as to the whereabouts of the crocodile!

'It's . . . behind. . . you!'

The audience screamed as one! Though by this time, Sandra and Debby were holding on tight to each other – even though Sandra knew that Debby (who by now was looking just a teeny bit more terrified than excited) was really, still having a great time!

Then . . . in time honoured tradition, the crocodile snapped its jaws . . . shut!

Fifteen minutes later, after the show had ended with its traditional English "not so happy" ending; the exhausted Sandra and Debby sat with Aunt Betsy and Uncle John, at the Airport's "Calypso" styled cafeteria. The drained duo then, respectively, drank a well-deserved coffee and a strawberry milkshake, to ease their over strained throats.

Sandra had brought Debby to the airport, and the exhibition, to show her what England was like, as she (Sandra) was about to, temporarily, emigrate to England itself, in two months' time.

Although she felt content with her current life, Sandra had decided to try to boost it, by starting a re-vitalized one in England. Whilst in England, she also intended to take an Open University, Introduction to Counselling course. If the course worked out, she might well go on to take a higher education diploma, in Criminal and Psychological studies.

To all intents and purposes, the airport visit had been a success, and after reassuring Debby, that England was not full of crocodiles (or really stupid policemen!) and that she (Sandra) would be back in two years, Debby seemed (more or less) happy for Sandra to go.

Had Sandra known however, that her adventure to England, would have her dangling between the gripping laws of Crime Frontiers, and the snapping-sanity of Steven Chadwick, then she might well have chosen differently!

Never the less, Sandra, who was now 28 years old, was mature enough to recognize; that no one can out run their past, no more than they could overtake their future. After the murder of her mother, Sandra attended two years of periodic, grief based therapy, during which she also told her counsellor, in confidence, about her father's sexual abuse of herself. After another eighteen months of receiving paralleled counselling, Sandra finally felt "wholesome" enough to leave therapy all together. After leaving therapy, she spent the intervening time leading a comparatively happy and "normal" life – even though she was still a little confused as what Love was really about!

Now, finally (2 months after the Punch and Judy show) the day of Sandra's departure had duly arrived! As she walked along the departure gangway, and in spite of her relative upset after a much shared and tearful goodbye with Uncle John, Aunt Betsy and her beloved Debby, Sandra still felt good about leaving at last.

Above all the tears and regrets, as she boarded the plane, Sandra felt good to be putting at least, some time and distance between her past and her future. By the time the plane had surged into the sky, Sandra was looking forwards to a bright future. However, one of the main reasons why it is so tricky for us to let go of the past, is precisely because, it is not always that easy to fully recognize where it is, even though … *"It's behind you!"*

Chapter 7
CELLMATES

Quote: from the Crime Frontier's manual:

"At the very centre of every wrongful intention there squats a lie; which becomes our cellmate, from the very moment we begin to shut out the truth!"

By the time 28 year-old Sandra had made her life-changing move to England; George Harold Pipe, who had already been living in England for all of his 33 years, had already made a life changing decision at the age of 8.

However even though he was only 8 years old at the time, George knew that bravery was very important! Never the less, the very thought of climbing, let alone falling, from the tree was beginning to fill his body with dread!

Standing before the tree, and trying not to show his fear to his 9 years old playmate/girlfriend Jean, George wished he had chosen a 'Kiss' or a 'Promise' as a challenge, instead of a 'Dare!'

If George had chosen a 'Promise' or 'Kiss' then he and Jean, would have probably gone to the small hidden corner of their shared garden. Once in the hidden corner, they would then have kissed a little bit, and then explored each other's bodies, as they usually did on such occasions, and had done for the last few months. Of course, neither George nor Jean could have been, justly accused of lusting after each other's bodies. Their shared curiosity was natural, as was their shared respect for each other, it was all part of growing up and learning to live and indeed love.

But it was too late now, George had chosen a 'Dare' and Jean had dared him to climb the tree – and as far as George believed - Jean was hardly likely to love a coward!

Not that Jean, who lived in the flat upstairs, had wanted George to hurt himself! After all, it was only a week or more since, they had kissed their first proper kiss (on the lips!), and promised to marry each other (when they were both grownups of course!). It had been a hot summer's day, and to George that kiss on his lips, had felt hotter than the summer's sun that shone high above!

Now, standing before the tree, George realized that all Jean probably wanted, was to give him the chance of being brave, so they could both be proud of him; but then Jean didn't know about his terror of heights!

The beginnings of George's life-changing decision came to him, just as he was reaching up to the lowest branch of the tree, and those beginnings came as a thought, and George's thought was:

"What if . . . instead of climbing the tree, I took all my clothes off and stood in front of the tree, that way I could still be brave, but not have to climb the tree!"

When George suggested the idea to Jean, she looked doubtful … but seeing that he was in some sort of difficulty, she said, 'Yes!' After all, it meant that they could both be brave together – because if anyone else saw them, they would both be told off!

Their joint attempt at bravery, was of course, bravado, an emotional placebo for bravery! Something that made them both feel that they were being brave, but in reality lacked that essential ingredient of moral courage, self-honesty.

Unfortunately for George, relying on acts of bravado in order to avoid dealing with ones fears, can become problematic even for an eight-year-old! This is due to the reality, that no matter what stage of life one has reached, one's true-self will naturally always be cast as the "central character" in one's life – even if that central self is frightened of heights! Consequently, any act that tries to deny one's true character, would be like a heckling audience member, trying to upstage the lead actor! This in turn means that sooner or later one's true self, begins to feel more than a tad . . . pissed off!

Moreover, this all means that, the more and more reliant on bravado one becomes, the more undervalued one's true self begins to feel . . . and the more reliant on bravado one becomes, etc...! Which all means life begins to get totally confusing, and the whole dammed "plot" begins to appear and feel out of control! Anyway, (without getting too moralistic) that is when life start to become really confusing, particularly when it comes to issues such as self-identity – let alone self-control!

Of course, if young George had realised just how dangerous a "cell mate" his acts of bravado would eventually become, then he might well have chosen honesty, by admitting his fear of heights to Jean, and (bless their pounding little hearts) braved her reaction instead! Then things may well have turned out very differently! But then, how many budding psychopaths realise such things – let alone an 8 year old boy, who is terrified of heights?

It was some weeks, and many such similar dares, before someone else did see George, parading, naked in the garden. The "someone" was Jean's mother, as she looked out of the upper back bedroom window, which she nearly broke as she angrily rapped on its glass, to gain her daughter's attention!

Two hours later, in the shared kitchen of the house, George was confronted by an even angrier, Jean's father!

'You dirty little bastard! You filthy little …???'

George wasn't quite sure what the next name meant, nor many of the others words that the raging adult was furiously shouting at him. To George, even the walls of the kitchen seemed to be glowing with the same, heated rage, that he could see coming out of the grown up's bulging red face!

As George stood there, his own face and body began to alternately, flush with cold fear and the heat of injustice! Then George found a place … a place inside of himself; where it was quiet and cool … and once there, he just waited until the raging adult had stormed off up the stairs!

George stayed in his "place" for most of that evening as he waited for his parents reaction to the news, about him being caught "parading!" However, to George's great relief, his parents either never got to hear of the event, or chose never mentioned it! Never the less, during the days that followed, Jean was anywhere to be seen, and it became obvious to George that she had been banished from the garden and him!

Two nights later, a very defiant and very naked George crept out of his bedroom, stole up the stairs; laid down on the cool lynonium-covered landing outside Jean's bedroom door, and then he waited. He didn't care if he was caught by Jean's parents, though he rather hoped that only Jean would come out, for in his mind, he was, definitely, being brave! If Jean's parents did catch him, then he would stand up for Jean and himself – and he would tell them what for!

"We weren't really doing wrong just because we like each other, so how dare you call my bareness bad!" that would tell them what for!

Whether Jean's parents would have calmed down enough, for them to encourage George to see that "flashing" was an abuse of his nakedness rather than a compliment to it, was another matter entirely! However, as it happened, George wasn't caught that night, or the several other nights he climbed up the stairs, to lay on the cool lynonium.

Then five weeks later, Jean and her family suddenly moved away! They moved to a place far removed from the back garden and the landing – but not from that cool and quiet place in George's inner world.

It wasn't long before George took to "parading" alone, either partially or fully naked in other places besides the garden. At first he would parade alone in the garden and then, on one brief occasion, in a nearby park! Soon, the more daring the situation the braver George felt, and the more impressed he thought any passer-by would be, if they saw him in nothing but his "Bravery!"

Before long, young George was "parading' on a routine basis. He would go on parade whenever he felt fear or doubt, about the world or himself (bless, his little cotton socks … and shirt and … well … whilst we are at it we may as well throw in the rest of his clothes, which he used to carry so tightly underneath his arm – whenever he was on parade!).

Chapter 8
IT'S NOT EASY BEING A PSYCHOPATH!

So, we have met all but one of our main characters (Trisha) of our story, and they are almost ready to crisscross their ways upon the stage. All we need now is the stage, and that stage is the Crime Frontiers confidential phone line. We will catch up with Trisha in a while, but for us to get a better feeling of the Crime Frontiers Advice line call, it is best perhaps, to pretend that we are a first time user of the help line.

What type of user you, dear reader, may wish to play is of course up to you. Perhaps, you would like to take on the role of a worried and caring family member; a partner, sibling or perhaps a friend of someone who already is, or is about to be, involved in a crime ... Oh dear! Oh dear! Oh dear!

On the other hand, you may wish to play the part of a criminal, but one who wants to change for the better ... Mmmm ... that's nice!

Then again, perhaps you might be calling, wanting to taunt the do-gooders at the other end of the phone ... Naughty! Naughty!

No matter! You may be who you want to be, as you tap, press, poke or stroke the numbers in. Now you can hear the dial tone, and hear the recorded voice at the other end; it is rather a nice voice, the voice of a welcoming, casual-acquaintance, an informative voice, with just a mere hint of mischievousness!

What you, dear reader (as the caller), would do next in this fantasy is of course open to debate – and may not be as easy as you would think. You may for instance, having no experience of committing a crime yourself (Ahhh, that's nice!), change your mind and role, preferring to play the part of an Advisor-negotiator. As it happens that would have its problems too.

So perhaps the most convenient way to get a flavour of the Crime Frontiers line call, is to eves-drop on a couple of calls; they are lengthy, but as they tell us about the main "supporting characters" both the calls and the characters are probably worthwhile pursuing.

It may also be convenient, for it is the first call that Andy is taking that shift. We know that Andy is a man who has a quick and a street-wise mind, and apart from a few minor teenage scrapes, he has a clean criminal record. Although Tom and Sid the barman put Andy up for Crime Frontiers, he took to it like a duck to water. What is more, after going through six months paid training, he is now a full time Advisor-negotiator, and has been so for over a year. Andy now finds himself seated at the other end of the phone to a caller.

As for the caller, we already know him too; it is George. The last time we left him, he was parading his "bravery" around the local parks, but things have predictably changed. It is a common fact that most so called, "harmless" flashers will often cause great concern or even terror to their victims. It is also a common occurrence that so-called "harmless" flashers, eventually descend into indecent assault or rape!

As for the reasons why George phoned Crime Frontiers, well we can also eaves drop into George's thoughts, as well as his more recent past. Of course, such knowledge is an advantage that Andy does not have, but then you, dear reader, do not have the advantage of six months paid training, so overall it is fair.

George is now married to a very good woman, Mary, and they have two lovely children, Toby aged seven and Fern who is eight. Although his marriage had been going well, George struggles, and his struggles with his "inner urges" are not going at all well! This losing battle is a shame but predictable, particularly when you consider that in getting married, George had very much hoped to curb his growing deviances, which by now are psychopathic deviancies! However it isn't easy being a psychopath, as George was finding out (yet again!) on that rainy Saturday morning, shortly before he called the Crime Frontiers chat-line.

George has been standing, half-hidden in an alcove of undergrowth, roofed beneath a huge oak tree, flanked by a long line of trees and bushes of mixed varieties. The tree line runs alongside and overlooks a quiet semi-suburban road, which joins two small residential housing estates. George had been waiting in the cold and wet; and although his nose is blocked and his body is beginning to shiver, he does not totally wish to stop waiting, for he is waiting for any decent (or even a half-decent) chance, of a potential victim to pass by his lair!

As another gust of wind swept into the alcove, George blew his nose into his already sodden handkerchief, and at last, seriously thought about going home to his dry, warm, house. If he left now, he could be home to greet his wife Mary and his two children when they arrived back home too. As even more wind dislodged even more raindrops from the tree above, George's warm home seemed even more of a good idea to him – much better than waiting in the rain for …?

However, being a psychopath was not easy! It was difficult for George to go back home, it would feel like a failure, particularly if he had to retrace his steps; that would feel too much like retracting his intentions, and to George that meant cowardliness! He could go forwards, and take the longer, circular route to his home, but he would get even wetter and colder by doing that. Never the less the thought of sitting in his favourite chair, in the warmth, seemed more and more inviting. It was as he was imagining himself sipping a hot cup of tea at home, that George suddenly remembered the Crime Frontier's advert. He had seen the advert on the TV the previous night, as he shared some of his bedtime hot chocolate with Mary.

The advert had showed an archetypically dressed burglar, garbed in a striped jumper and eye mask. The burglar was in a back garden, vainly trying to reach a partially open window, some two metres above the reach of his gloved hands. The camera sequence followed the burglar's slapstick efforts; as he jumped then ran and jumped, then stood on and fell off an upturned wheelbarrow. He then stood on, jumped up and toppled off an upturned, plastic rubbish bin! The camera then panned in on the hapless burglar's glum face as he in turn looked glumly into the camera.

Then the voice-over said, "If you think this advert is of questionable taste, then just wait until you experience the real thing!'

The camera then panned out, to reveal four burly policemen and a petite policewoman standing around the burglar. As two of the police officers lifted their prisoner up to his feet, another officer handcuffed him. Then the officer turned to the camera, tipped his cap back in resignation and said:

'Our prisons are full to the brim with cases of mistaken self-identity!'

After that, a printed message scrolled across the bottom of screen, accompanied by a voice over, giving out the contact details including, web address and help line number. The advert continued with the voice stating:

'If you would like to talk, anonymously, about any crime you may be thinking of committing, then contact us in complete confidentially.' At that point one of the policemen stepped forwards and added, 'They won't even tell us!'

The advert ended with the burglar being led off and the voice over concluding, 'Crime Frontiers is ideal for people of questionable taste!'

George found the advert mildly amusing more than inspirational, never the less when Mary went into the kitchen he took the time to put the free-phone number into his mobile's memory . . . just in case?

Now, beneath his oak domed lair, George unzipped the inner pocket of his knee length anorak, pulled out a pack of cigarettes, his lighter and his mobile phone. It was dangerous to switch his phone on; criminals' movements had been back-traced via their mobile signals, and used as corroborating evidence. Looking up and down the deserted road, for the umpteenth time, it looked unlikely to George that he'd get the chance to commit any crime at this rate!

Besides, phoning the helpline might well be useful "I could use it as part of any mitigation plea; should I be caught for any past or future attack! At least it would show the judge, that I was trying to reform!"

In fact: It was unrealized by George, that any such attempted mitigation would not be possible. Any contact between the helpline and any caller, came under the Anonymity Code, and would neither be confirmed nor denied by Crime Frontiers. Even if George had given his own version, most judges knew that; part of Crime Frontiers advice would include; educating George about the damaging effects of rape or attempted rape (or any crime).

Therefore, if he were then to be caught for a crime, having already learned about its damaging effects, then it would be tant amount to knowingly, inflicting his victim with that damage! To some judge's way of thinking, it would almost be like deliberately infecting someone's with HIV, or some equivalent emotional/moral devastation!

To some extent, this was why Bell wanted crime education, to become a part of the school curriculum, so as to reduce crime, not to punish criminals more severely.

"Anyway! George concluded, "At least it will help pass the time, and if I haven't seen a suitable woman before the end of the call, I will defiantly go home!"

He then lit a cigarette and after returning the cigarette packet and lighter to his inner pocket, he switched his mobile on and rang Crime Frontiers! It was unusual for him to bring his mobile phone on one of his "excursions," but today he'd "forgotten" to take his usual precaution (but then again, perhaps, the Crime Frontiers TV advert had more of an effect than he realised?). Anyway, after pressing the appropriate numbers for a direct contact with an Advisor, George heard Andy's chirpy voice.

''Ello, this is Crime Frontiers confidential line, my name is Andy, what can I do for yer sunshine?'

Although the policy of the helpline is that Advisor-Negotiators, are advised to use a pseudo name for their help-line persona, Andy always chose not to.

Hearing Andy's voice on the other end of the line both bemused and reassured George. He felt bemused, because he expected a well-meaning, liberal, middle class person to answer, not some seemingly streetwise cockney. Yet George was also reassured because Andy did sound streetwise. But then again, telling all, to someone who wasn't likely to pull any punches was a bit scary! Therefore, being bemused, reassured and slightly scared, George did what he usually did; he stayed in the background by saying nothing whatsoever.

Andy however was not put off by George's silence.

'What's up, cat got yer tongue? Because if it 'as, then it must 'ave got 'old of something worthwhile then! Which in my book must mean it's gotta' be worth at least one word or two! We could start with yer name, you don't 'ave to use your real name, any name will do, it just saves me calling you "sir" or "madam" all the time.'

Continued silence . . .!

The silence was getting to Andy just a bit, but he had been trained to expect it, and he had experienced that many first time callers would mostly listen before talking, so Andy continued.

'Or even better, you could tell me of just one of the reasons why you decided to make the call?'

More silence . . .

'Fair enough,' Andy ventured, 'but yer know that cat ain't gonna' let go until you let it out of the bag my ol' sunshine!' he then continued, 'Believe me when I say, that I know it takes courage to call, but you've got this far, which is a lot further than a lot of people out there, would 'ave even dared to have come, so it would be a shame to not make it worth your while.'

Silence . . .!

'If it helps any,' Andy stated, 'I can show yer how talking can give you a surprising amount of power!'

At last George spoke, 'Power?'

'Well I can promise you, that talking, will give you a lot more power, than perusing or committing any crime will give yer! If that's what you are thinking of doing,' Andy answered. 'It's like . . .'

As Andy continued to speak, the sound of his voice suddenly became fainter to George; mainly due to the fact, that George had just lowered his phone from his ear and down to his waist level, because he was now looking intently . . . at a lone woman!

The woman was still some way off; she was walking quickly down the other side of the road, with her head lowered against the rain, and she was not taking too much notice of her surroundings.

Now George was taking off his left hand glove and was quickly pinching the end of his cigarette. Now he was watching the glowing cigarette-end fall towards the leaf covered, rain sodden ground beneath his leaf covered, rain sodden shoes.

Meanwhile, with Andy's voice being just about audible, George quickly plunged the remains of the cigarette-butt deep into the side pocket of his coat (didn't want to leave any evidence near a potential crime scene!). With his heart racing, he held his breath, and looked quickly back up the road again, to assess the approaching opportunity more thoroughly!

The woman was still there! Although the woman was still some way off, her face was clearly visible to George, and as far as he was concerned, both she and the opportunity were defiantly worth at least, half a chance. At that point, he decided that, "This one, will defiantly do!"

Bringing up his mobile again George said, 'Hold on!'

At first George thought that it would be too distracting, let alone dangerous, to keep the phone connection open, and he was about to disconnect Andy . . . but as went to press the disconnect button, George had a vision! The unfolding vision that George was having; was one of having a sworn to secrecy witness, listening into a "live" and real chase – and even, possibly, a real rape! The vision was influential enough for George to put his phone into his inside breast pocket, but still leave it connected to the barely audible Andy.

After partially zipping up his inside pocket, George pulled back the hood of his anorak; waited a second to see that no one was observing him, or following the woman, and taking care not to pull the cigarette butt out at the same time, he pulled out his woolly ski mask. Then taking two steps forwards, he was about to don and pull the mask down over his face, just as the woman was approaching the opposite point to his lair - when at the last moment – he checked to his left again!

Out of nowhere, a boy on a bike came racing down the road. As soon as he saw the boy, George quickly stepped back and shoved the mask back into his pocket!

The boy's name was Darra. Darra was on his way to meet Sarah and Pete. The three school mates were meeting for the fourth time in their newly formed friendship, which also meant it would Darra's fourth time being late!

In truth Sarah and Pete had already put Darra's time keeping down to being "Just a Darra thing," so they weren't at all put out when, seven minutes later, he duly arrived late! Never the less, as he sped down the hill, Darra did not slacken his pace one bit, as he furiously peddled past the stretch of trees on his right, and then sped round the rain-silvered bend in the road ahead.

If you had asked Darra about psychopaths, he would have probably said that they should all be called, "psycho-pathetics!" Like most people, Darra did not believe that he would win a Noble Prize, or become the Prime Minister of England, (although there was always hope!). But never the less, it would be nice if he could live out his "ordinary" life without it being made less-ordinary, by some, "Selfish fucking dick head!"

However, being wet, cold and very frustrated, George did not call out to ask Darra about any moral or mental condition George might be under, so Darra sped on! However, enough about Darra or moral and mental conditions – for George is about to fully move from his lair!

Even before the "idiot boy" on the bike was out of his sight, George had quickly decided; firstly, that it would be too difficult to catch up with the woman, and then drag her all the way back and into and then behind his lair. Secondly, it would be much better to catch her further down the road, where two half-built new houses, waited, in a poorly fenced building site on the very edge of the housing estate!

Rapidly stepping back, George spun around, took a deep breath, turned right and took five strides forwards. Then he stepped onto a rough path, that although lay parallel to the road, could not be seen from it. Racing and at one time almost tumbling down the path, he made up time and distance. Less than a minute later, he fully stepped out from the cover of the trees, and onto the shiny rain soaked pavement!

Looking to his right, he could see that the woman had reached the final bend in the road, only just downhill from him. Quickly crossing the road, he turned right and began to pace along behind the unsuspecting woman.

Back at Crime Frontiers, Andy had been waiting on the phone and was beginning to think about disconnecting the call and going to the staff canteen for a "nice cuppa!"

Meanwhile the building site, where George intended to grab the woman, still lay more than a minute ahead! As he quickened his pace to overtake the woman's own lively pace, George speculated on whether she would be, stepping out, quite so lively afterwards! If things went very wrong at the building site, she might not even be stepping out anywhere ever again! Although, of course as far as George was concerned, he didn't want that sort of thing to really happen!

Although the building site was still a minute, further down the road, when he was no more than eight quick strides from the woman, George pulled out his mask, pulled it on, adjusted it so he could see out of it properly and quickened his pace even more! At four paces away from the unsuspecting woman, George could feel his heart pounding, his forehead go cold, his stomach tighten . . . and a sudden burning sensation ... just above his left ear!

In a movie, it would have made a good comedy sequence, but to George it was all far from funny.

'Shit!' George almost cursed aloud! Distracted by his earlier phone call, and the sight of the woman when he had first seen her, he had not pinched his cigarette out fully – before plunging it into the same pocket as the mask!

Although the mask was still damp, from when George had been wearing it before, a partially attached ember from the supposedly fully extinguished cigarette, had ever so gradually but persistently caught on the outside of his mask – and it was this oversight that was now burning George, just above his left ear!

At that very same moment as George tore his mask off, Andy asked, 'Are you Ok there sunshine?'

To George (who had almost forgotten about Andy), the muffled voice coming from within his inside pocket, seemed sudden, rasping and very loud, particularly as he was so close to the woman, but George had more immediate things to attend to!

Unfortunately, Olla, the woman up ahead and George's intended victim, did not hear Andy's voice. Nor did Olla turn around to see George's completely unmasked face, as he frantically brushed his singed hair, and then plunged his mask into a nearby puddle. Nor did Olla see George remove the cigarette end from his pocket to put it fully out this time!

If things had been kinder, and the slight breeze that there was, had been in the opposite direction, Olla may have at least got a whiff of George's singed hair and mask, but Olla, like the heavily blocked-nosed George, smelt no such warning! Never the less, at least now Olla was more than pouncing-distance ahead of George!

Bringing the phone out and back up to his mouth, George half walked and talked in a whisper.

'I'm ok! I need a moment. I'm just a bit busy right now!'

As flustered as George was, he still had the presence of mind to put the now, definitely dead cigarette butt, into his inside pocket, along with his phone. Then putting on and pulling down the mask for the second time George fell in behind the woman again!

Once again, had fortune been more kind to Olla she would have turned around before George had pulled his mask down, which in turn would have changed everything!

Unplanned changes affected George in two ways. Such changes either made him feel lost and out of his depth. In situations he might well reach out to (or in his current predicament hold onto) the habitual emotional rescue, his commitment to committing a rape. Alternatively at other times and emotional states, he would see any such so called "rescue" as just another "Nice fantasy – but really dumb thought!"

Never the less, choosing to cling on to his current fantasy, George had hardly slackened his own pace during the whole cigarette incident. He was now only eight paces behind Olla, and was midway in retrieving his phone from his pocket yet again, to finally disconnect Andy, when two unexpected things happened! Up ahead, Olla suddenly slowed, dipped her hand into her shoulder bag and brought out her own chiming phone! The second thing was that George's phone slipped out of his grasp. By the time George had scrambled down and recovered his phone, Olla was talking into hers and was continuing further down the road.

As frustrated as he felt; George was not stupid! He knew that to try to attack any victim whilst they were on their mobile phone would be full of dangers! Part of the initial conversation on most mobile calls, are about where and what both callers are doing – thus pinpointing their exact location – he'd have to call the attack off… it really was not easy being a psychopath!

Slowing his pace, George let the woman carry on ahead of him, but as he walked he spoke into his phone, as much to double check that it was still working as anything else!

'Are you still there?' George asked.

'Yes mate, you Ok?' Andy replied, coming out of a daydream.

'Sort of,' replied George, with some irony. Still half distracted, he then saw the entrance of the building site coming upon his left … it would be a good place to calm down, and to readjust to the loss of the woman. Speaking into his mobile again he said, 'I'm Ok, give me one more minute and I'll be with you.'

Looking about to see that there were no still no onlookers, and to re-check that there were still no Saturday morning workers on site, George stepped inside the building and went up to the first floor. The room he chose to unwind in was still unfinished, having a door and window but no frames. Never the less, the room was dry and out of the weather, and it would certainly be good enough for him to reorganize himself, and maybe even listen to what this Andy was trying to say. Besides, disconnecting now would feel like admitting to a total defeat!

However, he did not want to overstay, although the building site was unfenced, there was a sign outside proclaiming that the site was visited by a security patrol. Sitting against the far wall facing the window, and relaxing as much as he could, George spoke into his mobile again.

'Sorry about that again, but I was distracted. What were you saying again … what were you saying about power?'

'Good!' Andy replied, 'What I was about to and am saying is, having knowledge is a form of power, but having knowledge inside of your 'ead, is not always the same as being able to safely use it in the outside world, if you know what I mean?'

'Yes I know what you mean,' George answered, again with irony as he inspected the small burn-hole in the side of his ski mask.

'So! What I'm saying,' Andy continued, 'is that talking with someone who already knows a lot about crime, can 'ave an almost magical effect on turning things around and to your advantage, and I do mean to your advantage!'

'I don't believe in magic!' George replied with a dismissive tone!

'Neither do I,' Andy replied just as dismissively, then qualified by adding, 'It was just an expression, but thanks for telling me, at least this way we both know that neither of us is going to stand for any bullshit! No, me ol' mate, this

is down to you, me, and our consciences!'
'What do you mean our consciences?' George asked dismissively.

'A conscience,' Andy quipped, 'is the moral lifebelt we all 'ave to stop us going completely under, which is particularly 'andy, if yer 'appen to be in a world of self-made shit at the time!'

'Go on,' George replied, as he stuffed the mask back in his pocket.

Being a fan of distraction and football, Andy decided to use both to his advantage, 'Do you follow football by any chance?' he asked.

'Sometimes,' George replied with surprise and annoyed caution.

Taking a deep breath, Andy then took a shot at what he hoped would be his first goal.

'So I'll tell yer what. I'll make a deal with yer. If you give me … your goal for today … I'll negotiate a way with you, so that you feel that talking about crime is more powerful than committing a crime, and I promise you you'll be the one who makes the final move.'

Watching a phalanx of low flying geese bank across the sky towards a near bye lake, George decided that he liked Andy, at least for the moment! 'Ok!' he answered and then stated, 'Well my … goal … for today and most days … is to rape someone!' then he added matter of factually, 'I had a victim in sight, just now, but things went wrong … but don't worry she's gone now!'

For what seemed a long three seconds, particularly to himself, Andy did nothing nor said nothing; then slowly but very firmly, he pressed the large green "HELP!" button on his desk top!

The "HELP" button was there for any Advisor-negotiator to press if she or he thought they were already or might be getting, beyond their abilities. When the button is pressed, it alerts one of the Standby negotiators, stationed in the Crow's Nest, which is a large glass booth on a balcony overlooking the "Hub."

All Standbys have hands on experience in the field. If necessary, the Standby will take over the call from the original Advisor-negotiator, but that is a last call move! In general, the Standby would listen in on the conversation, and prompt the original negotiator as and when the call went along. The caller would not be aware of the Standby, unless the Standby took over the negotiations.

But you, dear reader, in your role as an advisor, are not Andy, and you may well choose to continue alone with George, which of course you would be perfectly entitled to choose and do so. However, on this day there are two very good Standbys on hand.

On Standby, is Charlie Fenton, a good man, who had been at one time or another, a top negotiator for three of the top five corporations in the City. Charlie (he didn't like being called Charles) had made lots of money; far too much money to even be remotely excited by any more of it, but being a hunter by nature, he still preferred to be involved in high consequence dilemmas on a regular basis (as did George!).

The other Standby is David Bell. As mentioned before, Bell is the man who created and founded Crime Frontiers, against great opposition from many types of factions. It is David Bell who answers the "HELP" call from Andy. Up in the Booth, Bell acknowledged Andy's HELP call with a relaxed wave and smile, and Andy in turn continued his conversation with George.

'Ok! So your goal was to rape someone today?' Andy repeated to George, whilst acknowledging Bell's calm wave.

'Is . . . to rape someone, not was!' George replied tersely.

'OK! I got that,' Andy answered. 'But the woman you just saw, she has gone now, right?' Andy asked, mainly for David Bell's benefit, more than for any clarification from the caller.

'Yes, she is safe now, so let's forget all about her!' George replied – as much as for his own clarification as for Andy's benefit!

At the other end of the line, Andy blew a sigh of relief and looked up at Bell. Bell said nothing but nodded to Andy encouragingly. With that, Andy continued,

'Ok! So both you and the woman 'ave just avoided, what to most people would be seen as, a very dodgy situation. I mean anything could 'ave gone wrong! You could 'ave got caught by any one – anything could 'ave happened out of the blue! And let's face it sunshine, even if you 'ad 'ave raped, it would have been a bit of an own goal anyway!'

Although George did, in part agree with the "own goal" comment, he was not in the mood to give way. Getting up and walking over to the window, he sat down on a knee-high pile of plastic covered, bags of plaster, having sat, he too sighed as he replied.

'You're going on a bit about football . . .I'm talking about rape!'

Andy however was not put off, 'That's because in many ways,' he persisted, 'there's a powerful and solid similarity between, a football, and that, ball, of tension inside all of us, that we all get, when trying to achieve any important goal . . . even if that goal is rape!'

Before George could think of an answer, Andy pressed ahead, 'And what I'm saying is that, talking wiv' someone who already knows the score about your goal, which is to gain feelings of power through sexual-bullying, can have many benefits. Certainly more than any rape can get yer!

Besides, anyone, can be big enough to be a bully, me ol' mate, but the real question is George; are you big enough to stop yourself from becoming one? Because size really does matter, mate!'

For a moment, George was silent, then he demanded, 'Go on about power.'

'Well,' Andy continued, 'talking it through with someone, who you can trust, is a lot like gaining more power, through reliable knowledge. Particularly, the power and knowledge to get yourself outside, of that . . . ball of tension . . . that would otherwise carry yer right into a whole world of shit!' Andy waited a second for any reply then ventured on, 'And as it 'appens, it also means that you'll gain the ability to, step aside from being "sent off" to some sin-bin, of a poxy prison cell, for bleeding years on end!'

At last George conceded, 'Go on,' he suggested rather than ordered.

'Ok! It's like this. Trying to steer, or coach, your inner emotions, your inner world, can be like imagining yourself inside a large, clear plastic ball, a man sized . . . but real world ball!'

At that moment, George felt a strange with an unexpected lighting of his weight, as if he were having some, partial out of body sensation. Almost without thinking, he faced away from the door and back towards the frameless window. He could feel a slight breeze coming in, as the rain outside started to increase to a steady downpour. There was no point in leaving now until it had eased.

'Carry on.'

'Ok! As you called us, I am going to presume, that as well as wanting to commit a rape, there are times when you wish you could cease or control that desire, right?'

Again, the same sensation, 'Sometimes,' George replied with a cautious note in his voice. It was true. There were times when George had banged his head against a wall; and sometimes, he had even burned himself with a cigarette, trying to "Snap himself out of it!"

'Well what I'm suggesting,' Andy continued, 'is that all your desires to live a normal life, and your desire to live a life of a rapist, are all contained as one, by continuingly getting entangled up into that ball of tension you get, whenever you think about rape . . . or about living a normal life!'

'Ok!' George conceded.

'So we are calling this life-sized, clear plastic ball; your immediate intentions, inside of which you can see both of your goals, in one direction heading for a life of a rapist, in the other a life of a non-rapist!'

Looking out of the widow George felt a bit more grounded when he replied, 'Ok! I follow you so far.'

'So!' Andy carried on, 'You start heading for a normal goal in life, let's say its intending to go to the cinema for a night out, or even staying in. You start by walking the ball, i.e. your intentions, from the inside, towards your intended goal, let's say a night out at the cinema.

However, whilst you are determinedly heading for the cinema, or even staying at ‘ome watching the telly, all your old habitual thoughts and feelings, about rape, are still bouncing around inside you – blocking your intentions, putting you off balance or even barging you completely off intended course! Then before you know it, you’ve ended up losing possession of yourself, so to speak, and you find you are heading towards a bleeding disastrous own goal. ‘cause let’s face it sunshine, no one is going to be giving you a medal for raping someone!’

Back in the room, George grunted a begrudged confirmation, but added, ‘They don’t give them out for not raping either!’

Back in his booth, Andy juggled George’s comment for a moment then returned it to him from another angle.

‘True…they don’t … but they aint gonna’ lock you up for years, for not trying hard enough to rape!’

Andy’s answer caught George off guard for long enough to allow Andy to return to his original course, ‘Ok! All I am saying is that when you’re in those situations, talking with someone, outside of your ‘ead, particularly whilst you’re getting or ‘ave already got the urge to rape, is like ‘aving a trusted team mate, right there, alongside you, helping you to get outside of that ball of tension! And once you step outside of all of the old thoughts and ‘eavy ‘abits, then … you instantly become a lot more powerful! You’re gonna' also find, that the whole of your life is much lighter, and much more pleasurable, to move about and direct, in the way you choose!’

George had to admit the idea did sound ok, ‘Sounds ok!’ he stated.

‘Too right it’s ok!’ Andy replied, ‘It’s like being the star player, and the referee, both at the same time! Just as it might seem to do in rape, I guess! Except, that the opposing team aint made up of a bunch of shocked and defenceless woman … going about to doing … whatever!’ Andy paused for effect then stated, ‘But then that’s the real challenge, Sunshine; using your own balls, to tackle life’s fair and foul challenges, and not someone else’s! That’s the real fucking buzz, and that’s how you score a fucking outright winning goal . . . Sunshine!'

Looking into the dark depths beneath an ancient row of hawthorns across the way, George got up and moved about to avoid a mild case of pins and needles in his left leg. He then stated, without the slightest bit of humour, 'Are you suggesting that every time I feel like raping, I phone you, because if you are, then I'd never be off the phone!'

Then, unheard by George, David Bell made a suggestion to Andy, 'Try to get him to consider the residential course, I have checked, and we have a two week placement, starting on the third, in three weeks' time.'

Andy lifted his hand to acknowledge Bell, before replying to George's question, 'If you feel that is what it would take, then yes! You can call us at any time, and every time! But we would also be giving you some very good, real-time, hands on, tips, on handling those situations, yourself.

Plus we will suggest some very different, achievable, alternative goals and aims too. Moreover, we can give you some very good exercises to balance your different emotional strengths. Particularly for the times when you will weaken, and we both know there will be times like that . . . me ol' mate! There's nothing like a touch of the ol' emotional ecology, to empower the natural tools you've already got!'

'What . . . tools?'

'Well yer feet, for a start, which are great for whisking you away from any potential crime situation! Then there's yer 'ands, which could dip into yer pocket, pull yer mobile out and give us a buzz 'ere. Yer eyes; which can look out for any, distractions, which can attract you away from a potential rape situation. That's called "The surprise!" exercise.'

'The surprise exercise?' George asked.

'Well it's a bit like counting heads, you know, when yer gotta count 'ow many people there is in a room or sumink. Well instead of just counting by heads or numbers, you count by hairstyles; it's a lot more fun, and is much more likely to keep yer mind on the job . . . which in your case, is keeping yer away from thoughts about rape! I do it when I'm walking down the street some times, to pass the time, except I count the different types and expressions on faces, it makes walking down the high street very … interesting!

Anyway, the surprise exercise can be used when there aint many people about. There is loads of distraction exercises you can do to keep yer mind away from rape, no matter where you are or 'ow far you are down the road, so to speak! Of course, they are in themselves only distractions, but they are powerful, and very so when they're used to back up a gradual changing of perception about rape! But that all comes clearer if yer can phone us!'

'How powerful?'

'Very! 'cause they lead to you changing your course of action! It's like finding out a room you thought was locked, is unlocked! It leads to physical action, and that is a very immediate and a very powerful tool for stopping yerself from committing a crime! I mean 'ave you ever tried committing a rape whilst physically sitting on yer 'ands?'

For a moment George frowned then answered, without a humour, 'You could if she done all the work!'

Quick as a flash Andy replied, 'Well in that case, then sit on hers!'

Even George couldn't help but smile at the other end of the line, before answering, 'Ok I get your point.'

With that agreed, Andy carried on, 'In short, the daddy of them all, is yer mind, and that can beam you up and far away from any bleeding desire to commit any sort of crime! Of course, first you have to think of these things, before you can act on them. But that's the $64,000 question, 'ow do you make sure you can at least start thinking of walking away when yer in the heat of the battle, as it were. And when it comes down to it, me ol' mate, we are talking about a battle of wills, your will to rape and finding the free will to walk away. But like we said, as far as giving up crime is concerned there aint no magic wand, even the wand of physical action. That comes down to yer conscience. But we can help in many ways.'

Suddenly, George felt physically tired and his answer showed in his tone of voice.

'Ok!' He sighed, 'I've got to admit . . . Andy, what you say does make a lot sense.'

In spite of Georges waning energy, Andy kept going and gradually and calmly, alongside Bell's background assistance, went on to successfully introduce and negotiate with George, the possibility of a residential place, starting on the third of next month. The negotiations had to be steady and precise. George already had an option of six days extra holiday time due, from previously working days off, and with bank holidays, he could also negotiate the extra needed days.

George was also figuring out how all of this could be done without letting Mary his wife know the truth – after all he didn't want to worry her! The residential, was to take place at "Lantern Place," just outside of London. There would be an optional; one evening or afternoon a week, full year follow up with a specialist, from the Crime Frontiers volunteer support arm, as well as any necessary outside help.

In the end, George agreed with the plan, but was still uneasy about the mountain he would have to climb, 'But how can a fortnight course change me? To be honest, I can't even trust myself, even when I'm determined to give up. How will it allow me to trust myself enough to give up the . . . urges?'

'Yourself trust will come!' Andy answered. 'But first, it will be much more about you learning to mistrust rape!'

George looked over at the tree line opposite, but did not heed the easing rain. The residential placement was a good offer, and George knew it! To get such help would require months of being on some waiting list, or for him to be caught for rape, or at least an assault; or to give himself up for at least one of his previous attempts! Neither option was at all appealing to him for even a millisecond!

The only fly in the ointment was that the two-week placement would not start for almost another three weeks. And he'd still have to find a way of avoiding telling Mary his wife – for as far as George was concerned, there was no way he would burden her with the appalling truth! However, if he told her that he was going to go on a training course for his work, which ran regular mandatory and voluntary courses, he could probably just get away with it!

Andy also offered George an immediate place at "The Oasis" a semi secure hostel, for people who are considered to be a "live and dangerous" risk to the public! However, George refused The Oasis!

With that said, George suddenly began to feel exhausted again. Never the less, before he rang off, he promised Andy, that he would phone the helpline, on a daily basis, and defiantly whenever he got a rape urge. Then with the good wishes of Andy still in his ear, George finally rang off!

Back in his office, David Bell congratulated Andy on a good negotiation, and then set a time with him to have a case conference. Bell then slumped back into his chair with some satisfaction, having just solved a particularly awkward, Dingbat, from his puzzle book. The Dingbat was a picture of three descending stars and the word PENNY running along the bottom.

As for Andy, he went off and enjoyed his good result as a negotiator, with a nice cup of tea and some Hobnob biscuits. Indeed, dear reader, if you had done a similar negotiation, you might well have felt pleased too!

However, unbeknown to Andy, Bell and even George, the "game" was about to go into "extra time!"

Chapter 9

THIS ONE!

Had George known that, Olla, the woman he had previously targeted, was only "popping" to a nearby friend's house, to return some borrowed money; George might have decided to leave the building site immediately after disconnecting from Andy! David Bell would certainly have advised so!

However, George rested for a while, and had another cigarette, which he managed to finish, before he saw his fantasy woman returning, up the road, and without any site of sight of her mobile phone! By the time George, had ran out of the half finished building, and half way across the road, Andy and all that he had said, had become no more relevant than any other telephone-sales "pitch!"

As it happens, "This one!" was different! "This victim!" was not submitting without fighting! "This one" even fought for the very paving slab, from which George was trying to snatch her from. Unbeknown to George, "This one" would have fought for anyone's freedom to walk unmolested. "This one!" would have even fought for George's freedom to walk in such places, unmolested by his urges!

However, not all fights are equal, and taking into account age and weight, George could overpower most men of his size! Therefore, he was not at all surprised, that it took him no more than a minute, to drag the brawling woman into the half-finished building. Then it was merely seconds, until they had reached the bottom of stairs leading up to the very room, in which he had been talking with Andy, only ten or so minutes before!

Nevertheless, Olla, continued to kick out and struggle, and to make matters worse, two dogs from the garden further down the road, had started and were continuing to bark, very loudly!

Then, Olla began biting George through his glove – and that hurt!

In the end, George pushed the woman into a pile of building rubble, then pulling his glove fully back on; he stepped forwards – then stopped! For, although Olla was sitting down and obviously very frightened, she held a house-brick in each of her shaking hands!

Seeing the woman's determination, George decided to tactically-retreat! Grabbing the woman's discarded bag, he took out her mobile phone, and sprinted out of the building and into the road!

Looking back to make sure that the woman wasn't following him; George pulled his ski mask up around his ears, and continued pacing down the road, whilst casually not looking around. Just before he reached the more built up area, he threw the woman's mobile into some bushes and slowed his pace to a normal one. As he walked, George tried to make it appear as if the persistent yells of his victim, were no more worthy of attention than the whining blare of some tedious car alarm! Blare! Blare! Blare! … Yell! Yell! Yell! … Moan … Moan! ... Moan!

The fact that George had never learnt to casually ignore his own tedious inner wailings (about how "helpless" he was to stop himself offending), did not correlate in his mind as he paced down the pavement.

George always made a never-ending drama out of his inner struggles:

"I mustn't!"

"But I can't help myself!"

"But I mustn't!"

"But I don't know how to stop! I must … do it … I have no choice!'

Moan! … Moan! ... Moan!

Ironically, the ability to dismiss such ignoble infighting was well within the easy reach of George's abilities. All he had to do was treat his whining about rape, with the same stubborn indifference, that he showed to the dilemmas' of his victims!

Never the less, back on the pavement, George was making a conscious effort to appear casual and in control. He knew that if he could just make it to the next side turning, then he would be out of sight from the growing number of "Fucking do-gooders" who were probably already looking out of their nosey, fucking, windows, right now!"

Then almost before he realised it, George had made it around the corner! The sound of the woman's yells and screaming grew fainter now, and less frequent. By the time George had gotten half way down the side road, the woman's alarm calls had stopped altogether. To George, that probably meant that his victim was about to try some other tactic, or one of the bloody do-gooders had reached the scene – and would certainly be phoning the police!

Then George suddenly stopped!

'Fuck it! Fuck it! Fuck it!' George cursed, as he realised that the side road, which he had never used before, was in fact a cul-de-sac! It really was not easy being a psychopath!

'No! Wait!' there was a narrow ally way at the end of the road, if it led into the woods behind … he could be away and gone before any do-gooders or the police could arrive! To George's immense relief, the ally did lead into the woods!

When he finally arrived home, George's shoes and trousers were so spattered with mud; it took almost a quarter of an hour to clean them. Never the less, clean them he did! He also carefully and firmly bandaged his hand; the bite of "that" woman, had not drawn blood, but it had drawn teeth marks and a nasty bruise! He would have to pretend that he had hurt his hand, whilst searching for some tools in the shed.

Fortunately, Mary was rather squeamish when it came to injuries and the like, so it was very unlikely she would want a closer look at his injury.

Even if either of their children injured themselves, it would be George, who would dress any wounds or grazes. If he weren't about, then Mary would end up take the injured child to a neighbour, or the doctor's, or even the Out Patients at A & E, a few miles away (the same hospital as it happened, where Olla was being treated for her injuries, at that very moment).

For the moment, Olla was being treated for things like, cuts, grazes and bruises. The emotional damage done by anger, fear, embarrassment and even guilt (in spite of her knowing that it was undeserved and irrational), would have to be treated later on. Moreover, there was her concern about what her family and friends would think and feel about her and her attacker. Plus there was a whole lot of other related "stuff," not to mention her sadness about her favourite skirt, which had been totally ruined! It wasn't easy being a victim!

Never the less, as he surveyed his bandaged hand, George wanted everything to appear, absolutely, normal as possible; for when Mary and the children returned at around six thirty, from the specialist hospital (situated in the neighbouring town) young Toby was due his quarterly, asthma check-up.

Therefore, when the doorbell suddenly rang, shortly after four o'clock, it sounded to George like the shill jangle of a burglar alarm!

As he moved cautiously towards the front door George's mind was thinking furiously. "Fuck, surely they couldn't have traced me all the way back here! They must have used bloody sniffer-dogs!"

To his relief when George looked through the door's spy hole, he almost laughed out aloud. It was only his next-door neighbour, a man that George usually found to be so boring, as to be physically annoying! Nevertheless, this time George was so relieved, that he actually invited the neighbour in. Then for over half an hour, George listened to the saga of his neighbour's recent holiday. However, George was not only pleased to listen, he was genuinely grateful for the man's ordinariness, even though George still found him boring!

In the end, George even managed to invite the grateful bore over for the following night, "At around seven?" so he could give his "Thank you gifts!"

to the family in person! The gifts were a bottle of "Rather tantalizing" Rumanian wine: "For you and your dear lady." There was also a box of "Made in Rumania," sweets for the children. The gifts were a "Thank you!" for looking after Geronimo, the neighbour's slightly less boring, tortoise!

After the neighbour finally left (with Geronimo), George at last flopped into his reclining chair and switched the TV on, then he sighed and smiled to himself, after all, when all was said and done – it really was quite easy being a psychopath!

When Mary, Toby and Fern arrived home, there were many things to talk about. Amongst the news there was; young Fern falling in "Lurv" with Toby's new doctor; and the latest news about how the long-term prognosis for Toby's asthma was improving! It had however, been a long and tiring day, and even Mary went to bed by nine thirty!

For the rest of the night George watched the telly, apart from a wild life program; to George the programs were rubbish, as was usual on a Saturday night! George watched the programs paraded themselves before his half-vacant eyes. To George, the programs were like a parading bunch of over pretentious, strippers! As the night crawled on, George began to "channel hop" between the telly, and the exclusive fantasies showing in his inner mind. The advantage of this was, that as he watched, George edited, by fast-forwarding the boring bits! However, even the highlights of his past escapades, soon began to lose their allure!

By the time he was climbing into bed, besides the already sleeping Mary, George was fantasizing about more future escapades. Each fantasy image beckoned him with allure of a destitute, ballet dancer, turned striptease artist, who was not only demanding George to watch her – but to join her on centre stage!

But for now, we must leave George to his fantasies, but we will renew our acquaintance with him, at a more convenient time in the future.

Chapter 10
THE TALES OF "TRISH-TRASH" TRISHA

If anyone had offered Patricia Hammond (known to her friends as Trish, Trisha, or "Trish-trash") a job as a striptease artist, she would have jumped, hopped, skipped and twirled to take up the chance!

Unfortunately, for Trisha, there would be little doubt; that the numerous pockmarked needle-scars running along her undernourished arms and legs, would have undoubtedly turned away any potential employer, let alone (most) audience members! Therefore, instead of striptease, Trisha had taken up the tradition of many female drug dependants, that of prostitution.

Standing in the centre of the musty smelling room for the third time that day, Trisha felt a rush of "goose bumps" as she noticed several shafts of sun-beamed sunlight, streaming through the gaps in the boarded up window. Feeling her emotions stir inside of her, she roughly pushed them down – emotions were more trouble than they were worth in this business! For a start, if it weren't for "emotions" she wouldn't have fallen in so-called "love" so many fucking times! What's more, if it wasn't for their so-sensitive emotions, her punters (customers) wouldn't get so many fucking erection failures!

Erection failures were a sore point with Trisha. There were some days (particularly cold ones), when her jaw ached something chronic, from trying to kick-start a punter's hard-on! However, the worst of it was, if he couldn't get one at all. Some punters refused to pay if she hadn't kept her end of the deal (as if it was down to her to control his emotions!). Fortunately, most punters paid, but it still left an awkward ending!

For a short time, Trisha had tried ripping prospective clients off via "Cash and run!" She would get the payment up front, then send the punter to some location or tell him to wait until she came back – then she fuck off and spend the money, leaving the punter standing there waiting … derr! A friend of

Trisha did C&R on a regular basis "You've just as much chance of getting beat up, as you would if you give them the sex anyway!" However after a few goes at it, Trisha felt too frightened and too guilty to carry on!

Back in the room, Trisha came back from her thoughts. Fortunately, this punter didn't suffer from erectile failures. However, by now the dancing sunbeams seemed no more "uplifting" than the abandoned floral-printed, brassier that "skulked" in the far corner of the room! Never the less, she knew that it was important that she at least, appeared, to be "uplifted" by the company of her punter. Although he was a "submissive" he did not like his women to be miserable.

"Anyway … what the fuck!" Trisha thought, as she put on a dominant stance beneath a sweet smile, then ordered and watched the punter pick the bra' up and then put it inside a plastic bag, that lay nearby.

After obeying Trisha's instructions, the punter turned around and asked, 'How much?' The man, a regular punter, knew the price already but he always asked and Trish always replied.

'A tenner for a blow job, full sex costs a score, whilst anything "extra" will cost some extra more!' then nodding to the bag, she added, 'You can keep the bra as a freebie, Sweetheart!'

To her mild surprise, the punter seemed genuinely delighted when he thanked her. Both outwardly and inwardly, Trisha dismissed his gratitude, with the thought that "Bra's were only meant to support tits not potential – just as erections were meant to support cocks – not promises!"

Of course, it was not that unusual that Trisha got the "goose-bumps" selling her holes and lumps, but it wasn't always due to the cold. Sometimes she would get them in a punter's presence, whether it was friendly or not. Of course, she'd rather sell herself wholesale, like in love and marriage and all that (you know; respect, loyalty and all those things!).

"Anyway it wasn't worth worrying about now," Trisha decided as she rubbed her arms and then gave a small smile to herself, whilst wondering if she should charge "extra" for her goose-bumps!"

"Besides," Trisha concluded, as she hastily covered up a spent condom with the remains of a cardboard box, "Why knock a good day, and a good place come to that!" The derelict house that she and her co-workers used, had been "available" for over six months now, and that was a feat of good fortune if nothing else!

Getting back to business, she turned to face her punter.

'Money first please, Sweetheart!'

There was no real need to demand upfront payment from this punter, he always paid, but even though he was a submissive, Trisha did not like to take her punters for granted. Besides, as submissive as he was, she had still walked him the slightly longer way around, from her corner, ensuring that they passed beneath the street CCTV monitors; at least that way the police would have his face, if he ever did seriously turn on her.

The punter settled for a tenner's worth of "tit and fanny show" with some "dirty talk" whilst he masturbated. As Trisha reamed off her "dirty talk" she was suddenly reminded of her days back at school, when she was reciting her multiplication tables.

Amongst other things (such as becoming an Olympic swimmer, a concert pianist and a Vet) Trisha had also wanted to be an eminent doctor when she grew up (whilst also being a brilliant wife and mother!). So as a moral booster, whilst watching the wanking man, Trisha reflected (not for the first time) that even though it would be considered as "fringe medicine," in her own way, she was giving a sort of therapeutic health service, to her "sick" clients!

Eventually, after giving and getting their tenner's worth, Trisha and the punter made small talk as they readjusted their clothing, and then left the room to the buzzing meanderings of a lonesome, bluebottle fly.

As the punter and Trisha left the room, she phoned Jake, her drugs supplier, but got a leave message reply, so she left one telling… no …asking him to call back ASP. Then the satisfied pair made some more small talk, whilst they walked in single file, down the stairs. Turning to say something to her punter, Trisha suddenly slipped and almost toppled over – as she stepped on yet another discarded condom!

'Fucking untidy bastards!' Trisha complained as she massaged her ankle.

Seeing that Trisha wasn't seriously hurt, the punter joked, 'This place wouldn't exactly pass the Health and Safety inspectors!'

Flexing her ankle, Trisha scowled at the punter and replied, 'That load of fucking wankers can come down and lick my fucking arse!' then as an afterthought, she added with a smirk, 'Mind you … at least I'll know their tongues will be nice and hygienic!'

With that said, Trisha laughed aloud and poked the punter in his ribs, 'You've no idea what you could catch from some of my punters,' she informed him whilst she banged the bottom of her shoe on the top of the banister rail, until the condom fell away! Then giving the punter a knowing nod and another scowl, she replaced her shoe and started back down the stairs, as she stated, 'They should try living in the real fucking world for a day!'

'Who … your punters?' the punter asked.

'No!' Trisha sharply corrected, 'Those fucking health and safety wankers! Before you know it, they'll have us working girls behind fucking shop windows next, like in Amsterdam!' Then turning to look up at her punter and showing him her scarred arms and legs, 'I mean can you see me prancing around in a shop window for fuck sake?'

The punter just shrugged his shoulders.

Then after a second or two of reflection Trisha added, 'Mind you, they're not all the same!'

'The … health people?' the punter tentatively suggested.

'No! My punters! Try to keep up for fuck-sake, darling! You men are all the same once you've cum your loads – you haven't got a clue what's going on!' then giving her punter a big smile she assured him, 'But at least I'm lucky to have someone like you.' In truth, Trisha paid that sort of compliment to most of her punters, but there were also times when she believed that there was some truth in it!

After squeezing through the kitchen's broken back door, the two of them made their way across the rear garden, and then each in turn, squeezed through the partially broken rear gate. As Trisha and the punter entered into the ally, that ran the rear length of the block of houses, both of them, who didn't normally interfere in other people's disputes, walked straight into a shocking one! Bumping into the back of punter, Trisha could immediately see what had stopped him in his tracks! For a moment, she hoped that the fight might be just some horseplay, between two friends – but deep down she instantly knew differently!

A thickset man in his forties was leaning over a man, who was kneeling hunched up on the ground! Behind them a woman, who Trisha thought looked like a "working girl" was backing away. As the obvious victimizer became aware of Trisha and the punter, he immediately half turned and told them both to:

'Piss . . . the fuck off!'

The victim, a taller and younger man, said nothing, but looked pleadingly up to both the punter and Trisha. The punter and Trisha; both of whom would normally be ashamed to be seen as a coward, even by another coward, promptly swivelled around, and then ran along the ally way, until they both came out onto the open road. Without further talk or a wave goodbye, the punter quickly paced of towards the high street, two hundred or so metres away.

Meanwhile, still shocked and trembling, as soon as she was in the open and on the road, Trisha immediately felt safer . . . and in some way . . . more . . . outraged!

Once out of the ally way, and in the relative safe surroundings of the road, things seemed somehow different to Trisha! Everything felt somehow, cleaner, than what lay back down the alley! The right answers would come from such clean place! Further up on the same side of the road, and on the opposite side to the fleeing punter, three normal people, two men and a woman, were chatting normally besides a parked car. These people would help; they would never reject a call for help!

As Trisha moved towards the group, they in turn began to get into the car – just as the loud engine noise of a passing lorry, drowned out Trisha's shouts of, 'Excuse me …wait …!' but by the time the noisy lorry had passed the people, they had got into the car and had already closed their respective doors. By the time, the car had moved off, Trisha had slowed to a standstill, and had given up!

Looking up and down the now empty road, she quickly realized, that she was on her own, even the punter had completely disappeared. Feeling panicky, she looked back towards the corner of the dreaded ally, and she knew with certainty, that the opportunity to do something to help was steadily ticking away "thump!" by "thump! by "kick!"

But then maybe it was all already over! Maybe it was too late for her, or anyone to stop any more violence! Maybe all anyone could do now was to call the police or an ambulance or someone!

Then without any conscious commands, Trisha's shaking legs brought the rest of her adrenalized body, right up to the very corner of the ally way! Next, Trisha's light-headed-head seemed somehow to, float, towards and then around the corner of the dreaded ally way itself! However, to Trisha's disbelief and relief the ally way turned out to be empty; there was no one down there!

But her relief was only temporary, and it was quickly shoved aside by questions! Had the three people gone their separate ways? Or had one been dragged off by the other, to some quieter place, where no one else could accidentally disturb them? Maybe they were even in the room that Trisha and her punter had just left! If so Trisha knew that, the victim (or victims?) would no way be a willing submissive! There was no choice left, Trisha decided, as she reached into the front pocket of her jeans and then drew out her mobile phone!

But the emergency operator would ask her awkward questions!

'Is the victim badly injured? Is the assailant still in the vicinity?'

'What is your name caller?'

'You don't want to leave your name?'

'Why don't you want to leave your name caller?'

'That's OK! Not to worry caller, we can trace your name, from your mobile signal, or maybe we'll just look it up under the heading of "Cowardly Wimp!" Go back and find out what is happening – you spineless fucking wimp!'

For an indecisive and time warped moment, Trisha stood motionless as a completely unexpected, but distinctive memory, appeared to her. To her utter amazement, she suddenly found herself obstinately recalling the days when she had been part of a wannabe girl's rock group, called, "In the Touch!" Trisha had even written the lyrics of one of the group's songs, "Just cloning about!" and in spite of herself, and her situation, the words just sang themselves in her mind.

"If could make a clone from me
I'd have it cross a raging sea
Then I'd have it climb a mountain or maybe two
Then write a poem about the romantic view
Written of course with its own heroic blood
Then it could move the mountain to dam some flood.
Oh! If only I could make a clone from me
And I had the courage to set it free!"

The group did have some great times together, but due to two pregnancies; neither of them Trisha's, a lack of money and the lack of a good lead singer, the group had only lasted a little over a year. Never the less, Trisha often recalled that it was, by far and away, the best time of her life!

But now, years later, standing in the empty road, alone, with her goose-bumps erupting all over, it was all getting … just a bit too much for her! "Somebody else should have come along – it just wasn't fucking well fair!" Well, she wasn't going to get her head kicked in (or worse!) just because some poor bastard was in the wrong place at the wrong time!

If further proof were needed of the whole situation being unfair, then Trisha got it two minutes later! As she reached a near bye public telephone, from which she definitely intended to call the police, she found that the handset had been vandalized!

It was indeed all too much! With a mixture of guilt and anger, Trisha strode off towards the home of Glenda, a working pal and good friend, who was putting Trisha up for a few weeks.

But it wasn't all over! Now Trisha had to deal with the problems of using or even passing by that house and ally, in the future! Bloody hell! It was part of her place of work for fuck sake – and a good place at that!

But what if the attacker … or even the victim … should be there, one day or night, waiting or patrolling in the vicinity! How would she face either of them, and what would she say and do if either did find her?

Trisha decided that in the future, there would be no safe alternative but to choose a new area. But what if the attacker or the victim was already living in her new area? Or maybe one of them would use it as a roundabout, alternative route to get where they really lived, so that they wouldn't bump into each other or herself … or maybe they would want to find her … very, very much so!

"Fuck! It just wasn't fucking fair!"

For the future, Trisha decided, that if something was wrong, then at least some sort of attention should be drawn to it. For a start, there was that vandalized public phone which should be reported, that would at least be a start! But for the moment, she couldn't remember the name of the road it was in, and it was already some way back. Then with the fading rhythms of her song echoing in her ears, Trisha decided to … Blah! …blah! …blah!

Drip … drop, drip! Drip, drip, drop, drop, drop!
'Oh! That's fucking great!' Trisha cursed out aloud, 'Now it decides to rain! That's just fucking well … great!'
Pulling her thin cotton jacket up around her neck, Trisha began muttering to herself as she walked along, 'I should have known better than to trust those wankers (weather people), they always get it wrong! You can't trust no fucking body; they're all just a fucking load of wankers – all of them!'
As Trisha paced along, she repeated the phrase "Fucking wankers!" out aloud; and although it was to no one in particular, several by-passers on the other side of the street, did look over towards her, whilst several others on her side of the street, decided to give her just a slightly wider path! However, Trisha was used to such commonplace, public rejection by now … although it was not always so!

In the days when she earned a living as a street beggar, Trisha had developed a good technique (or funnel). Firstly, she would stand by a bin, preferably one in a park. Then, when she saw a potential donor or donors approaching in the semi distance, she would pretend to search the bin (supposedly for food etc.). As the potential donor/s got nearer, Trisha would lift out and poke around inside an empty "McDonald's" (or any other brand name) burger bag; (she always made sure she brought a clean and empty bag to work). Then after a further fruitless rummage inside the bin, Trisha would forlornly return the empty bag into the bin! At that moment, she would look up to be "surprised" and "embarrassed" by the appearance of the approaching donor/s … but never too embarrassed to awkwardly ask, "Any spare change please?"
In truth, even though not all the donors quite believed the "situation," they were still quite willing to shell out their change, for her "performance" anyway! As it happened, that is where Trisha got her nickname "Trish–trash" from, after telling one of her working pals, about searching in the trashcans.
Never the less, as the signs of her heavy drug use became more obvious

(and more repellent); donors became less generous and a lot more suspicious. In the end Trisha resorted to prostitution; it would not have been her first choice by a long chalk, but at least in this business, she could insist that the punters paid up front before her "performance!"

To give her fair due, Trisha had tried many ways at earning a living before she chose to be a "street worker!" At one time, she even tried her hand as a "street performer!"

Going under the stage/street name of "The Joke Busker" Trisha's pitch was half way along the long pedestrian tunnel, running between Kensington tube station and the museums. Whenever she saw a prospective donor or donors approaching, Trisha would start reading out jokes from her notebook, (to boost her courage she had a joint or two before performing, which unfortunately also affected her ability to memorise the jokes).

It was also unfortunate, that when most prospective donors caught sight of the scruffily dressed and be-draggled red-haired Trisha, nervously "ranting" out aloud from a small black book, they presumed that she was probably a maniacal religious preacher, which in turn meant that most of the public had passed hurriedly bye, without realising their own or Trisha's mistake! Neither did it help matters, when Trisha tried to get them back, by suddenly grinning and shouting out her favourite joke, without the necessity of quoting from the book. Trisha's favourite joke was:

"What's the difference between an elephant and a paedophile?

Well with a paedophile … it's the victim that never forgets!" After a few outings Trisha gave up her joke busking, judging it, as a bad joke!

What lay at the deeper levels of Trisha's being, that led her to become who she was and now is, had long been submerged in the depths of time. However, as we rapidly rise to the very surface of her being once again, the bedraggled Trisha has far more pressing things on her bedraggled mind, as she let fly yet another curse!

'Fuck them all!' she shouted out aloud! Although Trisha aimed her curse at the world in general, it was received by a heavily, pregnant mother to be, who rapidly blushed as she silently and hurriedly passed on bye.

'They're all useless fucking… wankers!' Trisha warned the retreating woman.

It is surprising; how when we finally decide to give up on something, it sometimes has the opposite result, or more accurately, the paradoxical can result. As soon as Trisha had given up on everything, as well as everybody, she recalled the poster for Crime Frontiers!

The poster had been strategically positioned, in an area in which petty and serious crime sprouted as regularly as the cysts, boils and hard-luck stories of the local junkies! Trisha also remembered the easy to remember free-phone number, displayed beneath the phrase.

"For when you feel like you can't trust anyone – particularly yourself!"

Trisha also remembered that anyone could call … completely anonymously!

"Ok!" Trisha finally decided, "It's that or fuck all!"

However, when Trisha tried to report the crime that she had witnessed in the ally, it was Sandra who answered her call, and it was Sandra, who told Trisha the news:

'That the Crime Frontiers Advice line, never, handed any information onto anyone outside of the Advice line centre, whether it be to the police, ambulance services – or even to a potential victim! It was always left it to the caller them self to so, if they wished!'

To her credit, Trisha did not shout or scream into her phone, in fact when she did reply, she sounded rather resigned.

'You must be fucking well … joking!'

Sandra listened to the disappointment that spilt from Trisha at the other end of the line, and she tried her best to convey her own empathy, 'I know it sounds like a silly rule, but that's the way we have to do it! If it helps, at least I do know how you're feeling, and I would feel the same as you right at this very moment!'

In truth, Sandra did feel bad about the rule, but she understood that the reasoning behind it, protected the sanctity of total-confidentially.

Trisha however was not in such an understand mood; she suddenly wanted to throw her phone so hard that it would smash into a thousand pieces! However, the phone was her prized possession; it had been an advanced birthday present from her ten-year-old daughter, Nina, on one of the bi-monthly visiting days to the foster home of Trisha's two children; Nina and Harold. In fact, apart from a few clothes, the phone was all Trisha possessed. Besides she needed the phone for work, some of her regular punters would call her on it.

'Fuck it!' Trisha cursed aloud! Absolutely nothing was going right for her! It was with more resignation than with any hope, that she managed to listen to Sandra's further explanation.

'Look Trisha! I know we are both in a horrible situation. I also know that having a sense of duty, a conscience, can feel a bit like having an unplanned pregnancy at times, but we got what we got!' Sandra suddenly thought that she might be coming over, as a bit clichéd and superior, and she felt a rush of doubt. She almost pressed the HELP button, but deciding against doing so, she made a quick alternative decision.

'Listen angel, I also know that I shouldn't cut a caller off, or advise them to hang up, but I'm going to do just that. I know you're going to think me a … dick 'ead … for doing so. But I'm going to ask you to hang up – for at least a minute – and take that minute to look at the world around you, the physical world, the trees the sky … anything real, then, decide if you are going to call the police or not.

Then, if you want to phone back immediately after, and tell me what happened, you're free to do so. My name is Sandra and I'm in booth 17, which means that's two rules I've broken, as we're not supposed to give our real name out! But I want you to hang up, think for a minute … and then call back! I would really like you to call back, no matter what you decide! Ask for me by name, my name is Sandra!'

Sandra looked up and saw that even though there were no trainees working that day, it seemed that neither Standby was by chance, listening to her call. At the other end of the line, Trisha was still silent, so Sandra continued.

'If you want to phone the police or an ambulance, to tell them about the attack, do so! I know you said you don't want to use your mobile, but if there's a shop or house near bye, ask to use their phone, I'm sure they'd let you. After that, you can disappear, quicker than a ra' …!' Sandra was about to say the well-known English phrase she had recently learned: "Like a rat up a drain pipe!" but she quickly ad-libbed it into '… a ra …bbit … into Wonderland … Angel!'

Sandra was rather pleased with her, rat into rabbit escape, and in spite of the serious of the situation, she could not help but grin to herself. Sandra's narrow escape had not escaped Trisha either and she too, could not help but giving an unseen smile as she answered, 'Thanks for the compliment, but believe me I'm no angel, I didn't get the nick name of "Trish-trash" for nothing, darling!'

Without a pause Sandra asked, 'So what! Angels can come in all sorts of guises?'

Trisha was now feeling forgiving but not forgiven, and answered, 'Does that including in the scared shitless guise too?'

'Of course it does, even angels get scared.'

'And how would you know, Arc Gabriel?'

'Because you just told me they do!' Sandra answered.

At that moment, Trisha felt her stomach tighten, and then unexpected tears began to well up in her eyes! She then deliberately disconnected the call!

As soon as Trisha rang off, Sandra again looked up and reconfirmed, that neither of the Standbys appeared to have been listening. Relieved, she half turned, to get up and quickly stretch her limbs, and it was not until then, that she saw Andy!

He had been waiting with a small pile of the Crime Frontier's in-house, daily, newsletter.

Innocently handing Sandra a newsletter, whilst raising one eyebrow, Andy spoke with a teasing tone to his voice, 'Sorry to listen in on you, Angel, but I thought I'd see how a smooth operator, like your good self, handled things!'

Andy's tone and the look on his face, told Sandra that he had heard enough of her conversation, with Trisha, to realise that she had at least ignored the "No name" advice and broken the basic "No cut off" rule!" With all that being obvious, Sandra held up her hands in surrender, dropped her head in acknowledgement, and then she sheepishly looked up into Andy's eyes.

'Don't suppose we could talk about this, over a beer or coffee, after the shift? I'll buy the beer!' Sandra added without smiling.

'I suppose I could manage a quick beer,' Andy replied then added, 'But if you know, as I do, of a very nice pub that serves a really good malt whisky, I could give it some extra time – presuming it's a double, of course!'

Sandra grudgingly grinned and said, 'What more could a condemned woman wish for?' With that, they agreed to meet at the reception area at the end of the shift, and Andy carried on delivering the newsletter around the Hub.

Twenty minutes later, one of the other advisors diverted a call to Sandra – after discreetly reminding her that she should not give out her real name. Sandra thanked her and began to wonder, that at the rate she was going, she might have to buy quite a few people whiskies, before the end of the day!

Taking a deep breath Sandra took the call. At the other end of the line, Trisha was a still shaky but no longer uptight. She told (a much relieved) Sandra; that using her own mobile, she had told the police about the assault in the ally way, and then promptly rang off, without giving her own name or number.

Trisha then told Sandra, that about ten minutes after she had rung off from the police, the police operator had phoned her back. The operator told Trisha: that neither an ambulance nor a police patrol, had not been able to find anyone matching the descriptions that Trisha had given, either in the ally or the house or in the vicinity. The operator thanked Trish for calling and then asked, if she would like to come into the local police station, to make a statement.

Alternatively, an officer could come to her. Trish told Sandra, that she had "declined" the offer. She would take her chances that neither of the "ally men" would go out of his way to meet her again.

Trisha also declined Sandra's offer to talk about any counselling, but she did agree to keep in touch. In truth, she quite like talking with Sandra, and would have continued, then and there, but time was getting on and all this business, had lost her real business. It was fast approaching school leaving time; there were three schools in the close by area, and the local police would scoop any "working girls" off the street during that time-period.

Thanking Sandra for her help again, Trisha was about to ring off, when Sandra said, 'Remember Trish, you do have friends and even more importantly, you do have a choices, and even though they may be difficult sometimes, it is no use throwing the baby out with the bath water.'

Although she did not mean them to be condescending, as soon as she said the words, Sandra instinctively regretted them! For the space of several heartbeats, there was silence from the other end of the line. Never the less, when Trisha did speak, her voice was quaking with anger!

'Excuse me! Did you say I have a fucking choice! Listen and listen good, bitch! I was dragged up by my arm, by my hair … and when I was old enough, by my cunt! And when I say old enough, I mean when my so-called fucking arse hole of a so-called fucking "uncle" thought I was old enough! I am a drug user, and my kids are in a foster home and are embarrassed whenever they see me! The only true friends I have are my drink and drugs – and my best fucking friend is heroin! And when I say best friend, I mean best fucking friend, because it is the only one that can fucking, kiss, all the bullshit and pain away! So you tell me, Arch fucking Angel Gabriel, what fucking choices I have?'

The sound of pain and anger in Trisha's voice, made Sandra squirm in her chair; for a split second, she warmly recalled her own mother's kisses and hugs when she had tried to comfort her as a young child. However, she had also learnt that kisses and cuddles were not always enough!

'Now you listen, Trisha! I was brought up by my cunt too – so don't you start shoving yours, in my face! But no matter how either of us were brought up, you still have exactly the same choices as you had when you took your first hit, puff or whatever you take. And you will continue have those choices, no matter how bad or even great your life gets!' With that, Sandra again looked up and around to see that no one else was listening in.

Sandra's answer was not exactly what Trisha had been expecting, especially from someone who seemed to be such a nice girl, and for a change, Trisha's wits offered nothing.

Using the silence as a space for another idea, Sandra suggested a way.

'Listen to me, Angel. You, very rightly, sound very angry about your childhood abuse, but have you ever thought seriously about some serious counselling? We don't do long term counselling here, over the phone, but you can go our web site, lots of the site's sponsors advertise such services and many other services, and many of them don't charge!' We also have our own in-house resi …'

At the other end of the line, Trisha suddenly twitched with uncertainty, but answered, 'I've done all that crap! Of course I'm fucking angry …'

'And have you also realised,' Sandra insisted, 'that some of your anger, may be aimed at your own attempts to lead a normal life?

'What the fuck do you mean, my own attempts…?'

Sandra was on free roll by now, and she was speaking not just from the manual but her gut, 'Listen Trish, no one likes to admit or show they are damaged, it makes them feel and appear vulnerable. It makes them an easy target! So like a sick or wounded animal, they will try and hide their vulnerability, no matter how much pain or further damage it will cause! It is a form of camouflage, for whenever they feel threatened or challenged! Other people even try to hide their damage from themselves – and get angry at any attempt to live a normal life – including giving up drugs!"

'What do you mean?'

'I mean that every time you try any attempt to give up drugs, and live a normal, undamaged life, without having first repaired the damage your abuser caused, then you get angry, and that anger will sabotage your efforts to be normal, every time!'

Trisha answered, laughing, 'If you think I blame myself for being abused, that I'm on some self-punishment kick, then darling, you got more than one fucking screw loose – you're completely unscrewed! '

For a moment, Sandra waited to collect her thoughts, before she continued.

'Some victims do punish themselves, out of a false sense of guilt. Yet others continually self-harm, in order to keep their wounds, open.'

'Why the fuck should I want to keep my wounds open?'

'To ensure that the, *injustice*, of the abuse is not *diluted*! Let's face it, Angel, if the abuse has caused no harm, then where is the wrong? And how can you condemn the abuser '

Once again Trisha found that her wits came up short, so she said nothing.

'It is a form of martyrdom "justice," Sandra continued, 'that can be very tempting, even if their abuser is caught and publically punished. Either way, I'm not saying that you don't blame your abuser, Trisha. But justly blaming someone for damaging you, is not anywhere nearly as, just, as taking the steps to heal that damage.'

'What do you mean … martyrdom?'

'Look … you might feel very upset at … say … being burgled. Yet even if the burglar were caught and punished, how would you feel about yourself, if you then decided; that you didn't really need to even bother to try to get your property back, because it had been somehow, tainted!

Especially if your property included valuable things like … we'll you tell me Angel. What precious qualities do you think your abuser, or any such abuser, devastates? Or perhaps I should say makes … worthless?'

There were, of course, several precious qualities that Trisha could name. But saying any one of them, out aloud, suddenly seemed to become rather difficult, so once again she stayed silent!

'And when you've thought of some of those, stolen qualities, tell me what you think of someone who, abandons them?'

Sandra was not meaning to insult Trisha, but she was meaning to goad her – and she did!

If the heavily pregnant woman, from before, had blushed at Trisha's previous emotional outburst, then had she been with her now, she would have given birth on the pavement, right then and there!

'Are you fucking crazy? You stupid fucking ... cow!' Trisha screamed! It was a rhetorical question, but when Trisha carried on, her voice was full of menace, 'I didn't abandon them! They were fucking taken from me! I try every day to get them back, you stupid fucking *cow*! And just because I take drugs and work the fucking streets, doesn't mean I'm a fucking nobody! I am who I am, and I do what I do! But I have respect, and I give respect – you fucking disrespectful . . . cunt!'

However, Sandra was not pregnant, and although she was easily moved, she was not easily embarrassed.

'So like I said, how would you feel about someone, who didn't really try and claim those precious things back?'

For a long moment, Trisha was speechless then she said, not screamed, 'I have tried! I . . . I . . . just don't know where . . . to find them anymore!'

At that moment, Sandra was moved, and when she replied, it was with sadness, rather than any sort of accusative tone or manner. 'That may be because you've hidden them too well!'

As Trisha stood there, she felt an urge to run, but she remained.

Then Sandra continued, 'You may have hidden them, behind a sense of martyrdom, or even some other reaction – including that of safe keeping - to protect them from further damage. But protection is a double edged sword. And as long as you continue to use it, you will get doubly angry at any attempt to bring your true loss, into the open.'

The emotional tension between both women was beginning to tell, as both began to feel drained. But Trisha attempted one more thrust.

'Look sweet-heart, I know you are trying to do good. And I'm not saying what you say is wrong. But to be frank with you sweet-heart . . . I don't give a fuck! Life isn't perfect at the moment it's true, but I get by. That stuff, in the ally way was a one off! But it proved I do have a good heart, telling the police and all that. So don't worry about me. When the time is right I will get off the drugs – and when I do, maybe I'll give you a call, in fact I promise I will . . .!'

Sandra however was not easily fooled. 'Thanks, but to be frank with you, sweetheart, any attempts to give up your drugs and lead a undamaged life, are just fairy stories!'

'Well thanks for the vote of confidence, Miss Know it all!'

'OK! How many times have you tried to get of the *habit*, and carry on as if you're living a normal life?'

Trisha's answer sounded tired rather than angry, 'A few times, I was clean for eighteen months one time . . .!' Never the less, when she heard the word "habit," she also made a mental note; that Jake her dealer hadn't called back yet. If his wife (June) was very busy, at their gift and card shop, then Jake might even be picking up their kids from school. In addition, if she (Trisha) hung up very soon, she might still have time to get another punter!

However, she decided to give Sandra just a while longer, but as there was no point in ending up with nothing, Trisha turned and headed towards "her corner," even though it was no more than three minutes away from the dreaded ally way! Then speaking into her phone she continued.

' . . . I've tried many times to change!'

'And sooner or later failed!' Sandra stated, 'Because deep down, inside of you, you believe that any such attempts, by themselves, are just trying to carpet over the missing floorboards, the missing sense of complete justice! And until your efforts go hand in hand with identifying and healing all of your damage – the missing qualities, then sooner, rather than later, you're going to put your foot through one again, and again, and again . . . Angel!'

Then almost as if speaking to herself, Sandra added, 'It's a lot like sentencing yourself, to a life of imprisonment, for a crime your abuser should be serving instead! But like my Aunt used to ask, "Why pluck a chicken when it can't even fly?'

The relevance and reference to her own past life, did not escape Sandra, and she was suddenly full of doubts that she might be straying too far from the Crime Frontier's documented help advice.

'Ok! Forget the chicken bit!' she said then genuinely stated, 'Of course you have tried, many times … and in the end they all failed. I also know that it takes a huge amount of courage, to try again, and again. But sometimes, it's the small things that trip up our big hopes. Like even small upsets, that can throw us off balance, and stop us from moving on.' Sandra then continued (whilst referring to her Advisor Training Manual, under the heading: "The one step escalator."

'Have you ever stepped onto an escalator, that isn't moving? Yet, when you step on it, it feels, as if the escalator and you are moving? Well having your commitment being thrown, off balance, is like being on an escalator that's stopped working. But, not taking that extra step, that extra effort to keep you moving, can leave you stranded, going nowhere!' Then putting the manual aside, Sandra decided it was now or never, and trying to sound as reasonable as she could, she said, 'Ok Trisha! What I'm about to ask you is a question, not an accusation.'

'OK! I get that!' Trisha replied, pensively.

'Ok! What I am saying is that; if you want to keep on putting your foot, in it, and crippling yourself, then although it's not fine, it is your choice! But … if you want to fix the whole floor … the whole house, then we can help! It will take time, but we have tools and people, good people to help you make it easier. So what do you want to be Trisha, a cripple … or carpenter?'

Silence …!

Then Trisha replied, more in humour than self-condemnation, 'When I had my own flat once, I decorated it all by myself, never done any carpentry though!'

'That's OK!' Sandra replied, 'It's your home, it's your life. All you gotta' do is keep knocking those nails on the head!'
'I can do that,' Trisha replied.
'Good!' Sandra answered, 'Because you're going to be the one holding the nails … Angel!'

The next ten minutes were spent with Trisha, waiting for any punter to show up, and discussing the possibilities of how she could enter the helpline's, drying out clinic, in London. After which, she could then, perhaps, attend the Crime Frontiers residential course. After getting a firm promise from Trisha, that she call back whenever she wanted, and would visit the clinic (just to have a look) by the following afternoon, Sandra said a final, 'Good luck and thank you!' and Trisha rang off.

After Trisha had rung off, Sandra went to the canteen, and enjoyed a well-deserved break and a coffee. Sandra was also enjoying the fact; that she had done well with Trisha – and with only referring to the helpline manual twice!
Of course as pleased as she was, Sandra knew that she still had a lot to learn. Some of the negotiators were able to conduct a "Fair Exchange Swap" no matter what crime the call was about, even first time callers. The exchange was run on a, good news bad news basis. For every advantage the client saw by committing their crime, the negotiator would point out an unavoidable disadvantage. Some of the best negotiators would even point out "advantages" that the caller hadn't thought of yet. In some exchanges, a few swaps were enough, at other times the exchange would last much longer. In the end, the client was left to decide for him or herself.

Never the less, as she drank her coffee, Sandra was very pleased with herself! The only thing she did regret; was that Andy had not stayed, to hear her success!

Back on the street, Trisha headed back to her friends flat. It was too near the "sweeping up time" to stay around her usual spot. However, two minutes later, Jake, her dealer, returned her call! Fifteen minutes later, Trisha had "Put her foot in it" yet again! But then, yet again, it did feel such a . . . *snug* . . . fit!

Chapter 11:

CHIEF INSPECTOR MILES RUPERT

In spite of young Debby's fears about England, being full of crocodiles and very stupid policemen, Detective Chief Inspector Miles Rupert, knew that (with a few exceptions) the truth was opposite. Never the less, as Rupert speed dialled his home number, he was very much hoping that it all didn't "Kick off!' For although being a good negotiator was part of his abilities as a good police officer, Rupert knew he was no match for Julie, his wife, when she felt that she had been wronged! Moreover, being stood up for their ninth wedding anniversary meal, especially as it was a special home cooked one, would undoubtedly make Julie feel rightly, wronged!

Unfortunately for Rupert, he also knew that, if the only solid leads to the "The Face Painter" murder case, were not chased down that very night, then by the following morning; they might well be worth no more; than a trail blood-stained footprints left in a fast thawing snow!

In this case, the "footprints" were a series of mainly typewritten letters, from the Face Painter himself! The letters (surprise, surprise) taunted the police about their lack of progress in catching him. On each letter, the murderer had carefully made sure that none of his DNA or fingerprints were on the letter, envelope or stamp. However, whether through a sense of self-importance, or self-delusion, the murderer had signed every letter "The Artist of Death," in his own handwriting!

It had been Rupert's call to put a part of one of the letters, with the handwritten signature, on "Crime Watch," the popular TV show that tried to gain the public's help in solving crimes and in catching criminals. Rupert's gamble was that someone "out there" would recognize the handwriting and call in with a name. Particularly as there was the added bonus of a substantial cash reward.

The "melting snow," was the ever-increasing possibility, that whoever the

Face Painter may be, he would see or get to hear about the Crime Watch appeal, and then flee to any place that Rupert and his team could randomly stick a "damned" pin in!

On a personal note, the melting snow effect for Rupert was the reality that; if the Face Painter was not caught that night, or very soon, the case would be taken over by another senior detective. But more than being dropped from the case, and from any prospects of near promotion that went with catching the killer, the thing that horrified Rupert; was the taunting boast, typed at the end of the first letter from the murderer! The boast was that, he would face-paint each of his victims a different colour and design, so they could all be part of his "bigger picture!"

Within one hour of the Crime Watch appeal, there had been six names put forward by the public. Another twenty two names were eventually added, via the wild fire spread of the appeal and letter on the internet. By 11 am, the following day, Rupert's team had narrowed the "names" to a handful of probabilities. However, the most probable "name" was that of a Keith Longbottom, a man with a history of violence. It was to Longbottom's last known address, in a quiet suburb just outside of London, that Rupert and his team were getting ready to "knock!" on.

Back in the operations room, Rupert heard a bubbly Julie, cheerfully answer the phone by the third ring … and slam it down by the fourth explanation that he had apologetically offered, for not being home by seven o'clock that night!

'We're all ready to go sir!' Rupert's right hand assistant, Detective Sergeant Tom Vanner earnestly shouted, as he poked his frowning face around the Operation room's permanently squeaky door. 'If we don't get a move on, he'll have flown … if it is our bird that is!'

Rupert pressed the re-dial button but the dial tone came back as 'message receiver.' Still holding the door open, the sergeant frowned even harder, whilst Rupert paused for another agonizing minute…!

The breaking news of the "Spectacular arrest of The Face Painter serial killer," came on the "Ten o'clock News" that very evening, as Rupert and Julie watched it with mixed emotions. Rupert and Julie saw and heard Rupert's boss, Chief Constable Pitch, state that a 39-year-old man was in police custody, on suspicion of murder. Pitch also stated that further charges, relating to the recent spate of strangulation murders would, 'Most definitely be brought within the next 24 hours!'

After the news about the capture of the Face Painter, Julie and Rupert watched the news item on three other news channels. After they both finished their anniversary champagne drinks, Julie switched the off the TV and they both went to bed. At 11.47 p.m. a hot and panting Julie, answered the bedside phone, 'It's Pitch for you!' she said, as she handed the receiver to an equally hot and panting Rupert.

Rupert could tell by the "squeaky" Operation's room door, going fourteen to the dozen; that the team were back at headquarters. He could only just hear Pitch's elated voice over the din, even though Rupert's boss was almost shouting down the phone.

'Sorry to interrupt you on such a special occasion, Tom Vanner told me about your anniversary. But thought I'd give you a bell to say we've definitely got the bastard! It was Longbottom alright! We've got photos on his mobile and everything, we've even got the face paint he used.'

Rupert tried to calm his breath before replying, 'That's great sir! I'm sorry...'

'I'm sorry you weren't here too!' the Chief Constable interrupted, 'but no apologies needed! You did what you felt was the right thing to do! If there's one thing I've learned over the years Rupert, it is that a good detective knows how to prioritize feelings, as well as the facts!'

'Thank you sir,' Rupert replied.'

'Come in tomorrow at midday,' Pitch replied, 'and not before! If you want to lead the interview with Longbottom, you're welcome of course. Bye the bye, if you and your dear lady, would care to come over for lunch on Sunday, me and my better half would be delighted . . .after all we need to discuss your future . . . Miles!'

Before Rupert could check with Julie about the Sunday, the phone went dead. Rupert then put the phone down and smiled at Julie, 'Fancy doing … it … on the spare bed?' he suggested.

'But you keep complaining it squeaks,' Julie replied.

'I know.' Rupert grinned!

The next Sunday found Rupert and Julie enjoying a traditional Sunday roast dinner, on the patio of the Pitches'' well-kept garden. After lunch, Julie and Miranda Pitch swapped gardening tips, over a casual sharing of the clearing and washing up. On the patio, Pitch and Rupert enjoyed a surprisingly good homemade beer.

'It's another one of Miranda's priceless skills you know,' Pitch volunteered as he raised his 18th century pewter mug to Rupert. 'Don't know where I'd be old chap, if she took off with some one more deserving,' Pitch admitted with a wry smile, then looking at Rupert he said, 'You know of course, that your promotion is almost in the bag, now that this bloody Face Painter animal is too … in the bag that is!'

In response, Rupert tried to look interested and pleased in the same moment, but as Pitch was turning to refresh their beer at the time, it was academic. After topping up both tankards, Pitch carried on with his drift, though Rupert detected that it had not reached its final destination just yet. Pitch then took a long gulp of beer and wiped his mouth.

'Of course you know what these things are like old bean, things won't be final for months yet – bloody procedures you know. Just like these dammed bloody road humps – can't put your foot down when you want to, even if the road is clear ahead!'

Rupert outwardly nodded in mutual acceptance, whilst inwardly smiling at the well-known fact; that Pitch, had twice partially written off his official limousine whilst driving along the winding, hump free road leading to his house. In the end, Pitch was only allocated another car, after the Home Secretary's insistence, (via Marjorie's gentle hinting to the Home Secretary's mother) that he could only use the car with a chauffeur.

'Anyway' Pitch offered, 'thought you'd like to fill in, in the meantime, by taking over a new case!'

"Ah!" thought Rupert, with another attempt to look interested and pleased, "Now we're getting there you canny old bastard."

The "Canny old bastard," stopped in mid-tankard-rise and looked with one bushy eyebrow raised at Rupert. Rupert looked questioningly back then Pitch broke the silence.

'Of course it would be nice if you could wrap the new case up before your promo' is rubber stamped. But if you don't manage to do so, it probably won't affect the eventual outcome of the promotion, old chap!'

Rupert's stomach felt as it were doing a bungee jump out of his midriff and towards his feet, as it always did whenever a new case was on offer. Never the less, he managed to sound calm when he replied, 'It all sounds like a good idea sir, what's the case?'

Pitch downed some more of his beer and then smiled. 'We code-named it "Achilles!" Partly on account, of this bastard's nasty habit of leaving different body parts spread all around London. We also call it "Achilles" in the hope, that his seemingly insatiable craving for notoriety, will be his Achilles heel.' As Pitch further described the case, Rupert already knew what the case was about, but he let his boss unfold it in his own way.

'You probably know some of the case,' Pitch continued, 'through the grape vine and newspaper reports. They are calling it the "Body Part Murders!" You can get the full update from the op's room. Whitney Jones has handled it so far but he's off to Scotland, he's got a good team in place already, but you can pick your own team of course.'

Rupert had indeed heard about the case, it would have been difficult not to. Over the last two years, three men and one woman, all considered attractive and successful, had been abducted and murdered, or murdered in their place of residence. In all cases, a body part of the victim had been found in an "appropriate" place!

The first known murder victim was a self-made property millionaire. His severed and bagged feet, were found outside a shoe shop, along with a note saying: "Try size 9"

The second victim, a prominent political writer, had his ears posted through the letterbox of the "Society for the Deaf and Partial Hearing." Along with the ears, there was a local map, with a cross on it, pinpointing the rest of the victim's whereabouts, plus a printed note stating: "Ears the rest of him!"

A charity shop received the hand of the serial killer's next unfortunate prey, a high profile barrister. Her hand was clutching a note saying: "I thought you needed a helping hand!"

The penis of the fourth poor soul had been mailed to a "Sex Advisory Clinic." Once again, there was a note; the note had only one word on it: "Oops!"

The Body Part Murder case had been just about the most high profile case that there had been for some years, and Rupert knew it. Rupert also knew that it was no mere "fill in" job, if he messed this up, he might well mess his promotion up too!

Now, the rest of Rupert's internal organs seemed to think that bungee jumping was in fact, a jolly good idea, as they proceeded to follow his stomach's example, whilst his runaway mind seemed to deny all association, as it in turn, skipped along the top of the Pitches' well-maintained garden hedge!

It was Pitch, who brought Rupert's scattering self-awareness back together.

'We don't have any concrete information about this bastard at all, I'm afraid. There has been a country wide newspaper appeal, and we even managed to get two spots on Crime Watch.' At that moment Pitch looked around, almost as if he were checking that he was not being overheard, 'Now Whitney Jones has phoned me this very morning, to tell me, that this missing girl, Rita Knightly, severed head has turned up this morning – outside a bloody hair dressers if you please! There's no note, as far as I know, but it looks to be this bastard's latest! Apparently, the poor girl had recently been crowned her county's beauty queen . . . the poor girl! Anyway . . .'

At that moment, Rupert's boss stopped speaking as a smiling Amanda Pitch appeared. Miranda laid a tray of tea, milk, sugar and plate of very appetizing homemade pastries, onto the iron cast garden table. Reminding her husband, not to spoil his appetite for dinner in three hours, she then returned to the lounge through the French windows. Mrs "P" had heard her husband detail many saddening cases over the long years, too many to want to be saddened or appalled by them anymore.

Once Mrs "P" had closed the French windows, Pitch continued. Sitting down in his deckchair again, Pitch looked up at Rupert, with plain exasperation and informed him, 'We do know, that all of his victims were given a cocktail of powerful sedatives, before death and dissection. But so far, we have zilch! No prints or DNA, no description, the notes are all printed by different, but common laser printers, in short there are no forensics to speak of at all, not at even one of the crime scenes!'

Then delicacy picking up the smallest of Mrs P's pastries, but not raising it to his mouth, Pitch looked painfully towards the weathered bronze nymph, almost hidden by the hanging leaves of an ancient willow tree at the far end of the garden.

Then he concluded, 'So far, we haven't even managed to get a sniff of the bastard – let alone a bloody name!'

Chapter 12

GLITTERING HORIZONS

'My name is . . . *Steven!*'

As soon as Sandra heard his voice, she knew that this call was different from the sixteen other calls, she had dealt with that day. She knew it was different because this voice, felt different. Other voices had been sad, brave, frightened, hurt, friendly and even insulting; but this voice was deep, very cold and bored! Never the less, using her Advisor pseudo-name, Sandra replied as non-plussed as she could.

'Hello Steven my name is Susan, how can I help you?'

'How can you help me?' Steven replied, speaking into his unregistered "pay as you go" mobile phone. Then, pausing to look disappointedly down at the home cooked spare-rib, which he held in between his forefinger and thumb, he continued.

'Well let us see . . . Susan . . . is that your real name? No matter it will do. How can you help me? Well . . . at this moment Susan, I seem to have all that I need, so perhaps you cannot, help me. Unless that is, you can somehow . . . magic, some mango chutney to me?'

Sandra blinked once, in curiosity, and then consciously watched the lie detector readout, that automatically rolled across the bottom of her screen. As soon as any caller to Advice line began to speak, the detector automatically started reading the caller's voice patterns, pitch and nuances, then the detector gave an opinion as to the "honesty" of the caller's statements.

Various versions of the detectors are in use by a multitude of private and governmental, fraud prevention bodies, including the Welfare Benefits Fraud Detection dept. The Crime Frontier's version is a good version, but it is viewed as a guide, rather than any absolute reading. Never the less some Advisers-negotiators find the detector a useful aid.

When Sandra looked at the readout, she noted that it had not budged from -

TRUTH – whilst and since Steven had told her his name; however it was early days yet.

‘This is a crime advice line, to help people to deal with crime, Steven,’ Sandra answered. ‘I’m afraid we don’t do deliveries of chutney, mango flavoured or otherwise. Perhaps there is something more we can help you with?’

Steven answered immediately, ‘But it is too late to help me with my crime … far too late Susan! However some chutney would help no end, in making my latest victim, a little more … digestible!’

Almost without thinking about it, Sandra looked at the readout on the truth indicator, and then she immediately pressed the HELP button!

After she had silently returned Bell’s acknowledgement, Sandra then asked, ‘I’m not sure of your meaning Steven, could you be a bit plainer?’

‘Well it’s like this Susan,’ Steven painstakingly explained, ‘At the moment I am sitting on a bench, in a shopping arcade, and I am eating the remains, a rib to be exact, of my latest victim. I am eating a portion of her ribs, out of the Kentucky Fried Chicken box, which I serendipitously saved from last night’s last minute meal. Unfortunately, in my effort to do justice to Rita, my latest victim, I did not use any herbs or sauce … do you know what serendipitously means Susan?’

Sandra found herself feverously trying to rally her emotions and thoughts as she also realised, that the degree of underlying coldness and boredom (and apparent truth) in her caller’s voice, had hardly fluctuated since he began talking.

In his glass booth, unsure about the look of high discomfort on Sandra’s face, Bell prompted, ‘It means a lucky providence,’ then he added, ‘You are doing very well and I am here.’

‘Yes I think I know what serendipity means, it means a lucky providence or chance!’ Sandra answered Steven.

‘That’s right!’ Steven congratulated. ‘You get a gold star, or should it be a silver star and a stripe, judging from your good ol’ US of A accent, Southern if I'm not mistaken?'

'Let's just leave it that I'm from the US of A, Steven. Though I'm afraid that if you want to earn a star yourself, then you're going to have to tell me a bit more about the reason you've called. We only give stars for complete openness here. For instance, if it is too late to help you to stop a crime, why did you phone today?'

Steven suddenly looked up from his newspaper, and then wondered about the people passing by; as they trudged or hurried past or into the usual shops and stores, he then returned to his call.

'Oh! I phoned out of sheer … vanity! It is one of the few things that I have left! In fact, it is my most loyal trait amongst the continuingly deserting pleasures, of this disloyal life! Apart from free choice, of course, but then you can abuse that, time and time again, yet it will still mindlessly spring back up again! Which means its freedom and therefore its loyalty doesn't really count for much.

Vanity however is far more discerning! Though my guess is that you are not a hard line user of vanity, or if you are then you're still in denial, and are calling it pride, or positive self-thinking! You must feel, very, proud, when you manage to re-route some lost and undeserving soul onto the path of righteousness, Susan!'

'I think … or at least, I try to help some times, that is all I can do,' Sandra replied then added, 'but if I'm completely honest, I'm just a sucker for a bargain!'

'Bargain?'

'Well, when I first applied for this position, they told me that the two most powerful motivations in life are; the survival and evolution of one's self, and that of one's own kind! So, I thought, what the hell, if I do this job, then I'd get two powerful motivations … for the price of one! But then that's just little ol' me, Steven. What's your reason for doing what you do?'

Back in the shopping centre, Steven smiled, paused and then replied, 'Oh I do not need a reason, I just am!'

Some people who contact the advice line, needed to be listened to, some needed to be gently but firmly guided, whilst others required education, in the consequences of their crime, both to the victims and them self. Sandra however instinctively knew, that any of these approaches would be seen as a weakness by this man, and something to be preyed upon!

Trying not to be too overwhelmed, Sandra replied, 'Is that the biblical version of "I Am what I Am" or the one from "Pop Eye the Sailor man?"

'Oh be assured Susan, it is strictly my own!'

'Well I'm not sure that I do find that so reassuring! 'Sandra quipped then added, 'But I take it, that, you do not you think that you are undeserving, or lost?'

Steven's reply was instantaneous, but for the first time his tone expressed some emotion, it was anger, 'Lost, No! You have to care about your destination to feel lost, and as for feeling undeserving … then my answer is no! What I have gained I have gained by naked ambition, Susan – and you have no idea of the tedious troubles I've had to go to, to get the freedom that I deserve!'

For a moment, Sandra said nothing, and then she replied, 'There is massive difference between freedom and free-loading, Steven!'

'Really?' Steven replied, 'Then let me ask you a question. If you could take a long-lasting pill, to make you a permanently good person, would you? Not that I'm suggesting that you are bad, but if you did take it, you'll just be a better version of you, than you otherwise would have turn out to be. Would you take it Susan?'

For a moment Sandra said nothing, so Steven continued.

'Or perhaps you would crush one into a junkies "fix,' so they'd be forever saved? Or you might give such a pill to your children, if they misbehaved, Susan. And after you've given them their medicine, and put away their temptations, along with all their other childish toys, would you sleep easy in the knowledge that their troublesome free will is finally at an end? Would you feel a better person, for doing that Susan?'

Again, for a moment Sandra said nothing.

'No?' Steven asked and then added, 'Then be careful before you mock how I celebrate my, freedom, to do as I please!'

Then Sandra spoke, 'Can I ask you a question?'

'Yes!'

'If you could make a short term, free-choice, that would turn you into a better person . . . would you?'

'I make such choices every day!' Steven replied, with a touch of annoyance! At that moment, and though Steven would have disputed its findings, for the first time the needle on the indicator flicked towards "LIE."

Noting the needle flicker, Sandra continued, 'Yet you still haven't told me want you want from calling today.'

'My, my . . . you are a persistent little saviour aren't you?' Steven retorted. 'Well . . . the reason I called today is . . . because, I want to share . . . and to warn! But not just to warn you Susan. I want to warn all the little lost souls who call you in the future. You see, just because I happen to be a completely misunderstood serial killer, it does not mean, that I do not have a sense of philanthropic duty!'

When Sandra did not respond, Steven continued, although the lie detector did not show whether the mounting helpfulness in his tone, was false or genuine.

'I am here to share, Susan, to tell you and your future callers. That although this is something I haven't tried before, eating a fellow human's flesh that is. I must never the less, share the truth! And that is, that for the life of me, I cannot see what all the fuss is about! It really isn't worth all the effort!'

Sandra did her very best to control her nerves, by answering, 'I'm glad that you think so. But to be honest, Steven, cannibalism is not something that we'd be recommending to our callers anyway! Never the less, if any of them are thinking of trying it out, then we will pass on your comment – anonymously of course!'

After trying her very best, Sandra stared in an almost trance at the bottom of her screen, which continued to declare that this man was telling the truth. She then indicated that fact to Bell, who in return told her that if she wanted him to take over he would, though he still thought she was doing fine.

'Thank you! But I must admit,' Steven continued, 'I was wondering what the reactions of the passers bye would be, Susan. If they realised, that the freshly homemade and chopped up portion of rib, that I am holding to my lips, at this very moment, came from the very same … wait a minute … let me see the headline again.'

Steven returned the rib he was holding into the box, wiped his fingers, and turned the national newspaper to the front page. Reading the banner headline out aloud, he quoted: "Beauty Queen Still Missing!" then scanning down the page, he added, 'Oh! Yes, here it goes on: "Police intensify search for abducted beauty queen, Rita Knightly, who according to worried police sources is still missing!"

Then putting his newspaper down on the bench beside him, then quickly surveying the surrounding shops and shoppers, and then leaning forwards, he added in a conspiratorial tone of voice, 'But as you know, Susan, you should never believe everything you read in the papers! In fact, I can reliably tell you, that this news is way out of date!' Pausing to think and to pick up the rib again, Steven then carried on, 'But I will say, that I can now also tell you, Susan, what by now, the latest TV news will already be eagerly, telling its viewers. And that is, that dear Rita, may, have become the latest victim of "The Body Part Murderer!"

Then leaning forwards even further, Steven triumphantly informed Sandra, 'But on that fact, I can give you an exclusive! I can tell you that poor Rita has become the latest victim of The Body Part Murderer!'

In her booth, Sandra felt she should say something, even if it was the obvious, 'Are you saying you are this man, this Body Part Murderer?'

'My, my! Persistent and astute! We really are on the ball today aren't we,' Steven quipped. 'The police found poor Rita this morning, or at least they found her once proudly, crowned head, in the doorway of some hairdressers. Which is, where poor Rita's head and I, parted company, last night!'

Then, bringing the late Rita's rib, up to his mouth again, Steven apologized in advance, 'But for now you must excuse me, for just a moment Susan, for I must return to eating Rita's homemade, barbecued rib. And as far as I am concerned, I really do believe that it is the height of bad manners, to speak with one's mouth full . . . even if it is to an American!'

In her booth, and to her total horror, Sandra could hear the unmistakable sound of Steven chewing, with what sounded like his mouth deliberately left open! As she listened in horror, she felt an immediate rush of nausea – and then her own ribs suddenly ceased to move! She stared at the computer screen, waiting for the indicator needle to move towards LIE, but it didn't budge from the TRUTH!

Slowly but instinctively, Sandra tried to push herself away from her desk, whilst the sounds of Steven's chewing, drowned out all other attempts at any logical thought from her brain. With a super conscious effort, she tried to remain in touch with what was happening. Never the less, she hardly heard Bell's voice in her left ear, as her eyes closed, her head fell loosely forwards, and then her inner world began to frantically spin!!

The fact that the computer screen had read TRUTH since Steven had given his name, seemed a minor point to Sandra by now. It had no more significance than some channel logo in the corner of a TV screen. However, the channel now playing on the inner screen of Sandra's closed eyelids, was strictly for her private viewing!

Unbidden images of two giant hands appeared first. In the palm of the left hand, various miniature body parts lay, like dice, waiting to be thrown. On the palm of the outstretched right hand, there sat a Kentucky fried chicken box, which was overflowing with miniature limbs! As various limbs fell onto the palm of the giant hand, the index finger of the hand reflexed, in such a way that appeared to be inviting Sandra to take some of the dismembered limbs from the box. Then suddenly, both giant hands, silently, but quickly, high-fived each other, and then disappeared!

The next image to appear was a line of very tall shoppers, marching out of a toyshop doorway. All of the shoppers were carrying lumpy, blood-smeared, clear plastic shopping bags, bulging with a variety of blood drenched body parts. Then Sandra envisioned herself running towards the toyshop entrance, out of which, a very tall headless man came out and stood still, whilst he used his thumb and forefinger to silently "mouth" words to himself. Inside the man's clear-plastic bag, various aged and sized heads were talking to each other! Sandra could even hear some details of the conversations.

"Do you know, it's just murder trying to find a dress to fit me!" one severed head was telling another, who replied, "Tell me about it … if you don't I will never trust you again!' Then a neighbouring head speedily interrupted, 'She's listening!' The three heads then swivelled round to look at Sandra, and then turned again to look at each other, and then slowly closing their eyes, all the heads fell silent!

Still inside her own head, Sandra slowly walked towards the shop doorway. However, as she pushed the door open and entered, instead of a toyshop interior, she found herself inside a real memory! She was suddenly in the TV lounge of her childhood home; staring at her blood drenched dead mother's body. Then the fantasy seamlessly returned to one in which Sandra was back at the shop, except now she watching her mother's corpse, being auctioned off!

The main bidders, were a pair of obviously decomposing zombies, who were leaning side by side against the right hand wall. The zombies' main opposition, sitting at the front of the shop, was a large woman, wearing a pair of painfully fitting white shoes that had dark blue chunky heels; that she noisily stamped on the floor whenever she made a further bid.

When Sandra desperately tried to raise her own arm, to bid for the body of her dead mother, she found that for some reason she could not … then the reason became abundantly clear! Finally, the star of the horror made its appearance. Behind the auction rostrum, stood Sandra's own headless torso – with the bulging eyed, drunken head, of her father, stuck on top!

Her father's head was screaming, 'Five dollars! … I bid five dollars for the bitch!'

Then her father's head shouted out, 'Sold … to the lying bitch of a bitch's head at the back of the room!'

With that, the "auctioneer" brought the hammer slowly down – not onto the rostrum, but down towards Sandra's upturned face! As she watched the hammer's head slowly become bigger and bigger, she could see the word TRUTH embossed across its face, growing larger … and larger … and …!

Meanwhile, back in the real life-shopping arcade, Steven finally managed to swallow the scrap of Rita, which he had been resolutely trying to chew! He was also by now, growing piqued at the silence on the end of the line.

'Well Susan you're very quiet, a penny for your thoughts?'

Silence …!

'I was wondering, Susan, how you think the passing shoppers would react if they knew what, or rather who, I was tucking into?'

Supported by her desk and chair in the Hub, Sandra's inner and outer visions began to swap over again, as she began to black out altogether. Then in an act of physically painful, but primal rebellion, Sandra's ribs and diaphragm took charge as they filled her starved lungs and brain with an explosion of oxygen – but along with the oxygen came a flowing of primeval rage!

Without any real conscious decision, Sandra sprang up from her chair as if she were a released Jack in the box! Then with her jaw jutting forwards, she made chewing movements as if she were trying to gnaw at the phone's mouthpiece, and then she screamed out.

'What?'

Up in the Crow's Nest, Bell rose out of his chair, as all heads in the room swivelled in Sandra direction, but Sandra was way past the point of any self-consciousness.

'What is it with you fucking people! Just because we try to do some good … you somehow believe … that we are some kind of fucking doormat for your fucking … emotional bullshit!'

Back in the shopping centre Steven's head jolted slightly, then he replied, 'Actually . . . that is not my belief! I just choose to treat you like so!'

With that, Sandra lost it completely! *'Listen, you fucking idiot! I wouldn't save your fucking soul, if God all fucking mighty came down here and told me to! In fact if he did, I'd tell him to go and fuck himself too, which if you're so called pathetic, vanity, will allow you to register, Buddy, is what I am telling you to do! You fucking, full of shit, asshole!'*

With that said, Sandra sat down and with a trembling hand reached to stab the disconnect button! Her whole body was shaking with something that, at first, she did not even recognize, let alone try to understand! It was only then, that she realised, that there was a very loud silence coming from the rest of the room, and that every head in that room faced her direction.

However it was not embarrassment making her hand pause over the cut-off switch, it was recognition. Recognition that she had felt and expressed the power of her own rage, it was not the first time she had felt it – but it was the first time she had spontaneously expressed it!

Having never wholeheartedly admitted to himself, that he felt anger, let alone rage; Steven was both fascinated by it and fearful of it, so much so, that his hands were beginning to tremble. At first his right hand; the one holding the remains of Rita's rib, began to quiver ever so slightly, now more so, now it was shaking so much, that he began to worry that people would notice, so he dropped the rib back in the box.

Breathing quickly but deeply, Steven relaxed as much as possible to cover his own anger at being, so disturbed by this woman! Never the less, his attempts at calming himself were easily and defiantly, thrown aside, as he blurted, rather than merely spoke, into his mouthpiece.

'Then report me to the police!' he ordered, almost as if he were morally flabbergasted that she had not done so already! 'I am sitting in the Queensway Shopping Centre, in Paddington. My name is Steven and I am 42 years old, I have dark hair and a small scar on my right forearm, from a boating accident when I was young!'

Looking around to see that no passer bye had heard his outburst, Steven breathed deeply. His own, spontaneous, revelations, threw Steven almost as much as they did Sandra (and Bell up in the crow's nest!). Never the less Steven continued – as if it had all been deliberate!

'True!' he said, 'I am about to leave, and the phone isn't registered in my name, but if you give that number to the police, they could pinpoint my whereabouts, to within a few metres. What's more …' Steven continued, in an effort to assert his apparent control of the whole situation, '… I will make sure to have it with me, at all times!' then relaxing somewhat, he added, 'It will even be by my bedside, when I am asleep!' then relaxing even more he added, 'Why … you could even give me a call tonight, Susan … when I'm tucked up in my bed. Then you could tell me a bedtime story, wouldn't that be … cosy!'

The thought of being any way near this man's bed filled Sandra's mind with sheer spite; however, her reply was quite calm, even official sounding.

'We do not pass on anything that any caller says to our Advice line. We do not tell the police or any outside source – our Anonymity Code is an unbreakable rule, it is … absolute!'

There is a place, on some journeys, where the purpose of the trekker's original destination becomes, diverted or side tracked, by new possibilities on the horizon! Sometimes, those glittering horizons indicate the very borders of a more, wholesome, land.

At other times, they are mere illusions rather than practical possibilities! Glistening on the distant horizon of Steven's mind, and only hinting at a land full of even greater possibilities, was an idea! It was such an audacious idea, that Steven was now encountering, that his jaw dropped open, with the sheer audacity of it!

On such occasions, anyone can suddenly find him or herself plunging from their original path, and onto unplanned paths, or even onto pathless lands.

Sometimes, even though he might be sitting in a shopping centre, Steven liked to liken himself to the olden day explorers! Heroes, who willingly risked life and reputation, not to mention their sanity; to explore the treasure troves of, as yet, unchartered and unclaimed domains! What is more, although Steven regularly explored the "out of season resorts" of human morality, it was not as a mere tourist! In such places, Steven felt a kind of welcome! Not from the so-called local inhabitants, the likes of Rita or Mary or any other of his victims, their lives and morals merely served as "holiday" souvenirs!

No! Steven felt welcomed by the harshness of his explorations. Time and again, he would overcome; and the more he overcame, the more welcomed he felt, and just as importantly – he felt welcoming!

He welcomed the dread that he could, and did cause in such places! He was thankful for the hostility, and the insults, which his hostile actions created. Such reactions were like inspiring signpost; that pointed towards even more outlandish exploits!

Where the olden day explorers found new routes, Steven found new ways to bypass the meaningless of his own, every day, mundane, needs. Where the intrepid traveller conquered mountains, Steven rose above his mounting fears. Where pioneers planted their countries flags, he planted his terrifying signatures! In such places he, Steven, felt complete, and at home!

There are of course, other influences! Even for Steven, there were of course other forces at work – there always are! At other times, some stowaway of humane compassion would rise and grab the moral compass! At such times, Steven felt as if at some point in his past, he had been tricked somehow, and that he had been pressed-ganged into "serving" his ever more demanding compulsions!

Such mutinous compassions were infrequent, but when they struck, they left Steven feeling marooned, by the ever circling, sharp-toothed crimes from his past; whilst he in turn watched his hopes of a heroic rescue, disappear beyond the horizon, like floating ships deserting a drowning rat!

However, this was no time for stowaways! Sandra's comment about the "rules of anonymity, being absolute and unbreakable" had given Steven a completely fresh horizon to head for, and a new domain to explore and claim – for his very own!

'Rules are made for breaking … Susan … even absolute ones!'

Sandra did not hesitate to reply, 'Not so!' she stated with a defiance of her own, 'They are made to stop us breaking each other!' then she added, 'Didn't your bedtime stories teach you that, when you were a child Steven?'

For an instant, Steven felt the vulnerability of his childhood fears climbing aboard – but it made him lash out!

'Oh! Well done Susan!' he congratulated. 'You are pitifully wrong about rules of course. But well done, in letting me know your intimate feelings a while ago. You see how well we are getting along together! We have only just met, and already you have shared your deepest and most private thoughts and feelings about me. And on our first date too! Mind you, I hope that this doesn't mean that you're some kind of emotional slut … women can be a bit promiscuous when it comes to sharing their feelings … don't you agree?'

For a moment Sandra thought, then replied, 'I would ask you to return the favour, by telling me about your own feelings, but as I already know enough about you, it seems an unfair swap!'

'Really,' Steven quipped, 'well this could be amusing, do tell.'

Sandra looked up at Bell, who said, 'It's your call!'

Returning to Steven she replied, 'You are driven by fear …!'

'Everybody, is to some extent,' Steven interrupted, 'I do hope this is not going to be one of these caricatures, where one size fits all!'

'But not everybody is a criminal Steven!' Sandra replied.

'Of course they aren't, they haven't the courage!'

'Suppression of fear; doesn't always mean courage, Steven. Besides, like most criminals, you're more frightened of what will happen if you *don't* commit the crime, rather than if you do!' When Steven didn't answer, Sandra continued, 'And as for sharing my feelings, well at least my passion should also have told you, that I have feelings. And in spite of my outburst, I still do have caring feelings for you, Steven!'

Back in the shopping centre, Steven felt strangely barbed by Sandra's admission. However, he consciously noted that his hands had already ceased to tremble! He was feeling in control again.

'Oh! But I do have feelings Susan.' Steven said in a "hurt" tone of voice. 'You see, I too cried when Bamby's mother died …and when "The Snowman" melted!'

Glancing at her monitor, Sandra saw that the indicator had still had not shifted from "Truth." Leaning slightly forwards, she then whispered into the phone. 'What's it like to be a slave to your own homemade fears Steven?'

Up in the crow's nest, Bell looked up and momentary frowned with concern!

Back in the shopping centre, Steven felt a surge of anger, but remained steady enough to recall his fresh horizon, and then he plunged forwards!

'Fear …I'll show you fear!' before Sandra could say anything Steven continued, 'So, let me see, for fear … Mmmm … let me see … our fear … will be … I know!' Steven exclaimed then deliberately paused for effect.

'How about seeing, if you … can stop me killing? Not just killing anybody mind you, but killing one or more of your … Crime Frontiers chums!'

At that moment Sandra froze, but Steven continued, 'While, I in turn, will try to get you, to break your so-called, unbreakable, and absolute, Anonymity Code! By forcing you, to hand over my details … to the police! That way I'll have something to fear, just as much as you will! Then we will see who blinks first shall we, Susan?'

As the enormous implications of Steven's challenge slowly thudded into place, Sandra felt a surge of rising dread that she had not felt so intensely since her childhood. Never the less, she was no longer a child, and her answer was assured and calm, 'It's not wise to hope that others are as weak as you!'

'Anyone can be corrupted!' Steven answered menacingly, 'and once corrupted, anyone can break laws, including their own laws.'

Now Steven's voice became confident and far from bored, as he continued along the new purpose of his call.

'Well, my philanthropic sharing has turned out quite well, don't you think, almost karmic. As I said, all I wanted was to do was help, by sharing my views and disappointment, about eating poor Rita. However, now I have been rewarded with a new challenge, and that is to start killing your fellow employees, one, by one, by one!

And you have a new purpose too, which is to stop me from killing them. Stop me by fair means or foul, including breaking your precious code of anonymity! All you need to do is hand my details and phone number over to the police, so they can trace my exact whereabouts.

If you fail to do so … then I will trace, track and kill your fellow … Goody-goodies! And after each kill, I will inform the media clowns that I will continue to kill, until you do break your precious anonymity code!'

Sitting in her chair, Sandra could not think of an answer … neither could Bell ... and a deep silence followed!

'So!' Steven eventually ventured, 'Keeping your cards close to your pounding chest are you. Never mind, perhaps you would like me to open my heart to you! Would you like to know what I really think of Rita, in spite of having to kill her?'

For what seemed a very long time to Sandra, there was silence! But it was Sandra who spoke first.

'Yes I would like your honest opinion of Rita, Steven, I really would!'

'Oh!' Steven reassured, 'I am always honest, Susan. And I can honestly tell you that out of the two, poor Rita … that was … and last night's take away chicken, then I can honestly share with you, Susan, that the chicken … was far tastier! My name is Steven, my mobile number is 07815900350, and I shall have my phone with me, at all times!'

Bringing his phone down to his lap, Steven circled his rock steady forefinger over the disconnect button, and then with a satisfied sigh, he stabbed it, with a great amount of … relish!

Back in her booth, Sandra heard the line disconnect and saw the caller screen go vacant; but not before she noted, with a gut wrenching feeling, that even when Steven was giving his opinion of Rita, the indicator had not flinched as much as one iota from displaying the TRUTH.

Chapter 13

A MATTER MORAL-INDIGESTION

The serendipitous take-away box to which to which Steven referred to, came with his previous night's take-away chicken meal. The box had eventually allowed Steven to eat his homemade barbequed "Rita-ribs" in public, from an appropriately normal looking box. The original chicken meal had been a last minute affair, because Steven had spent most of the previous afternoon and night, disposing of the late beauty queen's not so "tasty" body parts. It had been coming up to 11 p.m. before Steven had deposited Rita's bagged head outside the hairdressers.

Steven had pondered whether it was worth cooking a meal at home, but decided against it; he already had Rita's roughly chopped ribs ready to prepare fully later on, and now he was feeling tired. He eventually went to the "Kentucky" near his place, and bought the last minute and as it turned out "serendipitously boxed" take-away.

As for the death of Rita, from his moral point of view, Steven judged that he could hardly take the blame for the series of events that had happened, so easily! In fact, in Steven's mind, it would have been ungrateful, if not downright rude, to refuse such an appropriate chance. Indeed, any such refusal would deserve every bit of clasping, clammy, regret that would have certainly hounded him, if he had not at least tried to kidnap and kill Rita! The fact that his efforts had been successful, were a bonus.

However, the conversation with the Crime Frontiers people had not gone as easily as Steven had presumed. It was true that the call to the helpline had served his purpose; that of providing some "spice" to the blandness of Rita's ribs. Never the less he had felt, disturbed, by the Susan woman! The rage of the American, Susan, had stirred something inside of him, and that was not part of his plan – nor was his impulsive challenge to her and Crime Frontiers! Now he had to figure out a way to either back down . . . or carry out his threat!

As far as Steven was concerned, the Susan woman's rant was impotent; and would remain so unless she did decide to give the police his details! However, in her rage she had given him a clue; for the amount of passion, which she expressed in her rage, had not diminished when she also "calmly" told him, that the Anonymity Code was "Absolute!" Sitting back down on the bench Steven relaxed somewhat, "Yes!" he concluded to himself, "I am safe . . . for now!"

Sitting on the shopping mall bench for a while longer, Steven drew some comfort from the partial safety that Susan's blanket rage had given him. However, there was a hindrance! The blanket did not quite cover him …entirely! His own reactions during the call had somehow left him feeling, exposed! It was as if there were a draught coming from … where …? For the moment, he could not identify its source, and it was this lack of self-knowledge, this gap in his own self-identity, that left Steven feeling unsure about his next course of action.

Dropping the newspaper and the remains of the ribs into a convenient nearby waste bin, Steven got up and walked off. However, he had hardly gone a few steps past the bin when he was "wrenched" back!

Retracing his steps, Steven stared into the full-length mirror, conveniently stationed outside a clothes shop. Frowning at his reflection, he was struck by how unhealthy he was looking. He decided that from that moment on, he would start a healthier diet and exercise even more than he did already. Invigorated by this latest idea for his wellbeing, he immediately went to buy some organic fruit and vegetables from "Marks and Sparks."

As he sauntered through the clothing isles of Mark's, Steven was hardly noticed (clothed as he was in his invisibility-cloak of normality!) to his fellow every day, normal shoppers, he seemed:

"Well . . . just . . . normal really! I'd have a beer or two wiv 'im."

"He looks like anyone else! Slightly … unapproachable I guess, better looking than some … better looking than my old man, that's for sure!"

"I think he's rather cute – a bit old for me, but you never know!"

Having arrived at the deli' counter without being lynched by a howling vigilantly mob, Steven was eventually served by a polite and enthusiastic woman, called Stella. As it happened, Stella was feeling a bit hyperactive because she wanted to be home and gone! Gone, to the circle-dance classes, to which she had been going to for six weeks now! To Stella the evening classes were a whole, fresh new world to explore, a bit scary, welcoming, challenging and exciting and a lot more!

Seeing that the shop assistant's bubbly mood matched his own, Steven easily started a polite conversation with her, and she even began to tell him about her dancing lessons. Then suddenly and for some reason beyond his conscious compression, the combination of Stella's obvious eagerness to be away and gone for her circle dancing, and her clear sense of duty to be a helpful counter assistance, somehow … touched Steven! In fact, Steven felt so mysteriously moved, that before he knew it he could feel himself (almost) wanting to cry!

To Stella, seeing Steven's discomfort, was as disturbing to her as it was to Steven. Whilst Steven's own reaction was to wonder, "What the fucking hell is happening to me?"

Stella's next reaction was that she began to panic! Presuming that she had overstepped the line, she quickly went back into being a normal counter assistant, and promptly gave her customer the space to make up his mind. After a quick exchange of cash, goods and awkward politeness, Steven eventually walked away with a slice of Stella's politely, recommended, leek and potato pie.

Heading towards the clothing department, Steven decided to leave the fruit and vegetables for now. As he walked, he tried to put his moment of "weakness" aside. He had, had a stressful few days, enjoyable stress it was true, but stressful never the less.

"Perhaps" Steven thought, "I should take up a hobby … not circle dancing though!" He had however played and enjoyed badminton a few years ago, so perhaps, "I should go back to that," he mused.

Whilst in Mark's, Steven also bought a shirt, a pair of plain trousers, underwear, shoes and a deep hooded top, to replace at least some of all the clothing he had burnt and disposed of after the abduction, dismembering and disposing of Rita.

By the time Steven got home with his shopping, he was suffering from indigestion! For a moment, he played with the idea that his physical discomfort; maybe caused by some deeply emboweled moral reaction to eating human flesh, as opposed to merely butchering it. However, he decided it was more probable; that his discomfort was more likely due to his preference for his meat to be under-cooked! Either way, he hoped that a dose of Alka-Seltzer would conveniently dissolve the problem.

Going to his bathroom cupboard, he popped a tablet into a glass of water and sat on the loo. After a short while, he got up again and added a pre-cautionary extra half tablet, calculating that this time his discomfort may well be due to some deep moral reaction. After all, when all was said and done, he had really quite liked Rita. She had even offered him sex, once she had gotten over her initial terror!

Although he was liberal about sex, he chose not accept Rita's offer. Accepting it would mean leaving his DNA trace all over and inside her body. Besides, it would be tant amount to rape, which as far as Steven was concerned was on par with aggressive begging; no matter how aggressive you got, you were still a beggar.

However, when Rita had offered to be so nice to him, Steven had pondered about keeping her as a sort of secret Love experiment.

Love had always a been a bit of a puzzler to Steven. So after her offer, he had seriously pondered about keeping Rita, and seeing if it were possible to, induce, her to love him. If he used an extension of the Stockholm principle (where bye a victim of kidnap can end up seeing his or her kidnapper as a saviour), could Susan come to truly love him? Unfortunately, to test if her love could be validated as true love, he would have to eventually free her, to see if she stayed with him or went to the police.

Steven was *fairly* sure that he could trust Love to overcome Susan's everyday morality, but to risk his very freedom, for what was essentially an academic pastime … ?

All in all the whole idea would be too dangerous, so he killed her instead. After killing Rita, it was just a matter of editing her remains for his and the media's taste for the sensational, then waiting for the reviews.

Steven hoped that the resulting news coverage of the "find" outside the hairdressers, would give the national newspapers a "head-line" to kick around for days; thus, full filling his ever-present hunger for needing to feel full-filled.

Unfortunately, for Steven, being morally-anorexic, required that he starve himself of empathy, which of course meant that he inevitably ended up feeling, somehow … empty! In reality and unfortunately for both himself and his victims, deep down, Steven could never dislodge the deeply emboweled and bulimic-self-hate, for what he had allowed himself to become!

Never the less, as he got up from his convenience, Steven let out a series of satisfying belches, and decided that if he indeed could not corrupt the Susan woman – then he would kill her!

Belching a satisfying final burp, Steven closed the bathroom cabinet door and walked out into his lounge, feeling almost light hearted, apparently, the 'Alka-Seltzer' had worked!

CHAPTER 14

FINGER TIPS ACROSS THE OCEAN

Anyway, enough of criminals and their like! Let's get back to Sandra and Andy, who are about to get on together like two peas in a pod!

Immediately after her gruesome and gruelling session with Steven, Sandra went for a "talk down" and case conference with both David Bell and Charlie Fenton. Bell decided that the threat from Steven was to be taken very seriously. In the meantime, Bell ordered that a memo be sent to all of the Crime Frontier's in-house employees, telling them of the basic facts of the threat. The memo would not include Steven's name or his telephone number.

The memo would also advise the staff about personal security. All duty Advisors/negotiators would be instructed; that if any caller asked for "Susan" they were to place the call straight to Sandra, or if she were absent, passed to Bell or Charlie Fenton. Bell assured Sandra that he would try to make sure that he would be the Standby, whenever she was in the building.

However, it was also decided not to inform the police about Steven or his threat; for that would be a breaking of the Confidentiality Code. Therefore, at least for now, the threat posed by Steven would stay, in-house. It was of course almost inevitable, that the news would leak out to the press, never the less, for the present, Bell would wait and see if Steven called again.

It was also inevitable that most staff would put two and two together. Indeed, after the memo went around, a few of the staff did ask Sandra for further information, but when she stated that she would not reveal any more than what was already in the memo, such questions ceased.

To his credit and Sandra's relief, when Andy saw Sandra, in the staff canteen the following day, he did not even mention the Steven incident! It was Sandra, who opened the conversation, when she approached Andy at the otherwise empty table.

'Thanks for your support the other day, with my indiscretion, and don't worry, I still know I owe you a whisky!' As it happened, Sandra had already told Bell and Charlie Fenton about asking Trisha to ring off and call back! However, the matter was brushed off by both men, with the proviso, that when she was in doubt, it was best to ask for help.

Smiling at Andy, Sandra concluded, 'I felt so tired after the shift, I decided to go home, but I couldn't find you to tell you, so I left a note in your mail box!'

'No problem, I got the note thanks!' Andy replied, whilst reassuringly raising his hand, which held a fork full of drooping spaghetti bolognaise, then he added with a playful condescending grin, 'Always ready to 'elp out a poor damsel in distress!'

Sandra stopped midway between sitting herself down, and decided not to tell Andy about the "blob" of bolognaise sauce that had just dropped down the front of his white cotton shirt! Instead, she laid her egg-mayonnaise salad on the table; smiled sweetly back at him, and then replied in her most demure voice.

'Oh! Why thank you, Oh true English gentle knight,' she then made a half curtsey as she sat down and un-wrapped her lime green, cotton napkin. Smiling a crooked smile, Sandra then added, with an emphasized mock southern state drawl, 'And here's little ol' me thinking, that such shining chivalry, was just some ol' long lost part of your Oldie World history!'

For a brief moment, the two of them looked at each other with sparring eyes above half parted lips.

Then smiling again Andy spoke first, 'Shows you what you know about 'istory then don't it … but then you are American!' Then without ever dropping his gaze from Sandra, he picked up his napkin, dipped it in his glass of water, and began to clean the bolognaise stain from his shirt.

As she held Andy's gaze, a ruthful smile curled along Sandra's top lip, and then she replied in her normal accent, 'Yes I know, but then we Americans, do have a reputation for looking forwards. But I guess that's why the rest of the world is always trying to catch up with us!'

For a moment, the two of them neither moved nor said anything – amid a growing almost sensual silence, then Sandra decided to offer a truce. Gently flapping her table napkin fully open, she said, 'Talking of looking forwards, I have been looking forwards to meeting you, out of hours so to speak. I liked some of your questions in the weekly workshops. You're not as dumb as you look,' with that said, she raised a forkful of sliced oiled tomato to her half opened lips.

'Are you saying that I'm dumb looking?' Andy challenged.

Sandra's fork dropped slightly, as her left eyebrow rose and she answered, 'Yeh!' You do, ever so slightly!' then returning to her mock southern state drawl, she added, 'But in a kinda' sexy way!' She then looked straight into Andy's eyes; opened her mouth, and then slowly began to chew her sliced tomatoes; being very careful not to wipe away the trickle of oil that was escaping down the right side of her chin.

Seeing the flicker of uncertainty in Andy's eyes, Sandra thought that she had been too open, too quickly! Wiping the napkin across her mouth, she half smiled.

'I'm sorry! I can be a bit straightforward sometimes! I . . .,' Sandra put down her fork and smiling once again she said, 'You know I seem to remember our old history teacher telling us about our involvement, in the Second World War. If I remember rightly, he said something about there being some sort of rallying call . . . something like, "Hands across the sea?" Sandra then held her right hand palm out to Andy.

Andy grinned widely, and then gently high-fived her, 'As it 'appens it was the ocean!' he replied, ''ands across the ocean, but what the 'ell . . . what's an ocean between friends?'

After their agreed truce and lunch, the two of them were just as eager to meet for a drink after their shift, and agreed to do so. Moreover, as each went to their respective booths, both Andy and Sandra were feeling a prolonged flush of expectant excitement!

Just over a "tediously-long" four hours later, Sandra and Andy sat across a stained oak table, in a secluded area of the almost deserted "Jar and Pepper" pub. The "Jar and Pepper" was the focal point in a small, thirty (odd) house village, situated seven miles from the Crime Frontier's complex.

It was only after Sandra had informed Andy; that she had told Bell and Charlie Fenton about her rule breaking, that both she and Andy were able to begin to fully relax. Andy then told Sandra, that for the record, he would have left such a call up to her anyway.

For the next fifteen minutes, Sandra then told Andy about part of the phone call from Steven (including about his "Take away" and his admission to being the Body Part Murderer). She also told him about the meeting with Bell and Charlie Fenton.

Andy then bought Sandra a "well earned" whisky and offered his support in any way he could give it.

For a while afterwards, both Sandra and Andy swapped summarized histories of their lives. Although Sandra did tell Andy about her father's murder of her mother, she made no mention of her father's abuse of her, and although she did briefly mentioned her last visit to her father in his jail, she most certainly gave no hint about leaving her father her "special little secret!"

Over the next round of drinks (two coffees) the couple, who were for to all intend and purposes, looking and acting like a couple, exchanged their stories about how they each got to join Crime Frontiers, with Andy ending the swap, with the tale of Almost and the twenty pound note! As Sandra settled down after laughing out aloud (for the first time since he had known her), Andy decided to risk their good fortune even further. He "nonchalantly" ran his fingertips along the inside of Sandra's bare left forearm, and for a lingering moment, they both shared a most definite sensual silence!

Looking at Andy and then at his hand, Sandra whispered, even though the bar was still almost empty, 'Err! As good as your hand feels where it is, I'm not sure that this is the right thing to do – you know "flings with work colleagues" and all that?'

'Fair enuff!' Andy replied, withdrawing his hand but adding with a mischievous smile, 'But I've known my hand for thirty two years, and it's never been seriously wrong yet!'

An hour and a half later Sandra and Andy sat, cuddled, on Andy's couch. Although neither of them had exceeded their drink-don't drive allowance, it was Andy that drove them both to Andy's comfortable, rented, one bedroom flat. The flat was a well-furnished and maintained, in a Victorian period house. Andy had moved to the flat shortly after he had committed himself to Crime Frontiers, on a year's contract (leaving a trusted pal to run his market stall). The house was some ten minutes' drive from Crime Frontiers.

Cuddling even closer together, Andy moved his "trusty" hand along and in between Sandra's legs, causing not only them, but also her already open mouth to open even wider. Then with a half laugh, half a gasp and a lot of will power, Sandra closed her legs, trapping Andy's hand where it was, she then closed her open mouth onto his! After some moments of passionate kissing, Sandra pushed her self slightly apart from Andy.

'I'm sorry,' she apologized, 'it's not that I don't want to, but I think we need to wait a while!' Then levering herself further away, she said, 'I'm not the woman you may think I am.' For a moment, she thought about telling Andy about her father's abuse of her, and of her therapy, but now was defiantly not the time she decided.

As for Andy, he could feel Sandra's hand trebling on top of his, and he wanted to be inside her, but on his other hand (which was stroking the back of Sandra's slowly arching neck), was his watch! His watch showed Andy, that he had less than fifty minutes to go before he was due to back on duty, for the start of a series of pre-arranged shift swaps!

Andy could of course phone in, and cancel his appearance, even though it was in the busiest period. Although Advisors/negotiators were normally only allowed to be on phone-duty, for no more than eight hours in twenty-four, he was going to do paper work for most, if not all, of this initial leg of the swapped shift.

In view of the time, and Sandra's hesitation, and although he inwardly cursed his decision to agree to go in to work, Andy slowly walked his hand back down Sandra's left calf. His fingers did dawdle half way along, but eventually his hand moved onto the back edge of the couch, where it sat like some dejected partygoer on the kerbside; having just been refused an entry into a very exclusive and exceedingly desirable club!

In truth, Andy had been thrown out of less exclusive and desirable "clubs" in his time. Equally, in truth, Sandra had not always been that exclusive! During her time in counselling for dealing with sexual abuse, she went on a sex binge for four months! It is not only the obvious things, such as the victim's sexual views and habits, which sexual abuse or any abuse alters. It is the small things too; such as the sounds of childish laughter, the sight of an approaching friend or the smell of clean sheets, it is these "simple things," which sexual abusers also vandalize. Never the less during her sex binge, Sandra did finally manage to dislodge the worst of her long held views, about sex – even the one of likening pubic hair to "A nest of entangled spiders!"

During her sexual binge, Sandra always took the usual precautions about health and pregnancy, but little discernment in the way of partner choice.

Then one morning she woke up next to somebody's gentle snoring, but for the life of her, she could not remember who he was or what he looked like!

However, what really got to her was the reality; that she didn't even care who he was, or what he looked like! She never did find out his name and called him "Mr. Whatshisname" in her mind ever after that. Since that morning, Sandra gave up any thought about sexual promiscuity being her substitute of choice, and her "binge" was over. In fact, Andy was the first man she had chosen to, date, since those days!

Sandra wasn't concerned that Andy would try to abuse her, as far as sex was concerned, he seemed fairly traditional (thank goodness!). No Sandra was worried that if they did, it, that in spite of her strong and growing feelings for him, that the sex would somehow feel the same, as before, with Mr. Whatshisname and the rest of them – that was her fear!

'I am sorry,' she said, leaning forwards to Andy 'but it is for the best, at least until we know each other a bit better!'

At that point Andy, gently held both of his hands in the air and said, 'That's Ok! I'm not taking it personal,' then putting on a forlorn puppy dog look, he added, 'Miss Goody Two Shoes!'

Sandra smiled, kissed him on his down turned lower lip, and retorted, 'That's right, and I'll stay that way for now, thank you!' She then kissed him on his forehead; got up from the couch, then turned to Andy and added reassuringly, with her own mischievous smile.

'But it was a much closer call than you might well think!'

Andy just looked and smiled at her, before replying, 'Oh! I really needed to hear that!'

'I'm sowwy,' Sandra replied.

'Just my luck,' Andy retorted.

'What is?'

'I wait years waiting for something to look and feel so bleeding good, and then would you believe – three of them come all at once!'

'Three?'

'Yeh! You … me …and …' Andy paused as he stood, then took and kissed the inside of Sandra's right forearm, before looking into her dark brown eyes, and concluding '…and us!'

With that said and done, they both gave each other an excruciating look, laughed, and shook their heads, then quickly kissing once more, the two of them got ready to leave.

Andy offered Sandra a lift back to Crime Frontiers; he also ended up explaining about his new shift change. When Sandra heard that he was in fact going to be a bit late for his new shift, she jabbed him, twice, in his ribs, as a half mocking retribution, for his double cheekiness!

As they sat inside Andy's car, now temporally parked outside the main gates, Sandra placed her hand on his shoulder and gently but firmly turned him around, until they were face to face. She then gave him a gentle but firmly committed, kiss goodbye, then got ready to get out. Several kisses later, Sandra eventually got out and went off to her car, and Andy rushed into the main building itself.

As she drove home, Sandra recollected her actions and motives. She was wary, not so much of sex; it was more about the trusting, trusting her own judgment about relationships.

Thirty five minutes later, she flopped herself onto her duck down, lemon yellow duvet covered double bed and concluded to herself, that the best answer was "To get well and truly fucked, by a well, and truthful man!" Then turning on to her front, Sandra cuddled into her duck down pillows and then decided, that Andy fitted both of her requirements . . . exactly!

CHAPTER 15

TRYING TO GET RID OF A COLD BY SNEEZING IT OVER SOMEONE ELSE!

It is a little understood fact, that committing a "successful" crime can often surprise the offender almost as much as it shocks the victim/s. In fact, Garfield Trueman, known as "G" to his street friends (and Gary to his parents and little brother), was continuingly surprised at how easy mugging people was.

However, even "G" had to admit that it was surprisingly unusual, for any of his victims to wish him, 'Good luck!'

"G" was particularly surprised, as he had just mugged the said victim of £85 and a mobile phone! But then "G" also did an unusual thing; pulling his hood further down against the cold rain, and against showing his face too clearly, he turned around and went back.

'Are you fucking with me?' he asked menacingly.

'No!' Steven replied, without smiling. 'It's just that if you are so desperate, that you have to go around mugging people, you're going to need a lot of luck . . . which is a shame and a waste.'

'Desperate!' "G" said, bringing the knife back up to Stevens' neck. 'You want to see how desperate you can get, bitch!'

Apart from slowly nodding towards the knife, Steven did not move, but he did have something else to say. He casually looked at "G," and then he looked up and along the ill-lit railway bridge walkway, he then returned his gaze to "G" once again.

'You know if any one sees that knife they will call the police . . . and I can assure you that neither of us wants that!'

"G" again found himself puzzled by the man's behaviour and by what he had just said. Cautiously lowering his knife, until it was half way down the man's body, he looked into the man's eyes! Never the less, as the man slowly raised one gloved hand, "G" immodestly brought the knife up again.

Steven however, merely, slowly took a handkerchief from his pocket and offered it to "G," then he nodded to the pocket in which "G" had put the stolen mobile.

'Do you think that you could give me the SIM card out of my… I mean ... your … mobile?' Steven asked, 'It's got an important number on it. If you drop it into the handkerchief, I will wipe it clean, so you won't leave any prints on it.'

"G" had to admit the man had balls, but then so did "G," and he liked to protect them. Stepping back, "G' swiftly brought down the knife; took out the mobile, prized open the back lid, then using the blade's tip, he eased out the SIM card and let it fall to the rain sodden ground.

'It's all yours Fuck-head, all you go to do – is get on your knees!'

It was an unnecessary comment, and what Steven did next was, strictly speaking, also unnecessary! He had secured the SIM, and that probably would have done, but Steven also had his "vanity" and his plan!

He had left his phone's number, as the bait for Crime Frontiers to break its anonymity code! In truth, Steven knew that he had made a mistake in not removing the SIM from the phone, before he had ventured out. However, his vanity would not allow him to break his word to Crime Frontiers; that he would always have the (activated) phone with him.

Admittedly, it was unlikely that the police would get their hands on the stolen phone, but given this "idiot" before him, it was not impossible! If the police should by chance get hold of the phone, and try to trace its original owner, via the history of text and calls – then anything could happen!

Besides, the truth was that Steven did not want to lose the phone or cash, and he was very reluctant to surrender either to this "petty criminal!" particularly as he had spent time and effort in tracing and baiting, the idiot, in the first place!

'Thank you!' Steven replied, letting the card stay where it fell, 'It's just that I noticed how much your approach, to solving your problems, also, depends on so much on luck. Luck that passers do not disturb you, luck on whether your victim has cash or valuables, etcetera! Yet you have intelligence I think?

Yes! Also daring? Yes! So why should you risk such hugely valuable qualities, on such a thing as mere luck?'

Once again, Steven scanned the bridge then he added, 'Besides, using crime to solve some personal problem, is like trying to get rid of a cold, by sneezing it onto somebody else!'

Looking back into the eyes of the man before him, "G" could not help but wonder what lay behind those eyes. Then he also checked to see if the walkway was still clear.

Steven cocked his head to one side and said, 'It's just a thought, that you might interested in a far surer way of dealing with your …shall we say immediate financial problems. Also and perhaps, if you would agree, you could help me to solve one of my problems at the same time?'

'I aint no dog, licking scraps from your plate, motherfucker!' "G" replied, then stepping forwards and raising his knife again he added, 'My teeth can rip your pussy-heart right out of you!'

Steven smiled, 'All you have to do is make one phone call, the call may be recorded, so you had better disguise your voice a little. When the phone is answered, all you have to say is that you want …!'

At that moment, Steven quickly looked left and up the walkway, then at the knife that "G" held, 'I think it is better that we go somewhere less suspicious, if any one should happen along?' then pointing with his open hand to the SIM on the ground, he added, 'But I really do have to retrieve the card!'

"G" eyes followed the man's gaze, then he too looked to his left and right along the walkway, but apart from the two of them, the bridge was still completely deserted. It was only as "G" began to swing his focus back to his "victim" that "G" realised that it was already far too late to repair his mistake!

"G" did at least manage to side-glimpse the man's gloved fist, before it hit him on the right temple! The next sensation that "G" felt, was the rush of nausea flooding into his brain! Then with a final effort, he tried to bring his knife up, but it was more like a last second plea, than any recognizable attack! By the time "G" had collapsed onto the concrete floor, he was completely incapable of caring any further!

Slowly kneading the side of his fist, Steven again checked for anyone coming. Seeing that all was well, he squatted down, picked up the SIM; the knife, and then he thrust the single-edged blade, deep into the young man's shallow breathing chest, and then he waited! As he waited, Steven retrieved his stolen phone and property; then he also removed the now dead man's mobile phone, and it was this addition act, which gave Steven an added idea! Walking further along and off the bridge, he opened the text feature and typed in:

"Tell miss America at Crime Frontiers if they do not ban their anon code, I will continue to kill and I will choose one of them next. Tell them cos i told pigs about this one, he is a freebee!"

Steven then addressed the text to some of G's many contacts. He pressed, "send" and walked back to the corpse, took a photo of it, and sent the image to the same contacts. He then pushed the phone into the open mouth of the corpse, checked everything else was in order, and then he began to walk away.

Of course, Steven had not deliberately set out with the vague hope he might, randomly be mugged. As with all of his victims (apart from Mary and Wolfe) he had gone to some trouble and pleasure to research "G".

Using a computer search of his chosen area, the first step had been trawling through past local news and court reports. Having found four potential candidates, Steven used the social networking sites to prune his choices down. Fortunately, "G" had provided plenty of helpful and up to date information, about his likes and routines. The tricky part had been physically following "G" who, by his egotistical nature and occupational precaution, was continually conscious of being potentially observed.

Although Steven had, had to improvise at the last minute, by setting himself up as a potential mugging victim at the bridge, it had been relatively simple thereafter. Never the less, although "G" had grabbed the potential mugging situation with surprising speed, Steven adapted quickly. If "G" had not fallen for the ploy, Steven would have attacked him anyway!

In truth, Steven considered himself fortunate that "G" had been so helpful. However regardless of "G's" assistance, he was not the king-pin in Steven's main plan. He had intended to further warn Crime Frontiers by targeting their chief accountant, on the following Saturday, and he still would! However, using "G" as ago between, had the beautiful advantage of supplying a potentially perfect alibi that of self-defence – if things eventually turned pear shaped!

In short, "G" was the perfect criminal! Steven however was not overly impressed at such good fortune; he had always felt that he somehow seemed to be just, plain lucky, when it came to matters of so-called crime!

As he finally disappeared into the cold, rain swept darkness, Steven let out a very loud . . . sneeze! However, that would not have surprised any one; for it was the sort of night that anybody could catch their death of cold!

Chapter 16

RUPERT GOES TO SCHOOL

The next day, after Steven had murdered the luckless "G" and left the photo and text messages, the story hit the national media. Amongst the newspaper headlines, there were such as:

"Killer threatens to silence Crime Frontiers line!"

"Will Crime Frontiers be gagged?"

"Monster uses victim's own phone to text-threat Crime Frontiers!"

"Killer tells Crime Frontiers to stop protecting criminals!"

Augments about the help-line's Anonymity Code, resurfaced on almost every TV talk show and in pub debates. The Crime Frontier's phone and website were overwhelmed, with messages from supporters and critics.

When Chief Inspector Miles Rupert and his assistant, Detective Sergeant Tom Vanner, showed up at Crime Frontier's office complex, (which had been nicknamed, "The Wrong School" by many of its staff), they had to run a corridor of cameras, microphones and questions, before they finally reached the sanctuary of the school's reception area. Never the less Kirra the receptionist, was even friendlier than she usually and naturally was.

Since its conception, Crime Frontiers had gone out of its way to let it be known, that it was an alternative for people, who, for whatever reason, did not want to go to the police – and it was defiantly not a competitor to the police.

The company also took care to explain, that their refusal to employ any serving police officer, was due to the conflicting legal requirements that any such arrangement would create. However, the fact that Crime Frontiers would employ an ex criminal (who had not been convicted for any serious offence for ten or more years), did not always help the situation. Even though Crime Frontiers pointed out, on regular occasions, that having such an experienced-based knowledge of giving up crime, was only a beginning and not a be-all, in becoming a Crime Frontiers Advisor-Negotiator.

Never the less, in spite of the company's stand for the police, there were many in the police ranks, as well as outside of them, who looked upon the Crime Frontiers helpline as moral and legal danger. As for Rupert, he was undecided about the usefulness of the crime-chat-line. He could see the moral and practical potential of having such an alternative, but he still had deep reservations about its potential dangers. For one, there was the still the un-answered question, of prevention of further crime verses justice for previous crimes.

Rupert had seen and heard Bell before, at a conference that Bell had given at the Police Federation annual meeting. Contrary to quite a few peoples assumptions, including Rupert's, Bell had far from come over as some a well-meaning, but head above the storm clouds do-gooder. Nor was he, in Rupert's opinion, some wanna' be anti-establishment anti-hero.

To Rupert's mind and feelings, Bell and the helpline were best summed up by Mathew Frome, the senior political advisor to the Met' Police Board. Frome had been sitting next to Rupert during Bell's presentation. As Rupert and Frome rose at the end of the talk, Frome had turned to Rupert and said, "Well at least they are on our side and not the others!' Then looking at Rupert quizzically in the eye he added, 'Otherwise I think we'd all be in deeper trouble!'

However, such moral pros and cons about the Advice-line's existence were not at the top of Rupert's agenda, this particular sunny morning.

When he and Tom Vanner were ushered into Bell's spacious top floor office, to meet the already standing Bell and the seated Sandra, Rupert knew that he had to tread carefully. As Bell moved forwards and firmly shook Rupert's hand, the two parties were formally introduced, and then Bell opened the conversation.

"Thank you for coming to see us Chief Inspector, I know your time is much appreciated in many places,' Bell then warmly smiled, then indicating to Sandra he added, 'In view of your phone call earlier this morning, I took the liberty of asking Miss Lott to join us. Sandra is the only, American speaking, member of our Advisor and negotiating team.

And as I mentioned to you in our telephone conversation this morning, both she and I were present when a threatening call was made by a caller; who may or may have not been, the man that you are inquiring about. I should also point out that Sandra has volunteered to be present, in her free time, and not the school's.'

Sandra gave the policemen a helpful smile, and both men smiled back, as Bell re-seated himself at his desk. However, before Rupert could say anything further, Bell stood again and politely but firmly raised his right hand; in the fashion of a policeman stopping traffic.

'Of course Inspector we will do our utmost to help in any way with your enquiries,' Bell said, as he then lowered his hand and placed both hands, knuckles down, on his smoked glass desk top. He then looked pensively at Rupert and stated, 'As long as we do not have to compromise our code of caller anonymity. Which as I am sure you are aware . . .,' Bell continued as he again sat in his chair and opened his arms in a gesture of frankness, '. . . is a legally, albeit sometimes controversially, protected right, protected by act of parliament!'

Rupert lowered himself into the central of the three waiting chairs, and looked from Bell to Sandra and back at Bell, and then he leaned back and mirrored Bell's open armed gesture. Tom Vanner, whose job it was to observe, rather than give out any opinions, sat in the right hand seat, mirroring no one.

'Of course we respect your legally binding commitments Mr. Bell, sir,' Rupert replied, then deciding to get to the point, he added, 'But this is not an enquiry into the helpline business, or your codes of practice. This is an investigation into a possible murder. In which the perpetrator has threatened to kill or attempt to kill one or more of your employees – which we are also, legally bound, to do our utmost to protect.'

Then briefly holding up his left hand (being left handed) towards Bell,

Rupert turned to Sandra and said.

'Although you were not directly threatened Miss Lott, in the text this man sent, we are very concerned for your safety. We are afraid that it is a possible direction, in which this man may be heading. Indeed our forensic profiling people believe it is almost certain, that you may, or have already become pivotal to his main aim!'

Turning to Bell, Rupert then stated, 'That aim, in our opinion, is to undermine the Advice line's Confidentiality Code, and therefore make it appear hypocritical and untrustworthy!'

Rupert raised his hand, yet again, only to find that Bell had already raised his. For a moment, the two men faced each other off, both with one hand raised like two wizards, battling for supremacy. As Sandra watched, she wished the two of them, "Would stop all this posturing crap, and get down to catching this deranged Steven bastard, before he killed someone else – or her!"

It was Rupert, who carried on talking. Turning to Sandra and bowing his head in an apology, 'The forensics profiling team, as well as myself and sergeant Vanner here, are agreed. Although, you are, as it were, a catalyst in this man's plan to bring Crime Frontiers into disrepute … you may also be the key to catching him, Miss!'

Bell lowered his hand and nodded as if he already knew the Chief Inspector's theory was correct, then he said, 'And here we come to the nub, Chief Inspector. You and Sergeant Vanner are correct of course. Indeed, I would be disappointed, if not very concerned, if you had not come to your conclusions. So! In all honesty, it is very reassuring that we all agree that this is not, only, an investigation into a crime that has already been committed … is it?' It was a rhetorical question, and Bell did not wait for Rupert to answer it.

'It isn't even a sole matter of preventing, goodness willing, a further crime,' Bell stated, as he turned to Sandra and bowed his head in an apology. 'No! It has turned into a fight, Chief Inspector, a street-brawl, for the very survival of Crime Frontiers, and just as importantly, for the moral evolution, of a humane society.'

Bell then rose out of his chair; went to the wide expanse of window and looked out at the sky, and spoke. 'I'm also sure that this man's main aim is to force us, to compromise our Anonymity Code. He hopes that we will be forced to reveal facts about him. Facts that have been gained, from his confidential conversation with Sandra, and which in turn may help your enquiries. He hopes that by his threats, or even worse by our capitulation, the trust in the anonymity of any caller will be broken beyond repair, because we will appear to be two faced, and untrustworthy!'

On that point Bell then turned to face Rupert again, then taking the few steps back to his desk, he placed both palms on his table and continued, 'However, Chief Inspector, compared to that of the general public's preference for … revenge over prevention … this man's threats are … almost laughable! The, almost, being the safety and wellbeing of my staff and the public.'

'That's very noble of you sir!' Rupert replied, in such a way that even his sergeant couldn't clearly interpret.

Sitting down again, Bell looked to the sergeant and then to Rupert, 'But perhaps there is a different conclusion Chief Inspector.'

Rupert politely smiled and replied, 'If it will lead to this man's arrest I would like to hear it.'

'As yet I'm not free to disclose that, because as yet it is untested!' Bell responded.

Standing once again Bell then quickly added, 'I have great admiration for the motives and abilities of the law, and its enforcement bodies, Chief Inspector. Indeed, when it comes to the matter of catching the perpetrators of any crime, your capabilities have and are growing remarkably in their powers. I also have little doubt that those powers will soon become an all-powerful deterrent, to those who would otherwise feel, unrestricted by their own conscience or intelligence. In summary, I believe that it will not be too far away before the time, when all acts of crime will be corralled into the sad province, of the insatiably insane or the incurably stupid!'

Whilst Rupert and the sergeant listened to Bell, Sandra gazed out of the window; she had heard this speech twice before, and felt that her belief in it did not need to be re-confirmed, besides it at been a long . . . night!

She had spent the whole night and half of the early morning, thinking about: "This maniac Steven, the helpline, courage, fear, life, and to crown it all – she couldn't help fantasizing about what it would be like to just hang . . . from Andy's shoulders! "Jesus, that Andy ticked so many of her boxes!"

But in Sandra's mind, as far as this Steven was concerned; at around 2.30 am that morning she had decided that, "There was no point in sitting on the fence and playing patter-cake with this maniac!" She would have to find a way to become "The writing on the wall!" What is more, if that wall ended up being one in this Steven's future prison cell – then so much the better for all! However, as far as how and what she'd be writing, then Sandra had to admit, that she hadn't quite worked that out yet!

Whilst Sandra continued her daydreams, Bell was looking from Rupert to the sergeant and back again, 'It may not be too long before the very nature of your work becomes, predominantly, one of preventing injustices, rather than being restricted to your more tradition role, of being the repairers of injustices.'

Again, Bell stood and shrugged his shoulders, 'Yet Chief Inspector, as long as the law is intrinsically shackled to punishment, it will also inevitably be seen as no more, than the perpetrator of non-violent-revenge! However, Chief Inspector, although revenge, albeit non-violent, may help numb the pain, it is never the less equally true, that it is the unfelt-shackles that bind us the most! And there many steps to take, Chief Inspector, before our legal systems can evolve beyond their present role of dishing out rubber stamped, pre-packaged dollops, of karma!

So, Chief Inspector,' Bell concluded, 'To ask us to break our code of anonymity, is like asking us to break the only leg we have left to stand on . . . and against . . . crime!'

Rupert did not answer straight away, but looked from Bell to Sandra several times, and said nothing.

Seated in her chair, Sandra was oblivious to her surrounds or the continuing silence in the room. Neither did she see the sergeant, who had been looking at her intently for some time. The sergeant was looking at her with both curiosity and some concern. He was about to ask 'Are you ok, Miss?' when Rupert spoke to Bell.

'Is it possible to get a trace on his phone calls to the helpline, either his past ones or any future ones?'

When Bell did not answer, but just looked away, Rupert continued, 'We think he is between 30 and 50 years old, white, male and medium build.'

Breaking off from her thoughts Sandra suddenly asked 'Did your profiler come up with that?'

'Yes,' Rupert replied and nodding to Sandra. 'The young man he killed, on the bridge, had previous, including four convictions for street robbery. His name was Garfield Trueman, though his street name was "G." One robbery we caught him red handed for! The other muggings he held his hands up to, after he was shown, that victim's descriptions of the suspect, fitted him perfectly; even to the designer sports top that he was still wearing when he was apprehended.

We think that this man killed "G" after "G" had tried to mug him. The knife used to kill Garfield, was identified as his own, as were the only fingerprints on it. So it is a fair presumption that it, the knife, belonged to him too!'

Sandra looked up at the detective, 'It seems a lot to pay for a foolish mistake,' she said.

Rupert looked back at her, 'I do not condone any type of vigilantly or revenge type actions, or any breaking of the law miss. Garfield was in the wrong place at the wrong time I guess, just like the people he himself, terrorized and mugged.' When Sandra didn't reply Rupert carried on.

'We guess, and it is only a guess of course, that this man fitted Garfield's victim MO. All of his known victims were medium build, they were also white, as was Garfield, though younger. Of course the boy "G" may have changed his MO, but for now that's what we're going with.' For a moment, there was a silence that was long enough to notice, until Rupert continued.

'It's not much of a profile but it's a start. It would help if you could give us any help at all, in adding to it.'

Before Bell could interrupt, Sandra replied, but she replied to the sergeant rather than the Rupert.

'Yes! I have had contact, he is a . . . client, and because he is, I am not going to say anything else about him or what he said.' Turning to Rupert she said, 'If that means I am violating your laws Inspector, then you must arrest me or do whatever you have to do. Until then if it's ok with every one, I would like to get back home, I have a lot's to do, as I'm sure you do Inspector.'

Sandra gave Sergeant Vanner an almost apologetic smile, and stood up to leave.

'No you haven't broken any law miss,' Rupert answered, 'and of course you are free to leave. But I must warn you! This man isn't constrained by any laws, apart from the ones he creates for his own ideas of justice. And if you want an example of that, you can find it at the mortuary basement.' When Sandra continued to stand there without reply, Rupert softened his tone.

'I apologize for seeming somewhat blunt, Sandra, but we are bound by more than a duty to the law to protect you, and anyone else that this man threatens.'

Sandra sat down again and nodded to Rupert. Rupert nodded his thanks back and turned to Bell, 'We'd like to place two plain clothed officers, at your main reception, if it is all right with you sir. We believe that this threat from this man, is a potentially very serious one, and you and your staff are entitled to protection like any member of the public. As it is us, that called you, and it is us, who are offering to keep some sort of watch on these premises, I can't see how accepting such an offer, would compromise your ethical code. Of course we can keep surveillance from the outside, without your permission sir, but we would much prefer to work with you.'

Turning to Sandra once again Rupert added, 'We would also like to keep a 24 hour, plain clothed surveillance and armed escort with you Miss, if you've no strong objections that is? If you want us to catch this man, it may well speed his capture. I presume that you want us to catch him before he commits any further crimes.'

For the briefest of moments, the thin cordiality in the room changed, and all present tensed . . . all but the sergeant, who just sat and observed.

Rising up from his chair, Bell answered before Sandra could give hers. 'We will of course step up our in-house security Chief Inspector, and we shall be offering Sandra an escort to and from her home.' Briefly nodding in the direction of Sandra, Bell stated, 'Sandra is more than capable of deciding if she needs added protection, and I'm sure she will let you know if that turns out to be the case! But for now and I must say for the near future, we will neither be requiring nor condoning, any form of police presence inside the building.'

When Rupert began to try to speak again, Bell raised his hand, 'Even if we gave you enough information, in the hope of to finding this man, what makes you think that such information is correct and not some bait. He may well feed us enough details, so that we in turn give that "lead" to you. You then can make a raid at some location or other – and find nothing there but the media, and your and our, own embarrassment! Can you be sure that your denial that we helped you, even if you should make such a denial, would hold up to the scrutiny of an enquiry?'

Rupert said nothing.

In answer to Rupert's silence, Bell said, 'I thought not!'

Looking at Rupert, Bell spoke easily. 'But there is another reason why we will not divulge any information we receive or conclude, from this man's conversations with us.'

Pausing for a second, Bell then stated, 'You know Chief Inspector . . . you can surround someone who, let us say wishes to rob a bank. You can surround him with a dozen police officers, and you will stop him robbing that bank!' As he spoke, Bell cuffed his blue cotton shirt cuffs and began to walk forwards towards the office door. 'But you may still not stop him from, wanting, to rob the bank.' At the door Bell turned to the two policemen and said, 'But with one word or phrase . . . one idea . . . you can stop him wanting to rob any bank!'

Opening the door and inviting Sandra to leave with him, Bell looked the Rupert squarely in the eyes, 'We handle the truth here, Chief Inspector. We use it to pull aside the lies that a criminal shields his or her, false hopes behind! Whilst with our other hand, we exchange the truth. We exchange it for the sanctity of complete anonymity. It is our promise to any, and every caller, no matter what their crime, their lies or their truths . . . Chief Inspector.'

As Sandra joined Bell, she turned to face Rupert, and to give her own opinion about Crime Frontiers, 'If someone phoned the helpline wanting to share their peodiophililiac, masturbatory fantasies with me, Inspector. Then as long as they realise that I have a voice too, then they are more than welcome to call me, in complete anonymity and confidentiality, including this Stev'. . .!'

Although she managed to stop, before she fully divulged Steven's name, Sandra knew from Rupert's look, that she had said enough! Blushing profusely, she never the less completed what she intended to say.

'However if you can offer us something better, than their guaranteed anonymity, or offer me a reason why I should break my promise, then please let me know!'

Bell raised an eyebrow at Rupert, and then softened his physical stance but not his piercing gaze. 'Naturally we could break the Anonymity Code,' then putting his hand on Sandra's elbow he continued, 'and we'd all be applauded for our successful efforts to put this, *monster*, in his cage.

There are even some criminals, who would courageously slap their own guilt-soiled palms together. However, there is one thing of which I am certain of. Whichever they decide to do, neither cheerer nor jeerer, would ever choose to phone the helpline for any, serious help. No matter how desperate or monstrous they felt . . . or would come to feel!'

Taking his hand from Sandra's elbow, Bell stood silent for a moment more, and then he concluded.

'Promising monsters … can be a highly rewarding but very serious undertaking … Chief Inspector!'

He and Sandra then left, leaving Rupert and Sergeant Vanner to look at each other, and then simultaneously raise their eyebrows.

Two minutes later, at the end of the corridor leading from Bell's office, Rupert and the sergeant waited for the lift to arrive. Rupert was looking at Tom Vanner, who had a frown on his face, but said nothing.

"I know that look Tom, what are you thinking?'

Turning to Rupert but looking to the ceiling, the sergeant spoke, 'I was watching that Bell … when you asked the American … Sandra … If she wanted us to catch this maniac.'

Rupert ignored the opening lift doors and said, 'And?'

"And … It was only for a half of second … but I swear … just for a moment …' the sergeant turned to look at his boss and stated, 'I'll swear that he didn't want us to catch him!' the sergeant then looked down to the floor again.

Rupert began to considered Tom Vanner's opinion. Through years of experience, he did not underestimate his sergeant's ability to read people. Indeed, it was one of the many reasons, why Rupert had asked him to be his permanent right hand man! However, Rupert was the main problem solver in their team, and it did not take long for him to put his sergeant's "hint," together.

'He doesn't want us to catch him because he bloody well wants to catch him, himself! He wants to try to talk with him – negotiate with him! Fuck! The silly bastard wants to try and get this maniac to back down, or even give himself up!' Looking at his sergeant again he asked, 'What about the American, Sandra?'

The sergeant pondered for a moment, then looking up at the ceiling once more, he replied, 'She's deep that one!' then addressing Rupert, he added, 'Oh! For sure, she wants this character caught and she won't mind who catches him! The fact that she let out the name, Steve, tells us that, even it was partially accidental. But whether she'd purposely break this anonymity rule thing, is another question.'

Looking down and up again, Tom Vanner added, 'I don't think she's fully chosen yet … but one thing's for certain,' he emphasized as looked back along the corridor, 'She'll make her own mind up, and no one else is going to make it up for her!'

The sergeant looked down at his shoes and slowly nodded, then he shrugged his shoulders and re-pressed the button to re-call the lift. As the lift doors opened, Tom Vanner smiled and he looked up at Rupert, as if wanting to say something more, so as he and Rupert walked into the empty lift, Rupert asked, 'What else?''

The sergeant pressed the ground floor button; looked back towards the empty office and replied, 'Nothing important!'

'What?' Rupert insisted.

Sergeant Vanner smiled again and looked at Rupert, 'Well …' he replied, '… that American don't half have nice tits!'

Chapter 17

THE CALLINGS

Bell's calling:

Although Sergeant Vanner's opinion of Sandra's physical qualities were subjective, his measure of David Bell was almost but not fully spot on. Forty minutes after leaving Sandra at the elevator doors, Bell went back to his private room behind his main office. He had long grown weary of the day-to-day running of Crime Frontiers.

It was not that Bell had grown disenchanted with the principles and aims of the helpline; it was more a case that he was bored with his involvement with it. As an answer to his dilemma, Bell had decided, that bending, rather than breaking the Anonymity Code, would at last "nudge" him out altogether!

Bell unlocked his small safe and withdrew a small notebook, then going to his desk he sat down and withdrew his mobile phone from his jacket pocket. Turning to the last page of his notebook in which he had made an entry, he stared at the number that Steven had given as his mobile number.

Bell held no intention of breaking the Anonymity Code, by handing the information to the police. Nor did he have many illusions that he could persuade Steven to hand himself to the police. Bell knew that criminals rarely handed themselves over to the police, and Advisor-negotiators never advised for or against such a choice.

He could of course, try to obtain a private "ping-track" trace of Steven's phone, and maybe even find and confront him personally – he could even kill him – however, if "grassing up" threatening clients to the police would be viewed as hypocritical by the public, then murdering them would be defiantly be seen as a case of "sour grapes!"

In fact, Bell did not even intend to try to speak with Steven directly, not yet at least. Instead, he wished to use the situation to try to re-take the initiative, and the use of a text messages, would be the perfect tool to do just that. So using his own personal mobile phone, Bell sent the following text to Steven's phone:

"Welcome to the dark side. No! Don't look back, that's what cowards do, and we both know that's not really you. In here you can hide from almost everything, except of course from the things that you bring!"

Question: Would you like help with your unclaimed baggage?

Satisfied with his text Bell entered Steven's number and pressed, "Send."

Sandra's calling:

Although Sandra's mind was deep, it was not dark. Sitting in her favourite chair in Andy's front room, whilst listening to her favourite piece of music, "Pachelbel's cannon in D major," Sandra could clearly see the basic reasons, both for and against keeping the code of anonymity. However, for the past hour or so, she had been also trying to see beyond those basic reasons, but still she could not choose.

It would be so easy to give the police the information they wanted. It would be even easier to do so, when she thought about the risk to innocent people or even her fellow workers. Yet deep within, Sandra knew that there was another person to consider, and that person was herself.

Putting her writing pad on the floor, Sandra got up and went into the kitchen to refresh her coffee. As she waited for the kettle to boil, she edged deeper into her thoughts and feelings, until she began to think about the numerous lies that she told her father, in order to escape or at least postpone her father's abuse of her. She also recalled how she lied to her friends, in order to keep the abuse a secret from them. As she had grown, Sandra had begun to dislike the lying with intensity that almost and indeed sometimes even passed, the revulsion she felt about the sexual abuse itself.

Now many years later, Sandra saw any lie as an abuse against herself, just as much as it would be against another person. In short, betraying the anonymity code would be like betraying herself!

Suddenly Sandra recalled a distant memory of sitting in the bedroom of her best school friend. They were both drinking homemade milk shakes, and her friend was reading aloud from a book of poems. Although Sandra could not recall the poem as a whole, she did recall the end of the poem as clearly, as if her friend was suddenly in the kitchen with her, and her friend's words were:

"It is foolish to try and defend innocence by arming your guilt."

At that moment, the kettle clicked to a boil – and Sandra stepped back from "the line!" She had decided two things. The first was that when she returned to America; she would go and tell her father about her lie, about killing her mother – though whether he'd believe her now could be in some doubt. The second decision, was that that no matter what Bell, the police or Steven said or wanted, she had given her word to Crime Frontiers, to Steven and herself, that she would keep her promise to obey the Anonymity Code – it was her law!

Steven's calling

It is night time, and Steven sits, as he recalls the many moral-borders he has crossed. He sits in his chair and stares out and far beyond his bedroom window. It is almost as if he's not quite all there, like an off stage actor waiting for his entrance cue, in a play as yet fully un-written – because others may try to improvise! He rises as his "audience" calls him … though what they will call him, he already knows.

Rising out of his chair and closing the window against the chill night air, and still looking out at the lights below, he ponders. He has already worked out that Bell, wants him to give up his quest and maybe himself to the police, he has concluded this from the fact, that someone, probably Bell, has sent him another text on the phone that, he exclusively, used to call the Crime Frontiers line. The last text started by asking:

"Question: How do you recognize a criminal genius?

Answer: It's the one who has worked out that crime doesn't pay!"

The text then went on to inform: "The prime purpose of any decent law, is not to tell you that you are about to disobey that law, the prime purpose, is to inform you that you are about to … make a mistake! If you are about to break a law, then it is because you are trying to carry too great a weight. of responsibility! If you would like to exchange some of that responsibility, then give me a call."

As with the previous text, Steven did not bother to send any reply. He already knows that the police, in the form of Chief Inspector Rupert and his sidekick, want to catch him unawares! Steven has seen the pair of detectives outside Crime Frontiers on the TV news reports.

Moreover, Steven knows of Rupert from old – though he and Rupert have never actually met. For Rupert was a prominent detective in the investigation of the Mary and Wolfe killings! So Steven has another ending, and it is one where he is neither caught, nor gives himself up, nor gives his challenge up! "No!" Steven concluded to himself, "It will be them who will be surrendering to him, including the American Susan!"

Drawing the curtains, Steven returns to his chair, it was time to lure all the Goody-goodies in!

Chapter 18

Unrequited acquaintances

When Steven woke from his night's sleep, he felt refreshed and clear-headed, even before he had had a shower! After his shower, he felt quite exhilarated, so much so, that he went for a short jog. Then, after another quick shower and during breakfast, and as if sent by some express karmic reward for all his work so far, Bell sent another text:

"We are more than just a pair of random points, drifting through a universe of chaos. I am me! You are you! So how about we meet, face to face, so that we may move forwards side by side?"

Even though Steven had hoped for such an offer, and had even planned to suggest the same to Bell, that very day; as he read the text, Steven almost choked on a piece of crispy bacon! After clearing his throat with gulps of fruit juice, he eventually began to relax somewhat. Steven then began to trawl through each phase of his plan, until once again all of his intended prey seemed to be squirming within his net of subterfuge! All he had to do now; was to get Bell, the policeman Rupert, and the American woman, to meet in the same place at the same time, and his net would be full!

Now, it was time to turn hope into action! After quickly finishing breakfast, Steven saved Bell's text, then texted back:

Meet me in Trafalgar Square, under the Spare Plinth, at 8.30 pm. Do not be early or late!

Then he dialled the helpline, asked for Susan the American and was put through straight away. After checking with her that nobody else was on an extension, Steven got to the point straight away.

'Meet me in Trafalgar Square, at 8.30 tonight, under the Spare Plinth, be alone, or I will have killed someone by nine! If you tell anyone about this, including Bell or the police, I will kill whoever you told. The square will be crowded, if you come as I say, then you have my word that you will come to no harm. I will not harm you!' Having made his point, he hung up!

Next, Steven went back to his bedroom. Taking a seat in front of the dressing table mirror, and having been pre-prepared, he open the bottle of clear nail varnish, he then changed his body posture to that of a woman, or at least as feminine as he could imitate.

Using an unused mobile phone, he dialled 999 and asked for the police. Ten minutes later and after being put through to various departments, Steven was at last put through to the person he wanted. Even though Steven knew before hand, that he could have asked for Rupert directly, it was important to Steven that all should be seen to be done, properly.

'Hello, is this the senior detective in charge of the Mary Francis murder?' Steven asked.

'Yes, this is Chief Inspector Rupert, how can I help you?' Rupert replied, noting that although the caller's deep voice was obviously a man's, it had a notable feminine lilt to it.

At the other end of the line Steven slightly feminized his body posture even more, and then started to apply the nail varnish to little finger nail of his left hand. Although the act of applying nail varnish was, primarily, a role-playing act to support the character he wanted to portray to Rupert, Steven took as much care in applying the varnish as any well-presented woman would.

'Oh! Thank goodness!' Steven replied, putting even more emphasis on feminizing his voice. 'I wasn't sure who to call, or who had retired or something, even though I looked it up the web site about Mary and her dog's murder!'

When he had heard, via his receptionist, that the caller's enquiry was about Mary, Rupert was immediately interested. Apart from his own original involvement with the case, he had also been recently been approached by detectives from the Cold Case Unit, who were re-inquiring into Mary's murder.

However, Rupert's initial feelings towards the caller was not that expectant. As with all high profile murder cases, even old ones, Rupert knew that the Mary Francis murder had a variety of web-based information about it. Like many so called cold cases, it still regularly drew calls from well-meaning people who believed that they had relevant information.

Rupert also knew that Mary's case had attracted a lot of media attention at the time, due to the near "ferocious" strangulation of Mary, and the added macabre fact that Mary's dog, called "Wolfe" had been "murdered" then ritualistically placed on top of Mary's body. Rupert even remembered that the RSPCA had been brought in on the fringes of the case, due to the possibility that a charge of animal cruelty might be brought against the dog's killer!

Back in his office Rupert, sounded cautiously enthusiastic as he replied to his caller, 'No they haven't pensioned me off quite yet sir, and Mary's death is still being investigated. Do you think you may be able to help, sir?'

Applying the varnish to his second finger, Steven nervously replied, 'Yes! I think I may know who killed her … in fact I know who killed her!'

When Rupert detected fear in the caller's voice, he stopped fiddling with his pen and he pulled his note pad in towards him.

'Please continue sir. What makes you think that you know who Mary's killer is?'

Steven's reply was immediate but still carried a note of fear, 'Because I am his … lover!' But since he told me about what he did … I am sure he will kill me!'

Hearing the heightened fear in Steven's manner, Rupert deliberately added a reassurance in his own, 'In that case sir, we must do all in our power to see that you are and remain safe, could you tell me your name or the name of this person?'

Hearing Rupert's attempt at reassurance, Steven increased his own "panic," 'No! Not yet! I daren't – it's too dangerous! I can't tell you unless I can be sure that you can lock him up!'

Rupert however, had been in many similar scenarios before and he knew that any such sureties would be useless, 'I appreciate your situation sir, but we cannot arrest anyone without good cause or evidence. If you tell me what you know, we will take it from there. I can tell you that what you say will be treated in the strictest confidence! What made you first think that this … man … may be Mary's murderer?'

Pausing for effect, and to inspect his finished fingernail, Steven swapped the varnish brush over to his partially completed hand and started on the little finger nail of his other hand. 'Ok! I understand you. But if I tell you what you need to know, I cannot be there when you arrest him!'

Taking a deep breath and pausing for effect again, Steven then launched headlong into his "confession," 'I had no idea he was a murderer, no idea, not the slightest … until we had the row … last night! It was all so stupid; it was more a tiff than anything! But he was drunk and I just said, I was leaving! I didn't really mean for good, though believe me Chucks he's not as great as he thinks he is! Anyway, all I meant was to go and stay at a girl friend's for the night … but then … well he just went mad!'

'Mad?' Rupert asked with concern.

'Yes! Mad!' Steven replied, enjoying the passion of his character. 'I thought he was going to attack me right there in the living room! I didn't know what to do, and then suddenly he grabbed me!'

Steven gave a short pause for effect, and Rupert encouraged Steven to carry on, 'It must have been a very frightening experience for you, what happened next?'

Having reached the nail of his next finger, Steven started to apply the varnish, but stopped, 'That's when it all happened!' he emphasized. 'He dragged me up to the bedroom, threw me on the bed and … well … I just thought he was just going to rape me! To be honest it wouldn't have been the first time … fortunately his not that big … down there, if you know what I mean!'

Rupert shifted his weight and winced as he replied, 'Never the less sir, rape, is a very serious crime!'

But, Steven carried on as if the comment was either unnecessary or disbelieved, 'But he went to the wardrobe instead, then he knelt in and threw a floor board out. Then he brought out this cloth. It was like an oily towel, then he came over to the bed, and when he flipped it open, I thought a knife or a gun was going to drop out, I know he keeps a gun – but it was a dog's collar and lead!'

When Rupert heard the words "dog's collar and lead" he nearly bent the tip of his fine tipped pen against his note pad. One of the facts that had been kept from the public in the Mary case; was that "Wolfe's" collar and lead were never found.

In truth, as Steven had followed the reports of the case at the time, and he already knew of this "secret" information; however, he had destroyed the lead, collar and Mary's gloves the very same day of the killings.

Changing his pen over for another one, Rupert carefully did not ask about the gloves that Mary habitual wore when walking her dog. Instead, Rupert asked, 'That seems a strange thing to happen . . . what happened then?'

'It was then that he told me!' Steven answered . . . then deliberately paused.

Rupert could not hold out, 'Told you what sir?'

'He said, "That the last, bitch, that owned the lead, had ended up on a police mortuary slab and that if I didn't want to do the same, then I'd better take it back! I said, take what back, and he said, "About leaving him!" Of course I said that I didn't mean it, and said I'd never really leave him . . .then after a while . . . he seemed to calm down . . . then he told me to put it on!'

'Put what on sir?'

'The dog's collar and lead! I did of course – if he had told me to wear a priest's dog collar I would have.'

'This must have been very frightening for you sir,' Rupert interjected, 'However I must ask you. What makes you think this has anything to do with Mary's murder sir?'

Steven's answer was immediate, 'The name! The name on the collar, it was the same as the dog that, that poor Mary had. I remembered it from the newspapers, and let's face it Chucks, there aren't that many dogs called "Wolfe" and certainly none whose owner ended up the way, he said she . . . ended up . . . poor love!' At that moment, Steven suddenly thought about adding, "It shouldn't have happened to a dog!" but thought better of it, so he waited for Rupert's response instead.

Rupert considered his next words carefully. Obviously, this man knew far too much for it to be a coincidence – and equally it was obvious that he was terrified that he knew so much! Never the less, Rupert knew he would take it step by step.

'Right sir, I've listened to what you have said, carefully, and my immediate advice is that you leave where you are, and go to your nearest police station – '

'I'm not walking into any police station,' Steven exclaimed, 'what if someone should see me, he has lots of friends . . .?'

'Well we need to get to somewhere safe, sir, where we can meet!

At that moment Steven thought "At last!" then he said, 'Well I can meet you at Trafalgar Square, under the Spare Plinth, I work close by. I could meet you at 8.30 tonight, but I won't meet you or give any names until I know that I can be safe! But you mustn't be late, I'll have to be back home by nine thirty or he will be suspicious!'

'Don't worry sir, I'll be there on time, and if you need us to help in any way we can, just tell me what it is. But I must be honest with you. We have good CCTV of the surrounding areas near Mary's murder, and if this man can be placed in the vicinity at the time, it would be of great assistance, but it would not prove he killed Mary.

Nor would the possession of the dog lead, he could easily say that the real murderer dropped it, and that he found it in the area. From what you have told me so far, we would still need you to come in and make a statement sir, about what he said to you. Even then, alone it may not be enough to ensure a conviction! It would however allow us to arrest and investigate him further, and once we do that; we can very easily prove his involvement, or completely eliminate him!'

Back in his room, Steven was more than a little surprised about what Rupert had just said! So much so, that he over-painted his finger-nail – a clear subconscious reflection that he had, literally, over-played his hand!

'How do you mean easily prove?' he asked.

At that point, Rupert leaned back in his chair and relaxed somewhat as he explained, 'We have a DNA sample. It was thought at the time, that the dog might have tried to defend itself or Mary, so a saliva swab was taken from the dog too, in case any human blood traces were found. There were blood traces found, but at the time, they were too indistinct to use. But with the new techniques, we obtained a more accurate reading about seven months ago. Unfortunately, we found no match on our DNA data base, then or since. But it would not take long for us to eliminate or match this man sir!'

The news of the DNA evidence came as a huge shock to Steven! The fact that the police had CCTV evidence, possibly of him near the scene, was not news to Steven, and it had never worried him. However, the news that they had his DNA, not only worried him – it scared him!

Gathering his wits as quickly as he could, he replied, 'Really … I didn't see anything about that on Mary's web site?'

'At the time it was thought to be, prudent, to keep it from general knowledge that the case was being re-investigated. But since the DNA find, we were going to put out a fresh appeal on Crime Watch, as soon as we could get a slot.'

With that said and pretending that it was all good news, Steven played out the rest of his sham, as best as he could, and then rang off!

After Steven rang off, Rupert tried to trace his number but to no avail, never the less he did call Sergeant Vanner in from the outside office. When the sergeant came in Rupert grinned and said, 'Good news about the Mary Francis murder!'

Back in his room, Steven was … furious! The whole purpose of subversively calling the police was so; that he could manipulate everyone to Trafalgar Square, so as to make it appear, that the police and Crime Frontiers had at least colluded, in trying to trap him! Now not only was his plan ruined – he was in danger!

In fact, he had been carrying a time bomb around for God knows how long! A bomb that could he could have triggered, by breaking any one of the minor laws, requiring that an offender's DNA be recorded.

However, after a moment of reflection, Steven began to calm down. Although it was the only good result in this mess, at least he had found out about them having his DNA!

Never the less, Steven was deeply disappointed. He had intended to mix in with the tourist crowd at Trafalgar Square, and film the moment when Bell, the Susan woman and Rupert showed up for the meeting.

The police, the Susan woman and Crime Frontiers, could deny collusion until the cows came home. But with the video proof, the texted invitation from Bell, and his (Steven's) reply, the doubt and distrust would be planted, both in the public and media minds. It would of course mean that he would have succeeded by cheating, but he would have succeeded!

However, if he sprung the trap now, and the American was caught in it, then she just might well feel, outraged, enough to try to take him down – by telling the police about his admission to Body Part Murders! If that happened, the publicity would be hugely widespread, as would his self-description, after that who knew what would happen! Clearly, he had been far too generous at the shopping arcade!

Never the less, the fact remained, that he sincerely doubted that the police, would be able to prove his guilt in the Body Part Murders, without more proof than his mere ramblings on the phone – for he had been meticulous in not leaving any forensic clues! However, they would have enough reason to take his DNA, and then he would be sunk, by "Bloody Wolfe!" for the Mary murder!

Going to his bed and laying on the top of it, Steven thought through his options. He could of course abandon any further involvement with Crime Frontiers, or any sort of further crime come to that – even minor ones! But one thing was for sure, somebody was going to pay for this! As to who and how much, he hadn't decided yet!

Putting the future aside for the moment, Steven decided that for the present he needed apply some damage limitations. At six p.m. Steven (as the "boyfriend") phoned Rupert. Steven then told him, that it couldn't be his boyfriend who murdered Mary, because he already had lots of convictions, and that his DNA would defiantly already be on their files.

Moreover, even if his DNA hadn't showed up yet it would, and they could arrest him then. All this could be done, without any need to put himself in danger from his boyfriend's family and friends!

Besides, whatever happened, it was all getting too much! The whole business was getting all too complicated, and he wanted nothing more to do with it! In fact, he was leaving London and his boyfriend altogether that night, and he obviously wouldn't be at Trafalgar Square at 8.30!

Steven then texted Bell and simply cancelled their meeting. However, as he snapped the lid closed on his mobile Steven had a feeling of vague unease, similar to the feeling one can get on hearing the sound of a breaking twig, in a forest . . . at night!

When Steven discreetly went to Trafalgar Square at 8.40, he saw that all appeared to be normal. However, when he realised that American woman had not turned up, his mind was instantly made up about exactly who, was going to pay for all his disappointment!

Steven concluded that the American's absence was because; either she had told the police, and they were lying in wait. That she hadn't taken him seriously! Or, as far as protecting the Anonymity Code was concerned, then she just may be incorruptible after all!

As he walked towards his car, he began hoping that it was the latter reason, for that could be the very insurance that he needed to re-establish and carry out his, original, master plan!

As it happened, Steven did not randomly kill any one by nine, nor out of spite later on; there was no point in being childish! Besides, if he was going to hang, it would be for the whole sheep not for one of its fleas. However as he travelled home, he began reorganizing his priorities about Trafalgar Square.

Knowing that his Trafalgar Square subterfuge had not worked, or at least not been given a chance to fully work, was disturbing to Steven. However, its abandonment did have a sort of silver lining, or strictly speaking, a more proverbial lining.

For even if his Trafalgar plan would have worked, it would have been somewhat, cheating, and Steven didn't like cheating; what's more he particularly didn't like to cheat himself! The Trafalgar Square plan would have cheated him out of a more moral success, that of truly forcing Crime Frontiers to betray their promises of absolute confidentially.

Now with the Trafalgar fiasco behind him, he could perhaps return to his earlier plan. A more risky plan it was true, for it would require him to be in the thick of the action, and on offer of direct arrest – which would be no minor effect, what with the "Wolfie" waiting to pounce!

Nor was the master plan fully formed, yet, and it would require a great deal more planning and manipulation, but the rudiments were there, and more importantly, to Steven, it was more … sporting! More … honourable and therefore, more … morally correct! In fact, the more he thought about it, the more glad he was, that Trafalgar had met its "Waterloo!"

As he continued to drive, his spirits began to rise once again, for was already planning how to build a more robust, Goody-goody trap, and how to obtain an irresistible bait! Fortunately, as far as the latter was concerned, he already knew just where to find it! However, he already knew that just choosing the right bait – was only part of setting a good trap!

As far as Sandra was concerned, her reasons for not obeying Steven's demands were two fold. When Steven had given his word to her, that she "would come to no harm," Sandra immediately looked at the truth indicator – it indicated a LIE! When Steven had said that he would kill someone by nine o'clock, the indicator once again indicated he was lying! The same applied to Steven's threat to kill anyone who Sandra told about the meeting – though Sandra noticed that the reading was not so strong.

The definite LIE readings probably meant that Steven had not fully made his mind up yet, about what to do if she did not turn up at Trafalgar Square! As far as any reasons for not telling the police about Steven's demand, there was only one main one; and that was her promise not to break the code!

When Steven arrived back and began walking from his car, he began cheerfully and absent-mindedly humming a tune, it was from an Abba song, and it was, of course, "Waterloo!"

Chapter 19

"There's a bright-green elephant in the room!"

After provisionally accepting the offer of a month placement at the residential course, George Pipe deliberately tried to take things easy. The only fly in the proffered healing-balm, was that the residential itself would not start for another two weeks!

Although on many conscious levels of his understanding, George knew that rape was wrong, on a deeper emotional level, his rape urges served as an act of self-medication, protection, against his various feelings of discontent, and at such a level, rape even took the guise, of a friend!

Rape of course was no real friend to George; unless befriending a bully can be valued as a true friendship. What is more, if you had of asked the 8 year-old George, as he stood before the tree, he would have certainly condemned rape as a terrible and bad thing!

However, he has changed since then, and so has his desire for a more potent "medication" than "parading!" Now, an urge to rape could feel just as rewarding as any act of self-protection. In some ways it was like a form of proxy parental love, and could of course be just as demanding as any parental *demand!* Equally of course, it could also be just as passionate, and as such, just as capable of being deluded and damaging as any delusional love, passion, or parent!

"Would you steal to save your love, and if in that moment when you did, would that mean that you love to steal? Would you kill to save your love, and if in that moment when you did, does that mean that you love to kill? Would you die to save your love, and if in that moment when you died, does that mean that you loved to die?

Passion's autumn rose I'll tend it not, for when its heady scent is gone its petals will rot! I'll not imprison the stench of love's decay, inside a mouth to mouth rescue of "Our last day." I'll not swap angel wings for those of a fly's, who squats and succours on wherefores and whys and then sucks on memory's thinning meats, each thinning day, until reality's dustcart takes the garbage away. No! Passion's autumn rose I'll tend it not ... but the pollen of true friendship ... I'll forget-me-not!"

Yet to shame love as being a terrible thing, even if it is an imperfect love, was a potentially dangerous thing to do! It would be like throwing the shield away with the sword! In truth, George felt he needed to rescue some sort of honour from defeat!

Yet George knew that if he could hold out for long enough, to attend the residential, then he might then have the opportunity, to retire his "blind-duty" towards rape – not in shame, but with the honour deserving a once loyal but now dangerously deluded, old soldier !

Never the less, this particular old soldier didn't seem to want to be stood on the shelf that easily. Soon the initial "feel good" feelings of the residential, began to attract thoughts of foreboding, fear and guilt. A sense of, unfinished business, began to wriggle and search from within George

An unsettling emotional "itch" began to spread throughout his day and decisions. This uneasiness crept into every waking hour, and at seemingly random moments, a spasm of frustration suddenly rose from within him, almost physically suffocating him!

These panic attacks; left George shaking and almost gasping for air, movement, and a craving for something, anything, that would free himself! In these moments, George longed to get himself self out and away from whatever place he was in, whether it be his work place, his home or in between.

To be fair, since his phone call with Andy (leaving the attempted rape on Olla aside ... for George, that, was just in the "heat of the moment!") George had tried very hard to contain his urges. However, his habitual urge to rape was like any living entity, unless contained, it would do all in its power, to survive and multiply!

Then one day, when Mary and the children had gone out for the afternoon (attending a birthday party of one of Fern's friends) George was out of the house – almost before his family had reached the end of their road!

Although, the two mid to late-teenage girls, that he spotted some twenty minutes after leaving his house, were a bit on the young side for George's taste, they were never the less – old enough!

George was following two girls, Laura (aged 16) and Sulanda (aged 17), as they walked across the local common! To most northern Europeans, either of the two girls would have been considered as being averagely attractive. However, in southern Europe, the slimmer of the two girls, Laura, may have been judged, as being a tiny bit scrawny!

Moreover, in the inner New Guinea jungle, Laura, would have even been looked upon as being so skinny, as to be ill or possessed; and any one "dating" her would have been severely frowned upon. In other parts of the world, the slightly plumper Sulander's skin colour, would have been a certain no-no, and she, would have considered any boyfriend as very brave to be seen going out with her.

However, sexual depravity, has the universal ability to dismiss even the most lowest forms of prejudice!* So in the end, it didn't really matter what part of the world they might be in, or have come from, it just meant that George found both girls, acceptable, as potential victims!

(*Whether that places sexual depravity on a higher moral platform than racial prejudice, is of course arguable).

Never the less, the two teenagers were some way ahead of George, but near enough for him to hear most of the words of the song they were singing, and as they sang the chorus, the words became louder and much clearer. Although Laura and Sulanda sang in harmonic unison, each girl sang slightly different words.

The chorus was melodic and could easily be sung, even by the tone deaf. The lyrics of the song were simple: Firstly Laura would sing, "You lurv, you lurv, my singing!" Then Sulanda would then sing, "I lurv, I lurv, your singing!" After a few lines of the chorus, the chorus changed to "We lurv, we lurv, our singing!"

When both Sulanda and Laura reached and turned onto a side path that led off the main and well-used track, they both looked behind them, and although they saw George, they seemed not to be worried; for other people could be seen in the semi-distance, and further down the main track.

Then as the girls walked, they not only sang louder, but one of them would suddenly change the song's pitch, often with a deliberate cringe making result, whilst the other girl tried to mirror the change.

However, after several goes of mirroring each other, Sulanda changed her voice to as deep as she could reach, and the change was so striking that even George was impressed! Sulanda's singing was far too deep for Laura to mirror, and both girls burst out laughing; even George could not help but have a small smile himself!

As he continued to follow Sulanda and Laura at a safe distance, George suddenly thought about phoning Crime Frontiers. All he had to do was take out his mobile (in his rush to leave his house he'd forgotten to leave all phones etc. at home), press in the numbers … and he'd be in a completely different world before he'd could say "That was qui …!"

What is more, it would be a much cleaner and consequently a much healthier world too, what with his loving family and close friends alongside him! He even began thinking about buying some ice cream for the kids as a treat, for when they got back home. At face value, things were looking good for everyone, but then suddenly a stroke of bad fortune "appeared!" as a dumfounded George looked straight ahead … he realised that the two girls ahead had just turned left!

The small side-track that the girls had taken, was a shortcut, which joined the main track further down the way. However, this shortcut, passed through a small, but densely wooded area, which was patched-worked with ditches and dense undergrowth.

But at the centre of the wood, there was a disused and partially ruined Second World War air raid shelter. George had visited the shelter on occasions, and had fantasized about committing a rape there many, many times; for in spite of its dark, musty smelling interior – it was his "Fantasy rape palace!"

"Fuck!" George inwardly cursed, as he stopped in his tracks, "What do they think they are doing! They must know I'm still behind them; are they mad or just plain stupid! Or were they just, teasers, daring to see if I would follow them?"

To give him deserved credit, in that moment of moments, George did try to think himself out of it! "No they weren't teasers, they were too nice for that!" he decided. However, he did not go as far as completely dismissing the idea of continuing to follow them . . . just to test the situation!

As he started to walk, George began to think about turning around and going back home! At that moment and from seemingly nowhere, a powerful vision dropped into his mind. The vision was one of watching, the slimmer white girl, doing exactly as he was telling her to do! As he continued to watch the inner vision unfold, George almost unthinkingly, quickened his pace, until he reached the side-track that the two girls had taken.

It was at this point; that George remembered something that he had read, on the Crime Frontiers website: "If you wouldn't marry her, then it won't be worth raping her – if you would marry her, then it won't be worth raping her!"

For about ten seconds George stood motionless. As he stood, he imagined himself with the slimmer girl at his home, with his children, with his neighbours, his friends. Even without his wife Mary in the picture, it didn't take George long to realise that he would never marry the girl. After that, the point in raping either of the girls seemed to be . . . blunted!

The effectiveness of the "marriage exercise" both surprised and impressed

George. He was so impressed (and pleased), that with the exercise upper most in his mind, he turned away from the side-track that the girls had taken! However, he did not turn towards his home! Instead, he continued along the secondary path. Even so, George had resolutely passed by the chance of directly following the girls, and he felt quite pleased with himself!

After a few moments, George was quite amused to feel, that somehow, he felt not only lighter, yet in a curious way more solid, and for some time, so it was with his view of the world.

The good feelings about himself and the world, stayed with George as he travelled along the secondary path. In fact, George had hardly thought about the two girls at all, until he reached the place where an offshoot of the side-track that they had taken, joined the path that he was walking on! At that moment his inner visions of the girls returned, shutting all else out and making his earlier valiant attempt of escaping his "cell mate," seem no more worthwhile, than the doodling of a key hole upon a dungeon door!

As George stood in the open air, the girls were nowhere in sight, not in the distance ahead nor up the side-track. This meant that the girls would probably still be in the wooded area, and maybe at or even in the air raid shelter itself!

Although George did not feel trapped, he did feel as if he were being, unfairly tested. Not by the girls especially, but more by life itself – and for a moment he again thought about calling Crime Frontiers!

Then whilst he was debating exactly what to do next, two dog walkers appeared in the distance up ahead. Suddenly George had an overwhelming feeling that he did not want to be seen just "standing there!" Nor did he want to look suspicious by appearing to turn back. So having apparently been "trapped" George "escaped" onto the side track; that lead towards the air raid shelter!

As George walked, he thought through the situation. "This is simple, if I meet them, I will just pass safely by!" However, each time he decided that (or something in a similar vein) he immediately got an inner vision/urge about rape!

Shooting the moral messenger:

It was unfortunate that George had not yet been, advised, about such things as "Moral memos," let alone about "Ghost urges!" Moral memos (according to the Crime Frontiers theory), have long been used by the sub-conscious (sub-conscience?) and certainly long before we used words to "signpost" our thoughts throughout the day!

Moral memos occur; when a person's subconscious, instantly and automatically sends a success or failure themed, fantasy or memory, to symbolically reflect, the degree of potential success (or failure) of that person's current thought or actions!

In short; if the sub-conscious wants to reflect, that the person's current action or thought is likely, to result in a high degree of success, then the seemingly "out of the blue" memory or fantasy (memo), will also reflect a high degree of success in its story line.) The same applies to high degree of failure, and anything in-between. It's a bit like using a personalized memory or fantasy as a symbolic segue, between the conscious and the sub conscious (or sub conscience?). It's a sort of "moral" traffic lights!

Unfortunately, people who have, unusual ideas, about what "success" is, can easily misinterpret the message behind such symbolic (success or failure based) internal memos! What is more, such misinterpretations, are particularly relevant to George, who (unfortunately and consistently) interprets rape – as a powerful symbol of . . . success!

So . . . it was not at all surprising, that whenever George valiantly thought about successfully avoiding rape (by successfully "passing safely by") he also automatically received, a powerful success-based fantasy about raping one or both of the girls. It was also of no great surprise, that George then went onto misinterpret the fantasy (or memo) as a powerful urge to commit rape – even though the fantasy (urge?), was meant to reflect the high degree of success that he would achieve by (successfully) "passing on safely by!"

Of course, on a more day to day practical level, having all these damned moral memos flying about his brain, was somewhat unsettling for George (bless his poor confused mind … and grubby little heart). But then again … it's not easy being a psychopath!

However (dear reader) for now, we will have to hurry on by such things as moral memos and the like, for although we will hear about them a later on, George is already in a great hurry!

As we try to catch up to George, he is already striding towards the last bend in the track, that in turn leads into a small open space, in which the abandoned air raid shelter stands. Now, with the inner "urges" of rape held firmly in his head, George is moving fast!

Then suddenly … he slows, as a cat slows, when it reaches the border of its prey's terrain! For now George is on the very edge of the air raid shelter clearing, and deep into his hunter mode!

Holding his breath, George stopped, and inched his upper body around the trunk of a tree that in turn, is part of the trees surrounding the clearing. Then, as he slowly tilts his head forwards, hoping the two girls won't see him – George sees the two girls and quickly steps back!

Pressing himself against the trunk of the tree, George inwardly cursed, "Fuck!"

The two girls were there, for sure, but so were three other teenagers! Two boys and a girl! As he stepped back even further, the reason the two girls had taken the shortcut in the first place, suddenly became obvious to George. They took it, not to tease him, but simply to meet up with their friends. In fact, the only person or thing teasing George – had been himself! With a mixture of emotions, including frustration, relief and guilt, George had little choice but to turn around and make his way home!

Twenty five minutes later, George was thoughtfully walking down the familiar residential streets towards his home. As he walked along, he was beginning to realise; that giving up rape, by his own volition, was not going to be as easy as it should be!

Then three minutes later, he finally turned the key in his front door and entered the relative sanctuary of his home. Then, before he knew it, his family had returned, and his daughter, Fern, was eagerly showing him her painting (of an elephant) that she had painted, at the party.

The elephant was a bright-green elephant; with bright pink ears, a mauve trunk and three tusks, one yellow, one deep blue and a red and white, striped one.

George took Fern's picture and looked at it for some time, and then he turned to the grinning and expectant Fern, looked into her eyes and said, 'That is a very, very, splendid elephant!'

Chapter 20

Better the angels you hardly know – than the devils you think you do!

After the disappointment of the Trafalgar Square no-meet, Steven was eventually cheered up by Bell sending another text:

"Although Crime, by its very nature, will happily cleaver the laws of humane kind, it is not however able, to even dent the bond between cause and effect. Just as the laws of physics state "Whatever is taken from one body is given (in kind) to another." the first Law of Crime states: "Whatever a crime takes from its victim, it will give (in kind) to the victimizer – unfortunately for criminals, Crime, by its very nature, does not give kindly!"

If the text was meant to get Steven to alter his intent, then it was about as much use as a Go Slow! sign on a roller coaster; for Steven had long decided, to deepen his commitment, by upping the stakes!

The following morning, a revitalized Steven has booked (under a false name, well made and applied false moustache, wig and clear glasses) into a hotel overlooking Hyde Park.

He has decided that it would be better not to direct his operations from his home. The possibility of the Susan woman or Bell, giving the police his mobile number, is too great a risk. If the police should try to pinpoint the signal location, he would be a sitting duck at his home, particularly if they cross-referenced the rough location with his first name! However, they would have a far harder job finding him amongst the several hundred rooms here. He could of course destroy the phone, but that would be losing face, regardless of whether or not anyone else found out!

Never the less, having raised the stakes, Steven unpacked his bags! He unpacked some every-day clothes, a retractable knife, a revolver (along with the remaining five bullets) and several new, un-registered pay as you go phones! Hooking the earpiece of a brand new mobile phone onto his right ear, he dials the Crime Frontiers number but not the help-line number; instead, he dials the general business line.

Having been connected to the operator (within the target maximum waiting time), Steven asked to be put through to the accounts department, he then asks the receptionist for the name and initials of the Chief Accountant. The helpful receptionist gave Steven the required name: D. B. Smyth and Steven thanked her. As soon as he disconnected the line, he trawled through the telephone directory app'. There was only one plausible D. B. Smyth and his address was in Surrey.

The time and day is the following Saturday in the afternoon. Although he arrived into the area by car, Steven is wearing a crash helmet with a combined chin protector and a pair of tinted goggles. For a moment longer he stares out of D. B's kitchen window, then turning and picking up the remote control, he switches D. B. Smyth's television to mute.

Outside the window of D. B's Smyth's kitchen, low clouds scurry overhead and disappear behind the trees at the bottom of D. B's garden. The tops of the trees are swaying inconsistently to the impromptu gusts of wind. In the mid-distance, a glider plane is arching low and tight into the wind, as the pilot makes ready for a landing at the small private aerodrome, hidden behind a distant hill.

By the time the muted newsreader has made way for the muted weatherman, Steven has formed an answer. The question; was from Donald (The Crime Frontiers Chief Finance Officer). Steven carefully closes the kitchen window curtains against any potential observers, such as neighbours, visiting dustmen or low-flying glider pilots with high-powered binoculars.

Donald is at that moment bound to his kitchen chair, which stands in the middle of his open-plan kitchen/diner. Donald's so far unanswered question was, "Who in Christ's name are you and what in the hell do you want?"

Noting the various religious pictures and paraphernalia, dutifully placed around the kitchen, Steven, although a long time non-believer, replies in his best improvised cockney accent.

'Well for a start, we'll 'ave less of taking our Lord's name in vain, if you fucking well please!' then squatting in front of his captive, he added, 'And to be fucking well 'onest! It's better that you don't know, who we fucking are!'

Without more ado, Steven pulled Donald and his chair to the computer consol. The computer sat on Donald's work desk, which in turn, formed the central part of the ergonomically designed workspace, which Donald used for his "home office." The PC is on, but unconnected to any web site.

Steven then continued, 'As for what we want? You are going to give, us, the password that will access this PC 'ere, to your company's financial files and company accounts!'

For a moment, Donald thought about lying, but realised that the various work related printouts laying on his desk, would betray any such lie, so he said nothing.

Steven however was not so reticent, 'After you 'ave given us the files, you are going to remain tied up for a few 'ours, until we've made good use of those details. And all this is going to 'appen, Donald …' Steven stated as he came around to face Donald's flushed face, '… because if you do, do as we ask, then in a few months' time, you will get a nice little … earner … dropped through your letter box, for your troubles. Because we are not unreasonable people … Donald!'

Steven then pointed his forefinger into the air, and qualified his offer, by sharply jabbing his forefinger into Donald's left ear, 'Unless that is … I get (jab) … fucking (jab)… angry! Do you want to see what it's like (jab) when (jab)… I (jab) … get (jab) … angry (jab, jab, jab) … Donald?'

Steven was of course, fully aware that Donald could still hear perfectly adequately with his right ear. He was also aware, that Donald would be aware, of the greatly publicized death threat to helpline employees. Never the less; it was of course important to Steven to give the impression to Donald, that he (Steven) and his "gang," needed the financial data purely to commit some sort of financial fraud, upon Crime Frontiers or its associated companies.

It was of course, equally important to Donald, that he convinced this man, that he (Donald) did indeed believe; that Steven (and his "gang") were only after financial gain, and were certainly not wishing to endanger the lives of the Crime Frontiers staff! For that (revelation) would have ended any hope that Donald could come out of this, complete and utter nightmare farce, alive!

But then, both Donald and Steven made one of those, silly mistakes!

You know the sort of thing; you must have made similar ones yourself (dear reader), though perhaps in less hazardous situations (probably)! The first mistake was that Donald glanced down and to his left! The second mistake was that Steven (following Donald's gaze) saw the wickerwork waste bin and the discarded newspaper, with its headline about Crime Frontiers; the killing of Garfield, and the threatening text, etc.).

Donald's mistake however, was not wholly in glancing down; it was in trying to smile apologetically! Steve's mistake was in misinterpreting Donald's smile as one of those "You can't fool me" smirks!

Quickly tying a gag across Donald's mouth, Steven then asked (rhetorically), 'Are you 'aving a fucking larf!'

Then returning to face Donald he asked again, 'Are you 'aving a good old fucking laugh? Or are you just 'aving a funny moment?' Steven then kicked the side of Donald's left shinbone, then grabbing the chair and Donald; he slammed both onto the parquet kitchen flooring!

Hauling Donald up from the floor, Steven slapped him, very hard, five times! Then squatting in front of the up righted Donald again, Steven said in his best reassuring (but no longer cockney) voice, 'Because if I were you, and let's face it Donald, who would want to be you. I would most definitely change my sense of humour. Because it really is not a healthy one to fucking well have, Donald!'

Steven then rose, and slammed Donald down to the floor again, then he stood up and turned away from the prone Donald, who for some unaccountable defence-mode reason, had started to giggle through the gag.

Steven was annoyed, that his sham (of wanting the access codes for fraud only reasons) had unravelled so soon. Turning around again, he picked

Donald up, and then kicked him down to the floor again, by which time Donald had stopped giggling!

Quickly striding over to the kitchen worktop, Steven pulled out a bone handled, carving knife from the knife block and returned. He then re-squatted down beside Donald, who was vainly trying to struggle out of his bonds! However, Steven had learnt from a previous near-escape of one of his Body Part victims; that such bonds had to be secured with diligence and measured patience. He had also learned that, these were two attributes in themselves, took time and experience to acquire, particularly under fraught situations!

For over a minute, Steven watched the struggling accountant, so that he and his captive could appreciate his bond securing achievements, then Steven spoke again.

'That's all right Donald, there's no reason to get up!' Patting Donald on the head, Steven added, 'In fact all you have to fucking well do, is to tell me the password to the finance and personal files. Because I know that you want to. And if you are having a funny moment, then get serious!' Steven then pressed the point of the knife into Donald's neck and said, 'Just as I am about to do with you!' With that warning, Steven, using his free hand, hit Donald across his mouth, very hard!

When Donald regained some of his senses, he murmured something inaudible though the blood filled gag. Steven nodded, put the knife down; walked over to the PC worktop, picked up a pen and a half used note pad. He then read the neatly written shopping list on the top page, tore it off, and then returned with the remainder of the pad and torn off shopping list.

Squatting down again, Steven looked at Donald in his remaining un-swollen eye, and pointed to the shopping list, then said, 'I like Ovaltine too!'

Raising Donald up from the floor, and un-strapping the tape from Donald's right wrist; Steven put the pen into Donald's visibly shaking hand, and then placed the pad on Donald's trembling knees. Then Steven ordered him to, 'Write it!'

For a moment Donald genuinely thought that Steven wanted the word

"Ovaltine" written down; and he began to write it, but then realising his mistake, he stopped writing. In that moment, both men knew, he would do exactly as the "nasty man" wanted. With that matter settled, Steven carefully removed the gag from Donald's mouth and said, That's the spirit! You see! I knew you could get serious if you really tried.'

Seating himself at Donald's P.C. Steven cheerfully quipped over his shoulder, 'You talk me through it and I will do the typing.'

Ten minutes later, Steven pocketed a memory-stick containing the National Insurance numbers and other financial details of every Crime Frontiers employee. The data also included all employees' home addresses and contact details! A minute later Steven clicked on to and out of several random web sites, then switched the computer off. He then walked over to Donald, and squatted in front of him.

'There! Steven said, patting Donald on his head for the final time, before giving him a playful poke in his good ear. 'It's all over now! Now you can go back to being one of the normal people!' Steven then rose to his feet and concluded, 'And I can carry on with what I normally do.'

A little over two hours later, after returning home from her regular Saturday morning visit to her mother, Francis, Donald's wife, found Donald still alive and still tied to his chair.

Although Donald and Francis did not know it, Donald owed his life to the late "G". If Steven had not been able to use "G"'s death, as a "signature," he would have used Donald's death instead!

Four hours later, Chief Inspector Rupert learned that Steven had "upped the stakes" by obtaining the names and addresses of all, 364 Crime Frontiers employees and volunteers – plus the details of its many associated businesses and organizations. After a hurriedly called meeting with his boss Chief Constable Pitch, it was agreed that the Crime Frontiers case would take priority over any other current case, even the "Body Part Murders" case would be temporally co-headed by another senior officer.

At 10 o'clock the following morning, Rupert and Sergeant Vanner arrived at the reception area of the Crime Frontiers building. At 10.45, they left;

having gained no more than they already hadn't on their previous visit.

'If we're going to catch this crazy fucking … monster,' Rupert told his sergeant, 'we're going to have to do it on our own!'

Chapter 21

A collection of motives

Chief Inspector Rupert's calculated profile of the "monster" was accurate as far as it went. Steven did look middle class; he was above average intelligence and at 42, he was in the profiler's age range. As to whether he had killed in self-defence, or had murdered "G" then it would have been a pointless question to the monster. Killing the mugger on the bridge, and assaulting the accountant were neither morally wrong nor right; both had been the product of successfully combining opportunity and logic.

Besides, to Steven any crime was like a "holiday" away from the bland landscape of his otherwise every-day life.

However, on this particular day, Steven was still in an explorative frame of heart and mind, in spite of receiving yet another text from Bell, stating:

"The concept that 'No' can be a floor as well as a ceiling; can also mean, that is there is no shame or weakness in obeying the law. Just as the laws of physics states: For every action, there is always an equal and opposite reaction, it is important to remember that opposites can often find a mutual attraction. This means of course, that 'No' and 'Yes' are not necessarily opposites at all, but rather your 'No' can be the push and your 'Yes' be your pull, just like the ladder rungs leading to a new horizon!"

The text also stated that the Bell was offering Steven a two weeks stay at the Crime Frontiers residential, with two daily crime-workshops!

As amusing as the prospect of the residential might be to him, Steven did not feel any overwhelming urge to re-pack his bag and rush off to take up Bell's offer.

Yet even now, Steven's master plan was not fully ready, there was a problem, or more accurately, two separated halves of a problem. He still had not fully formulated a way of getting all of his intended prey in one place at the same time, to make it appear that they had colluded.

Yet at the same time he had to be sure that, someone from Crime Frontiers had not grassed him up to the police, or indeed, the police themselves had not plodded their way onto his identity! So being a creature of habit Steven (the monster) decided to take his unfinished quest, for a walk.

The monster started the walk, by catching public transport to the Guildhall in London. Then, he walked to the small gardens at the rear of Wood Street Police Station. In the small square of garden, half a dozen or so office workers were dipping into their lunch packs before returning to the surrounding, clean cut, shiny glass, office blocks (no twitching lace curtains around here!).

In the centre of the garden, there stood a modest four-sided plinth and bust. The plinth bore a dedication to John Heminge and Henry Condell, the recorders and saviours of William Shakespeare's plays and works. Whenever he visited the garden, the monster liked to sit and recall some of the Bard's plays. However, it would have been debatable if even the Bard's works, could have bettered the tragedies and comic pathos that dwelt within the Wood Street Police Station records!

From the gardens, the monster strolled down towards Lower Thames Street; popping into "St Magnus the Martyr" church on the way. Although the church was unremarkable in itself, the monster liked to pop in to ponder the glass encased, model of the olden day bridge that spanned Southwark and the City of London. The model bridge even had model houses, people and livestock. In those far days, the central street running down the length of the original bridge was crowded with people, tradespersons, and all manner of livestock! The bridge was continually in use, and the gauntlet of two to three story houses with their shops and stores, overshadowed all users.

Each building, room, window and even the cobbles of the street itself, were all part of the tales of those who lived on or passed over the bridge. The monster usually liked to dwell in the church and imagine all about such tales.

Occasionally, religious buildings such as the church and its like touched the monster, though usually it was on his funny bone, rather than on any deeper level of his being.

On a deeper level of the monster's being, religion lacked personal accountability! "Purposely pursuing a twisted, even malevolent sense of power, through blatant wrong doing, was one thing; but to try and claim innocence and even respect, in the name of some "fairy-tale-God figure" was tantamount, to using Love as a cover story for child abuse – and therefore beyond Steven (the ordinary and Steven the monster's) contempt!

So, with the self-absolving, not to mention self-dissolving selfishness, of all dedicated psychopaths, the monster left the church, unrepentant.

Now it was out of the church and into the fresh air! Then down the narrow alley, right again, and down to and along Three Cranes Wharf. Here in the olden days, the wooden cranes of Three Cranes, were never endingly groaning and creaking as they swung back and forth throughout the day and night. Now days of course, the groaning cranes had been replaced by the pneumatic-whine, of their single arm successor, as it occasionally passed the pre-sealed containers of city's garbage into a waiting river barge. Now days, the once putrid stench of the wharf, no longer served as a gastronomic (and socializing) beacon for the city's vast community of fat, shiny bellied, bluebottle flies, who would constantly swarm around the nourishing flesh-pot, whenever they felt like a spot of dinning out!

However, today, as he idled by, there was barely a whiff of corrupted flesh or rotting garbage to offend (or perversely delight) the monster's nostrils! Instead of having to dodge the stamping hooves of whipped carthorses, the monster took care not to step onto a discarded piece of chewing gum. Neither did he have to compete for any 'rights of way' with drunken, sweating, barge loaders, or snarling feral dogs! Instead, the monster merely stood politely aside, as he returned the short nods and grateful smiles of a small group of tourist, as they in turn passed politely by disturbing no one, apart from a sense of dockside history.

From Three Cranes Wharf, the monster idled along the Thames Riverside walk, occasionally stopping to look down at the river. On such occasions, the monster would sometimes stare at the river's hypnotic surface, as it meandered down to the sea and then beyond, to be dispersed amongst the world's oceans; from whence all forms of original life had begun their personal quest! On such occasions, the monster would sometimes ponder about Life; with its endless-cycles of creation, destruction, war, peace, good and bad, that without which, this glitter-ball of opportunity that we call "Our Planet," would not shine so nearly as brightly!

However, there were no such ponderings today! For as he strolled along River Side Walk, the monster suddenly identified the primary requirement of his quest! He realised that what he needed, was a – collection of motives!

A collection of the motives, that would navigate the minds and actions of his adversaries, yet had the potential to lure them, shocked and aghast, into the grinning mouth of his Goody-goody trap! It was only a beginning of course, but it was an essential beginning, and one that the monster could slot into its place, with a hearty . . . thunk!

Looking up from the river, the monster noticed in the semi distant the, final, version of the Millennium Bridge, although the bridge was still known by many, as "The Bouncy Bridge!"

When the bridge was first opened, people used to complain (and praise) the fact, that when enough people crossed it at the same time, the bridge used to . . . bounce! Although the modern "Bouncy Bridge" was perfectly safe (for a start, it didn't even have a single-story house on it!) the bridge was closed for health and safety reasons, until its bounce had been neutered!

From a semi distance, people crossing the bridge had the appearance of Lowry "matchstick men," which seemed appropriate enough to the monster, as the bridge led directly into the mouth of "The Tate Modern Art Gallery."

The Tate's art works themselves, are displayed within the monolithic carcass of the former Bankside Power Station, which after being de-bowled of most of its industrial inners, had then been re-stuffed with the pickings of the nation's modern art collection. As far as the monster was concerned:

"True art, is the blending of two or more, previously separated or even antagonistic entities, into a single empathy, of mutual co-existence!" but then what else is a monster supposed to think about art?

Squatting next to the Tate Modern; was another powerhouse brought back from the dead, the Globe Theatre. The Globe was the original playhouse of William Shakespeare's plays. Now the two resurrected powerhouses sat side by side, their respective diminutive and outsize shapes appearing comically at odds with each other. The course of future art, seemingly, antagonizing the cause of past art . . . but the monster knew far better!

At times, the monster would prowl inside the Tate's bowels, but not today. Today he searched for inner inspiration. Turning right and away from the river, he dropped into the Café Rouge at the side of St Paul's Cathedral. As the monster sat, he drank a coffee and listened to French songs being playing in the background.

Then in a "complete" moment of inspiration, he had an answer to the Sandra problem – but it would all depend on the premise, that she was corruptible, and would betray the Anonymity Code! If she did, then his plan would succeed! However, if she did not act in line with his judgment, then her unyielding stance would become the unbending arrow; piercing the hearts of his enemies; with one foul . . . thunk!

From the café, the monster wandered to Smithfield Meat Market, the area of his childhood. He had had a reasonably upbringing, and his family had never lacked for anything financially. However, after the death of his father, a pharmacist, the monster sold the family house and small pharmacy shop, and moved to his present home. Although he was not very rich, he was comfortably well off.

Whilst he wandered around, he passed by his family's old house and pharmacy shop, now turned into town flats. These days the Smithfield area was neat, clean and respectable, though it was not always so. Muggings, pickpockets and ruffians were common in the early nineteenth century, as were public hangings, tortures and floggings, as well as occasional wife auctions (divorce was very difficult to obtain in those days!).

In his own youth, the young monster liked to sneak into the Smithfield's meat market, when he was on his way to school. He used to love the smell of the place, as he watched all the bustling activity around him. He also liked to hear the surround-sounds of the of butchers' cleavers, as they severed the various animal carcasses into manageable joints, thunk... thunk . . . thunk!

However, by the time the monster arrived, the market was closed to the public for the day; never the less he wandered around for a short while. From the market, the monster decided to, call it a day, and he hailed a taxi. Never the less it had been a very useful walk!

By the time he had reached his hotel; had his evening meal, showered, combed his hair, brushed his teeth and then snuggled up into his cosy hotel bed, he was a very exhausted monster! Laying his sleepy monster's head upon the hotel's sleepy-soft pillows, he let out a sleepy monster yawn, and then he sighed a small, clear, satisfied sigh!

Finally, the monster was ready to fall asleep, snuggled up in the knowledge; that all the strokes of his master plan were no more than a final decision's away, from becoming a single empathy of mutual understanding and co-existence! Moreover, as he finally closed his fluttering eyelids, that decision was hovering no more than a dreamless night's sleep away … from becoming our monster's uppermost . . . desire!

Chapter 22

Nice one Harry

When Rupert and the Sergeant Vanner arrived to their office, neither were feeling optimistic, even the usual perkiness of the sergeant seemed somewhat suppressed. Therefore, when one of the "computer geeks," (as Tom Vanner called them) greeted the detectives with a wide, and very geek like grin, neither detective perked up. Never the less, the "geek" pointed back to the computer console that he had left.

'We got a match, on a car reg-number placed in the vicinities of both the crime scenes; the bridge killing and the Crime Frontiers accountant job. Stuart got it about an hour and twenty ago!'

For about three seconds, the two detectives swapped a double take between themselves and the "geek" and then back again between themselves. Then as both men looked on questioningly, the "geek" did not let them down.

'We started off with a combined, automated back trawling of the vehicle registration recognitions, within the duel geographical and time related catchment areas. We got eight reg's, but only one fitted the offender profile indicated, and including the name Steve, which you mentioned as a possibility!' Then seeing Rupert's and sergeant Vanner's raised eyebrows, he triumphantly stated, 'It's a chap called … Steven Chadwick! We have an address. I also took the liberty of dragging up a photo, from Passport House. He has no criminal record though, I checked that too!'

Then, with a big grin on his face, the 'tech' handed over two sheets of A4 paper to Rupert. The name on the sheet was indeed STEVEN CHADWICK. There was also a mine of related information, which included a last known address, work, education, health records, and a whole lot more.

'He's also lives, five point four two kilometres, from the Crime Frontiers head offices, I checked!' the "geek" added.

'Nice one Harry!' Rupert congratulated. 'It's a great start, keep trawling. If you come up with anything else on him, his car, you let me or sergeant

Vanner here know, immediately, do you understand?'

'Absolutely! Of course, right away Chief!'

By three o'clock that afternoon, Rupert and sergeant were in Bell's office. Bell, Sandra and Andy were all there.

'We have what we think may, may, be the identity of a suspect,' Rupert was telling the assembled trio. 'His name is Steven Chadwick, we also have an address and a photograph obtained from passport records.' Handing Sandra a plain cropped, photograph of Steven, Rupert asked, 'It would help if you, or any member of the staff, could tell us if you have heard of him, have seen him or know him?'

Sandra looked at the photograph for a long while, handed to Andy and then disappointedly replied, 'I am sorry Chief Inspector, but I've never seen him before – but if you have his address why don't you go and pick him up?'

'I'm afraid that it's not as simple as that Miss! At the moment he is a person of interest. However, we do know that this man, or at least his car, was in the relevant areas and times of the crimes that are connected to Crime Frontiers; though of course that could be entirely coincidental. Unfortunately, there is no hard evidence that could be used to obtain any arrest warrant, or even a search warrant. We could question him of course, but I have a feeling that would do more harm than good at this stage.'

Ignoring the baleful looks of Bell and Sandra, Rupert continued, 'We have of course made enquiries. If he returns to his home address or his car is spotted, we shall be keeping a very close surveillance on him, you can be sure of that . . .'

At that moment Bell interrupted, 'Are you saying Inspector that you think this man has already fled?'

In answer, Rupert shrugged his shoulders, 'He hasn't been seen at that address for over 20 hours!' Then looking straight down at the floor, he added, 'We think that he may have been . . . spooked . . . somehow.'

Again, there was a distinct baleful look from Bell, 'I hope that you are not suggesting, that any one from our organization, somehow, tipped him off,

Inspector?'

'No sir we are not,' Rupert answered, then he paused to look at Bell in the eyes, 'that would be a seriously dangerous thing to do with this man. However, information can be accidentally, released, without even knowing it. It would help to know if anyone has been contacted since the last time?'

Bell's reply was instant, almost abrupt, 'To tell you that would be a betrayal of our confidentiality code Inspector, as I am sure you well know, I am amazed you asked.'

From the look on Rupert's face, it was clear to all that Bell's answer had annoyed him! However, before he could say anymore Bell asked him, 'Tell me, if the evidence about this Steven Chadwick, is as weak as you say, how come you are focusing so much time and effort on him?'

Rupert answer was unexpected but correct, 'It is you, your staff and the danger you all face, that we believe are worth spending so much time and effort on!'

The answer silenced any repost Bell might have had, and Rupert turned to Sandra, 'If this man is the one that threatened you, the possibility that he has gone to ground, may mean two things. One he has given up, or two, he is about to try to fulfil his threat to harm you, or another member of staff.'

'But if you could get enough evidence, you could bang 'im up?' Andy asked.

'Not necessarily!' Rupert replied, 'Even if there were such evidence, the killing of the young man, Garfield, could have been one of self-defence. Whoever our man is, he could easily plead, fear of revenge by the victim's family or friends, as a reason for not reporting the incident. The fact that he used such a tragic incident, to text his threat could still bring no greater charge, than that of threat by text. Any half-decent defence would have him out on bail in a jiffy! As far as the assault on Mr. Smyth, he has already confirmed that his assailant wore a helmet and goggles, and used a disguised voice at different times throughout the assault.'

Then turning to Sandra, Rupert stated, 'We must provide you with adequate protection Miss! And with that in mind we would very much appreciate you wearing a light weight tracking device, we will be offering a similar device to any of your fellow employees who wish to take it.'

On cue, Sergeant Vanner brought out a small quarter-palm sized box, with a strap attached, and offered it to Sandra, who took the tracker and nodded her agreement to the sergeant and Rupert. 'The box automatically sends out its GPS position without you touching anything,' Vanner informed Sandra. 'There is, as you will notice, a button on the top that you can press, three times, if you feel alarmed; once pressed, three times, assistance will reach you as soon as possible.'

Sandra gave Tom Vanner a smile of genuine acceptance, 'Thank you, I do take this man's threat seriously,' then nodding towards Andy she added, 'I am staying at Andy's place for a while.' She then turned fully to Andy and gave him a smile, 'At least until things have settled down.'

Andy returned Sandra's smile, and giving Rupert a cheeky look, he quipped, 'For a moment I thought you were gonna to tell us you've gone and caught the bastard – just when all my dastardly plans, for protecting Sandra 'ere, have come to good!' Then passing the photo of Steven to Bell, and looking at the two policemen, Andy added more seriously, 'I aven't seen him either!'

Rupert smiled at Andy and then turning directly to Sandra, he informed her, 'We know you moved last night! We do try to keep an open eye for the obvious as well as the unexpected. In fact we've had a plain clothes detective discreetly escorting you since our first visit here, Miss!'

The looks on Sandra and Andy's face told Rupert, that in spite of their heightened sense of precaution about being followed by Steven, the escort had indeed been discreet.

At that moment, Kerri came in with a tray of coffee, tea and biscuits. Bell returned the photograph, with a negative shake of his head, and went over to the tea tray to play "Mum" whilst Rupert continued with his summing up of the situation.

'We think, and hope, that the killing of Garfield Trueman was opportunistic and out of character,' Rupert said. 'But the fact that he then went on to leave the text messages, for us and others to find, suggest that this man's underlying motivations, are driven by an egotistic desire for recognition! It was certainly powerful enough to override, what we believe to be his normally calculating and methodical MO, as shown in the way he obtained the companies personal records.'

Bell stopped his serving and looked expectantly at Rupert, who carried on speaking, 'However, we believe that, if he thought that it would make him infamous enough, then this man will do anything to satisfy that desire – even if it meant that he would certainly be caught!'

Bell picked up a coffee and handed it to Rupert, 'And how infamous does this man need to be before he . . . jumps?'

Rupert took the coffee and looked at Bell, 'Well! We are not sure, yet, but we are certain of one thing, sir. We do not believe he is the type to jump without out trying to take any would be enemies, or rescuers, with him, however well-meaning they might be!'

If Bell took the obvious hint, then he did not show it, instead he returned to his desk and stirred his own tea, then almost cheerfully he asked Rupert, 'If you do find and arrest him, is he the sort of man who would give up information . . .that might also enhance his desire for infamy?'

Rupert shrugged his shoulders, and then turned to Sandra, 'We could however interview him, and thereby obtain a recording of his voice. But only you, or Mr. Bell, could identify his voice as the same man as the one who spoke with you on the phone. You wouldn't necessarily have to tell us what this man said previously, just confirm that in your opinion, the two voices matched. Armed with that corroboration we could at least get an arrest for him, and search warrant for his address and car.

Whether that would give us any further evidence, is of course open to question. However, it could mean that we could greatly deter this man before he harms or kills again. The alternative is to wait and hope that he leaves some forensics or other type of evidence, when he does strike next!' Then using a very deliberate tone Rupert he added, 'He is going to kill again you know.'

For a moment sergeant Vanner thought he recognized some doubt in Sandra's face, but it was only about choosing the right words to reply to Rupert.

'If I hadn't joined Crime Frontiers, Chief Inspector, I wouldn't be in this position, but I choose to join. Just as this … this man chose to target the helpline and what it stands for,' Sandra then paused as if asking herself a question, then looking at Rupert she asked, 'Tell me Inspector if you could catch this man by breaking the law would you?'

When neither Rupert nor the sergeant replied, Sandra carried on, 'Then unless I break your laws, please stop asking me to break the laws that I have promised to uphold!'

For a moment, everyone in the room fell silent until Bell intervened.

'I think you'll find Sandra's stand point will be echoed by all of our employees, Chief Inspector, including Donald Smyth.'

Rupert turned to Bell and informed him, 'We will be increasing the uniformed and plain clothes watch on these offices Mr. Bell.' Then returning to Sandra, 'We will also be putting a 24 hour, armed, rolling tail on your movements.' Rupert smiled briefly and nodded to Andy, 'which means some of your movements too sir.' Then Rupert stood up, as did the sergeant, 'Needless to say we will be continuing with our other avenues of enquiry.'

Holding his hand up to those still seated, Rupert concluded, 'We may know who he is because he may have made an impulsive mistake, by letting his emotions rule his head, at the bridge. However, when this man makes mistakes, they cost other people their lives. Let us hope for you or any of your co-workers sake Miss Lott that you or they, will not end up as yet another one of his … mistakes!'

Chapter 23

Preparations

The skill in laying and baiting a trap, for a specific type of prey, relies on three equally important choices. One is to obtain the correct bait! Another is to choose an appropriate place to plant the bait, and finally, but certainly not least, is how the bait is presented!

Having taken the decision to proceed with his, Goody-goody trap, Steven caught the underground to Angel tube station, north London. From The Angel he took a short bus ride up to Waterlow Park, from there he went straight to the world renowned, Highgate Cemetery.

As he expected, by the time Steven arrived, he found the gates of both East and West cemeteries locked, and the staff long gone home. Walking up the steep hill, he stopped outside the rarely used access gates, which served as an upper maintenance entrance to gothic like West Cemetery; it was also a direct and short walk from the Catacomb.

By now it was early evening, and easy to see that the windows belonging to the overlooking houses, appeared to be empty of any potential onlookers. Using a short handled bolt cutter, Steven sheered the padlocked chain securing the iron gates. Stowing the bolt cutter, the original chain and padlock into his newly acquired sports bag, he took an almost identical lock and chain from his bag, and then he re-shackled and locked the gate.

The whole process at the gate had taken less than two minutes. Twenty minutes later, whilst travelling back to his hotel, Steven was standing on a late-rush hour Northern Line train, reading an article in the Evening Standard newspaper.

The Standard article was a critique on the football authority's failure, to suspend a football player who had been sent off, for pretending to be fouled. Although Steven did not follow football, he much preferred cricket, tennis and golf, he did however agree with the article. In the mind of Steven, the tacit support of cheating was the same as condoning theft by buying stolen goods;

they are a cause rather than a symptom of a society's or family's moral decline.

The choice of the Highgate West Cemetery, to stage the final act of his master plan was not difficult for Steven to choose. He had originally thought about using the, East Cemetery, for distributing the parts from one his "Body Part" victims. The East Cemetery could be accessed from the adjoining Waterlow Park, especial at night. In addition, the kudos of placing various body parts on the gravestones of the cemetery's more famous residents; was very tempting to Steven's flare for the dramatic!

Never the less, during a web search of the cemetery's details, Steven also discovered; that due to a recent spate of vandalism, the cemetery's charitable trust had hired a night security, with a dog patrol, to patrol both cemeteries! In the end, the risk of transporting and distributing the body parts, without being discovered, seemed to be a bit too hazard prone, so Steven had thought better of it! However, the vandalism and dog patrols had long ceased.

Steven had of course already made most of his preparations. Never the less, almost the very last preparation, before booking the hotel, was to bring along his revolver!

The revolver was an 2nd World War army revolver, which Steven had unexpectantly found and unrepentantly stolen, many years previously. He had been an occasional semi- professional burglar in those early days, and he had entered the unattended house, via a small un-secured window. The detached house was in a semi-rural area of Surrey. When Steven first saw the gun, just lying there in a dining room drawer, he was nervous – and even shocked! At first, he quickly closed the drawer and then he backed away. As far as he was concerned at that time, such things were out of his league and asking for trouble!

After leaving the revolver where it was, Steven had continued with searching the rest of the house. However, although he had taken the precaution of dropping the latch on the front door, he realized that he had not even checked, let alone secured the back door. It was only when he was halfway across the broad upper landing, leading to the bedrooms on the other wing; that Steven realized his oversight. If the owners should suddenly return, then unable to open the front door they might well try the back and get in! Then realizing that someone may be in their house, they may well also go to the dinning cabinet drawer, and take the revolver out, as protection, or even in anger!

So, supposedly, fearing for his life rather than merely his freedom, Steven did not go to the back door, but returned to the dining room draw – and took the revolver out! Before he knew it, he had checked the weapon was loaded, stuffed it into his waistband, and without making a conscious decision, or without bothering to search the rest of the house – he was out of the front door! One minute later, he was walking down the quiet and secluded road, whilst his heart was noisily pounding in his chest!

Since the night of the burglary, Steven had only fired the gun once! The urge was too great, and a week after he had stolen it, he had dug the revolver up from his hiding place. He went to a nearby wood, where he "fatally" shot a tree! At least, the tree would have been, fatally shot, if the chalked white heart on the tree's trunk had been a real heart. Steven's delight in shooting the tree in its heart, was somewhat diluted by the deafening explosion the gun had made. Never the less he was very pleased with his "find" and his ability to use it.

However, since that time, the gun and remaining five bullets, wrapped in wax paper and canvass, inside a Tupper ware box, had remained re-buried.

Although he had thought about the gun on occasions, Steven had not been overly tempted to retrieve or use it – even for his Body Part Murder adventures! As far as he was concerned, the revolver was a last resort, and only to be used on the most desperate, or important occasion. To be caught with a firearm meant a certain prison sentence, regardless of any other crime he might have been committing – or even just intending to commit!

However, there was another reason to keep the gun buried and safe. If he had "Possession of a firearm" on any potential police record, then any police hunt for him thereafter, would automatically mean that the police would be armed – thus making any sort of confrontation highly improbable to win or escape from!

Now, many years later, Steven felt that all of his patience and prudence had been, truly rewarded. For above all other crimes he had or may yet commit, including the Body Part Murders, this crime was to be his most important and … personal crime!

After re-checking that the empty sixth chamber, would be the first to be fired, Steven stuffed the revolver into his trouser waistband; as he had done so many years ago, though this time his decision was fully conscious and his heart rate was (almost) quite normal!

Chapter 24

Obtaining the bait

When Sandra and her best friend Lizzie were about 150 metres from the 'The Thai Delight' restaurant, midway along the high street, Lizzie asked the driver of their unmarked police car to pull into the side. Being the person that Lizzie is, she would be far too embarrassed to explain to her friends, waiting inside the restaurant, that she of all people was driving around with an escort of three armed police officers! Being the person she is of course, meant that she would, enthusiastically tell her all of friends all about her marvellous adventure, for months if not years after; or at least whenever she thought it not boastful to do so.

Lizzie, like all the other Crime Frontiers employees, had been issued with a small, easy to read, basic pamphlet on personal security; she had also been given the quarter-palm sized emergency bleeper. However, police, alarms and spooky men, were all put aside by the time Sandra and Lizzie arrived and greeted their dinner companions.

The visiting friends of Lizzie were originally from her hometown of Cheam. Neither guest nor any other diner, apart from Lizzie and Sandra, paid much attention to the smartly dressed man and woman, who entered the restaurant a few minutes later. When the third police officer arrived five minutes later, he was almost completely unnoticed by any one, except that is by Steven.

Steven had entered 'Rialto' some three minutes after Sandra and Lizzie entered their restaurant on the opposite side of the High street. It had not been difficult for Steven to follow the unmarked police car's short journey. He had bought a second hand car that very afternoon from a pimply faced youth, for "bargain" £1,745. In fact Steven greatest difficulty was, in choosing what to order from the menu, particularly since he found Italian food to be his favourite food.

Being the man that he is, Steven had no illusions about how difficult it would be, to kidnap Sandra from beneath the noses of her police escort; which is why he had no intention of trying to do so. No, Lizzie would be a far more sensible … kidnapee!

Sandra had accepted the offer of a lift from the police escort on this occasion, because it meant that she could enjoy the wine without worrying about exceeding the alcohol-driving limit.

Inside the restaurant, the two friends recounted to Lizzie's friends about the previous day when Lizzie had, walked in, on Sandra and Andy as they were passionately kissing, in an unused office at Crime Frontiers! As soon as Lizzie realized the situation, she said, in typical Lizzie fashion, 'Oh wow! Are you two going to have sex … because if you are, then the boiler room is never locked and it gets so hot down there, that me and … someone who shall remain nameless, were dripping with sweat before either of us had even got our glasses off!' Without doubt, next to Andy, Lizzie was Sandra's closest friend!

When Sandra and Lizzie had entered the police car, Steven had instantly recognized Lizzie from the files that he had downloaded from the school's staff accounts. It came as no surprise to Steven that when the time came for the dinner party to break up, Sandra went back with her escort and the two visitors went back to their hotel by taxi, and Lizzie got a lift in the her friends taxi, to the top of her road.

Although most people, (including Lizzie herself), would consider her as a bit of a "scatter brain," her one bedroom flat was, by most people standards, noticeably clean, neat and well ordered. Lizzie liked the warm secure feeling that she received, when coming home to a cared for home. It was worth the optimistic effort of pampering every room with that extra touch, tidy, and brush of love! After all, as Lizzie often remaindered herself: "With all the ups and downs of life, it's good to have at least one place that's ship-shape!"

However, no sooner than Lizzie had finished brushing her teeth, then the sound of the doorbell suddenly disturbed her! It was after all very late for someone to be calling. So feeling curious and cautious, she went to her front door peephole and looked through.

When she saw a man she did not recognize, she debated whether to go and get her police-bleeper, but it seemed silly; after all, there was a solid and locked door between her and the man, so she called through the door instead.

'Hello, can I help you?'

Steven held up an identity card, which Lizzie could not possibly read, through the spy hole, and then he said, 'D.S. Marlow, Miss! Is Constable Beadley with you?'

Thrown a little off balance by the question, Lizzie answered, 'Constable …? No, no one is here but me.' Through the peephole Lizzie could see the man step back, then forwards again as he shouted, 'Could you tell me, if or when you did last see him miss?'

Worried that the man's volume might disturb her neighbours, Lizzie deliberately lowered her voice when she replied, 'I haven't seen anyone since I arrived home, just a while ago!'

Dipping into his inside pocket, Steven brought out, flipped open and consulted a small notebook. Stepping closer to the door, he lowered his voice to a below normal level.

'I am speaking to Miss Lewis, Miss Elizabeth Lewis?'

By now, Lizzie was confused rather than cautious and answered, 'Yes. But I'm afraid I haven't seen any one!'

Keeping his volume low, Steven replied, 'It is just that he is supposed to arrive here, to inform you in advance, that we are coming here, Miss. Chief Inspector Rupert has asked myself, and my colleague, DC Read, to escort you to Saint James's Hospital, Miss.'

When Lizzie heard the words, Saint James's Hospital, she was even more confused – and worried! Perhaps something had happened to Sandra! Lizzie reached for the latch ready to unlock it, but did not, instead she asked, 'Hospital? Why does he want to see me at the hospital?'

'I don't know miss, Steven answered, 'All I know is that he wants to see you there, as soon as possible, I don't think you are in any trouble Miss, but if you would prefer I can contact him by mobile, does he have your number, Miss?'

Although it was all confusing and worrying, the man's last words were enough for Lizzie to be convinced; that he was a genuine police officer. Therefore, without further delay, she unlocked and opened the door and said apologetically, 'I'm sorry to be a silly-billy, but this is so confusing! I'll have to put some shoes on and get my things, but I'll be with you in less than a minute!'

As soon as Lizzie opened the door, Steven caught a waft of spearmint-flavoured toothpaste. However when he saw Lizzie, still dressed in her smart dining out clothes – but with the surreal addition of a pair of white, bunny rabbit slippers on her feet – he could not help but smile, and then assure her, 'That's all right, Miss, your bunny wabbit slippers will be just perfect!'

Twenty minutes later, Lizzie was getting her fourth "lift" of the night (including the taxi to Andy's place to meet Sandra). Moreover, although the rear passenger floor of Steven's car felt cramped, even for Lizzie's small frame, the semi-comatose, sedative-hazed world in which she inhabited for the whole ride, did at least manage to enhance her relative comfort.

Steven and Lizzie arrived at his hotel just over an hour later. Having been pre-warned by Steven, the hotel night staff were most helpful in assisting Steven, and his obviously handicapped younger sister and wheelchair (which Steven had "borrowed" from the Whittington Hospital), up to their double room (with separate beds). Being satisfied that Lizzie's absence would not be noticed until her absence at Crime Frontiers; Steven sent a text to Bell stating that he would phone Sandra, sometime, the following afternoon or evening. After tucking Lizzie up with another shot of powerful sedatives, Steven climbed into his own bed and fell fast asleep . . . it had been a long day!

CHAPTER 25

Trisha goes to war!

The following morning, and after getting an update from David Bell, Sandra and Andy each went to their separate booths. Although she did not see her best friend Lizzie at her usual booth, Sandra was soon too busy to give Lizzie's absence much further thought.

For the early part of her shift, rather than twiddling her thumbs waiting for Steven to call, Sandra dealt with a dozen calls; most of which, she either passed on details of useful organizations specific to the caller's needs, or she gave the caller advice or facts from the Crime Frontiers own crime data base.

The database included the statistical averages for a host of crimes, from petty pilfering, gang related statistics, and murder. The database included; such facts as average financial or personal satisfaction/dissatisfaction from the relevant crime (with and without time served in prison), the likelihood of not being arrested for the crime, average sentencing for first offences and beyond, personal consequences to the victim/s and offender, and a host of other useful information!

Incidentally (dearest reader), the average drugs user, owns far less than the average shop assistant, and the average sex offender, has less fulfilling sexual encounters, than the average shop assistant. However let us not get, too involved, with such diversions, for as interesting as they may be, our dearest Trisha, having had many a dealings with a variety of criminals, could tell us a host of anecdotal facts herself!

Unfortunately, that very morning (after Lizzie's kidnapping), Trisha, like poor little Lizzie, was still in a bit of a drugs-haze herself! However, when Trisha received a phone call from her dealer, Jake, she not only perked up, but she was also taken aback! Jake rarely if ever called her, it was nearly always her that called him. When he further asked to meet her, so she could, "Quality test a fresh batch pastries (heroin)" Trisha became wary.

Trisha already knew that Jake always had various quality controls performed on all of the deals that he bought. Being an "L-reg" (loyal) customer, Trisha also knew that Jake would also give out his genuine rating to his loyal customers, it was one of the reasons why they remained loyal. However, Jake had never asked her to be a guinea pig! Although she had previously, knowingly, bought some poor quality deals from Jake, she had never had any bad results. Never the less, to Trisha, Jake had sounded different and not his usual buoyant self. On the other hand, it wouldn't do to offend her best and main supplier – or refuse a freebie! Finally, after Jake reassured her that she should look on his offer, as getting "reward points" for being a loyal customer, Trisha agreed to a meet.

When she eventually arrived at the dilapidated crack-house, most of her previous doubts began to seem a bit silly to her. She even thought that her unnecessary anxieties had been prompted as a result, of her talking to and thinking about her conversation with Sandra. However, she was about to be a guinea-pig for a batch of heroin, so when she pushed open the un-locked front door, Trisha could not help but feeling tense. Once she was in the hallway, she called out Jake's name and was immediately answered by Jake, cheerfully calling out to her from the top floor.

With some caution, Trisha reached the first floor landing and unsuccessfully attempted to step over what seemed to be a semi-naked, doped up female, hunched, foetal like, under a multi stained blanket. Never the less, even when she did accidently tread on the woman, Trisha deliberately ignored the woman's moan of discomfort.

When she was on a drugs campaign, Trisha had learned not to get too concerned about the discomfort of herself or others. As with many a warzones, including that of drugs, any upright morals of human kind are treated as walking wounded; and more preferably as walking hazards! Such fine moral luxuries of compassion and empathy, were found in such far-flung-rations across the mind-fields of Trisha's inner conflicts that morality had more or less taken on the role of trench-humour!

In truth, she had felt so united in victory and blown apart by defeat, so many times, it was difficult for her to tell who she was for most of the time – let alone what side she was currently on! Never the less, if ever she saw a cavalry charge of heroin on the horizon, she would always be ready to be hobbling into battle yet again!

Never the less, as she carefully tiptoed over a second prone druggie, and without any conscious reasoning, Trisha suddenly changed her mind! For a moment she stood there, then without making a sound, she began to very, very, carefully, turn arou . . .!

At that very moment, Jake called her name out again! So returning to the "fray" once more, Trisha turned back, and with the gait of the dispossessed, she headed back up the flight of stairs.

If Trisha had known that the man she had seen in the ally way, the man who had so mercilessly beaten the other man, was at that moment waiting in the top floor room, alongside Jake, she would have continued turning and then ran for her life, but she did not!

As she climbed, Trisha's legs began to tremble and her mouth began to feel parched. Whether her symptoms were prompted by the anticipation; of suckling at the brestless nipple of her addiction, yet again, or whether they were stirred by the far deeper instinct of terror, was hard for even Trisha to tell.

Yet undeniably, she began to feel as if her sense of, self, was disappearing once more! So as she climbed up the stairs, she tried to hold on to the only thing she felt she had left . . . her very breath! Still holding onto her depleting breath with every footfall, Trisha continued to creep up the creaking stairs.

As she approached the next landing, a partially torn film poster appeared, advertising the film "Alien" along with its famous quote stating that: "*In space ... no one can hear you scream!"* Except that someone had crossed out the word "space" and replaced it with the words, "*this place.*" Only for some further comic to add their observation, by crossing out "*can hear ...*" and replacing it with ... "*is bothered if ...*"

The man waiting alongside Jake, in the attic room, went under the street name of "Big Man." He had only been in the business of supplying bulk narcotics for three years, but he knew his cliental from top to bottom. Knowing of Trisha's addiction, Big Man had baited her confidently.

The revolving relationship between any addict and their habit, are in many ways, like that of any masochist towards their chosen master! In that, in satisfying their hunger, the addict merely postpones a far crueller punishment!

Big Man felt no sympathy for Trisha or her kind. As far as he and more than a few people were concerned, addicts (no matter what their addiction) were all just "a load of winging hypocrites" who deserved all they got!

In the one hand, they clutched the "burdens" of their chosen habit, and in the other hand, they snobbishly held onto their "freedom from personal responsibility – let alone responsibility for others! So that when it came to making any real effort to cut the noose of their pathetic obsessions, they conveniently found that their, hands are tied ... behind their aloof and arching backs! In Big Man's opinion, if it weren't for the money, he'd hang them all in a pretty line – and piss on them!

By way of paying some condescending-compensation to Jake, Big Man had promised him that he could have a new area to peddle his wares. The new area was "protected" by Big Man himself. He had also promised Jake, that if he co-operated, then he would not suffer the same fate as the uncooperative man in the ally!

As far as Jake was concerned, he knew that in possibly loosing Trisha, he was losing a valued customer, but not as valuable as his new mentor! Besides, as much as he liked Trisha, Jake knew that such losses to "friendly fire," were an unfortunate but inevitable statistic of the double-cross fire that daily strafed the city's drug wars.

As Trisha reached the last flight of stairs, she heard a small commotion from one of the landings beneath. Quickly looking over the banister, she feared that the disturbance might even be a police raid, but they then would have made much more noise. Realizing that the druggies she had passed on the way up, were probably causing the disturbance below, Trisha became angry with herself, and decided to run up the remaining stairs.

When she halted outside the almost closed door, Trisha took two much needed deep but quiet breaths, knocked on the door once, and without waiting for a reply, opened it! As she stepped into the threshold of the room, the partially loose floorboard beneath her foot did not give way completely – but it did give out a very distinct and habitual . . . groan!

As soon as she entered the room Trisha was struck by how overfilled it seemed – mainly because it was filled with the presence of Big Man!

'Hello Trisha . . . good to see you again,' Big Man greeted.

To gain some time, Trisha pretended to look from The Man, to Jake and then to another heavily set man to Jake's right. It wasn't much time gained, but it gave her enough to decide – that denial was the best tactic! Trisha also knew that the man, had at best, only caught a partial glimpse of her behind the back of the punter. She also knew that she had been wearing her blonde wig, which she had not used since!

Looking at the man again, Trisha put on her curious face and asked, 'Do we know each other Sweet-heart?' Then without waiting for any reply, she added apologetically, 'I'm sorry darling, if we have met already! It's me not you, I've got an awful memory for faces – particularly if I'm out of it!' Then turning to Jake, she added, 'And I usually am out of it! Why . . . I've even walked past Jake here before!'

Jake, however, said nothing to confirm or deny Trisha's testimony. However, Big Man seemed to look at Trisha as if she had indeed spoken the partial truth, 'Then you must have been well out of it, darling, because we only met the other fucking day! Not that I blame you! In fact if it wasn't for a little birdie, telling me it was you, I might not be sure myself!' With that said, Trisha suddenly heard a shuffling noise behind her, but she did not turn around. Instead her attention was fixed to the man before her, who was looking into Trisha's wide open eyes, with such an intense knowing look, that she felt as if she were being given a wisdom beyond all of her previous understanding!

At that moment and without breaking eye contact, the man beckoned to someone behind Trisha.

Then Big Man smiled and stepped forwards, and with the patient air of doctor ushering in a casualty, he invited his "birdie" in!

To Trisha's horror, she recognized that the "birdie" was the woman from the ally! Yet even then, at first, Trisha did not fully recognize the woman – but the woman certainly recognized her. Fixing Trisha with a blood shot eyed stare, the woman slowly raised her right hand, and with her nail gnawed, grimy forefinger, pointing accusingly at Trisha, she spoke.

'That's her! Her hair is different from before, but I'd know her anywhere! We used to play truant together! She was with the other man, in the ally, they both ran off.' Then, turning back to Trisha, the woman proudly stated, 'I was in the ally too, when you and that man came out!'

Given the situation she was in, it was of no great surprise, that it took Trisha some time to gather in what the woman had just told her. Particularly, what she had said about playing truant? In fact, it wasn't until the woman smiled a characteristically, slightly crooked smile, that Trisha at last recognized who she was, and when she did, she was deeply shocked!

The woman was called, Chelsea, Chelsea French! When Trisha had last known Chelsea, they were both at the same school, but never in the same grade. Although Trisha couldn't remember playing truant with Chelsea, (Trisha had played a lot of truant), she did remember her, and her crooked smile. But at that moment, Trisha's brief nostalgia was interrupted by Big Man.

'Jake here says you'll keep your mouth shut,' he said looking Trisha up and down, 'Maybe he's right … maybe not!' Then stepping forwards until he was less than an arm's length away, he demanded, 'But what I want to know is … who the man with you was. What's his fucking name?'

Trisha answered truthfully and quickly, 'He calls himself Frank. I don't know any last name. I see him about once a month. I don't know if it's his real name, but I do know he was scared shitless. He ran off like a scared rat! I doubt if he'll be back! I hardly saw anything, he was blocking my view, and even if I had, I wouldn't say anything … I'm not stupid!'

'We'll see about that,' Big Man retorted. 'Where's this fucking Frank live?'

'I honestly do not know,' Trisha emphasized. 'I think he works for the council or someone, in an office maybe. He said that he has to catch a train and bus home, so I think he lives out of town. If I see him, I'll tell you straight away, if he turns up!'

'If you don't, you already know what going to happen to you don't you!' Big Man, informed, rather than threatened her.

'Yes! I know!'

Big Man then said nothing but just nodded.

In truth, Trisha was grateful to answer any questions about the punter – for it took the main focus away from her. She was well aware that if she had been the only witness, she would have been in instant danger, either back in the ally then, or now. But it was clear that the man was more interested in the punter. If the man before her knew that she had already told the police and Crime Frontiers about the ally way, then Trisha knew that all deals would be off!

The Big Man looked at Trisha and then at Chelsea, then back to Trisha, 'You see him, you phone Jake immediately! I'll make it well worth your while, when you meet him you call Jake, you understand?'

'Yes! I understand!' Trisha confirmed, then with equal emphasis added, 'You can rely on me!'

'No I can't!' Big Man contradicted, 'But you can fucking well rely on me! Now fuck off!'

As soon as Trisha felt the fresh air outside, she felt lightheaded and her legs began to shake. However, it was not just the threats of the man and her narrow escape that shocked her most – it was also the shock of seeing her ex school mate! Even now Trisha could picture the young Chelsea. It was true they had never been good friends, but they had never been enemies either. Trisha still didn't remember playing truant with her, she did however, clearly remember, Chelsea's face, and that was the shock!

When Trisha suddenly recognized Chelsea's crooked smile, amongst the drug abused remnants of her old school chum's face, it felt as if she had been thrust into the middle of some ghoulish episode of "This is Your Life!" Or more accurately . . . "This will be Your Life!"

By the time she had returned to her girlfriend's flat, Trisha had already phoned the helpline, and was impatiently waiting for Sandra to finish another call and phone her back. Whilst she waited for the call, Trisha raided her friend's fridge; and binged four slices of ham, a tin of sardines, a whole large tin of peaches (including the syrup), three mini bottles of Actimel yogurt, five cheese spread triangles and a tin of low calorie baked beans!

Twenty five minutes later Sandra phoned back, and Trisha told her about the whole sordid incident at the crack house, the man, and about Chelsea French!

Sandra listened without interrupting, then she said, 'It must be horrible to go through such a terrible ordeal,' then after waiting for any reply, she added, 'But in the end Trisha, you are 100% responsible for all of your actions! And before you think that I'm only trying to blame you Angel, I have to tell you, that I mean responsibility, in the sense of having the ability to respond, appropriately!'

Back in her friends flat, Trisha got ready for a reading of the riot act from Sandra; however, Sandra's response was different and far from condemning!

'And believe me Angel, you can respond appropriately! Because, I also have to tell you, that having total responsibility, also means, that whether you believe it or not, you do have the total ability, to change your old responses forever – no matter who you are or who you have been! Because, that is the power that, total responsibility, gives!' then for a moment Sandra paused for Trisha to respond.

Listening on the other end of the phone, Trisha response was to try to suppress the sudden and totally unexpected emotion of … hope! However, as she replied, the quivering in her voice could not be suppressed,

'What do you … mean?'

'I mean that you have and have always had that ability … my sweetest Angel!' Sandra answered, then again, Sandra waited, before she added, 'But, if you do not understand how to use that ability, then we can help you – but that will be your choice and total responsibility too!'

Twenty minutes later Sandra had re-contacted Trisha, to tell her that she had secured her a place at one of the Crime Frontiers associated safe houses, for that very evening! Trisha then packed her carrier bag of belongings, not forgetting the half-pack of Andrews (as an opiate user she'd be constipated for ages after her food binge!).

Trisha also left her friend, a thank you and goodbye note: which also stated that she had not decided where she was going to yet! In truth Trisha left the note not only out of genuine gratitude, but also to cover her friends back, should Big Man trace her to her friend's place. Then Trisha finally left her friend's flat and the surrounding area, she was never to return to either! Nor did she ever phone Crime Frontiers again; which meant that Sandra never did find out why Trisha was nicknamed "Trish-trash!"

After the phone calls from Trisha, Sandra sat back and shrugged her shoulders at David Bell, in the crow's nest. Bell gave the thumbs up sign, to congratulate her on her dealings with Trisha. Then both of them sat back, and waited, for Steven to phone! They would not have to wait too long.

Chapter 26

Planting the bait

When Steven drew his rented car to a mildly sharp stop, Lizzie slumped forwards in the front passenger's seat. The surrounding pub car park was about ten minutes stroll from the world renowned, Highgate Cemetery.

'Sorry!' Steven said, as he bent forwards to look into Lizzie's drug dazed, but still half-open, deep brown eyes. Un-clipping his own safety belt and placing his hand on the crown of Lizzie's crash/safety helmet, he gently brought her back into an upright position, and then undid her safety belt. He then checked to see that any of his disguises had not been disturbed, and then he sat back and thought a while.

Apart from a brief period, in which she had given her recorded opinion about her situation, Steven had kept Lizzie under sedation since kidnapping her. The hotel staff had seen nothing to be suspicious about a caring elder brother, tending for his handicapped, younger sister. In fact, they were rather touched by his obvious loyalty!

Steven had thought about ensconcing Lizzie in the West Cemetery's Catacomb, the previous night (the night of the kidnap), even though it would have been well past midnight. However, he had decided against it on the grounds; that there may not have been enough time for his trap to be completed, before the cemetery staff arrived early in the morning. They might discover Lizzie and raise the alarm before she could have been "found" and rescued, by the police.

Getting out of the car and going to the trunk, Steven removed the collapsible wheel chair, and then he brought it up to the passenger side door. With some difficulty and dedicated care, he then manhandled the semi-comatose Lizzie out of her seat, and then into the wheel chair. After strapping her into the wheelchair, and wiping her mouth and chin, Steven then wheeled Lizzie down Swains Lane, past the maintenance gate, and then down to the

East Cemetery, and then to the small building that served as the visitor's reception centre.

He then politely insisted that he pay for two, adult, entrance tickets, even though the well-meaning ticket sales girl had discreetly offered, to let Lizzie in for the free admission of a child's ticket. As far as Steven was concerned, the price of someone's dignity, whatever his or her apparent misfortune may be, should never be reduced to the level of a "bargain basement!"

Steven then took Lizzie for a leisurely tour of the East Cemetery. The pair stopped at the various graves and tombs of the cemetery's famous and forgotten occupants. Throughout the tour, Steven (using the guide pamphlet and his memory), gave Lizzie interesting details about the various dignitaries, such as Carl Marx, who were now behind death's door. Indeed, had Lizzie been more able to be attentive, she would have been both enthralled and (Lizzie being Lizzie) rather saddened, by their stories.

Then, about half an hour into the tour, Steven briefly left Lizzie unattended in her wheelchair. As he made his way along a narrow path, he came to a small, almost insignificant, mid nineteenth century grave. The only information, about the person that lay beneath the bramble strewn grave, was to be found on the remaining half of the broken stone scroll, the inscription read, "Aged 8."

For a quiet moment, Steven stood before the grave, and then he moved away to return to his charge. It was not the first time that Steven had visited the cemetery or indeed that grave. However, although he was capable of being moved, he preferred never to move without thorough recognizance and planning beforehand. Following the next part of his plan, Steven and Lizzie left the cemetery and went into the adjoining Waterlow Park. As Steven and Lizzie entered the park, he noticed that there were more people than usual. It was only then that he noticed colourful banner on the gate, advertising

"An Evening Concert of Franz Zimmer's Film Music!"

To Steven's further surprise, the concert, which coincided with a daylong film festival in the park's Lauderdale Hall, was that night. The concert itself was to be held in a cordoned off seated area, by the lake. People could of course hear and see the orchestra free, if they did not want to pay the modest price of a seat. The performance, scheduled to last until 10 pm, whilst the park was to close at the late time of 11.00 pm.

As Steven gently pushed Lizzie towards the lake to see what was happening, he was mildly concerned. Although he did not see any police presence, there were a few stewards around. However taking all things into balance, he realised that the gathering crowd would not interfere with his plan, and may well provide an added camouflage, into which he and Lizzie could blend. He could even see a few wheel-chaired concertgoers upon the hill.

Returning to the place where the main gates of the older West Cemetery could be partially seen, Steven sat down besides Lizzie and then began to eat and drink his bargain Tesco's Meal deal. Although by now, his meal did seem rather sparse compared to the small banquet that some near bye concert goers were enjoying, whilst being careful not to drop any vittles' onto their eveningwear!

Just over three quarters of an hour later, at 4 pm. Steven observed that the last of the West Cemetery guided tours were leaving, and the gates were being closed. There would still be one or two admin staff, left in the admin building/ex chapel, to the right of the gatehouse. However, at five pm all staff appeared to have left. There was of course, the possibility that one or two admin staff were doing a bit of voluntary overtime, but it was highly unlikely that any one would go up to the Catacomb at the top of the cemetery.

Besides, even if someone discovered Lizzie and Steven in the cemetery, if he left now, he could always state that he and Lizzie had wandered in, when the main gate had been accidently left unattended. Of course, if any one should discover them in the catacomb (which he would have to break into) then that would require a more drastic answer! Never the less, Steven knew that the point of no return (without consequences) had arrived!

However, although it was not essential, there was a far more preferential reason for starting now, and that was to give the police enough time to find Lizzie, before dark. For that would entail that, Steven, although having the normal night vision capabilities on his camera-phones, could film Lizzy's "rescue" in the clear daylight!

So, stowing the wrappings of his meal-deal inside the side pouch of the wheel chair, Steven wheeled Lizzie out of the park. He then turned right and (with some effort) wheeled Lizzie back up the steep hill, until they came to the service gate. Parking Lizzie in front of the gate, he unlocked the re-placed padlock, opened the gate and wheeled Lizzie in.

Having secured the gate from the inside, he then trundled his charge into the cemetery itself. He did not look to see if there were any onlookers, mainly because it was still daylight, and they (the onlookers) may be difficult to see, plus why would anyone behaving innocently look around?

This time, Steven did not give Lizzie a guided tour, as he wheeled her along the comparatively short distance to the catacomb. Indeed, for Steven, the whole effort of pushing Lizzie up the hill, and now over the rough path, was quite tiring! By the time they had arrived at the locked doors of the catacomb, he was quite, breathless.

Never the less, he had hardly paused for breath, before he repeatedly tried to force open the catacomb doors, with the chisel that he had brought for that very purpose. However, in the end, he had been forced to fetch a near bye sturdy spade, left by workmen, who had been previously working near bye the catacomb building itself. Even then, it took some effort, but by forcing the blade of the spade into the gap of the doors, he at last managed to spring them open!

'Sorry about that,' Steven said returning to the still semi unconscious Lizzie. Then after quickly pushing her inside and closing the door, Steven at last paused for breath.

As soon as he felt rested, Steven skilfully passed his charge beneath a waist high barrier, he then trundled her in between the two rows of ancient, wall tombs, which were stacked to above head height. When he reached the far end of the catacomb, he turned Lizzie around, so that she faced back along the gloomy corridor.

Taking a mobile phone out of his pocket, Steven switched it to the video app' and set it to transmit to his iPad. Flipping the top over to make a stand, he then placed and taped the phone onto the armrest of the wheelchair, so that it too pointed back up the aisle. After checking on his iPad, that the phone would capture and record anybody entering the catacomb, Steven returned his iPad to his sports bag.

Scrutinizing that everything was as he desired, he dipped his hand into the side pouch of Lizzie's wheelchair and pulled out a palm sized box. Taking a ready loaded syringe and medic' wipe from the box, he gave Lizzie the final injection of the powerful cocktail of sedatives. The dose was enough to keep his charge under sedation for another twelve hours, at least, thus taking her to the early morning; by which time, if she had not awakened or been rescued, Lizzie would be shortly found by the surprised cemetery staff!

Steven had no intention of letting Lizzie die, to do so would put him in the complete villain's role – and for the purpose of humiliating Crime Frontiers, that role would not be morally advantageous. Having done all that he could think of, he started to return to the exit – then looking to his left . . . he paused! It seemed that serendipity was looking over him once again!

Twenty five minutes later, and after leaving and closing the doors of the catacomb as best as he could, Steven placed and checked another camera phone amongst the nearby undergrowth, so that it looked directly onto the catacomb entrance. He then left and re-locked the upper cemetery gates and made his way back down to the main gates of both cemeteries. He then hid another camera phone, amongst the bushes of the adjacent and still open park.

The resulting camera view would show the main gate of the West cemetery. With his camera phones in place, Steven would have an undeniable record of any rescue – and therefore any collaboration by police and Crime Frontiers. Now at last, having planted his bait, he was almost ready to entice his prey!

Having first taken a twenty-minute car journey, Steven then sat a café, with a Latte and a slice of apple-crumble, he then got out the phone that he had originally contacted Crime Frontiers with, and stroked in the numbers of the helpline . . . and then waited!

Chapter 27

The presentation

It was not until Sandra was about to take a much wanted coffee break that the call from Steven was immediately patched through to her booth. Bell was in the crow's nest, and in spite of the occasion, Sandra took the time to indicate that she needed a coffee. Bell asked Sandra, on the extension, if she took sugar and cream and Sandra said no to both. Taking a deep breath she then re-opened her phone line, and said, 'Hello you have reached Crime Frontiers how can I help you?'

The tone of Steven's greeting was a mixture of optimism, with a hint of seduction.

'Hello… Goody … goody!'

When Sandra recognized the voice, her stomach tightened, but never the less she replied quite calmly, 'Hello Steven, you sound rather chirpy!'

Indeed as Steven sat at café, and took another sip of his Latte, he did feel most light hearted!

'I thought I'd call to, pre-congratulate, you for your forthcoming July the fourth celebrations, in two days' time. I do hope you have a nice Independence Day!' When Sandra did not reply, Steven carried on, 'After all, it's only once a year … and you never know how many such celebrations, you've got left!'

Again Sandra did not take the bait, so Steven carried on, 'Well you'll undoubtedly be pleased to hear, that I also have a present for you! But as giving presents is such a, personal thing, I want you to tell me if there's any one else listening in?'

'Yes, Mr. Bell, the founder is on an extension,' Sandra replied, waving to Bell again.

Still sounding upbeat Steven ordered, 'Then tell him to disconnect, and report back when we are alone.'

Up in the crow’s nest Bell shrugged his shoulders and disconnected his extension. Down in her booth Sandra told Steven, ‘We’re alone now Steven!’

‘Good,’ Steven stated, ‘because although my present for you, can also be appreciated by your work chums and even the police, who seem to escort you all over the place, I want you to be the one who opens it first.’

‘What present?’ Sandra asked neutrally.

‘Can't you guess?’

Silence . . .!

‘No?’ Steven inquired, then in a bemused tone he asked, ‘I wonder if your good friend Lizzie could tell you?’

When Sandra heard Steven say Lizzie's name, she felt as if a pack of wolves had just slinked into the Hub!

‘Let's see shall we,’ Steven suggested. At the other end of the line, Sandra could hear the rasping sounds of the Steven’s phone being handled, though in her earpiece, the noises seemed to be coming from inside her skull. Then once again, Sandra could hear Steven’s soothing voice.

‘I have a recording of your friend’s opinion, her opinion of her worthiness as a present, would you like to hear it?’

Sandra did certainly not want to hear it, but had little other choice but to reply, ‘If I must!’

After making sure that no one else was within earshot, Steven then put a small Dictaphone to the mouthpiece of his phone, and pressed play. Back in the Hub, Sandra could clearly hear Steven asking Lizzie her opinion.

“So . . .what do you think Lizzie? Are you a worthy present for Sandra? And whilst we are on the subject, is their precious Anonymity Code, more worthy than your life, even though it is rather a worthless little life . . . well . . . at least worthless to me! But perhaps you would you like to tell the nice lady, what you think?”

When Lizzie replied, her drawled words went straight into the core of Sandra's heart! ‘Hello, Sandy sweet . . . heart! I'm sorry to put you to . . . all this trouble Sweetie. I know you will do your best my darling, and if the worst

… does happen … just remember my lovely … you will have done better than I could ever have possibly … done!"

Whether Lizzie had anything else to say about the value of her life or the Anonymity Code, became a moot point, as all Sandra could hear was the sound of Lizzie's mouth being re-gagged. After that, Sandra heard the click of the dicta-phone being switched off, and Steven's voice reinstating his point of view.

'I knew that I should have scripted some reply for her, she's far too sweet to let her loose on her own. But as I am a believer of free speech, so I have to practice what I preach.'

Sandra reply was as instant, as it was predictable, and even before it was complete, it was casually dismissed by Steven, never the less she tried her best, 'But you don't want to give our callers the right of free speech. Lizzie has nothing to …'

'Now you mustn't worry too much about the wellbeing of your, present, Sandy Sweetheart,' Steven continued. 'Though I should warn you, it does have a death-by-date!'

Steven's voice then changed to one bordering on caring, 'Fortunately, being the forgiving person that I am, and having recently administered a strong cocktail of sedatives to our little friend, she is a sleepy little Lizzie. The drugs will not only dull her physical pain, but any emotional turmoil too!' Then after a few seconds pause he added, 'But unfortunately if she is not found and resuscitated, within the next, shall we say, the next 10 hours, give or take one or two procrastinations on your part; then I shall be forced to make her sleep forever!

Sandra reply was as repetitively hopeless as it sounded, 'Lizzie has nothing to do with this ...'

Steven interruption was sharp and assured, 'On the contrary, she is as much a part of the code as you and everyone else there is, and I will kill her to break that code!' Then returning to his caring theme, he added, 'But I am not an unreasonable man Sandra. If you want to collect your present, before it goes, off, then you can! Do you have a pen and paper?'

Back in her booth, Sandra replied, 'Yes!' She quickly drew her notepad and pen towards her, as she did so, she absently minded noticed that her hands were trembling! Although there was no way that she could have known it, as he began to play his trump cards, Steven's right hand was trembling too!

Steven then paused to take another sip of his coffee, 'By the way, Little Lizzie will have about eight hours before the effects of the drug wears off, ten hours if she's lucky. But as she is a plucky individual and will fight the sedative effects of the drugs, she probably won't be that fortunate. When she awakes, she will find herself inside a container and she will wake into total darkness! She will hear nothing apart from her own breathing, which may not last that much longer! If she can compose herself and not scream or move too much, she will be able to eke out the dwindling air for a little longer, but my guess is that she won't! If she is not to die of suffocation and the container is not to become her coffin, then you'd better do as I suggest!'

In a state of near panic Sandra was about to try a last ditch appeal, but she had noticed previously, something that gave her some glimmer of hope! Whilst Steven was saying that Lizzie would die of suffocation after eight or ten hours, the indication on the computer indicated that it was a LIE! Never the less, it did not mean that Steven would not kill Lizzie at any time of his choosing! Sandra continued as she was about to do.

'Tell me where she is . . . or will be . . . or let her go!'

Steven's retort had a smattering of annoyance and was quick! 'Now, now, little Goody-goody, let's not start off by trying to being a spoil-sport!'

Sandra did not answer, as she silently thanked one of her colleges for bringing her a coffee.

'I shall of course be taking the mobile, to which you have the number, with me at all times, as I promised. You do have that number?'

Leaving her coffee untouched, Sandra replied, 'Yes!'

'That way', Steven continued, 'you will have a chance of telling it to the police, in the hope that they will be able to track, capture and persuade, or even beat, Lizzie's whereabouts from me!'

Steven then paused to take another sip of his Latte, and then he continued, 'There is of course an alternative! But as I am now only feeling partly magnanimous, I will only tell you, part, of the necessary information, to workout Lizzie's whereabouts!

I am going to give you a page number … and it is your main birthday present from me! The page number is also your half, of my confidentiality code! Are you ready?'

'Yes!' Sandra answered.

'Then your part of the code is … page 44, of the London A to Z book. Somewhere, within the area covered by that page, little Lizzie will be waiting to be rescued. After I have finished this conversation, or should I say, negotiation, I shall send an e-mail and text to the good Detective Chief Inspector Rupert, at good old New Scotland yard. I will not give him any page number. I will however, give him the grid letter and number of the much smaller area, which can also be found on page 44, in the A to Z, and on just about half of the 134 pages of the book. Except, that he won't be aware of the page number that I gave you! Is that clear?'

'Yes, I understand.'

'Good! Steven replied, 'Not that I doubt your intellect to follow simple instructions, Sandra, but as I recall from our first phone call, your emotions may cloud your better judgment.'

Sandra ignored Steven's slight to her outburst on his first call to Crime Frontiers, instead she just replied, 'What do I do with the code, the page number?'

Steven ignored Sandra's question and continued with an amused tone in his voice, ' Now, the letter and number, or code, that I will send to Chief Inspector Rupert … you know I was going to call him the bear … after "Rupert the Bear," but it occurred to me that being American you may not have heard of our Rupert. He is a national treasure, and his adventures are a required bedtime story for many parents and children. Did your bed time stories tell you about him . . . Sandra?'

With a great effort to hide her frustration, Sandra replied, 'Yes, I have heard about Rupert the Bear.' Before her mother had taken to drink, she would regularly read Sandra many bedtime stories, including ones about Rupert, though Sandra's favourite bear was in fact Pooh Bear. To her self-wonderment, she dredged up the courage and patience to tell her tormentor this.

'Really,' Steven replied, 'he was my favourite too. Shall we explore our favourite Pooh Bear stories together, I am sure it will be fun, what do you think?'

To Sandra's turmoil of a mind, the stark contrast between the world of Pooh Bear and her current nightmare, brought a sudden welling of tears to her eyes, never the less she did her best to ignore them.

'Maybe another time,' she suggested, 'At the moment I am more interested in what you were saying about the codes.'

'Now, now, Steven admonished, 'impatience will get you nowhere fast, and even if it should, it will still feel too slow. So . . ..! I . . . was . . . explaining . . . about . . .. calling . . . Rupert the policeman . . . Rupert the bear. But seeing he is a policeman . . . and the police are called "pigs," I was going to suggest we call him, Rupert the piggy-bear! But now you have gone and spoiled it all!' Steven concluded in a mock crushed tone!

At the other end of the line, Sandra knew that her tormentor was now just playing games, to exercise his position of power. Never the less, she also knew that she would have to play along for at least part of the way.

'I'm sorry about that, it was just that what you said, about Lizzie having a limited time, well it seemed more important. I'm sorry if I was mistaken . . . I didn't mean to get your priorities wrong.'

Steven rather liked Sandra's answer and decided to relent, 'Fair enough! Now! Now that you have decided to be sensible, I will tell you about the code that I am going to send to Rupert the piggy-bear, do you agree?'

'Yes, I agree,' Sandra stated.

'Good! What an agreeable little Goody-goody you are! As I have said, the code I send to Rupert Piggy Bear, will be found on the pages of the A to Z. However, when the two codes, yours and Piggy Bear's, are cross referenced, they will show, within two hundred metres or so, where Lizzie will be waiting!'

At that point Sandra finished writing the co-ordinates and instructions down, and repeated them back to Steven.

Steven listened and then replied, 'Yes! You are correct! Of course, presuming that they recognize, that their part of the code comes from the A to Z book, Rupert and his little piglets, can try to use their part of the code to conduct a metre by metre, ground search, relating to every corresponding square throughout the whole A to Z book!

Incidentally, on average, each square covers about twelve or so roads or streets. Excluding the ten large scale sections of central London, at the end of the book, and the two small scale ones at the beginning, there are approximately seventy pages to which Rupert's code could refer to. Which means there are approximately 840 roads or streets in all. With, shall we say, a conservative average of 100 houses or buildings per road or street, giving a round total of 84,000 dwellings, plus quite a number of open spaces, such as parks and the like, which will serve as potential places for Rupert and his piglets to get access to and thoroughly search.'

'I understand.' Sandra stated.

'You of course could conduct a private search, armed with your exclusive page number, and of course a few trusted friends. All you would have to do, is get access to and search 42,000 residences, or their equivalent open areas!'

Steven paused awhile, so as to let the numbers sink in, then he added, 'Not that I'm saying, that such a monumental task, would be too much for you or the piglets to courageously attempt, in order to try and save poor Lizzie, as I am sure you will agree … Sandra?'

'Yes!' Sandra agreed.

'However, there is a far more certain alternative,' Steven suggested, 'The alternative is that you can help everyone, Sandra! By giving Rupert Piggy-bear, your part of the code, in the form of the page number that I have just given you. This will mean, that once I have given the good little piggy and his fellow piglets, their part of the code, they will be able to cross reference both codes, and discover the location of our sleepy little princess, give or take two hundred metres or so!'

Sandra suddenly asked, 'Why not tell me where you have taken Lizzie?'

Steven's answer was at first slightly annoyed, 'Because I choose to do it this way!' then he calmed as he added, 'Besides haven't you ever played Battleships, when you were a child? Trying to find the enemy battle fleet by finding which grid squares they are hidden in?'

'Yes I have,' Sandra answered.

'Did you enjoy it?'

'Yes, I did.'

'Well, it was my favourite game! So we will play my version of it now – and if you don't want little H.M.S. Lizzie, to be sunk, without trace, then you should pay close attention to the game . . . if that alright with you?'

'Of course, I was just curious that's all. . .' Sandra confirmed.

At that point, Steven paused and then mused, 'You know, what with Rupert the Pig-bear and his piglets, sleepy Princess Lizzie and your Goody-goody self; this whole adventure is beginning to sound, like a very good fairy story in itself, don't you agree? Mind you, I've no idea who could play the villain! After all, all good bed time stories must have a villain of the peace!'

Sandra thought for about two seconds and replied, 'We also need a hero, Steven. Perhaps you could play the hero – or would you find that too frightening a part for you to play?'

Suddenly Steven's tone changed and became very serious, 'But I am the hero, Sandra! Haven't you understood that yet?'

Hearing no reply Steven carried on, 'As I have given you your half of the code, under the so-called protection of the, Anonymity Code, the passing on of your page number, to the police will require . . . you to break your silly little

Anonymity Code! Though as I am sure you know already, Sandra, as all spy stories will tell you, to decipher any code, you will have to break the code first! Good bye and happy hunting!' With that said, the line went dead!

Five minutes later, and using a different mobile phone, Steven texted and e-mailed Rupert, and informed him of Lizzie's kidnap. He also gave him the partial code of "E1."

He also informed Rupert, that Sandra Lott, AKA Susan, of Crime Frontiers, would have the other half of the code enabling Lizzie to be found! Steven then sent the same message to the heads of several metropolitan police authorities c/o Chief Inspector Rupert. He then dismantled the phone and randomly threw the pieces away.

It took Sandra some time before she disconnected Steven's call from her end, and more time to stir from her seat. When she did rise, she did not speak to any one, or look up at Bell in his crow's nest. She did not even look at anyone in the room; she especially did not look for Andy. Nor did she speak to anybody in the corridors or elevator, even when Kirra the receptionist wished her "Cheerio!" Sandra gave no reply.

It was only as she turned the ignition key of her car that Sandra uttered any sound at all, and when she did, it was neither a moan of utter despair nor a cry of pain, but something trapped in between! As trapped as Sandra felt, she did not let herself cry, for to do that would blur her vision, and she would not be able to drive – and she wanted to drive!

Sandra wanted to "Drive to her fucking flat; pack her fucking bags, drive to the fucking airport, fly home – and never fucking come back!"

Although her eyes were blurred with near tears, Sandra managed to pull out from the car park and join the traffic; she also managed to see the unmarked police car following her! No matter! She would deal with them later. First, she had to form a plan – a plan of action!

But there were so many questions! For a start, should she let Andy know what was happening, or might happen – she owed him that at least, she felt guilty that she had not even looked over to his booth as she left the Hub! At least she knew that Andy would remain at the school, probably for the next seven hours, working the second of his three exchanged shifts.

Back in her car, Sandra began formulating her plan. At least she had the first steps of a plan in place, and that was; that she would call in at Andy's place first, before she would take another step!

Chapter 28

Guns and mirrors

As soon as she was safely in Andy's place, Sandra sat down and thought hard. After a few minutes, she got up; made a cup of coffee, came back to the living room, sat down, sipped her coffee and thought even harder. Her thoughts were interrupted several times by incoming calls on her mobile, from both Bell and Rupert, she did not answer either. Nor did she answer their text asking her to contact them. She mainly sat and thought.

We often plan certain things, when we have to keep appointments. We plan the route we will take to the appointed place. We plan what to take, what time we will leave, and what we might do and say when we arrive at our appointed place. In our minds, we create a story; about what type of person we are due to meet; what we are going to say and how we intend to deal with them.

To Sandra all of these things were a normal part of her preparations for her intended meeting with Rupert and Bell, back at Crime Frontiers.

Sandra's mind was deep but not dark. Sitting in her most comfortable chair in Andy's living room; listening to her best loved piece of music, 'Pachelbel's cannon in D,' she could clearly make out the reasons, both for and against keeping the code of anonymity.

She could clearly see the reasons for not further endangering Lizzie's life! However there were also the lives of the additional future victims, if the Anonymity Code should be broken and Crime Frontiers become compromised! Never the less, for the past ten minutes or so, it was this dilemma that Sandra had been trying to solve – but still she could not choose!

Laying her writing pad on the floor, Sandra got up and went into the kitchen to refresh her coffee. As she waited for the kettle to boil, she edged deeper into her thoughts and feelings; until she began to think about the numerous lies that she had told her father. Sandra had told the lies in order to escape, or at least postpone, her father's abuse of her. She also recalled the lies she told her friends, in order to keep the abuse a secret from them. As she had grown, Sandra had begun to dislike the lying with an intensity that almost, and indeed sometimes, even equalled the revulsion she felt about the sexual abuse itself; both made her be false to herself.

Now sitting within the temporary sanctuary of Andy's living room, Sandra saw any lie, as an abuse against herself – and the breaking of the anonymity code, would be tantamount to breaking her very being – again!

Suddenly Sandra re-called sitting on a bed, in the bedroom of one of her school friends. Her friend was reading aloud from a book of poems, which she (her friend) had bought herself as a present. Although Sandra could not recall the poem as a whole, she did recall the end of the poem as clearly as if her friend was there with her. And her friend's words were:

"It is unwise to try and protect innocence by arming guilt."

At that moment, the kettle came to the boil and clicked off, and Sandra made up her mind! She had decided two things. The first was that when she returned to America, she would go and tell her father about her lie to him, about killing her mother – though whether he'd believe her now could be in some doubt.

The second decision was that that no matter what Bell, the police or Steven said or wanted, she had given her word that she would *not* break her promise, her promise, of keeping the code of anonymity – absolute! She would not become a self-abuser!'

Having finally made her mind up, Sandra poured the boiled water into her mug, which ironically had a picture of Winnie the Pooh on it. She then made her coffee. However, she did not immediately return to her chair; instead, she put her coffee on top of her writing pad, that still lay on the floor, went over to Andy's glass cabinet that contained an antique, smooth bore, muzzle loading flintlock pistol, converted to the percussion system – and removed it!

When Sandra had moved into Andy's flat, he had shown Sandra how to load and fire the pistol. 'It was my old man's, he used to collect antiques' and that, well it was mostly bric-a-brac really. But this and the pair of porcelain figures over there are worth a few bob!' He then loaded the shot and showed her to work the, slightly dodgy, half-cock safety cocking system.

'It's just in case we get any unwelcome visitors!' Andy assured. 'Mind you, there's a slight problem with the shot," Andy added, as he tipped the pistol downwards, letting the ball of lead shot fall back out. 'It isn't the original shot and there's no ram rod or wadding, so if you don't keep the pistol upright, the shot will fall out – apart from that it's perfect!'

Looking at Sandra's doubting face, Andy reassured, 'I know it isn't an Ozzie exactly, but it will stop anyone who gets shot, and it will certainly make 'em think twice before they try anything!'

Sandra had then practiced loading the pistol shot, then she mocked fired it twice, before Andy returned the primed pistol to the gun case. He also left the shot and a ball of tissue (for wadding) to the side of the pistol case. They had talked about leaving the loaded pistol beside the bed, but Sandra had not liked the idea of the "slightly dodgy" safety cock, 'Wouldn't want it to go off prematurely!' she gently teased (on their first lovemaking, Andy had got a bit over enthusiastic!).

Now she was alone in the flat, Sandra slowly swung the pistol in a level arc. For a minute, she examined the pistol, checking that it was still primed, and then she loaded it with the ball of shot! Whilst awkwardly holding the loaded pistol, she took the box and laid it onto the table.

Next Sandra went over to a half-length wall mirror, and aimed the pistol at her reflection, aiming the barrel at her head and then her heart. As she held the pistol, Sandra deliberately let it slowly tilt forwards, until she could feel the lead shot rumble towards the barrel end. Letting the shot fall into her hand, she fully cocked the pistol and then mimed pulling the trigger, three times.

Fetching her large, pseudo, American Indian bag, she carefully placed the pistol, on half-cock safety, in an upright position inside the bag. She then placed the lead shot and the ball of tissue inside a re-sealable herb bag, from the kitchen. Stuffing the herb bag into the top of the pistol's barrel, she then placed various everyday things into the bag.

Although the bag was deep enough to conceal the pistol, Sandra brought over a large scarf to cover it up from any casual inspection. Finally, she placed the pistol case, still opened, back onto its tilted display stand within the cabinet.

Returning to her chair and coffee, Sandra began to relax and sip her drink. She was of course well aware; that by following the path she had chosen, she might well leave herself stranded, not only in a world of high moral quandary – but also in the world of Steven!

Laying her British bought and registered mobile on the table, Sandra then fetched her American bought phone, which she specifically used to keep in touch with home. Putting both phones into the bag, she then settled into the chair's deep, well-worn, upholstery and stared up at the empty gun case. Sandra's vision then slowly travelled along the grey metal band running along the side of the case. When her sight rested upon a point of light that, shimmered, under the discreet, blue tinged lighting of the cabinet, the whole effect gave the case a surreal form – it matched how Sandra felt about herself at that moment!

Then, without taking her eyes away from the point of light, Sandra spoke aloud but softly, almost as if she were not trying to wake some imaginary person in the room there with her.

'Well Mr. Steven . . . Sir! You have your rules for now! But you sure better watch your ass, if I ever meet you out of school hours . . . buddy!'

There only remained one last thing to do, not so much as an added precaution, but more out of an added hope; that all would end well! Andy was at the school and wouldn't be home until the end of his exchanged shift. Sandra went back to the living room and wrote a letter to Andy. After re-reading the letter several times, she then left it in the open gun case, and placed them on the dining table.

Moving to the front door she suddenly turned, and then rushed back into the lounge. Quickly going to the cabinet; she opened a drawer and took out an opened pack of blank mini-audio-tapes, that Andy kept for his hardly used palm sized Dictaphone. Removing the plastic covering, Sandra admonished herself on the head with a blank diskette, and then put it into her hip pocket. She then returned to the lounge door and looked around.

She then finally concluded, that there was, apart from a deep desire to return safely, nothing else she could take with her. With that decided, Sandra switched out all the lights, with the exception of the dining room table lamp, and quietly left!

The note for Andy said:

I am going to try and meet with Steven, he has kidnapped Lizzie. I am going to try to meet him by myself – it's my choice!

I have taken the gun – just in case! If I have not phoned you, by midnight, send the policeman Rupert, these numbers:

PAGE, 44, in the A to Z of London

P.S. I do love you very much – that is my choice too!

Sandra.

xxx

Chapter 29

Playing it by numbers

When Sandra got back to the school and hurried through reception, she answered, 'I know, thank you Kirra,' to the receptionist, after Kirra told her that, 'Mr. Bell would like to see you as soon as possible.'

Never the less, before she went up to Bell's office Sandra got out at the third floor. She opened the balcony door and edged towards the running rail, she then scanned the booths. When she saw Andy at his booth talking into the phone, she felt a deep pang of desire and regret. Then turning around, she left and headed up the two flights of stairs to Bell's office.

When she entered Bell's office, Sandra was not totally surprised to see Rupert and Sergeant Vanner already there too. Placing her American Indian bag on the floor to the side of her, Sandra sat down and stared at Bell. She then related almost verbatim what Steven had told her. When Sandra had finished, Rupert told her that he had received a contact from Steven; who had indeed left a set of co-ordinates. When Rupert asked Sandra for her co-ordinates, all three men turned to her.

After what seemed a very long pause, Rupert asked, 'Well, Miss Lott, if we could have your part of the instructions?'

However, instead of answering Rupert, Sandra turned to Bell and said, 'I'd like to hear what you think, before I make my decision.'

Bell smiled and looked into Sandra's eyes as he started to explain, 'Well it's a matter of short or long term gain. To hand over the coordinates, would mean breaking the confidentiality promise of our Anonymity Code, and that would mean ...'

But Sandra stopped him short, 'No explanations, no reasons or whys. Do I hand over the co-ordinates or not? A simple yes or no will do.'

For about half a minute, Bell studied Sandra, whilst Rupert and the sergeant looked on, then Bell gave his answer, 'No!'

Then, as all three men watched her, Sandra bent forwards; popped open the catch of her American Indian bag, and reach inside. Whilst never taking her eyes from Bell, she stood upright, with her right arm outstretched, holding her notebook in her hand. Sandra then turned to Rupert and demanded.

'I wrote the co-ordinates in here. If I were to give you this, would you give me your word, that if you have to tell the press where it came from, you will also make it absolutely clear … that Mr. Bell, opposed my showing it to you?'

Rupert nodded and said, 'Yes!'

Only then, did Sandra drop her open note pad onto the desk, right in front of Rupert's astonished face!

From the open page, Rupert read out the page number that Sandra had written.

'Page 140 of the London A to Z,' and then he stared back up at her. She did not flinch, and even Sergeant Vanner detected no deception in her face, after all why should she be lying!

Sandra in turn looked away from Rupert, back to Bell, and then back to Rupert, 'Is that what you need Chief Inspector?'

Rupert picked up the note pad and handed it to Sergeant Vanner, then turning to Sandra he said, with as much sincerity as he could muster, 'Thank you Sandra!'

Sandra said nothing in return, but just sat down, whilst being careful to avoid looking at Bell. As soon as Sergeant Vanner read the code; he flipped open his mobile and punched in some numbers, as soon as he was answered, the Sergeant spoke in a low voice. Thirty seconds later, he nodded to Rupert, who in turn took the sergeant's phone.

After nodding twice, Rupert asked, 'Where exactly?' then continued, 'I know the area well. Get the surrounding area secure, get the dogs and search teams. Inform and get the Parks Police, get some divers too! Do it as quietly as possible, but be thorough. We'll be there in 30 minutes.' Rupert then returned the phone to Sergeant Vanner, who then returned Sandra's note pad to her.

Bell rose from his chair and Rupert braced himself, for what he presumed was a last ditch effort to save the Crime Frontiers precious code. But all Bell asked was, 'Where is she?'

Rupert considered Bell for a second or two then replied, 'That is best kept as closed as possible until the area is secured.'

At that moment Sandra looked up and asked, 'May I come along? Lizzie is my dearest friend and if this ... raid... gets what this Steven wants, hopefully Lizzie will be safe! But it still might be a false lead! If he gets in touch, to negotiate, further demands? If he asks for me at the helpline, I can leave my personal mobile number, for them to pass on ...'

The desperate look in Sandra's face was enough to convince Rupert to agree with her request, 'You can come with Sergeant Vanner and myself, though when we get there, you must stay well out of sight, agreed?'

The look of sheer relief on Sandra's face said it all, but she said, 'Agreed!'

It was then Bell's turn to plead his case, 'I would also like to be present ...'

'There's plenty of room,' Rupert answered, smiling at Bell, 'though the same conditions apply.'

Within ten minutes, the four of them were in Rupert's limousine, with Sergeant Vanner driving. Twenty five minutes later, they had arrived at a small road called, Sussex Place, which faced onto the sprawling grounds of Regent's Park. As they pulled to a stop, three uniformed, armed police officers and a plain-clothes detective, quietly greeted Rupert.

Rupert got out and spoke in hushed tones with the plain-clothes officer. When he returned to the car, he indicated to Sergeant Vanner to join him. As the two men moved off, Sandra could see several police vans and cars; all empty of occupants, parked alongside the pavement. Just behind Rupert's limousine, the car that had been escorting Sandra previously, pulled in and parked up.

Coming back to the limousine and removing the ignition keys, Sergeant

Vanner then walked over to Sandra's escorts and indicated back to the limousine. A uniformed policeman got out of the car, put his jacket and cap on, nodded to the sergeant and came and stood by the limousine. The sergeant then re-joined his boss, and the two walked off into the main search area of the park; which had already been cleared of all members of the public. Meanwhile Sandra and Bell sat in a heavy silence!

When Rupert reached the inner cordon of the main search party, who were stationed besides the boating lake, he saw that seven armed, SWAT personal were about to enter the locked park café, which had been temporally closed for re-decoration. Five officers, weapons drawn, were crouching in front of the single story building.

Keeping low, Sergeant Vanner sidled up to the parked land rover and joined Rupert. Nodding to his sergeant, Rupert informed, 'We're about to make an entrance, there's no sighting through the windows, and there's been no contact from the inside so far, which can be good or bad! If there's no joy here, we'll have to search further in, and maybe the whole bloody park!'

Left alone in the back of Rupert's limousine, the increasing silence between Sandra and Bell, that had started since they had first stepped into the car, began to become unbearable. It was Bell who broke the "truce" first'

'He's won, you know. Regardless, of whether if Lizzie is here, or even if he hasn't killed her, he will have won.' Then looking directly at Sandra, Bell added, 'But many might well have done the same, if they were in your place. You had to do what you thought best for her – even though Crime Frontiers will suffer a greater damage.'

For a few more silent, seconds, Sandra just sat and stared out of the window, when she did speak, she did not look at Bell but her words were clear. 'Perhaps you'd like to explain that to Lizzie, if she's lucky enough to come out of this alive!'

Without missing a beat Bell replied, 'If she asks, I will.'

Looking at Bell, Sandra felt aghast, but she did not say anything in reply. After all, was what she was about to attempt any more just . . .or unjust?

'I did what I did for me, Mr. Bell. Not for you, the helpline or even Lizzie ... I did it for me!' With that, Sandra got out her mobile phone; stepped out of the car, slammed the door behind her, she walked towards the near bye, private, garden area of the Royal College of Obstetricians and Gynaecologists.

When Sandra came to entrance of the garden, Constable Latter, the policeman left to guard the pair of "civilians" began to walk towards her, and suggested, 'Perhaps you should stay in the car, with Mr. Bell, Miss.'

Heading towards a wooden seat Sandra turned and answered, 'I'd rather stay with this maniac, Steven!' then softening her tone, she added, 'Don't worry if the real Steven shows up I'll be the first to scream – very loudly!' then giving the constable a reassuring smile and then deep frown, Sandra said, ' I do hope they find her . . . safe and sound! It's such a huge park!'

The constable nodded reassuringly and answered, 'Don't you worry miss, they know what they're doing!' then indicating to his police radio, he added, 'They seem to be concentrating around the boat shed, so let's cross our fingers!'

Looking as though she had received some shred of comfort, Sandra crossed her fingers, smiled and nodded; and then walked over to the bench and sat down.

Suddenly, the police constable became distracted by the unmistakable sound of a megaphone being used. Even at that distance, he could hear what was being said.

At that point, wishing he were nearer the "action" Constable Latter (known as "Lassie" to his fellow colleges) turned his back on Sandra, and went over to face the direction of the "action." It was a mistake that he would regret for some time to come!

Further into the park, at the door of the "target" building, five armed policemen and two armed police women, shuffled, to the glass fronted, front doors. Within two seconds of SWAT team leader ordering, "Go!" into his police radio, what was left of the cafe door was repeatedly slammed open as the seven police barged inside!

Five minutes later David Bell, who had joined up with P.C. Latter, saw Sergeant Vanner and Rupert walking slowly towards them, as the policemen neared the limousine, Bell went forwards to greet them.

'Well?' Bell asked.

It was the sergeant who replied, 'No one! The buildings are completely empty of any one! We're conducting a search of the immediate area, but she could be anywhere, in the bushes, anywhere. That's if it's not all this Steven's idea of a red herring anyway!' then turning to Rupert he said, 'I'd better go and see the key holder, he's just arrived at the outer perimeter apparently. He won't be too happy about his door, seeing how he was bringing us the keys, but I'll explain our urgency.' The looking at Bell he added, 'The press have arrived too, but we won't be giving out any statements.'

As he went to go, the sergeant looked into the limousine, halted and asked, 'Where's Miss Lott?'

Bell and PC Latter turned, and then walked towards where they had last seen Sandra, and were rather taken aback to see she was not there – nor was she anywhere in sight!

'I don't know ...' Bell answered the sergeant, ' … we had a bit of a disagreement … and she went over there!' he added as he pointed towards the gardens, 'I thought she was phoning her boyfriend, Andy!'

For four different reason the four men froze! The sergeant was the first to express his fear, 'If this Steven character is about, and spots her … that may not be a wise thing to have done sir!' With that, and whilst speaking into his police radio, the sergeant raced down the adjoining side ally, which ran parallel to the garden!

Meanwhile Bell looked back to Rupert, and said, 'I can't imagine she would have gone far, not without hearing whether Lizzie is safe or had even been found!'

It was Rupert who suddenly paled the most. Turning sharply around, he went over to, and slammed the roof of his limousine!

'Bollocks!'

For about thirty seconds he thought through the situations – including the one of how to report the small but noticeable dent in the roof of his official car. He then turned to Bell and proclaimed, 'She wouldn't have gone ten bloody yards from here, not without knowing if we found her best friend Lizzie, first! Not in a month of Sundays!' Then turning to the confused looking constable, he explained, 'She left, because she already knew her friend, wasn't here – because the page number she gave us, was false! What she didn't know is, where here is! At least she didn't know, until we brought her to this place! Now… with the grid location of this place, and her genuine page number, she knows fucking everything!'

Then glaring at the, still confused, constable Latter, Rupert added, 'Which means, that you can bet any promotion you that you might have had coming constable, that this slip of a girl is now on her way, to try and rescue her friend … from the hands of a potential, if not already, murderer … on her fucking own!'

For a fraught few seconds, Rupert turned to stare at the dent in his limousine, then back at the constable. Though this time when Rupert spoke, it was with a worried rather than angry tone of voice, 'And if you think I'm pissed off constable … God knows what this Steven maniac is going to be when he finds out what's bloody happened!'

Wisely, constable Latter said absolutely nothing!

At that moment, Tom Vanner returned and breathlessly stated, 'I just spoke to the outer observation team. Bill Thorne said that he saw a woman, answering her description; hurrying out of the RCOG entrance about ten minutes ago! She must have walked straight through the building, from the gardens. She turned right along Park Road. He didn't stop or follow her, as far as he knew he had no reason to! We could check the surrounding CCTV coverage, and try and track her movements?'

Turning to Sergeant Vanner, Rupert nodded his affirmation then he asked,

'Do you have her mobile number with you?'

Tom Vanner shrugged his shoulders and shook his head. Rupert then said, 'She' probably dumped the tracker by now, but try and get her mobile number and get a warrant for a positional trace.' Then turning to Bell he asked, 'Do you have her number?'

Bell shook his head, 'But it will be at the school.' With that, he took out his phone and walked off towards the limousine. Two minutes later he returned, holding his phone up, so that the text message detailing Sandra's mobile number could be seen, 'This is her number.'

When the sergeant tried Sandra's number, and found that he was transferred straight through to the message service, he said, 'She's turned it off!'

After giving Rupert a glum look, Bell, politely said, 'I think the best thing I can do, is to return to the school and see if she contacts us. That is, unless, you have any other suggestions, Chief Inspector?'

Rupert nodded his acceptance, 'We'll let the search here continue. Meanwhile, we will tour the immediate area, if there is no joy, we'll drop you off at the school. Keep us informed if you hear anything at all. With your permission, Sergeant Vanner will come to the Crime Frontier's premises too, and he will conduct a search of Miss Lott's desk and any personal locker she may have use of. We can obtain a warrant if necessary!' Bell simply nodded his agreement and returned to Rupert's limousine.

Ten minutes later, all three men were in the Rupert's limousine, with Rupert driving, within the 30 mile per hour speed limit. After about ten minutes, Sergeant Vanner received a call from the communications department at HQ. After listening for about a minute, the sergeant repeated the message.

'According to com techs, the tracker is still sending!' then listening again he reported, 'the signal indicates she is travelling north, on Finchley Road, approaching Swiss Cottage!' Looking out of the window Vanner turned to his boss and stated, 'Which seemingly means, she is either directly ahead, right behind us . . . or she is in the car with us!'

Returning to his call Vanner said, 'Hold on!' Vanner then quickly checked the glove department and then he turned to Bell in the back, who began checking down the side of the deep upholstered rear seats. After he checked the seat that Sandra had been seated in, Bell brought up his hands; his left hand was holding the tracking device that Sandra had been issued with. In his other hand, was what he rightly presumed to be Sandra's mobile phone!

Thirty five minutes later, the limousine pulled up outside the school, thanking Rupert for his co-operation, Bell exited the car, walked a few paces, turned and waited for Sergeant Vanner, who was in conversation with Rupert.

Looking at the waiting Bell, whilst speaking to his sergeant, Rupert instructed, 'Before you conduct the search get one of the opp' cars to keep an eye out for our man there, in case he leaves the building. If he does, they are to follow and report. He may know nothing about this . . . or he may know a lot more than he's let on,' as an afterthought Rupert added, 'If her boyfriend is in there, question him, if not, try to find out where he is. Place a watch on his place and at Sandra Lott's old place, make it discreet, but have them give you any movements.'

As Steven sat at his chosen initial observation point, in the Waterlow park cafe, adjacent to the Highgate cemetery, he thought and pondered. The park was well used and he could blend in with the other park users. With a good few hours of summer daylight left, the warmth of the day still held sway. All in all, Steven felt reasonably satisfied. When he pulled his iPad out, to check that he was receiving the cemetery images, via his video conferencing app,' he was pleased that all was well.

From the three video phones he had placed at strategic points, all showed exactly what he wanted. The first view showed the outside of the main West gate; the second the entrance to the catacomb from the outside, the third showed the interior, from the perspective from the far end of the catacomb.

No one could approach, let alone rescue Lizzie, without it being recorded.

Steven was not overly disturbed, by the possibility that either Sandra or Bell may have "grassed" his personal mobile number to the police. But he debated if he should climb down and break his word, by switching his own phone off, or even dismantle it altogether! However, as he touched the butt of his revolver, tucked beneath his outer clothing, the idea of any police confrontation heightened his sense of drama (and superiority)!

The possibility that the American woman, Sandra; was on her way to try a single-handed rescue attempt, wasn't even on the fringes of Steven's radar – but then again, until Sandra had first thought of it, it wasn't on hers either!

Chapter 30

Slave Labour

As Sandra began her dilemma drenched quest to save Lizzie – after breaking Steven's code; back in the safety of his home, George Pipe was in a bit of a dilemma too!

Since his near disastrous own goal at the air raid shelter, George knew that he had, had a very narrow escape. He also knew that it would be very foolish to risk yet another outing. It seemed exceptionally stupid, when he realised that the future of his and his family's happiness, was possibly within reach, in the form of the Crime Frontiers residential!

However, the pressure of not exercising his desire to hunt was already increasing. And this was George's dilemma; in short, George knew that if he wanted to permanently contain his urges, then rather than being an indebted slave to them, he would have to be their honourable jailer! However, to George, suppressing his urge to rape was like being forced to play the role, of a mean minded zookeeper, from the poem:

'Tomorrow Land: June 18th'

"10.30 am: Johnny and Jenny are visiting the world famous MEE museum (Museum of Emotional Ecology). As they stare into the "Live Enclosure," their heart rate rapidly increases. Above the toughened one-way mirror, a sign says "Human Criminals" (Endangered Species!).

Jenny whispers, 'Apparently they're still found beyond the Outer Zoning, where they still reproduce without gene-erring or evo-cloning! But they're endangered whenever they come into contact with our kind, because all the kind love that we show them, permanently alters their mind. They too become loving and give up crime immediately, so now they are protected, by the law, from people like you and me!'

'But it seems so sad to cage them,' Johnny said with a sigh, as he walked away, turned back, waved, and then gently whispered, 'Goodbye!'

Never the less, it wasn't until after George, himself, had felt that he had been "attacked" (on a trip to the local corner shop of all places), that he finally phoned the helpline again. By the time he had phoned Crime Frontiers from his living room, George was pacing and his mind was racing! He immediately asked to speak to Andy, and he was glad to be put through to him almost straight away.

Blissfully unaware of Sandra's problems, as soon as Andy recognized George's voice as belonging to the man who wanted to rape, he was not overly perturbed, but never the less, he pressed the HELP button, so that Charlie Fenton could listen in, then he spoke to George.

'Hello Sunshine! Hello again, what do you reckon me ol' mate?'

Sitting down on his couch, George took a deep breath and began, 'That's alright! I like talking with you. I would have waited till tomorrow to call, but things are getting a bit . . . urgent!'

'What's 'appening?' Andy asked cautiously.

For a while, George was silent, and then he started to speak, 'I had another urge, but this time it was massive, I got it yesterday – but I haven't been able to shake it off since!'

'What happened, Mate, tell me?'

'Well it was yesterday morning. I got up, and although I was a bit tired, I was feeling good.'

'Sounds good so far mate,' Andy interjected.

'Anyway,' George hastily carried on, 'it was about half ten, I was on a normal, everyday Sunday morning errand, to the local shop. Mary had asked . . .!' suddenly George stopped in mid-sentence and then with sudden anger he blurted out, 'Fuck! I didn't mean to say that – I didn't mean to say her name!'

Back at his booth, Andy quickly interrupted, 'That's perfectly Ok! What you tell us, stays with us, including any names you say.'

But to George, naming his wife had been an unforgivable mistake, and he had to pay for his mistakes, so he answered, 'I'm sorry!' Then he followed his apology with, 'My real name … is George!'

'Ok! George,' Andy replied, 'I understand your misgivings about mentioning names, but the real important thing to remember is, we're here to do justice, to yourself and your loved ones, and to do that, you're gonna have to stop doing battle with yourself, George!'

'What do you mean?'

'Well! The first thing you'll be shown at the residential, is that not only is the pursuit of justice always a three-legged race, but that it's also a lot easier to win, when it's run side by side, instead of face to face, me ol' mate!'

'Ok! I get your point,' George replied, 'but what do you mean, how does that apply to me?'

'I mean,' Andy said, 'that firstly; you're desires to rape and your desire to give rape up, are going to be bound to each other … for some time to come! Secondly, the more you try to act as if either desire is not a part of you, then the quicker yer gonna fall flat on yer face!'

'Ok! I get that my urges won't go away overnight,' George replied rather testily, 'but what do I do about them?'

'Ok! There are certain thin …' Andy attempted to answer, but George continued over the top.

'You don't know how bad it gets! They're almost non-stop sometimes, it's like I'm at their beck and call, it's as if I'm some sort of slave to them!'

It was obvious to Andy that George needed to speak, so he said nothing and listened instead. For a short while, there was the old silence, but when George spoke again, he did seem to be more relaxed.

'Well as I told you, Mary, had asked me to get a few last minute things, for Sunday lunch, and I guess it was all this, normality, that made me feel really good, you know! You know… feeling normal is quite a treat for me!' George quipped, then without waiting for a reply he carried on, 'Anyway when I was returning from the shop, I just had some bread, flour and milk, you know … anyway, that's when this brilliant idea came to me.'

'Sounds good mate, what was the idea?' Andy prompted.

'At first I thought it was such a good idea, although it was simple really! It was, well … why not go back to the shop … and buy some ice creams for everyone!'

'Sounds a good idea!' Andy agreed.

George now began to sound more positive than Andy had ever known him to be, and Andy was quite surprised at the change in him.

George continued, 'You know, I know it might seem silly but I felt so, normal! I mean it felt like, I was normal … and that felt … well to be honest, it felt like … freedom … and I wanted to celebrate, by buying the ice cream … if you know what I mean?'

'That must 'ave felt good?' prompted Andy.

'Exactly!' George exclaimed. 'The only thing that I thought of was these images, of the kid's faces, when I returned with the ice creams!'

Andy somehow feared that the next thing George was about to say, was going to put a damper on things, and he was right in his fear. The change in George's tone was again dramatically different, and it was with anguish, more than mere disappointment, that George began to relay what happened next.

'Then suddenly it all changed! I was just crossing the road, and I was about to step onto the pavement … when this … other … thought … hit me!'

'What thought George?'

Now there was an edge of bitterness in George's voice, 'It was … that if the kids ate the ice creams … they would eat some … and they would spoil their appetite, for lunch, and Mary would hardly be pleased at that, would she?'

'Fair point!' answered Andy. 'But that's good thinking; you were being sensible.'

'I know!' George moaned, ' but it made me so miserable, but I still really wanted to get the ice cream, and then the next thing I thought of was … well I suddenly got this urge! It felt so powerful, so utterly … overwhelming, I felt powerless!'

Then Andy said, Go on, this is interesting!'

'Well,' George continued, 'as I stepped on to the pavement, I got this memory of standing outside a park … it was where I had previously … attacked a woman, about a … a year before. I didn't rape her, I never have raped anyone, so far! But in this memory I was standing there, at a different time, at the entrance to the same park … at that time I didn't go in, because it was too risky, so I went off into town instead …'

George began to sound as if he was becoming distant, 'The memory was as if I was there in the park itself, it was like it was calling me back! Even though I was trying to do good with the ice cream and all that … I still wanted to go back to the park, right then, and find someone to rape! I couldn't of course, I had to go home, but the urge hasn't left me since!' At that point, George's voice trailed off into silence. Then, speaking once more, in a completely defeated voice, he continued.

'I remember realizing, right then, standing on the pavement, that the ice cream … all the trying to do good … all of it, it was all useless!' Then speaking as if he were almost in awe, George stated, 'It was like I was possessed! I … can't overcome something that is as all powerful … as that … it has far too much power!'

Back in his booth, Andy already knew the answer to George's dilemma, he also knew that he would have to take things steadily, step by step, 'Well as it 'appens,' Andy answered, 'the pull of so-called good or evil 'ave exactly equal strengths me ol' mate, just as long as you are there to hold their hand!'

For a moment, there was silence, and then Andy continued.

'Can I ask you George, in that memory, about standing outside the park, when you went into town instead of into the park, did you commit any sort of crime or continue to look for a victim in town?'

'What?' George asked in frustration.

'Did you commit …'

'Err … No I didn't.' George answered, again with frustration. 'I just went to see if they had any good bargains in the charity shops, if you must know!'

For a moment, it was Andy's turn to be silent. As he looked up into the

Crow's nest, he saw Charlie Fenton shake his head in knowing resignation. At this point, any one of the Advisor-Negotiators could have told George that his urge; prompted by his sudden memory of the park where he had previously "successfully" attacked a woman, was in fact a "Ghost urge," born from a common misinterpretation; rather than from a direct sexual urge. However, Andy decided to, hopefully, let George feel a bit of victim empathy first.

'So when you were just going about your innocent business, with the ice cream, and then out of the blue, you were suddenly attacked by this outrageous and all powerful rape urge; do you think you felt anything like the woman must have felt, the woman you did attack, out of the blue, a year ago?'

After a moment heavy silence George answered, with despair in his voice and maybe more than a touch of anger! 'Yes… I guess so …a bit!'

For a while longer, there was a silence from George then Andy continued, 'Listen mate, I know that when you're in the grip of an urge, thinking about or doing anything good can seem like a real … drag! Even though that could be kind of 'andy, especially if you 'appen to be 'urtling bollocks first down a slippery slope at the time! But why didn't yer just continue wiv yer good thoughts, about the ice cream and all?'

'Because I was too upset – and the urge was too powerful! Haven't you been listening to a word I've been saying, for Christ sake?'

After waiting a few seconds, Andy replied, 'As it 'appens George I've been more than just listening, I've been thinking too! And it's unfortunate, that you 'aven't been told about such things as Moral Memos and Ghost urges!'

'Moral what?'

Settling down in his chair, Andy began to explain, 'There are many ways in which we are triggered to think of things. But the two most relevant, to you, are one, the comfort urge, which many people get when they are disappointed about something. We try to get compensated, by turning to a replacement desire. There is no doubt that some of your urges to rape are comfort urges.'

'I guess so.'

'However, me ol' mate, Moral Memos are not alternatives to a recent disappointment. Their purpose, is to reflect the likely future outcome, of your current or on-going thought or action. They are sent in the form of a symbolic memory or symbolic fantasy. They are messages, or memos, sent from your subconscious, or sub conscience, and they are instant and automatic seals of inner approval or disapproval. They've been around long before and long since we invented words! As it 'appens they can be sent even if you weren't 'aving any doubts, but they are often sent when we are in any doubt or emotional conflict, about anything - just like when you were 'aving doubts about the ice cream!

'The ice cream?'

'Yes, the ice cream. Even everyday things, like taking the lift or stairs can instigate a moral memo; or whether to eat some chocolate or not. But, and it is a big but, because a moral memo uses symbolic themes to signify their judgment or reflections, the symbols can be open to misinterpretation.'

'Misinterpretation?'

'Yes! Because, you were 'aving doubts about the ice cream, and the purpose of a moral memo is to reflect the potential success or failure of your current situation or intentions, in your case, the ice cream, you were also open to misinterpreting the memo or memory about the park – which in turn was just trying to tell you about taking the ice cream idea a bit further - not to go out and rape!'

Then with added emphasis, Andy added, 'In short, you've been *conned* me ol' mate!

It took a few seconds for George to get what Andy had just said, but when he did, he immediately questioned it, 'Hold on! You mean this, memo thing, is like some sort of inner guide, that's fucking with my mind?'

'Like an inner guide!' Andy confirmed, 'Except it uses the basic language of success or failure, rather than traditional concepts of good or bad – and that's where you might 'ave got . . . con. . .fused.'

If George was confused beforehand, he certainly felt even more so now. Trying to get a grip on what he was being told, he back-tracked a bit, 'So what happened to the good old concepts, such as good and evil then?' George asked with a heavy dose of sarcastic doubt, 'Or are they too confusing?'

'Well for a start, 'istory has proved time and again, that goodness and eventual success tend to follow one another anyway! As does corruption and failure! But never the less, that's a good question mate, and I'll answer it with another question.

Which is; that you may well try to stop yourself from committing a crime, or doing wrong; by go on and on about good or evil, or wevver it's legal or illegal. Or even the more high-minded principles, such as love or duty to God or society. But let me ask you this basic question, George.'

Pausing for effect, Andy then continued, 'Would you still carry on with, any action, good, bad, legal or evil . . . if you thought that action would . . . fail you?'

'No of course I wouldn't,' George replied.

'Then that's why a basic conscience, uses the basic concepts, of success and failure, above all others, as the constant and universal language of morality. Things like laws and social or religious decrees are too bleeding fashion conscious for yer basic conscience! And like it or not, when it comes to dealing wiv emotional stress, it's yer basic conscience that has the first word . . . or memo!'

'Ok, I can get that.' George replied, with genuine curiosity.

'Good!' Andy replied back, 'cause you certainly got a moral memo whilst you were debating whether to buy ice cream or not! That was the whole point of the park memory! It was trying to tell you, or reflect; that in spite of your doubt about the ice cream, your idea of buying the ice cream could still have the, potential, to turn out as a . . . success!'

'By sending me an urge to rape?' George asked with another heavy dose of sarcastic disbelief.

'No George,' Andy replied as evenly as possible, 'by sending you a memory or memo; in which you changed a potential failure, having to turn away from the park, into a potential success, by going to the second hand shops to buy something of value. As it happens, if your sub conscience was trying to reflect that your ice cream idea would be likely to fail, then it would 'ave sent you a memo that contained a story line of disappointing failure, and nothing else!

'According, to the Crime Frontiers theory,' George stated, with a touch of frustration.

Again, there was a short silence and then Andy carried on, with a touch of frustration himself, 'Well again, as it 'appens, according to the theory, yer basic conscience isn't so basic at all. It not only reflects potential success or failure, or gives you the equivalent of "you need more information," it even reflects the degree of success or failure, according to your benchmark of perfection or failure, of course!'

At that point, Charlie Fenton covertly "advised" Andy, 'Let's not get too complicated – or too full of it!'

In reply, Andy smiled and nodded his head in acknowledgment, then returned to George, 'My apologies' mate! Let's not get too technical, or up our own arse! Let's return to the basics.'

At the other end of the line, George smiled and relented, 'That's ok . . . I was a bit short with you too.'

'Ok mate,' Andy replied, then drawing a deep breath, he continued, 'And what follows are questions not accusations. But in that memory, George, about the park, did you go off to the second hand shops, because you felt that the park was a bit too risky?'

'Yes!'

'So do you think, that by sending you that, very specific, memory, about when you chose to go to the second hand shops, instead of into the park, would you say that your conscience was trying to reflect that . . .

One … your conscience was reflecting that, you should go and rape somebody?

Two … that the very idea of buying the ice creams was doomed to failure, and that you should go straight home and abandoned the idea all together?

Or *three* … your conscience was reflecting that; in spite of your current disappointment that the ice cream idea was too risky, just like the park idea was too risky, if you did go to the shop to buy the ice creams; just like you did on that day at the park, when you headed for the shops, to buy something worthwhile, then you might yet turn the disappointing failure of the ice cream, into a potential success?'

George did take his time, but when he did give his answer, he gave his genuine reaction!

'Fuck!

Andy sympathized with George by saying, 'I'll take that as meaning number three then!'

'Yes!'

'Ok mate! Simply put, George, you misinterpreted the memory or memo! But don't worry, that's not unusual, people misinterpret memos all the time, or put them down to random memory flash backs, or casual fantasies. Unfortunately, you misinterpreted the park memory, or memo, as a so-called urge, to go out and rape! It's what we call, a Ghost-urge! An urge that's based on a misinterpretation of what the moral memo, or conscience, is really trying to tell you!'

'It was bloody powerful ghost then!' George answered.

'Of course it was, me ol' mate! Although they're not always related, Ghost-urges often come from a Ghost Conscience. A Ghost Conscience is prompted by a resurrection of events, that 'ave been hastily and wrongfully buried, in a person's past, usually though not always, from their childhood.

Where as, a Moral-memo is meant to educate, the power of a Ghost Conscience lies in its ability to haunt! Or to put it more concisely; to haunt its owner with the feelings of inadequacy that were present at that hasty burial, or hasty cover up! So of course any message, even a misinterpreted one about success, that comes via a Ghost Conscience, will seem powerful.'

As Andy drew breath, Charlie Fenton reminded him again to, 'Keep it simple.'

Raising his hand to Charlie, Andy continued, 'Never the less, the bottom line is, that whether it's through, misplaced guilt, misguided cover ups or memo misinterpretations, when we start to mistrust our basic conscience, then it may well come back with a justified thrust – and that's how a mistrusted conscience can turn any everyday thought into a lust! And that, George me ol' mate … is how we all, including yourself, can get conned into crime – or perhaps I should say conned-fused!'

At that moment up in the Crow's nest, Charlie Fenton gave Andy a "thumbs up" sign, and then relaxed back into his chair – but not for long! No sooner than he had relaxed, than he suddenly noticed the figure of Sergeant Vanner, entering the Hub! Without any delay the sergeant went straight over to one of the staff, and asked him a question, after which the staff member then pointed directly to Andy! Charlie was about to warn Andy that he was about to be interrupted – but Andy was in full flow!

'The first time you phoned, I promised you, that talking would give you a lot more power than perusing or committing any crime! And that it was all down to our consciences. Well, the power of a shared conscience is to resurrect the truth, by uncovering the cover ups, or the lies!'

'Lies?'

'The lies that start any crime off! For a start, apart from the comfort urges, which are a sort of cover up anyway, there is the porky pie that rape can solve any problem – let alone an important one. Then there's the lie starting from way back when, which put you on the road to rape! Unfortunately, for you me o' mate, crime, including rape, is a road unto itself, and you, and yer victims, were just an inevitable accident waiting to 'appen!

I aint got a clue what yer original lie was, and maybe you don't either, but as I said, you chose rape to symbolize success. As it 'happens, you could 'ave chosen stamp collecting as a successes symbol, instead of rape. Once yer put yer mind to it, it would 'ave been just as emotionally exiting, and certainly more profitable!

Then there's all the countless bleeding Ghost-urges, then all the self-accusations, all of which led you towards rape, not that you couldn't have done a U-turn at any time me ol' mate! Cos' let's face it George, following the leader is one thing, but that's more like lemmings gone mad!

'I'm not disagreeing with you,' George interrupted, 'but lemmings don't actually follow each other over a cliff edge.'

'That's true, but try telling that to the countless rapist that are in prison – or their victims! Nevertheless, whichever way you put it, the bottom-line George is, that all along you've been conned! It doesn't matter whether it's been ghost urges, genuine urges, childhood baggage or a combination of all of 'em – you've been conning yerself all the way – and you've been conned rotten!'

Silence . . .!

Then Andy asked, 'Now all you 'ave to ask yerself . . . is do you want to go on standing for the same old three card trick – or do you want to learn – how all the cons are played and how to avoid them?'

For a moment, there was even a greater silence! Then George spoke.

'Ok!'

Then as if to start afresh, and take the initiative, he asked, 'So why, does my, so-called, basic bloody conscience, use rape as part of any bloody memory or bloody memo – even if it's to do with success! Why not just send me an image or whatever, about buying the bloody ice cream, why use one of rape at all?'

'Firstly, at the time George, you were indecisive about the ice cream turning out to be a success. You thought it would spoil the kid's appetite for lunch! Just sending you, another image or fantasy, about the kids enjoying the ice cream, wouldn't remove that doubt! That would require the cognitive part of your mind to kick into action, and come up with a practical answer – but I suspect you were too upset for that to happen!

Secondly, if you want to be listened to, then, when in Rome speak as the Romans do! In your emotional-world, George, buying ice cream, and rape, are both considered as symbols of success! Two very different forms of success, true, but never the less, as far as you're concerned, they both represent success.

Now as I said, although many memos appear not to be associated with what you are thinking or doing at the time, they are segued or linked, to the potential success or failure of your current thoughts or actions. And because you see rape as a symbol of success, it's not surprising, that your sub-conscience, might well send you a rape-themed memory, when it was also trying to symbolize the alternative, success, of buying the ice cream. Just as a banker, might get an image or memo of piles of money, or a tiger an image of a successful hunt.

You got a memo, which used the park memory as segue, to channel your thinking towards the alternative type of success, i.e. buying something useful, the ice cream! It is not only using the language that you understand, it is also using one that will make you sit up and take notice!

Now, I'm not saying a basic conscience is perfect, far from it, but it's a practical little bastard when it needs to be!

The fact, that you misinterpret the whole thing, is I'm afraid, just normal. But, when you got all guilt ridden about it, and then, started to self-condemn yourself, by blaming the singer instead of the song; i.e. yourself instead of the song of rape, you also conned yourself into the role of being a so called 'elpless, wanna' be rapist!'

Taking in what Andy had told him, George replied, 'To be honest … I think I understand what you say, but it all seems as difficult as it sounds!'

'Well!' Andy continued, 'Bearing in mind, that the very best person to con our self; is our self … and that you might still want to carry on regardless; let me offer you … a deal!'

Once again, there was a silence, then George asked, with genuine curiosity, 'What sort of … deal?'

'Well, for a start, identifying, that the vast majority of your so called rape urges are to do with confusion, and aren't even anything to with sex, let alone rape, will help a great deal! It will certainly 'elp, when it comes to dismissing them as a load of old bollocks!

But because you are so used to seeing rape, as a symbol of success, yer still gonna 'ave to deal with many such memos, or so called urges for years to come! Plus of course you're gonna get real, in yer face, urges too!'

'Thanks a lot!' George replied.

'That's Ok mate!' Andy answered, 'But, if we give you some real-time, tips, about dealing with any type of urge, Ghost or real, will you consider practicing and using them, in real time? And by that I mean when you get any type of thoughts about rape, at any time?'

'Well . . . I guess I'd certainly be interested,' George confirmed.

It was at that precise moment, that Andy felt a gentle "tap" on his left shoulder! When he turned, he was more than a little surprised, to see a smiling Sergeant Vanner! As surprised as he was, Andy nodded once, and then indicated that he'd be two minutes, he then promptly returned to George. Meanwhile, the good sergeant went to back to the aisle and pondered the large sign, that permanently hung from beneath the Crow's Nest! The sign was there to remind every Advisor-Negotiator of the quote, from John Huston's classic film noir 'The Asphalt Jungle' the quote simply stated that:

"*Crime is only a left handed form of human endeavour!*"

Returning to George, Andy continued, 'Well the next step is to get a list of some, real time, emotional blocks, that you can use against the very idea of rape – or any crime come to that! If that's alright with you mate?'

'Sounds good to me!' George replied.

Letting out a silent sigh of relief, Andy said, 'Ok mate! But first . . .can I suggest we both take a short coffee-break, me ol' mate, so we can get our bearings and refresh our energies!'

'Still sounds good to me, I need the loo anyway!' George replied, 'I'll make sure to leave the phone open just in case!'

Seeing that the truth indicator was showing that George appeared to be genuine, Andy replied, 'Ok mate I'll see you in a minute or two!' he then put his end of the phone into "mute" and turned around to wave to the gently smiling, Sergeant Vanner!

Chapter 31

Pinning courage down

By one of those coincidental occurrences, if anyone had offered or handed a cup of coffee to Sandra at that very moment, she would have nearly wrenched their hand off in taking it!

Not only was Sandra's mouth was feeling as dry as a desert; at that moment her whole body felt as if she were trying to find her way across one!

In short, the heavy emotional cost of trying to achieve what she was trying to do – was beginning to take its toll! She was in reality travelling on a Piccadilly Line tube train, heading towards the Holloway Road station, which is that line's nearest station to Highgate cemetery. Using the Google map app' on her American bought mobile; she knew that from Holloway road, she still had to catch a 271 bus, to Waterlow Park, adjacent to the Highgate Cemetery; the comparatively small area in which Steven's code, had said Lizzie would be!

During the tube journey, Sandra had a strong urge to leave a message for Andy. However she was cautious that the police might well be hacking into any calls Andy's phone might receive, and even though she wasn't using her English bought mobile, they might still be able to trace her movements.

Fortunately, for Sandra, four teenagers were distracting her thirst and frustrations! The group of three boys and two girls had started an impromptu game of "Guess the Celebrity," in which a player would give non-verbal clues, to a well-known book, film or personality.

The teenagers and their game had attracted quite a bit of attention from the other travellers, who along with Sandra, privately tried to guess the answers. However, Sandra's attention was repeatedly drawn to the bottles of fizzy drinks all five youths were carrying, and drinking from. By the time she had arrived at Holloway Road, Sandra had managed to correctly guess one of the mimes (Lady Gaga), but her thirst was by now painfully frustrating.

After Sandra exited the Holloway Road tube station, she was immediately further frustrated, to see not one, but two 271 buses disappearing up the road! Looking up to find that there was no rolling indicator, to show when the next 271 would arrive, she decided to release her tensions by quickly walking, at least to the next bus stop.

When she arrived at the stop, she was relieved to see that there was an indicator, and it was forecasting that the next 271 would arrive in 7 minutes, far quicker she judged, than she could walk to the park.

As Sandra looked down the sunlit Holloway Road, a sudden gust of cooling wind stirred thoughts of revenge against Steven. For about a minute, Sandra tortured her imaginary Steven, in various quick, slow and completely illegal ways. However, trying to not become too overwhelmed, she tried to distract herself by changing the image of Steven, for images of bus drivers, who arrived in twos or threes.

Nevertheless, it was only as she glanced across the road, that Sandra became completely distracted, by the sight of a young woman. The woman was obviously waiting for a bus to come down the road – it was also obvious, that some form of genetic disorder had permanently left her crippled!

As Sandra watched, the woman pushed her self away from the support of the bus shelter. Clearly, to Sandra, the woman had decided that she no longer wanted to pay for a complete waste of time. But try as she might, Sandra could not look away as the woman began to struggle her way up the road; with her arms and legs waving about in the air, as if she were some flaying insect that had been cruelly pinned onto, Life's "To do" reminder board!

For about a minute, Sandra watched the young woman as she, very slowly, made her way up the road. However, her pace was so slow that Sandra returned to her own thoughts instead. Never the less, some moments later (about four dead bus drivers' worth) she noticed that the young woman had stopped!

Then to Sandra's utter bewilderment, the woman folded herself downwards, and then picked up two empty burger cartons from the pavement. The young woman then started her way back down the hill, towards the bus stop again. Whether, she was aided by the slight, down slope of the hill, or by her fear of missing her bus, the woman made remarkably quick time back to the shelter. She then stopped, alongside a bin, and with the air of a loose stringed puppet, she elegantly, dropped the burger cartons into the bin besides her . . . then she sat back down again!

Back over the other side of the road, Sandra's jaw dropped wide open at what she had just witnessed! Had the woman struggled all that way – just to keep the streets clean? Sandra was still struggling to find an answer, when the 271 bus finally arrived. Whilst she sat on the bus, she tried to make sense of her own situation, and that of the young woman's sense of right and wrong! However, as she attempted to return her thoughts about what lay ahead, the only thing that Sandra knew for certain, was that whatever courage was, it would not be easy – to pin down!

Chapter 32

Keeping track

When Sergeant Vanner told Andy about the possibility, that Sandra may have gone to face Steven, by herself, Andy felt crushed! Never the less, Andy told Vanner that he knew nothing, and that Sandra had told him nothing. The sergeant believed him, and with that, he advised Andy not to act on his own, but to contact himself or Rupert, if he heard anything at all!

With that said, the sergeant took his leave and left to return to Rupert – but not before he paid a visit to the Crime Frontier's staff car park! When Sergeant Vanner easily found Bell's limousine in its named place, he took a decision. Walking up to the car, he reached into his pocket and took out the tracker, which Sandra had left down the side of Rupert's rear passenger seat.

Quickly squatting down and feeling behind the rear bumper, Vanner found the bar that secured the bumper to the limousine's body. Using the Velcro strap of the tracker, he attached the tracker to bar, and then stood up. Having checked that the tracker could not be seen from above or the side, the sergeant walked off.

Tom Vanner knew that he had no instructions to do what he did, but he did have the opportunity; and he knew that if one didn't take an opportunity, then it could vanish faster than a dust cloud from an accelerating limousine!

Back in the Hub, Andy was in turmoil, and when Charlie Fenton heard what had been occurring with Sandra, Charlie suggested that he took over the negotiations with George. It was a tough call, but Andy decided he would be more useful where he was. At least this way, he would be somewhere where any news might come to! In fact, as no personal phones were allowed into the Hub, if Sandra wanted to call him, his booth would be the only place she would be likely to call. Moreover, it would be better to have something useful to deal with, rather than sitting about doing nothing useful at all!

Not wanting to leave his booth, Andy stood and stretched his back and limbs. Then he called Keith, one of the roving staff, over. When Keith came over, Andy asked him for a coffee from the near bye drinks dispenser. When Keith came back with the coffee, Andy thanked him, and then he asked, whether he knew anything about Sandra leaving.

'I saw her go off with Bell and the two police men,' Keith answered, with a slight frown on his brow. Andy then asked Keith if he could check to see if there were any messages in his pigeonhole. All staff had such a message place, labelled under their work name, in case any client had left a message.

It was at that point that George Chadwick returned.

For a moment or two, there was the usual silence (which Andy found more frustrating than usual), Also, it was at that point, that Andy had a sudden vision of Sandra, and in spite of his Advisor training he added, 'Take yer time mate, I've got nowhere else important to go to.'

George once again took his own time, then he stated, 'I'll need time to take all this in. But it is beginning to make sense and …' at that point George searched his mind for the right words, then said, '… it all seems more … honourable … somehow! Anyway, one thing is for sure, some of these blockers would certainly help!'

'Ok! Fair enough George my ol mate!' Andy then signalled to Charlie Fenton and gave him the "thumbs up" sign. When Charlie immediately gave him the same sign back, Andy continued, 'And to do that, I'm would really like to hand you over to someone, who is the dog's bollocks when it comes to knowing 'ow to handle urges, whether they're real or misinterpreted ones! And if that's all right with you George? He'll also be able to explain a lot more about moral memos and ghost consciences, than I ever could. And don't worry, you'll still be protected by the Anonymity Code.'

As George pondered, Andy again thought of Sandra and again began to feel highly concerned for her. Then once again he stated, 'Take yer time mate, I still 'aven't got anywhere else important to go to.'

George took Andy at his word again, and took his time, but eventually answered, 'That's Ok! I think learning some of these blockers would be a very good idea!'

'Ok mate, Andy replied, whilst hiding his immense relief, 'for now I'll hand you over to Charlie, and just remember, you're not irretrievably mad, or bad George, or possessed …but like everyone else, you can sometimes get emotionally confused!'

'How do you mean? George asked.'

'Because part of the purpose of a, pre-word memo, has always been and is, to persuade you to do the right thing, even if it means that you may or may not end up, rejecting your pre-memo intentions.

But, like I said, if one of your memo happens to have a criminal theme, then you can find that, rightness of feeling, projected onto the crime instead, and end up feeling that, that is the right thing to do … even though you can't quite pinpoint exactly why. It's a subtle switch, and undoubtedly, when it comes to criminal behaviour, it's the main flaw of moral memos! It's also why, when most criminals are asked why they were, so stupid, they usually say something like, "To be honest … I'm not really sure!"

Once again George was silent. Then he asked, partly in humour, 'Does that make me sort of normal then?'

'You never know, George, you never know.' Andy replied, and then continued, 'Well, I don't know about you mate, but it sounds like that the two of us should wrap it up, for now, unless you have any more questions?'

George agreed and said that indeed, he had no more questions … for now.

'Well in that case, I'll leave you with a final tip!' Andy said.

'What's that?' George asked with a touch of amusement.

'That next time you have a choice, between rape and ice cream!' Andy said with a ruthful smile on his lips, 'Follow the fucking ice cream George!'

With that said, both men said their goodbyes and Andy was about to hand over to Charlie, when George exclaimed, 'You know I did come up with an answer afterwards – about the ice cream! I realized later, that if I bought the ice cream I could have hidden it in the freezer, until after lunch, and the kids wouldn't spoil their appetite! It was so bloody simple really!'

'Of course it was,' Andy sympathized, 'but like I say; sometimes it only takes a touch of the ol' moral vertigo to throw us completely of balance, my 'ol mate!'

'Moral vertigo?'

'Fear of reaching great heights, me ol' mate!'

George gave a short laugh in reply, then in spite of his growing concern for Sandra, Andy continued.

'On that point, in future, just try to remember this scientific fact,' Andy then paused to make sure that he had George's attention.

'Fact?'

'Changing trajectory . . . means widening the eventual gap!' Andy stated.

'How do you mean?'

'Well, although . . . thinking or fantasizing about committing rape, isn't the same as really committing it – it can still land you in deep shit! It is like rocket science; in that, even if you're only a millimetre off course at the launch; by the time you should 'ave landed on planet "Goody-two-shoes," you've gonna' find that yer landed yourself on a completely different planet, all together!

And speaking of rocket science,' Andy added, 'it may also pay you to remember. That to nudge yourself back on the right course, all you gotta do is to, behave, as if you were suddenly, already, back on the right course! Or to be exact, whenever you get a so-called urge about rape, then go back to what you were thinking about, immediately beforehand!'

Back in his room George gave a quick ironic laugh and paused for a while . . . then he said, 'Anyway I didn't think of the freezer idea until afterwards . . . until after lunch, and by then it was too late, we'd finished lunch by then, and the corner shop was shut!'

Andy just smiled, and then replied, 'Welcome to planet Earth – me ol' mate!'

With their final goodbyes exchanged, Andy finally handed over to Charlie. He then turned off his computer; sat back, and took short but grateful "drink" from the oasis of silence that his semi-sound-proofed booth provided against the continual, surround-sound of conversations, which constantly radiated around the Hub, 24/7!

However, Andy could not relax for long. Instead, he went straight to the crow's nest, and inquired of Charlie Fenton (whilst George went off to find some pen and paper), if he knew anything further about the whereabouts of Sandra, David Bell or the police. When Charlie honestly replied that he knew nothing, and that even David Bell wasn't to be found, Andy said, 'Ok then, that's it for me mate! I'm off! I need to find out what the hell is happening!'

At that moment, George returned, and Charlie Fenton gave his academic consent for Andy to leave.

Two minutes later, and after checking his mobile for any massages from Sandra, Andy was almost running past the outer reception desk – but at the last moment he paused and went back.

'Do yer know where Mr. Bell has got to Kirra?' Andy asked the receptionist.

'Not really,' Kirra replied, giving Andy an apologetic smile, 'He left about ten minutes . . .' then seeing the urgency in Andy's face, she added, 'I think he might have gone for a walk, down the lanes at the back, he often goes there when he wants to be alone and think. What's wrong, you look worried?'

'It's just that . . .well Sandra's gone missing and I need to find her.'

'Missing, well I hope to goodness she's alright! I knew something was up when she rushed out, went home, came back, and then left with Mr. Bell and the two policemen! But that was ages ago. Now you say she missing?'

'Yes . . .' Andy answered then asked, 'Went home? What makes you think she went home first?'

'Because she came back with a different bag . . . the big American Indian one, she used to wear it all the time when she first came here.'

Andy remembered seeing the bag, hung over the back of a chair at his place, that very morning, 'Then when she came back they all left together?'

Andy asked.
'Yes! But I've no idea where though!'

Three minutes later, Andy was pulling out of the school's main drive and "burning rubber" as he raced towards his home . . . at last!

Chapter 33

Negotiation

When Sandra finally got off the 271 bus, she went straight into Waterlow Park! By this time, most of the Hans Zimmer concert crowd; dressed in a variety of evening and casual dress, were already seated under the temporary awning in front of the orchestra, or spread around the fringes. The concert was well into its stride, and the orchestra were playing a selection from the film 'The Thin Red Line' the piece they were currently playing was entitled, "The Corral Atoll."

Pacing across the park and down towards the exit that lay adjacent to the Highgate Cemetery gates, Sandra drew little attention. Never the less, as she slowed to a walk, her heart was pounding, knowing that Steven could be watching her at that very moment!

However, Steven did not see Sandra go by his café observation point. The first he saw of Sandra was when she arrived outside the closed Highgate Cemetery gates. He had been watching three squirrels, playing a helter-skelter game of tag around a nearby tree, when, out of the corner of his vision, he spotted a figure on his i-pad screen monitor, the figure was walking up to the West Cemetery gates.

Initially he was unsure as to who he was looking at. At first, his head did not move as he watched the monitor out of the corner of his eye. Then reaching slightly forwards, he touched the screen, to bring the view of the gate up to full screen. When Steven did recognize the lone figure as Sandra, his heart began to race, and he was also unsure as to whether he was feeling excited or fearful! For a gut gripping second, he thought that that she had been prompted to do this by the police, in some baiting trap!

Motivated by his instinctive to fight, his hand crept under his grey cotton top and onto the butt of his revolver, still reassuringly tucked away in his waistband. Then Steven quickly realized that if the police were setting some sort of trap, they would never knowingly use an "innocent" as live bait!

Never the less, Steven had been taken unawares by Sandra's simple ploy, and for some unfathomable reason, he found that he did not immediately known how to react! Sandra's apparently defiant actions filled him with a strange mixture of feelings. Whether it was the feelings, or his inability to tell where the feeling came from, Steven unexpectedly felt lost and out of control! Something was making his throat swell with both compassion and rage! This was not how it was supposed to be; this was not how he was supposed to be like! This was not right! He would have to regain control. But Sandra moved first!

As he watched Sandra's image, Steven could see her bring a phone out from her pocket and press its keys. Three seconds later Steven almost jumped as his own phone chimed. Holding his phone to his ear, he said nothing, as the piece from "The Pirates of The Caribbean" wafted around the park.

'Hello Steven!' Sandra's voice said. 'I'm glad you have kept your phone with you, as you promised. I need to speak with you; I am outside the Highgate Cemetery gates. The police do not know I am here!'

Trying to regain some composure, and whilst not wanting to be overheard by a nearby elderly couple two tables away, Steven replied in a quiet but scornful tone, 'I know where you are . . . I can see you, what do you want?'

Sandra's reply was simple, 'To negotiate.'

Steven raised an eyebrow and sighed, 'So! I offered you and the piglets a chance to save your little friend, and instead, you've come here all on your little own to, negotiate, for her!'

'Yes!'

'Of course you have!' Steven reassured her, 'After all, where and what else would a Goody-goody like yourself, be doing outside such a place and at a time such as this . . . or perhaps you are just a Hans Zimmer fan!'

'I haven't come empty handed,' Sandra replied.

If Steven was intrigued by her statement, he did not show it, 'How did you get the co-ordinates I gave to the police?'

'How do you know they didn't just give them to me?' Sandra returned.

'Because they would not trust you,' replied Steven, with an acutely condescending tone. 'They are not allowed to trust people, the rules forbid it. They will try to protect you, but not trust you! And as it turns out, they were completely right not to do so, weren't they?'

'I guess they were,' Sandra admitted then added, 'Besides if they were waiting nearby, that would mean me breaking my promise to you about the confidentiality code. So let's hope that you can trust me a bit further. But what makes you so sure they are not waiting just up the road?'

By now, Steven was beginning to get impatient, 'Because the rules say they aren't, and Mr. Plod will do as those rules tell them. And the rules state, that innocent civilians are never deliberately put in danger, and certainly not used as live bait. They certainly wouldn't allow me to get close to you. No, I think we are both safe from their interference.'

'On that we can agree!' Sandra replied with some confidence. 'Is Lizzie near, and is she safe?'

Feeling that he was re-gaining some control, Steven smiled at Sandra's image, and then nodded his head to one side, 'She is very ... close ... very close!' then putting his head to the other side he stated, 'Is she safe? Yes, for the present. Yes!' Then looking deep and straight at the side on of image of Sandra, he added, 'At this moment, she's about as safe as you are!'

From his view of Sandra, Steven could see her shoulders drop with inner relief, then he heard her voice say, 'Then as we both have something each other needs, perhaps we have some grounds to negotiate!'

Whilst Steven watched a group of five depart from their table and head down towards the concert, he replied, 'Now what can you possibly have that I would need?'

As soon as Sandra heard Steven's question, she looked around, unsuccessfully trying to spot Steven or the position of the camera she presumed was watching her. Then she dipped her hand into her hip pocket, pulled out the blank-diskette and held it in the air.

'Your voice!' Sandra lied, 'I have been recording ever since you first killed the youth on the bridge, and sent his image to his friends in order to get your way. I needed to cover my back. No one else knows that I have this, and no one else needs to, if Lizzie and I remain unharmed!'

Whilst Sandra waited for Steven to reply, she desperately hoped that he was not aware; that anyone entering "The Hub" was electronically scanned, for recording devices as well as personal phones. But her hopes were not necessary, Steven knew of no such security procedures.

However, if Steven was in the dark about his thoughts and feelings beforehand, he was now completely clear – all of his thoughts were being highly motivated by sheer anger! Anger at his own stupidity, anger at the stupidity of the situation, but above all, he was deeply angry with Sandra!

Taking in and exhaling a deep breath, he rapidly tried to calculate the dangers; of having this woman running around with a recording of his voice, if indeed she did have one, let alone an incriminating one. Then without betraying any final decision at all, he gave his answer.

'There is a park behind you, go in take the first path on your left; follow it, at the top of the park there is a café, with outside tables, go there and wait until I arrive!'

With that Steven calmly disconnected the call and after watching Sandra move off, he returned the to the multi-screen versions of the cemetery to check that each screen remained unchanged. With the checks done, he sat back, and waited for Sandra to arrive!

When Andy arrived at his home and entered the dining room, he immediately saw the open and empty pistol case – he then read Sandra's note (with the true A to Z page number on it)! Sitting down on the couch, he tried to work out what to do next; whilst bearing in mind Sandra's obvious determination to neither betray the Anonymity code, by informing the police, nor abandoning her best friend Lizzie, to the whims Steven!

Dismissing any thought about immediately contacting the police, Andy took what he saw as the next obvious step, he phoned David Bell.

Bell had by then returned to the school. It took two minutes for Andy and Bell to exchange their latest news. At the end of their exchange, both men also realized that they each, separately, had the two parts of Steven's code to Lizzy's whereabouts! It took them another 30 seconds to agree to meet and work together, without involving the police. Having agreed that Bell would pick Andy up at his place, Andy waited impatiently. He still was far from happy!

When Bell rang Andy on his mobile, to tell him he had arrived outside his place, Andy rushed out and quickly got into the limousine. Both men immediately exchanged their part of the code, Bell having deduced his in the same way that Sandra had found out the police's half. Bell rapidly fed the co-ordinates into his car's sat-nav' and the result was instantaneous.

'It looks to be . . . near or probably at Highgate Cemetery,' Bell said.

'Let's go!' Andy urged. Bell then pulled out from the kerbside, performed a deft three-point-turn, then sped off!

As Bell's limousine sped down the road, it passed the parked unmarked police car, which had discreetly followed Bell since he had left the school.

Twenty minutes later, the driver of the unmarked police car, was joined by joined by Rupert and Sergeant Vanner, who kept a steady eye on the tracker readout emanating from Bell's limousine.

'Ok! If there's not something going on, then I'm a Dutchman's uncle,' Rupert stated. 'Keep well back for now,' he instructed the driver, 'we'll follow them on the tracker, at least until they get to their destination.'

'What about the SWAT boys?' Vanner asked.

Rupert pondered for a while then replied, 'Keep them informed, and tell them not to stand down yet. In fact tell them to keep a casual tail on us, I don't want them up our backside . . . but I don't want us to be caught with our trousers down either!'

Chapter 34

"A Quiet Moment"

When Sandra saw Steven that had disconnected the call, she breathed a huge sigh of relief. Even though she was very aware that there was a long and delicately dangerous way to go, she had at least achieved her first step – to get Steven to meet her!

How more delicate or dangerous her journey would turn out to be was yet to be tested! Never the less, without further thought on the matter, Sandra followed Steven's last instructions and turning around, and with the semi-distant sounds of the orchestra matching her footsteps she strode back into Waterlow Park.

In an effort to distract her fears, and calm her mind as she walked along, Sandra purposely used an exercise that she often gave to callers to the helpline; she called it the "Surprise!" exercise!

The exercise can be used, as a temporary, but useful distraction or diversion from various, real time, temptations or situations of vulnerability. It often went alongside the, somewhat poetic advice, called "The litmus test," for when a person felt, tempted, by wanting to find out if she or he could, resist temptation!

The Crime Frontier's Litmus Test for resisting temptation went as follows: "You can find out the acidity of a liquid by just, testing it with a paper that's called Litmus. But just like self-testing if you're vulnerable or not – it won't change the nature of the liquid you've already got!"

As she continued to walk along the path, Sandra began to look about her for unexpected things! It is of course true, that although our environment shapes us, in many ways, what we take out of our environment, can also refine our shape. It is also true that, as with many things in life, things remained unobserved until we look for them. So it came as no great mystery to Sandra, that no sooner than she looked for unexpected things, she found them; though, in some strange way it always appeared to Sandra that the "surprises" found her!

As soon as she started her exercise, the things in her surroundings seemed to take on a "presence" of their own. The experience was like being on a mild but pleasant cannabis "trip" but without having to pay the obligatory tax of paranoia.

About half way along the rising path, Sandra began noticing how welcoming the park appeared to her – even in such a dread time as this. As she passed a bush, the stiffly, spiked branches, seemed to jut out. But at the last moment she noticed, a pale white bud, sprouting at the end of the nearest branch.

To Sandra's eyes, every piece of the budding flower became both, independent and at one, with surrounding environment; which still included Steven, but who in Sandra's mind, had become no more imperative, than anything else around her. In her mind, the new growth also, somehow, gave some inner and calming strength to her resolve.

Twenty paces later, she saw a small child and his parents, coming out of some trees to her left. Noticing an almost hidden path going back into the trees, Sandra found herself being drawn to it. The main path that she was on, continued to the right and she presumed it led to the café. Believing she had at least a few minutes in hand, before Steven would arrive at the café; Sandra took the small path and then went into and along the almost hidden short side path. Then as if to applaud her reformed zeal, Sandra experienced one of 'Those-moments!'

Stopping and leaning on the wooden bars, that formed part of a ground level viewing platform above a small lake, Sandra found that she had wandered into a small-secluded nature reserve. By now the seclusion of the reserve was partly blocking the sound of the concert, as it continued with Zimmer's 'Silence,' however Sandra could still hear enough for it to affect her mood.

Looking along the length of waters, above which hovered a haze of drifting sunbeams, her attention was drawn to the tiny island, at the far end of the lake.

The "island" was in fact a small overgrown, bird-nesting platform, which "nested" an un-kempt, bright yellow wild-rose bush. To Sandra, the wild rose bush seemed to be radiating an aura of ecstatic pleasure towards a frantic halo of insects; which included a prancing-pirouette of pale yellow, flutter-winged, butterflies. All of this frenzied activity was set in contrast, by a backdrop of shadow-streaked trees and foliage, of the surrounding reserve.

Just a little way behind and to the left of the rose bush island, the drooping, pale green tendrils of a weeping willow, gently swayed and glittered in the dipping, yet still warm rays of the early evening sun! Just behind and to the right of the willow tree, a moss-mottled grey stone, peeked out from the deep greens and browns of the surrounding undergrowth.

Then, above all this array of splendour, Sandra raised her head to behold, an enormous slab of slate-grey-summer storm cloud; sliding its majestic way in between the swiftly darkening horizon, and the slowly vanishing blue sky above!

As she beheld the scene all around her, with an awed fascination, Sandra's very skin seemed to feel the chattering vibrations from a near bye clump of water-reeds, as they submissively quivered under the warm caress of an un-concerned passing breeze!

Then to Sandra's spellbound senses, and almost as if it were acting upon the reed grasses' cue; the frenetic dance of a nearby swarm of water-midges, seemed to suddenly slow in sympathetic harmony; as a deep rolling rumble of thunder proudly announced, the imminent arrival of the approaching summer storm!

As she drank in the panorama all about her, Sandra could even feel the beats of her own heart, donating its own rhythmic contribution towards this harmonic symphony of chaotic coincidences!

Inside the utter, completeness, of that "fairy story" moment, Sandra could have quite easily believed in – an Almighty God! However, in the next moment, the sight of a brown speckled, fawn winged moth distracted her attention, as it landed on the top of a nearby deep green, broad leaf!

Ignoring all else, Sandra gazed at the moth's slight movements, as it explored its way around the leaf's surface. Sandra knew that some butterflies smelt through their feet, so that they could tell whether a leaf was suitable for laying eggs, but she was unsure if moths did the same.

Then, suddenly, as Sandra watched the moth's minute movements, a streak of multi-forked lightening cracked clear across the increasingly malevolent horizon! Then once again, an ominous rumble of thunder rolled its way around the reserve, and across the surrounding park!

At that moment, the moth suddenly shuffled to the leaf's edge … then it crawled underneath, as if it too, were preparing to take shelter from the approaching … mayhem!

However, instead of seeking her own place of shelter, or proceeding up to the café, Sandra unthinkingly went to a nearby bench, as another rumble of thunder rolled across the sky. Then as if, she had all the time in the world to just wait; Sandra sat and waited upon the brooding anger of the approaching … monster!

Moreover, and indeed, up in the café, Steven was getting very angry! For if, Sandra was surprised by her own attitude to her situation; to Steven her "impudence" was "Fucking astonishing!" As far as he was concerned, even if she had been crawling, she should have reached the café by now! Then as he too sat and watched the approaching storm clouds, Steven began to doubt, not only his opinion of her, but that of his plan!

Had she fled? Were the police surrounding the park at that very moment? In an instinctive reaction, Steven's hand slipped over top and then curled around the butt of his revolver! Then like an owl searching for a mouse, he swivelled his head to the back and forth … though in truth it was more out of confusion than any wisdom!

'What the hell does she think she is doing?' Steven softly said to himself, whilst his hand gripped the butt of his revolver, but this time his grip was motivated a rising anger! For a moment he seriously considered rushing down to find this "pip squeak" – even if it did upset his well laid plans! However, he knew that such a move held as much danger to himself, as it would to her! She might have already hidden the tape of his voice in some place, so Steven withheld his anger . . . for a while longer!

As Sandra remained seated, and took what rapidly escaping time that she judged she had left, she deliberately tried to imagine the park in times that are more normal. She imagined children playing tag, or families and friends sharing a picnic. The thought of picnicking suddenly made Sandra remember two things; the first was her unquenched thirst, the second was Andy! In spite of their shared intimacy, she had never cooked a meal for him, she liked cooking; and then, deep inside of her heart, she felt a huge pang of loss!

As Sandra looked up and towards the approaching storm cloud, she concluded, that she was merely a good person, in a good place, at a very, very, very bad time! Scanning her surroundings, she then noticed that the bench that she sat on bore a weathered, green mottled, brass plaque, which bore an engraved inscription! The inscription simply said, "A Quiet Moment"

The "Quiet moment" quote made Sandra smile. Appreciating the wonder of the park and the approaching storm's enthralling power over her, suddenly seemed to make Steven's sick, evil intentions, feel even more grotesquely stupid than before!

In truth of course, the tortured twist and turns of Steven's intents, were shaped by the torturous turmoil's that raged across his own inner landscapes - not on some pretty park and it's local weather conditions; Sandra's comparisons were illogical and silly . . . but then she was only human!

After taking in more the scene before and around her, Sandra stared down at an empty water bottle on the ground nearby. Getting up she picked the water bottle up, and then she retraced her steps back along the path, and back onto her route towards the cafe. Pausing by a bin, she again looked around the park, just as if she were on a normal lunch break, on some normal day. It would be so easy for her to carry on walking, out of the park, as she would on any normal day. No one would blame her; no one would discourage her wish to live happily ever after with Andy, or at least to take the chance and try!

Never the less, for the moment Sandra stood still, neither wanting to move up nor down the hill. Below her, the round mouth of the bin seemed to be waiting; the more she stared into its cavernous yawning mouth, the darker its interior seemed to be grow, until it demanded the whole of her attention!

As Sandra stood hovering above the bin, she had an irrational, but incredibly strong urge to climb into the bin's darkness! She yearend to squat alongside the bin's other, discarded residents, unwanted and unlooked for by anyone, and to be of no use to anyone, at all! She wanted to hide in the welcoming darkness – until the waiting bogie man outside had gone far, far … away! However, Sandra had put her hopes in such dark places before!

As a child, Sandra had her own hiding place. She would hide there after school, particularly on rainy days, or when she had no other place to go at the end of school time. Sandra would hide from her father, who would habitually be in the TV lounge.

She called her hiding place, her "Quiet house!" On such days, the young Sandra would, very quietly, let herself in through the front door and quietly creep to the cupboard that lay under the stairs. Having reached the cupboard door, she would gently, move aside the coats that hung on the outside of the door. She would then un-clasp the hook that usually kept the door closed; go inside and close the door behind her – knowing that the lower halves of coats would swing back in place to re-cover the un-clasped latch. Once inside her "Quiet house" Sandra would … ever so … quietly … crawl to the end of the space, and then settle down. Quite often in such times, Sandra would read a book or do her homework; under the light of her rocket shaped torch, that she kept behind a pile of old and yellowing magazines – most of which she had read several times over.

The "Quiet house" would keep her safe until after her mother's return, at around six. Sandra knew that her mother (who worked on the fish counter of the supermarket in the next town) would immediately take a shower after taking off her work overalls. As soon as Sandra heard her mother return and go upstairs, she would creep out again, and close and latch the cupboard door. Then she would return to the front door, open it and noisily close it, as if she had just come in.

Once her mother, showered and freshly dressed, came down again to cook the evening meal, Sandra would tell stories about the things she had done at her best friend's house that very day. As Sandra didn't like to lie, the stories about her time at her best friend's house were true, except they were about the times when she had actually gone there after school, but not that day.

Back at Waterlow Park, Sandra shivered; she knew that Steven might be waiting by now, and he may even be watching her at that very moment. Never the less as anxious as she was, she could not help returning to her memory of the humiliating day that her father had to "rescue" her from her "Quiet house."

In spite of standing there by the bin, Sandra remembered that day in the past, almost as vividly as if she were back there. It had been a cold pale day, with a drained pale sun in an impartial sky. It was also the day, which unbeknown to Sandra, her father, whilst leaving the blaring TV on, had been called away to a neighbour's house.

As Sandra was sneaking in through the front door and creeping quietly into her precious Quiet house; her father was next door; helping to fix his buddy's car. He had also taken his toolbox from its usual place – from the cupboard beneath the stairs!

Ten minutes later, Sandra was about to complete the third page of her homework, when she froze in mid sum. With the sensation of dread erupting inside of her tummy, she heard the front door open and shut, and then she heard her father calling out her name! As she heard her father's footsteps coming along the hall, and then stopping outside the cupboard, Sandra's heart seemed to be pounding on the outside of her ribs - demanding entry! At that terrible moment, she thought; that without a single doubt, her father somehow already knew that she was hiding in the cupboard! Within two seconds those fears were compounded, when the door flew open and light flooded inside!

But her father did not know, and he had opened the door merely to return his tool box to its usual place, on the shelf along the back wall. To Sandra's relief, her father half put, half threw, the toolbox onto the shelf, and he did so without once bending to enter inside the cupboard; where he would have undoubtedly seen his daughter crouching at the far end! So, instead of discovering her "Quiet house" he simply closed and latched the door – shutting her inside!

It is rare that our bodies swirl with feelings of both sheer relief and dread, at the exact same moment of time! Never the less, for Sandra, having escaped discovery, by being captured, her thoughts and feelings were so confusing she almost fainted!

As she leant against the front of the family's old and now disused washing machine, Sandra felt as if she herself, had been thrown into some unstoppable, spin-cycle, of insanity! For what seemed ages she just sat quiet and helpless. But then another sensation began to rise up through her senses – it was the rising feeling, of utter and unavoidable humiliation! She then heard the steady clump … clump … clump of her father's footsteps above her head, as he returned down the stairs after washing his hands in the upstairs bathroom!

With sudden inner clarity, Sandra listened to the heavy footfalls, as they passed along the hall and into the TV room. A few seconds later, she heard the muffled sounds of a TV news reporter; apparently, if Sandra had heard rightly, there had been a sharp rise on the Dow Jones!

Putting the news of the Dow Jones aside, the young but now partially recovered Sandra, began desperately to try to think of a way to escape the inevitable – or at least limit the disaster! She had of course already made up an excuse long ago (for if she should ever discover in the cupboard) but she would rather she didn't have to try and make it believable – particularly to her father! Never the less, if she could remain hidden for about another hour, Sandra knew that her mother would eventually return home! And if her father had fallen asleep in front of the telly' which he sometimes did, then perhaps she could just tell her excuse to her Mom!

With that thought in her head, it was at that moment, that an even bigger, and in many ways more frightening answer came to the young Sandra! And that frightening answer was; that she could take this opportunity, to tell her mother the real reason, why she was hiding in the cupboard from her father!

It would be a course of action, which held many unknown outcomes! In his many efforts to convince his daughter (not to mention himself) that their "special little secret" was not to be revealed to anyone else, Sandra's father, Danny, had warned her of many dire results! Should she tell anyone else, one certain result was that, he would be sent to prison because of his "special love" for her!

There was also the warning that both she and her mother would also certainly get into trouble too! Indeed, although unbeknown to her father, Sandra herself had seen as much at her school, only a year previously! A girl who had told the teacher that her "step-pa had "done things" to her; had been teased and called nasty names by some of the other girls and boys, for allowing the "things" to happen in the first place! Like many misguided victims of abuse, Sandra already felt guilty!

For the young Sandra, there was also the matter of her own, love, for her father! For in spite of her great dislike of her father's actions, Sandra did feel that it was, in some way, his way of showing her his love – even if it was, not right, somehow!

And how would her mother react? Would she believe her? Sandra's father had told her, that her mother would never believe her, and even if she did – she might feel very jealous and very hurt!

Her father had also told Sandra, that if she did tell anyone else, she herself would be almost certainly end up – in a children's home! But in spite of all these dire warnings the young Sandra knew that "Things were not right" and that her father's strange love, was somehow very wrong! So, as she lay in the dark, Sandra, like so many other abused children, debated all the confusing and frightening courses that lay before her. However, despite all of the young Sandra's efforts "Mother Nature" was gradually but surely, taking its own inevitable course!

With all the emotional turmoil, the young Sandra's bowels were suddenly becoming uncontrollable! As she felt her insides move, she realized what was about to happen! She also realized that there was no way she could hold on for much longer – let alone for over an hour! She also knew, that there was no way, that the smell would not eke out of the ill-fitting cupboard door; then travel down the hall, and then across into the TV room!

Meanwhile, back at the café in Waterlow Park, Steven, was also approaching an emotional turmoil, of his own! And let's face it, dear reader, if you had the mind of a serial killer, who was at that very moment pacing back and forth; whilst waiting for "Miss fucking Goody-goody, to finish her fucking Goody-goody time taking!" then you'd be feeling rather … tense … too! "What the fuck does she think she is doing?" Steven asked; it was self-questioning and the only logical answer Steven could come up with was, "She must have gone; be drunk or got too frightened!" But to Steven the answer was immaterial, no matter what state she was in, she is not taking him seriously!"

As she looked into the threatening sky and around the park, for several moments more, Sandra tried not to think of her childhood memories, and instead she tried to concentrate on what she would say to Steven. It was at that very moment, that Sandra heard the sound, of a soft "metallic-click" to her left side! Looking down, she was immensely relieved to see, that in her tense thoughts, she had accidently pressed the clasp of her bag shut! It was at that moment, that another roll of thunder (nearer than before), and a squall of swirling wind, brought Sandra completely away from her childhood memories, and back to the park, to Lizzie, and to "this fucking maniac!" called Steven!

Sandra's conscious vision quickly re-focused, onto the various pieces of rubbish that lay at the bottom of the bin. Then dropping the empty water bottle into the bin, she immediately brought out and reset her mobile phone, and then headed off towards, where she judged the café to be! Two minutes later, at the café itself, the re-seated and re-calmed Steven watched Sandra climb the path, at last! Nevertheless, even as he unfolded his arms, he could not resist whispering.

'Oh, how so fucking nice of you, to come!'

Chapter 35

"Nice to meet, you!"

When Sandra entered the walled garden of the café, she immediately recognized Steven from the photo that the police man, Rupert, had shown her in Bell's office . . . it seemed so long ago and far away now! However seeing Steven, in person, for the first time, and albeit from a distance, Sandra felt almost shocked, by her immediate, physical attraction, to this man! Moreover, although she quickly tried to suppress such feelings, she could not deny that he was quite attractive . . . but then again so were many monsters!

As she approached the half-canopied seating area, she gave no outward clue that she had recognized him, for to do so would betray the fact that she knew far more about him, than he thought –and certainly enough to put her and Lizzie in immediate danger.

Likewise, as Sandra took a seat at a table, down and to the left of where Steven sat, for his part, Steven did not show any sign that he was ready to greet her, for before he did so, he wanted to study her. Looking at Sandra's angled profile for some time, Steven thought that she had an attractive face and figure. However, there was something; some quality, about her that he found unusual! Then he noticed that she suddenly looked pensive and deeply withdrawn; so for a while he changed his mind about breaking off his study and approaching her, and instead he continued to watch.

The reason for Sandra's sudden mood change was that, whilst being incarcerated in the limbo of waiting, for Steven to make up his mind to approach her, she had been irresistibly, drawn back into the feelings she had, from discovering; that her once precious "Quiet house" had been turned into nothing more, than a prison lavatory! Being faced with the meagre choices of being discovered by her father, sooner rather than later, there seemed little choice left, but to call out his name! After Sandra had called out for her father several times, he came and unlatched the cupboard door!

When she crawled out of the cupboard, Sandra kept her eyes averted as she told her father that: she was hiding because she had wanted to surprise him, by pretending not to be in, then suddenly appearing … but she accidently fell asleep!

On the surface, her story would have served as a believable camouflage, but unfortunately for the young Sandra; camouflage begins to lack any credibility if the hider, begins to tremble underneath it! And under her father's eagle eyed gaze, Sandra could not help but begin to tremble … then crumble, as she began to sob!

However, to Sandra's utter astonishment, her father at least pretended to believe her story!

'Trying to play pranks on your Pa' are you?' he said, putting his arm around her shoulders. 'Well never mind, just you go on up and change your school stuff, and into your comfortable clothes. Go on up now and be quick, you hear!' He then gave her a tight squeeze and wide smile – but the look in his eyes, told Sandra that he knew she was lying!

As she hastily climbed the stairs to the bathroom, Sandra also knew that she would have to pay for her "prank" sooner, or later! Doing as her father had told her, Sandra changed out of her school clothes a few minutes later, however, to the young Sandra, her forthcoming punishment was of little loss, compared to the huge loss of her "Quiet house!"

At that moment, Steven tired of his study, so he got up and then walked over! By now, the park's café had closed, and the nearness of the approaching storm clouds had driven all but Steven, Sandra and the two elderly regulars, away from the enclosed garden area. However, the two regulars were seated far enough away, to prevent them overhearing Steven's greeting.

'You should always check who's behind you,' Steven stated!

Looking somewhat "taken aback" Sandra looked behind her, stood up and then asked, 'Steven?'

'We meet in the flesh at last!' Steven replied.'

Holding out her hand, as if to shake his hand, Sandra replied, 'Nice to meet, you!' Then in one swift motion, she brought her mobile phone level to his face – and calmly pressed the photo app!

Before Steven could react, Sandra took three swift steps backwards, brought up the pre-set "send to" app, and then, in a soft, calm but assertive voice she said, 'If at any time I feel that you are going to harm me, then I will press send, and that image of you will instantly be sent to a dozen addresses!'

Half expecting Steven to lunge forwards and strike her then and there, Sandra added, 'I'm sorry! But I promised you that I have something that you would want,' Sandra stated whilst gently waving her mobile in the air as she added. 'And I never like breaking a promise!' she then went back to the table, sat down and added, 'I got the idea when I remembered you sending that photo of Garfield Trueman, the young man on the bridge, to all of his friends!'

Without moving, but not wanting to feel outsmarted, Steven replied, 'Well they say great minds think alike!'

For what seemed to Sandra to be an excruciatingly long time, Steven stared into Sandra's steady eyes. He was looking into the dark depths of her pupils, and for a fleeting second, Steven bathed in the imagined essence of her being. Then suddenly, like a swimmer who had found that he had entered into dangerous waters, Steven withdrew his gaze! For another second or two Steven tried to identify the quality of his experience, but again failed to find anything specific.

Feeling that the silence between them had gone on for too long, Sandra gently waved her mobile and smiled stiffly at him and said, 'I hope you don't mind, but I figure if you kill me – at least they'll know what you look like!' Re-seating herself more comfortably she continued, 'I know it kinda bends the anonymity rules a bit, and if I send it, it will break them. I'll probably be sent to hell or somewhere, but what the heck, we'll have plenty of time to talk it over down there!'

She then smiled again and put both hands in front of her, 'But whichever way you hang it, so far, I haven't broken my word to you about keeping your identity … anonymous! I have not told the police your phone number, and this phone …' Sandra held up her phone, '… is my own, that I brought from

America, my English one is … not here. That way they are unlikely to be able to trace my whereabouts!'

For a second or two Steven looked at Sandra, then he smiled, looked down at her mobile, back up to look into her eyes again, then he too smiled stiffly. Taking out his mobile, with which he originally called Crime Frontiers with, Steven casually took the back off and removed the chip and battery.

Sandra smiled back and said, 'As yet no photo, or copy of your voice, has been sent to any one, you are safe. If Lizzie and I are allowed to leave, alive and well, then I promise you I will delete your image, in front of you, as long as Lizzie and I are in a public place, with other people around … and that's a promise not a threat.'

With that made clear to him, Steven calmly looked into the sky as rain began to splash onto the ground around them. Pointing to the empty tables at the canopied rear of the café, he asked, 'Is there another copy of that voice disc?'

Not being the most confident of liars, Sandra paused for a split second longer than she had intended, but it was long enough for her to judge that it had too long!

'No!' There is no recording; it's a blank tape, I lied so you would meet me!'

Steven nodded twice, then replied, 'In that case, we will wait … for the rain to stop!'

Once they were re-seated, Sandra asked, 'You took a chance in keeping your promise, to keep your original phone with you, is that what you like to do Steven, take chances?'

For a moment, Steven stared at her in amazement, and then he said, 'What? Do you think you people are the only ones capable of keeping promises?'

Thirty seconds later, as the rain became near torrential, Sandra half turned and looked out at the deluge, whilst Steven (who had deliberately taken a seat on the opposite side of the table, being careful to make sure that he was not within an easy arms-reach of Sandra), looked out at the rain too … and bided his time.

As they waited amidst the drum tattoo of the rain, Sandra offered Steven a negotiated way out, 'If you allow Lizzie to leave, without further harm, David Bell has already confirmed a promise of non-prosecution, from Donald Smyth, the man you assaulted and stole the files from!' Sandra waited a second, but Steven's face did not even flicker.

'Plus!' Sandra continued, 'In exchange for Lizzie safe return, you are offered a safe haven, in our residential, if you choose to take it . . .'

'Bell has already offered me this rubbish in his constant text to me!' Steven interrupted!

Trying to hide her surprise and alarm, Sandra continued, 'In addition, Steven, I am offering you something worth far more, not just a way out, but a way forwards!'

Sandra then leaned forwards and a bit closer to Steven, 'We can go and get Lizzie . . .then afterwards . . . I promise you, that I will join you in your quest to reform the Anonymity Code! We can work together, in getting the code amended, perhaps to include a promise that if any caller names a potential victim, then Crime Frontiers must inform the proper authorities, so they can in turn inform the victim! You can do better than break the code Steven . . . you can change and create a new code!' Sandra enthused!

Steven studied Sandra then he replied, 'I need to think about this.'

At that moment, the garden area was suddenly near filled, with the stampeding, bedraggled, free-bee-concertgoers, seeking refuge from the storm! Then whilst the summer storm continued to release its downpour, and Zimmer's piece 'God Yu Tekem Laef Blong Mi' battled with the thunder, both Sandra, Steven and the crowd looked on; in that transfixing way that summer storms have over so many living beings.

After a while, Steven moved closer and asked with a genuine curiosity, 'What made you so sure you could get the numbers I gave to Rupert and co?'

'I wasn't sure!' Sandra answered. Although the babbling of the surrounding crowd, the tattoo of rain and the distant sound of the orchestra, made it almost impossible to overhear anyone's conversation; Sandra looked around her, as if she didn't want to be overheard, and continued, 'I had hoped to get the coordinates that you gave to the police, when I gave them my ones ...'

'So you gave them false ones,' Steven interrupted, 'you must have given them a false page number,'

'As you said, I gave them a false number. I gave them the first page of the enlarged central London maps. Page 140, that way I knew I'd be starting from central London at least. We ended up at Regent's Park.' Sandra confirmed. 'But they didn't tell me theirs straight away, but over the phone Inspector Rupert did tell his back up team, that he would be there within half an hour. After that, I knew that I would have time to be taken there; find out their co-ordinate, cross reference it with your genuine page number, and arrive here, probably well within your time you set.'

Sitting back, she held one arm up and said, 'Anyway, so I hitched a lift with them! They felt Mr. Bell or I might be of some use, if they needed to negotiate with you.' With that, Sandra lowered her arm and added, 'I would have told them what I had done, before it got out of hand!'

Nodding to Sandra Steven smiled then said, 'My, my, what a *sly* little Goody-goody you are!'

Sandra looked into Steven's eyes and simply replied, 'I guess a lot depends upon both of us being right then, doesn't it?'

Steven smiled and said, 'Of course it does.'

All the while throughout the rain and Sandra's recount of her reasoning, Steven had been searching, searching for a plan of his own. The news that there was probably no recording of his voice was a relief of course, but only a small one, now the photo image of him that Sandra held in her mobile, was the main problem.

Then as the rain began to show signs of decreasing and the distant sky show signs of clearing, the beginnings of an answer came! It came within, what at first seemed an unrelated memory, which was, that after the many plagues of London, the Victorians, so practical and superstitious in so many ways, had developed an almost obsessive belief in hygiene – even for the dead!

For a few moments more, Steven let the pieces fall into place. Turning his head towards Sandra, he smiled, then he tilted his head to the side and said, 'You know you really are quite plucky aren't you?'

At that moment, Sandra was not feeling at all plucky, so she did not answer but just looked deep into Steven's eyes. Once again, Steven tried to figure this woman out.

'Why do you fight me so Sandra?'

'Because I believe the things you do are . . . not good!'

Steven smiled as he would have smiled at some toddler, who had just fallen whilst trying to run. Although he cared little for human beings in general, he loved toddlers, they were so . . . unafraid!

As the crowd began to move out again, Steven asked Sandra, 'Do you think the ending of some greedy, property millionaire's ways, is such a bad thing to happen? Or the beheading of some dizzy, headed, bimbo queen, was of such a great loss, to the world, or her? Thousands are slaughtered each day, in slums, workhouses and on battlefields, devised solely to feed and protect the lives of such trash! Do you really believe such sacrifices are worthy of upholding? Let alone risking your and poor little Lizzy's life for?

'That's a fine sounding speech,' Sandra replied, 'but to be honest, it smells a bit … off! Besides, what gives you the moral authority to judge other people's mistakes or weaknesses?'

'I just empty the garbage when it's stench begins to offend my nostrils! Why do you fight me so Sandra?'

'Some things are worth fighting for, and against.'

'What things?'

'Respect, freedom, Love!'

At that moment, Steven laughed aloud, then exclaimed, 'Oh let us not forget Love!' Then looking into the sky, and raising his voice, so that even some of the crowd looked round at him, he partly quoted from Shakespeare's King Henry V, act 3, scene 1

'Once more unto the breech, dear friends, once more, or close the wall up with our English dead! …' then turning to Sandra once again, and looking deep into her eyes, Steven lowered his voice to an almost whisper, and then added with a sneer, '… for if the truth should ever break though, then we'd have to rely on our love instead!'

As Sandra looked back into Steven's mocking eyes, and for a briefest of moments, a shimmer of sheer hate for this man, rose up from the dark depths of her pupils, then just as quickly, it disappeared! Whether it had been snuffed out by feelings of fear or sorrow, was hard for even Sandra to tell!

But as brief as it was, Steven saw and recognized it, and asked, 'Why fight me so Sandra? Are we really so different, deep inside?'

Sandra did not answer at once, but looked down, at a coffee ring on the cafeteria table, then up again, and answered, 'I think that we are just two opposing ends of the same nightmare Steven, desperately searching for some glimpse of light!'

For a long moment, Steven paused, and then he stated, 'I believe that you will delete the photo of me, if I let you and little Lizzie go.'

Again, Sandra looked into Steven's eyes and stated, 'I will!'

For two or three seconds more, Steven held her gaze, then slowly stepping up and away from the table, he looked into the sky as the rain sharply decreased into an end of storm-fine shower. In the mid distance, and applauded by some of the leaving crowd, a rainbow made a very brief but dazzling appearance. By the time it had disappeared, Steven had finalized the end part of his plan, and it depended on Sandra's ability, to not panic, and his abilities, as a poker player!

Then he turned to Sandra and said, 'Then let us both leave and rescue poor … little … Lizzie … together!'

Chapter 36

The Catacomb

As Chief inspector Rupert Miles sat in the rear of the unmarked police car, that was discreetly following the route that Bell and Andy were taking, Sergeant Vanner's mobile phone chimed. After a short conversation, the sergeant flipped his phone shut, and raising his eyebrows he turned around to Rupert.

'That was Harold from HQ. They got some more hits on this Steven Chadwick's car reg' . . . three hits in all . . .and you're not going to like this sir! Two relate to dump sites for – the Body Part Murders! There's also one at the same time and part of town as Rita Knightly went missing!'

Even in the gloom of the car, Sergeant Vanner could see Rupert's face visibly flush.

'Jesus Christ!' Rupert whispered, and then looking towards the tracker on the dashboard surface, he added, 'Jesus bloody Christ!'

For a while, Rupert sat back and thought! Then he instructed, 'Get the SWAT team again, get them down here, right behind us, and give them our exact location and direction . . . now! Jesus Christ!'

Back in Highgate, and with the daylight rapidly failing, Steven slowly escorted Sandra to the upper-level gates of the West Cemetery. At that moment, the sound of a car coming down the hill broke the previously eerie silence! Steven quickly turned towards the road, as if waiting to cross, and Sandra instinctively followed suit. The car sped by followed by three more travelling at a more sober pace. When the road returned to its former quiet, Steven again checked that there were no onlookers from the overlooking houses, then satisfied all was clear, he turned and quickly unlocked and unshackled the gate, and then he beckoned Sandra to go through.

'Go to the end of the path and to the left, and then keep out of sight!' he ordered.

However, as she started to go through the partially opened gate, Sandra suddenly paused and turned, so that the gate was now between her and him.

Sensing resistance Steven stated, 'You do realize that if you should try to pull any heroics, I will not only kill you, I shall also kill Lizzie?'

Sandra nodded once and answered, 'Never the less, if you think I am going to walk into a deserted cemetery, at night, with a self-confessed serial murderer . . . without at least some hope of an heroic rescue, then you're very much wrong.'

Steven, narrowed his gaze and asked, 'What hope?'

Then from behind the gate, Sandra gave Steven a surprisingly warm (almost seductive) smile, and simply answered, 'You!'

For a moment, Steven said nothing in return, he just held Sandra's gaze and smiled in return . . . then ushered Sandra into the cemetery!

It is rare for someone, under middle age, to feel their own mortality. Perhaps if they come across the so-still body of an animal, or perhaps observe a deceased family member, the young briefly feel . . . mortal! Perhaps, and preferably, it may be as they lay on some beach, on some starry night, whilst listening to the roar, sigh and hiss of the relentless sea, as it crumples upon the uncompromising sea shore, perhaps if they then gaze upwards to behold the vast cosmos, then perhaps . . . !

Back in the cemetery, after doing as she had been told, Sandra reached a clump of trees and waited. The evening was nearly dark now, and although the storm had passed on northwards the cloudy sky still threatening to rain again, never the less the heat of the day persisted, giving the air a humid and clingy touch.

As she looked about her, the trees began to gentle rustle in the breeze. To Sandra, the "community" of ivy-festooned pale gravestones all about her, seemed to emanate a shared perverse glee at her presence, and she in turn, suddenly began to feel small and very mortal!

Hearing the approaching sound of Steven's footsteps, Sandra tried to remind herself that when she had volunteered for Crime Frontiers, she knew there would be moments of dilemma and even great regret! *"But this is fucking ridiculous!"* she thought to herself. Then, even though she was a long confirmed agnostic, she silently and quickly apologized to the surrounding "community," for swearing in their presence!

As Steven arrived beside Sandra, and not wanting to panic her into sending his image to all and sundry, he was still careful to keep at more than an arm's length away, 'If I had known that you'd come all own your own,' he stated cheerfully, whilst gesturing to the surrounding graves and tombstones, 'I would have brought some wine and a picnic hamper!'

Then as he beckoned Sandra to follow, he strode deeper into the cemetery, 'Mind you!' Steven cautioned, as he slowed, so as to allow Sandra to catch up, 'I shouldn't drink too much alcohol, it makes me more ….' for a moment or two he searched for the right word, then wagging his finger in the air, he added, '… reckless!

The stony-faced Sandra simply replied, 'So sorry! Next time I'll give you fair warning!' But as she said it she almost meant it, for by this time her thirst was becoming most uncomfortable, which also triggered her to ponder, "Am I trying to tell myself, that I have been purposely missing out on something, essential?'

As Steven and Sandra strolled along the dappled moonlit paths of the hushed Highgate cemetery, the daytime inhabitants had either already departed, or they had settled down and were already soundly sleeping. Now was the time for nocturnal residents to rise and do "their thing!"

In the surrounding bushes and unkempt under growths, other creatures were stirring, or were already awake and alert to every rustle, twitch or odour that a potential prey or hunter might make! Between the gravestones, a wily town fox strutted purposely towards an exit from the cemetery; from experience, he had found that the abodes of the living offered far greater chances of an easy meal.

Whilst Steven and Sandra proceeded, he spoke in a low voice that would not carry too far. As they passed the graves, he gave a running commentary, just as he had done with Lizzie, in the East cemetery. Except, whereas he had later taken Lizzie to the West Side Catacomb by the shortest route, this time he took Sandra the longer way. As with many things that he did, he had an underlying purpose. Firstly, the longer route both extended and increased the pleasure of his control. Secondly, the longer the route, the longer Sandra had to endure this highly charged situation, and the more drained and less able to, clearly think, she would become.

Had Steven been able to know it for sure, he would have been delighted that his extended tour, and purpose, were not only working, but were working overtime. To Sandra, the moonlit, ivy festooned statues and skewed ancient graves appeared truly "Gothic!" Indeed, were it not for the lack, of an occasional skeletal hand, poking out from beneath an occasional gravestone; the whole scene could have come straight out of a classic Horror movie! Except that, this was no movie set, and the only "Director" able to shout, "Cut!" was the grinning, homicidal maniac strolling no more than five paces ahead of her!

However, to some extent Steven's plan was only partially working! For as she carefully followed the path Steven had planned for her, Sandra's nerves were indeed as flighty as that of any cornered animal; yet her inner determination to rescue her best friend Lizzie, remained as level headed as any stalking lioness!

However, it was Sandra's very resolve, in not being deterred from securing Lizzie's life, that Steven was relying on to keep his prey from panicking … too early!

By the time Steven and Sandra came to the almost pitch dark entrance of the Egyptian Avenue, she was very wary, and as she began to walk though, she was petrified! However, when she then came to the Circle of Lebanon, domed by the silhouetted outreaching arms of the gigantic Cedar of Lebanon Tree; the menacing entrance standing before her; filled her with an undiluted terror! A few paces ahead of her Steven turned and inform her, 'Not long now! We are getting very close!'

With that, he turned and entered into the narrow circular avenue of family tombs, all of which were sealed, by sombre- black tomb doors! As Sandra followed, she half-dreaded that the baleful doors on either side of her would suddenly fly open, to release their life drained occupants! Never the less, in spite of her inner terrors, the other half of her dread, remained firmly fixed, to the living abomination that walked directly in front of her!

In this avenue of decayed death, even time itself seemed mummified! To Sandra, her very limbs and thoughts felt embalmed, as she followed Steven's dark form, illuminated, by the eerie light emanating of her mobile phone, which hung loosely by her side. Even with her forefinger gently resting on the send mode, if Steven had suddenly turned and attacked her … she doubted if she could have reacted in time!

However, Steven did not turn or attack! Instead he just walked, calmly and helpfully ahead … for this monster's traps were arched with cunning, as well as mere terror!

To Sandra's almost overwhelming relief, Steven brought her out of the Circle of Lebanon, unscathed! Increasing his pace he then lead her past many graves, though this time he gave no corresponding commentary, and Sandra had the ominous feeling, that her time as a tag-along tourist, was about to end!

As the two of them progressed along the grave lined avenues, the trees lessened and the graves became more set back. In the partially clouded night sky above, the flitting moonlight showed them the way ahead, until they eventually arrived at the almost airy open space that lay before the … catacomb!

To Sandra, standing under the flitting light of the three-quarter moon, the pallid face of the catacomb's outer walls looked alternately intimidating, then downright evil!

However, when Steven reached the catacomb doors, and thrust them aside, he turned, smiled and then; as if they had finally arrived at some long sought after tea room, he informed Sandra.

'We are . . . here!'

If you (dear reader) had asked Sandra; If there were any place on earth that she would rather have been at that moment … then her answer would not have been "here!" Though in truth if you had of been able to ask her; then Sandra would have been at least somewhat encouraged – for that would have meant that she was no longer alone with Steven – and would have at least someone to help her, if you dear reader, had of been there too!

Unfortunately, any possible help was at that moment, an infuriatingly short time and distance away! In fact, Bell and the gallant, street-wise Andy, were in a dilemma! Admittedly, Andy's experience of graveyards was sparse, and more on the side of a one time, erotic adventure, rather than an heroic one! Never the less, he was as at that very moment, trying to figure out which cemetery (East or West) Sandra may or may not be in!

The two men were standing in the road, in between the main gates of both cemeteries, and they were heatedly debating whether to split up and search each cemetery alone, or search each cemetery in turn, together! They had already worked out that if Steven was already aware, that Sandra was trying to rescue Lizzie on her own, he would undoubtedly try to stop her. It was also obvious, that if they just randomly shouted out her name, they might well put her in even more and immediate danger!

Then without further ado, the two men's indecision was decisively interrupted, by the silent, but obvious arrival of Rupert, Sergeant Vanner and six vanloads of police, including the SWAT team!

However, back outside the catacomb, any knowledge or hope of any help was non-existent. Standing proudly between the open catacomb doors, Steven bowed low and ushered Sandra inside. Then, as if to warn Sandra about her moment of peril; from somewhere near amongst the gravestones, a fox let out a warning yell to its partner – the yell was so sudden that even Steven could not help himself from jumping! What the fox's warning was truly about, Sandra could not tell, but at least it did return her to a greater level of awareness!

'After you!' she insisted to Steven.

Without further delay or ceremony, Steven then stepped through the yawning entrance and into the interior gloom of the catacomb. Even after Steven had disappeared into the darkened depths, Sandra, standing slightly to the left, waited! Then, keeping a tight grip on her mobile, and an even tighter grip on what was left of her rapidly deserting courage, Sandra was left with little alternative – but to follow Steven into the catacomb. True, she could have, even at that late moment, decided to turn and run, but then again, as Steven had previously assured her "Where and what else was a Goody-goody like herself, supposed to be and be doing, in a such place and at such a time as this?"

Therefore, following in the wake of Steven, the now petrified Sandra, took a very big breath and stepped into the gloom of the catacomb too!

As soon as she entered the catacomb, Sandra was thrown off balance! Firstly, she was taken aback by the fact, that the interior of the catacomb was not completely dark. In two glimpses, she could tell that she stood at the centre of two tomb-filled avenues. As she looked again to her left and right, she could see that several, consecutive, circular shafts of pale moonlight, spotlighted, the floors of both avenues. The moonlit shafts were coming through a line of skylights, placed along the roof. Meanwhile the walls stretching on either side of her, were grimly lined, to above head height, with stacks of coffin bearing, sealed tombs! To Sandra, it was as if she had stepped into some "Members Only" locker room of death!

The second, though perhaps not shocking revelation, was that her once attentive guide come guard, Steven, had mysteriously disappeared!

Unsure, whether Steven's disappearance was something to be relieved or very worried about, Sandra took her bearings. No more than a metre to the right of her stood the waist high, single bar barrier, beyond which, the first shaft of light lit the dusty floor, beyond that there were several more moonlit circular shafts extending towards the far end of the catacomb. Sandra then cautiously, stepped to her right, in order to get an unobstructed view past the line of moonlit shafts. It was only then, as she got her clear view, that Sandra beheld Seven's very own … *"Surprise!"*

Some of the more sensitive souls amongst us may well say; that the spectacle of a wheelchair bound, long deceased female corpse, dressed in a partially disintegrated shroud, and donning a modern day crash helmet, was, even for Steven, just a tad overly dramatic! Others, with more of an appreciation of the theatrical, might recognize the potential of the ironic humour in Steven's handiwork!

To Sandra, the use of the word "dramatic" would be have been a complete and utter, understatement, of her situation; and as for any suggestion of "humour" ironic or otherwise, that would, again, as far as Sandra was concerned, be better placed under the heading of utterly unforgivable!

For Sandra, the deep horror emanating from the enthroned corpse at the end of the catacomb, seemed to suddenly mirror her own body and mind! For she too, felt infested, with the very same sick, madness, as she began to feel her head spin with nausea! But she was saved from completely fainting, by the swift and sudden noise, of a creaking door!

At that very moment, a delighted Steven stepped out from behind the entrance door (proving yet once again, that the old tricks really are the best!). Then stepping forwards two more paces, he said in his diplomatic voice!

'Do try not to stare at her for too long, Sandra! The Victorians tend to feel rather embarrassed, at being seen in any state of undress!'

If Sandra had heard, let alone understood what Steven had just said, she did not show it – she was immobile! Indeed if Steven had chosen that moment to pounce, Sandra would have been completely incapable of defending herself – or pressing the "send" app' on her mobile!

But Steven liked to tease before he pounced!

'I found her,' Steven began to explain as he gestured to the corpse, then ducked beneath the barrier and walked several paces forwards, 'in here!' He then pointed to a head-high tomb whose front casing had been removed.

'Her name is Elizabeth too! I just couldn't resist it!' Steven pleaded, giving Sandra an apologetic look. 'Besides,' he added, 'it seemed so mean to blatantly snub such a serendipitous … gift!'

Then putting on a seriously concerned face, and pointing into the opened end of the coffin, he added, 'But don't worry … the real and perfectly alive Elizabeth … is now in here!' With that said, he brought up and switched on a large torch (that the tour guides normally kept by the catacomb's entrance) and shone it into the late Elizabeth's coffin – who according to the plaque at Steven's feet, was "*Much loved*" and "*Very much missed*"

'She's perfectly fine!' Steven informed the still immobile Sandra, 'Why don't you come here and see for yourself?'

For the third time, that night, Sandra mystified herself yet again; by actually managing to infuse her numbed lips with enough dexterity, so that with some degree of super-goody-goody strength, she was able not only to form some words, but to actually speak them too (without feeling the need to apologize to the community around her for any possible blasphemy!)

'Go … fuck… yourself!' Sandra defiantly mumbled!

It must also in fairness be said, that it took a super-monster effort from Steven, not pounce on Sandra right then and right there! However, instead of pouncing, he slowly laid the torch at his feet, and strolled off towards the far end of the catacomb.

'I will go and fetch the wheel chair,' Steven said in a considerate tone. 'We can get Lizzie out and wheel her down to the Whittington hospital, which is not even ten minutes from here. Though whether I come inside with you, is undecided as yet!'

As Steven re-continued towards the far end, Sandra desperately tried to infuse her limbs to move. Although she could already see the tip of Lizzie's head, peeping out of the end of the coffin, she wanted to see if she was still alive, preferably before Steven returned with the wheel chair!

However, Steven took his time, for his time was getting near … so very near!

Moving as quickly as she was able, Sandra came to the coffin and looked in. At first, she could see little inside the dark interior that lay beyond Lizzie's upturned face, which seemed ghost like under the moon lit gloom; a gentle ghost face in a cold harsh place! Then Sandra could hear that Lizzie was indeed breathing, softly but surely. Sandra was about to reach up into the coffin to touch her friend face, when, from the far end of the catacomb there came the sound of a distinct and unceremonious, *"Thunk!"*

The "Thunk!" was as a result of, Steven up-ending Elizabeth's (circa 1824) corpse, out of the wheel chair, and onto the stone slabs of the catacomb floor!

In spite of her own dilemma, Sandra did her best to look aghast at Steven!

'What?' he exclaimed, giving Sandra an insulted glare back, 'She's not only already dead, but she's also wearing a bloody crash helmet . . . for Christ sake woman . . . *lighten up!*'

Sandra continued to glare, but said nothing as Steven, holding up the mobile that he had rescued from the arm of the wheelchair, snapped the mobile shut and put it in his back pocket. Coming back towards Sandra, but leaving some room to spare; he then tipped the now empty wheelchair over on its side, slid it under the barrier, leaned over and up-righted the wheel chair once again, and then he turned to Sandra.

'We'll take her out, lift her over the barrier, put her in the wheel chair and wheel her out.' With that made clear, and as Sandra moved aside two paces, Steven went to Lizzie's left side. He cupped his right arm under her shoulder blades, slid his left arm down Lizzie's left side, in readiness to both pull and support her as she came out. He then slightly pulled her out of the coffin, then he looked to Sandra and waited . . . the time was so near now . . . that he dare not rush it!

Sandra, however did not move. Instead, she just looked at Steven, suspiciously. Then putting on an emphasized smile, and her emphasized southern drawl, she stated, 'I'm sure a big ol' strong man like yourself, can lift a liddle biddy girl out o' there, with no trouble at all!'

However, Steven did not smile back, but just answered, 'I already my pulled my back, putting her in! So I have no intention of making things worse, by trying to get her back out! And . . . as I don't entirely trust you to wheel us both down to the hospital, I suggest, that you stop playing games now . . . because quite frankly . . . I can only bend over backwards so far . . . Sandra!'

Facing what seemed to be little choice at all, Sandra made her choice. Ducking beneath the barrier, she carefully stepped forwards. Then making it obvious that her finger was still on the send button of her phone, she continued to step forwards, until she was at the side of Lizzie.

Then, with Lizzie's unconscious form between Steven and herself, and getting ready to take the weight of her friend's hips and legs as soon as Steven started to pull Lizzie completely out; Sandra cautiously slid her right arm deep inside the coffin. At that moment, Steven nodded once, and began to pull Lizzie out!

"Now …is the time!"

Now, is the time, for Steven's mal-contempt to bloom, within the coldness of the catacomb! As his once supportive hand, falls from poor little Lizzie's back - like the pivotal stone dropping from a cunning arch!

Now, all hope is doomed and all is lost, all that is, but a wistful lack! For now is the time, for Steven to relish his moment! For now is the time for his prey to pay, in full atonement!

Withdrawing his supportive arm, thus leaving the last barrier between himself and Sandra to disappear, Lizzie's upper body and thighs, jack-knifed with a resounding crash onto the front of tombs below! As Sandra, using her left hand, vainly tries to support her friend's upper body, there is now nothing between her immovable dread, and the unstoppable force of Steven's malice! There is not even a question mark – for now there is no question of what will happen next!

Moving with stunning speed Steven pounces! Crashing and crushing into

Sandra's already collapsing back, he lifts and pins her to the wall of tombs, whilst his right hand slides inside the open coffin and grips her right wrist – that still holds her phone!

Sandra almost faints with the horror of feeling herself, *sandwiched*, between the crushing weight of Steven and the unconscious body of her best friend Lizzie, who is now hanging upsides down, half out of the coffin! Meanwhile Sandra's twisted neck and face are being mercilessly pressed against the panel of the tomb to the left. Then Sandra feels Steven's snarling lips brush against her right ear, he lets out a low and triumphant . . . growl!

Sandra's reply was instant, 'I'll send the photo – if you kill me you'll spend the rest of your life in a prison cell!'

'Maybe?' Steven replied.

'They'll catch you! You know they will catch you!'

'Oh! … I should think that if they get my image, they will catch me – if they get your picture,' Steven teased, then added, 'Of course you could try to send it right now … and hope that I wouldn't dare harm you afterwards!'

'I might have already!' Sandra ventured.

Steven however was not put off by her answer, 'But then that would be a shameful waste!'

'What do you mean … waste?' Sandra replied, drawing some hope from her dread.

With that, Sandra felt Steven release her left hand; move his free hand along and between his stomach and her back. Next, she felt a hard metal object slide across her back, and then she felt the prod of the revolver press against the back of her head, then Steven said, 'As you can now tell, I could have killed you instantly, at any time! Especially after you confessed to not having any recording of my voice! Of course, you still might have instinctively sent my picture, during the last millisecond of your life! But either way it would have been a waste!'

'A waste?'

'No … not of your life! Though I do place some value from knowing you Sandra, but a waste of … three things!

'Three things?'

'The first, as I have already said, would be the waste of my finding the late Elizabeth's coffin here, and choosing to put her namesake, little Lizzie inside!

The second waste would be the one, in which shooting you beforehand, would have wasted all serendipity, there's that word again, that has come from all the efforts that the Victorian's have made, to protect the late Elizabeth, and her like, from being consumed by the nasty desires of evil spirits!'

'What?'

Easing the pressure on Sandra's back even further, but still gripping her right hand, Steven continued, 'Oh of course! I forgot to tell you during my little guided tour, that the Victorians insisted that every coffin must have a three-layered barrier! The barriers were made of leather, wood and … lead! It was the law… and they took it very seriously! As you can see for yourself!' with that he prodded Sandra's head down and to the left.

It was clear to Sandra that indeed the Victorians did take the law seriously. As she looked at the opened coffin's end, it was made of up of three layers, indeed it was like three coffins in one; and the middle of the three was made from lead. As Sandra stared at the plates, Steven continued.

'It took me some time to remove the lead end panel, but I thought it worth it for poor little Lizzie's sake. Every single coffin around us has the same the three-layered barriers, which means we are surrounded – by layers of lead!' At this point, Steven's tone became informative rather than mocking, 'The lead, a malleable but impermeable barrier, is there stop … the juices running out! It is said, it was also supposed to ward off evil spirits and nasty monsters, though under the present circumstances, I'm not really sure how successful that was or is!'

Then pressing the revolver against her head once more, he emphasized, 'But what I can tell you for sure, is that it is very effective in warding off modern day… tele-communication … signals!'

At that moment Sandra froze as Steven added, 'Including, the signals that allow messages, including pretty pictures, to be sent from one mobile phone to another!'

Steven crushed Sandra's face back into the wall, and continued, 'I know this, because when I placed a camera phone inside of this coffin, to record the final moment of the police rescuing Lizzie, it failed to send any picture or signal at all!' At that point, he wiggled Sandra's right wrist, 'Just as yours will fail! But if you don't believe me, have a look at your own phone.'

Steven then forced Sandra's head to the level of the open-ended coffin, and then he forced her hand that still held her mobile, around, so that she could see its glowing face. The face still showed his image, with the send option – but there was no indication of whether there was any available signal or not!

'Now press the, back option,' Steven suggested, 'and see if you still have any signal coming in – and of course the ability to send my pretty picture out!'

Sandra did not press the "back" option, instead she said, 'If I do that then you will try to grab the phone!

Steven moved his mouth closer to Sandra's ear, 'Maybe I will, maybe I won't. Of course, maybe, my story and my prediction about the worthlessness of what is in your hand are wrong!'

Although his mouth was still slightly away from her face Sandra could sense him smiling as he said, 'Maybe … I know it's wrong! Maybe… all I said about the lead lined barriers blocking your ability, to send my picture … is a total lie. Maybe I couldn't get a picture from this coffin because the interior of this coffin is too dark! And if indeed, you pressed send right now, then your picture of me would indeed be instantly sent … maybe!'

If Sandra felt sickened beforehand, she now had the horrible perception that what was to come, would be worse! But Sandra heightened senses had given her a finely tuned awareness of the situation.

'I have another option,' she stated.

'Really?' Steven asked, 'Do tell, I'm all agog!'

'Why don't you prove whether there's no signal, by showing me on your mobile – the one you brought from the wheelchair?'

Steven smiled and looked behind him and replied, 'fraid not! In the first place, that phone is in my back pocket, and I'm not about to let go of you, to get it. Besides! Even if it were within easy reach, it would not be an acceptable option,' he added, moving his mouth closer, so that it now brushed Sandra's ear, 'because that would spoil all this . . . fun . . . that we're having!'

'This is not fun Steven!'

Steven however was not put off by her answer, but the next question he asked her . . . confused Sandra!

'No? What about poker then? Have you ever played the game of poker, Sandra?'

For a moment, Sandra did not answer, unsure as to where his question was leading to, but then Steven jolted the revolver as an encouragement.

'Err! Yes, yes, as a teenager, we used to play it,' she answered.

'Good, then you'll remember the basic concepts and rules. I play it quite a lot. I prefer live games, where I can see every twitch and tell of my opponents,' Steven stated, as he let the pressure lessen on Sandra's back and neck, whilst still keeping a firm grip on her right wrist, and then continued.

'Here is the situation. You think that the picture of me, which you have in your hand, is a winning hand! Do you recall the concept of bluffing in your youthful games Sandra? Because the concept is, that it is not always what you have in your hand that wins – even if it deserves to!'

Shifting his weight a little, Steven continued, 'So! We now we come to the beating heart of the matter! Am I bluffing about the signals being blocked, or do you still in fact hold the winning hand? Though in fact, you have three choices!'

'Choice one; you can raise the stakes by instantly pressing, send, and hoping that I dare not harm you or Lizzie afterwards – if my picture has been sent!

Two, you can try and see if I'm bluffing . . . by pressing the back-app' and seeing if the "No Signal" appears on your screen!

But as an experienced player I would warn against either of those options, because either will automatically put you . . . all in!'

Sandra then heard the revolver's hammer being cocked!

'And I do mean . . . all in!' Steven emphasized!

'There is of course the final option,' Steven informed her.

'You can fold your hand . . . by laying your phone down!'

Feeling battered, bruised and bullied, Sandra felt helpless, but she managed to answer, 'There is another option!'

'What?'

'Why can't we just trust each other?'

'But I am trusting you. I'm trusting you to make the right choice,' Steven stated in his most reasonable voice, and then added, 'By the way . . . there is a clock on your decision! I shall count to ten, if you haven't made your move by then, then all bets are off . . . and Princess Lizzie here, will be waking up to discover, that the pieces of your once clever brain, have been splattered all over her once pretty dress . . . and bunny-wabbit slippers!'

Steven then began his countdown, 'And remember; number one is! If you press send and it fails to send, then I shoot you! Though of course if it sends my photo, then I will have to let you go and Lizzie . . . maybe!'

Two is . . . If you try to check if there is a signal beforehand, I shoot you!

Three is . . . If you fold your hand, by laying your phone down, I will keep your phone and my photo, and you can skip freely away with Lizzie and her nice . . . clean . . . bunny-rabbit slippers!

Four . . . means I have already been counting, and I am continuing to do so!' Steven emphasized with a another prod of the revolver, then he continued,

'Five . . . !'

As Steven continued to count at surprisingly generously slow pace, Sandra desperately tried to go through her options!

'Six . . .!' *"Should I risk everything on the hope that he is bluffing?"*
'Seven . . .!' *"Would he risk everything on the hope I would believe him?"*
'Eight . . .!' *"If I laid my phone down, could I trust him afterwards?"*
'Nine . . .!' *"What is the capital of Nebraska ...!!!!!?"*

Chapter 37

Dangerous empathies

'Ten . . .!' *Sandra instantly dropped her phone!*

As soon as he heard the phone drop, Steven threw Sandra across the catacomb! Grabbing her phone from inside the coffin, he switched it off and then shoved it into his pocket with a satisfied thrust!

Now was the moment when the Steven felt truly free. Taking three paces forwards, so that he towered over the half prone, but very conscious Sandra, Steven swung his revolver behind his back and then shoved it down the back of his trouser waistband.

Sandra just looked up at him and asked, 'Was it true? Does the lead really block the signals?'

Steven smiled a ruthless smile, and then he replied, 'Oh! I never show my hand once my opponent has folded theirs, Sandra . . . regardless of whether I was bluffing . . . or not!'

Feeling duped, defeated and doomed, Sandra shook her head from side to side, and then she looked up at the figure of Steven; casual, relaxed and quite comfortable in his domain! In a moment of shock, it appeared to her that for the first time in her life she was looking at pure . . . evil! To Sandra, his spiteful game of "poker" was beyond her forgiveness, and therefore truly evil . . . unless of course . . . he really was bluffing?

However, whatever he was, Steven was practical, 'I'll take the blank tape too!'

Sandra reached into her pocket and handed over the blank tape. Taking the tape Steven asked, 'If I find there is a copy of my voice, I'll kill you and everyone else I can find!'

'I know!'

'Thank you so much!' Steven said, 'So here we are . . . all alone . . . and with time on our hands. So, Miss Goody- goody,' Steven asked, 'What … next?'

For a moment, Sandra said nothing! Then without taking her eyes away of his gaze, she slowly and painfully brought herself to her feet. Then she stood fully, upright, and without smiling, without pleading, without anger, she gave her reply.

'We take Lizzie to the hospital, of course!'

There followed a moment of complete and silence …! Then Steven, slowly lowered and turned his head, so that he could see Lizzie, who was still hanging up sides down out of the coffin. Then he turned back to Sandra.

'And then?'

'After that,' Sandra suggested, 'we could go on to try and change the Crime Frontiers rules, so that potential victims are told of their danger. Or we can go our separate ways, either way we end up as the heroes, once we have taken Lizzie to the hospital!'

'Heroes!' Steven repeated, and then ominously added, 'There could be a problem … with making that, fairy story, come true!'

The look on Steven's face told Sandra that he was genuinely worried about something! And it was that, that frightened her more than she was prepared to let on! However, all she asked was, 'A problem?'

Turning away from Sandra, Steven went over to the upsides down Lizzie, who suddenly and bizarrely looked to Sandra; like some "extra" appearing in some vampire "B" movie! An image that was even made more surreal to Sandra; when Steven lifted Lizzie out from the coffin, then cradling her across his out stretched forearms, he then grinned at Sandra, whilst he completed several squat-thrust, to emphasis the well-being of his back, after which he then began to carry Lizzie towards the wheel chair!

As she watched Steven, and in spite of all her conscious logic; Sandra suddenly found that she was having to use all of her self- discipline and will power to stop herself from … giggling!

Whilst Steven plodded on towards the wheelchair, with Lizzie draped across his outstretched arms, Sandra bowed her head deeper and deeper into her already trembling shoulders; knowing without doubt, that the merest '*gig*…' of a giggle; would explode into every unforgiving corner, and streak along every arched buttress of that corpse-filled catacomb, and then detonate – every hope that she had left!

The only thing that stopped her exploding all of her pent up tension, was that she knew that both her own and Lizzie's life were hanging, by a thread, and that it would only take the slightest jolt, for this maniac to – snap it!

At that point, and even though Steven was as at that very moment, laying Lizzie gently down into the wheelchair … and now turning around to face her once again, Sandra was released of any urge to even slightly smile!

'The problem!' Steven echoed, 'The problem is that when I said we were safe from any interference from the police, it wasn't completely true. Unfortunately, I have learned from our dear Inspector Rupert, that a crime, that I once thought of, as being beyond any reasonable doubt of being caught for, isn't so safe after all! They have my DNA!'

At that moment, Sandra felt something akin to a mild electrical jolt run through the length of her body, but Steven carried on.

'Rupert doesn't know my identity ... I called him as the "lover" of the true murderer!' Steven said making the inverted comma sign with his fingers, and then he spoke rapidly, almost as if the whole scenario was hardly worth explaining.

'It was my plan "B" for getting the police and Bell …but it is no longer an option. Although they don't know who I am, they have my DNA!' Steven concluded, pushing himself away from the barrier and walking towards Sandra. 'And that means that should I be caught, for even a minor traffic violation, I will eventually be sentenced to life! And that does seem a bit steep for a minor offence, particularly if it were for the, minor offence, of trying to be a … hero! So, if it's all the same to you, I'll think I should remain anonymous … don't you agree?'

The only thing Sandra was thinking of was; that without a doubt, if this man knew that the police already knew his name, and full identity – then both she and Lizzie would be murdered then and there!

But Sandra had been in dark places before! However, this time she felt no terror, no fear, no doubt! Instead, she raised her self-up in such a way, that her presence seemed to fill Steven's vision! Then, looking deep into Steven's un-quavering eyes, she smiled, as she reassured him!

'If you don't tell who you are – then I won't!'

Then stepping in one-step closer, Sandra added, 'I spoke to Rupert before I came here, the police have no idea who you are… you are completely … anonymous! Then stepping in one more step closer, until her nose almost brushed Steven's nose, and felt as if her very being stood at the brink of a chasm, devoid of any life lines – and without even a hint of fear or a lie in her face, eyes or upon her lips, Sandra assured him.

'Your true identity, will be our very own … special … little secret!'

For a long moment, there was a deep silence, then she slowly stepped back – as if she had just remembered something essential!

'That's it! Do you know what the trouble with doing wrong is?' she asked.'

'What?'

Then she looked up into his eyes and stated, 'It creates loneliness. And let's face it, we only live once.'

Then Steven smiled a different smile. It was a smile that installed no fear in Sandra! Indeed if Steven had smiled at you, dear reader, in the same way as he smiled at Sandra, in that moment, you may have felt no fear either! Indeed, you may have done as Sandra did, and smiled back.

The exchange between the two of them lasted for no longer than four heartbeats. It was not love; or even friendship, it was a shared moment … a moment of equality! On what level of equality, was debatable, but the feeling of equality, felt mutual!

As far as Steven was concerned, it was a momentary, blending, of two previously separated and even antagonistic entities, into empathy of co-existence! As far as Sandra was concerned, it was a mutual sharing of dangerous empathies!

At that moment, Steven, looking straight and deep into Sandra's eyes simply replied, 'I'll wheel her to cemetery gates … and after that she will be in your …'

However, at that moment, the beat of Sandra's and Steven's hearts began to tighten, then suddenly race; as a single word … carried in from somewhere outside the catacomb, reached their mutually astonished ears! And the word was:

'Sandraaah!'

Snap! Whether the thread between Sandra and Steven would have held without this unexpected jolt, was debatable.

However, when Rupert had told Andy and Bell; that Steven was possibly the Body Part Murderer, the strain was too much for Andy. In three strides and a leap, Andy was on top of one of the police vans, and then over the cemetery wall. To his own surprise, Bell immediately followed, as did Sergeant Vanner!

As Sergeant Vanner disappeared over the wall, the SWAT Team Leader looked from the wall to the astonished Rupert, who in turn looked towards the arriving force of more police vans and cars! Rupert then turned back to the Team Leader and ordered, 'Get a fucking cordon around this place for Christ sake!' then turning back again, he added 'And if any other fucker tries to climb over that wall … shoot them!'

'Sandraaaah!'

It was the second time Andy had called Sandra's name but she did not shout back!

Trying to keep hold of the situation, she attempted to lessen the threat of it, 'It's just Andy, my boyfriend! I didn't tell him to come here, I mean I didn't ... I left him a note ... he wasn't supposed to read it until ... he must have finished early and found ...!'

Meanwhile, Steven also decided to lessen the threat of the situation, by immediately drawing his revolver out as headed towards the door! As he reached the open door – another voice shouted out!

'Sandra . . . its David Bell, shout out if you can hear us!'

Looking back at Sandra, Steven said, in a very peeved tone, 'I suppose you didn't invite him either!' then he added with venom, 'This is beginning to feel like a fucking drop-in centre, for wanna' be fucking heroes!'

As Steven raised his revolver and looked out of the door, Sandra quickly reached over, lifted and then opened her bag! She pulled out the flintlock pistol; removed the herb bag from the barrel, tore apart the herb bag, and dropped the shot into her shaking palm. Quickly dropping the shot into the barrel, she cocked the hammer fully back, and took aim!

She then ordered Steven to, '*Stop where you are!*'

Steven stopped where he was, and then looked back at Sandra; turned around to face her, smiled and then said, with genuine admiration, 'Oh! Well done!'

Then taking two steps forwards he added, 'You go straight to the top of the class! Tell me; were you a prefect at school . . . though I think you would call it a class monitor in America?'

Sandra did not move the pistol away from pointing at his head, as she replied, 'No I was expelled from two schools, for rebellious behaviour.' In answer to Steven's raised eyebrow she added, 'Let's just say that I had a peculiar upbringing! And if you think that I won't shoot you dead, I can promise you I fucking will!'

Steven simply answered, 'And I fucking believe you!' he then looked behind him whilst taking two-steps forwards, dropped behind Lizzie in the wheel chair, aimed his revolver and fired!

When Sandra felt the bullet slam into her left shoulder (Steven had aimed at her heart), most of her breath and senses were immediately knocked out of her. She was conscious however, and alert enough to see Steven come from behind Lizzie and the wheel chair. Walking over to her, he took her undischarged pistol from her limp right hand, scrutinized it, and after searching her bag for any more nasty tricks, he placed the pistol (butt first) back in the bag, and the bag over the back of the wheel chair. Sandra was also alert enough to wonder – whether the undersized shot was still in the barrel – or had it fallen out when she had been shot?

The "boom" of Steven's revolver shot had exploded all around the catacomb and out across the cemetery, startling various birds into instinctive flight! One panicking bird almost collided into Sergeant Vanner as he caught up with Andy and Bell. After Vanner instinctively ducked the bird, all three men stood as still as the graveyard statues surrounding them! Then as the last startled bird found a safe perch, all three "wanna' be heroes" raced up the hill and towards the catacomb!

By the time the men reached the catacomb, Steven was coming out the doors, and all three men could see him. In front of Steven, sat the wounded Sandra in the wheel chair, and it was obvious to all, that although she was still alive and conscious, she had been shot in her left shoulder!

'Let 'er go!' Andy shouted, 'If you 'urt 'er again I'll kill you!'

'My! My! My! This is a popular spot tonight!' Steven declared to no one in particular, and the he asked, 'So what has brought you three here tonight, and in such a rush … have you come for a bit of group-necrophilia?' Then directing his attention to the glaring Andy, Steven added, 'That's corpse-fucking to you!'

With that clarified, Steven then pointed his revolver at Sandra's head, and informed the three men, 'Because if that is so, then you're in luck, because if any of you come any closer,' he then re-cocked the revolver, 'then you'll all be able to fuck a nice … *fresh one!*'

Then looking as if he had just solved some simple equation, Steven exclaimed, 'No wait! I've got it! You are the hero lover, here to rescue his beloved!'

Andy glared at the man holding a gun to the woman he loved, then replied with an emphasized clarity, 'My name is Andy and if you harm Sandra any further, I will, fucking, kill you!'

'Really!' replied Steven, and then mimed as if he were trying to solve an even more difficult equation! Then pointing the revolver at Andy, he concluded, 'But what if I kill you, before I kill her?'

Returning the revolver barrel to Sandra's temple, and moving Sandra and the wheelchair forwards, Steven ordered all three men to, 'Back off or I will shoot her!'

For about 10 metres, the whole group moved steadily back down the path, whilst Steven held the pistol, with his finger wrapped around the trigger, to Sandra's right temple. When the group reached the rougher part of the path, Sergeant Vanner stopped giving his running phone commentary to his boss Rupert! Realizing that one stumble by Steven would likely end up with him shooting Sandra, Vanner decided to try and at least stop Steven moving further, and even better, to draw his revolver away from Sandra's head. Half crouching so he was partially hidden by a gravestone, with his police revolver in his hands pointing at Steven, Sergeant Vanner shouted out.

'Stay where you are and drop your weapon!'

When Steven saw Sergeant Vanner pointing a firearm at him, he stopped where he was! He then, slowly, half crouched behind the wheelchair and Sandra; reached down into Sandra's bag with his left hand and pulled out the antique pistol, barrel first. Then, fully standing up and holding the pistol up, as if it were some trophy; he let it drop and in one smooth movement, caught it butt first on the way down, then he pivoted and angled the pistol so that the end of the barrel came to a gently rest against Sandra's left temple! Then with his revolver aiming roughly between Andy and Sergeant Vanner, and the pistol still resting against Sandra's head, he addressed the sergeant.

'Sorry about that, but I was touch distracted! But don't let that stop you, for you were almost interesting. Please do carry on!'

For a moment or two, there was a very silent . . . Silence!

Then the sergeant shouted out, 'Stay where you are sir, and drop your weapon!'

For another moment or two, there was still a very silent . . . Silence!

Then temporally ignoring the policeman, and turning to his right, Steven addressed Andy once again, 'Of course if I shoot you and your beloved here, together, then you'll be able to die together!' then turning to Sandra he added, 'Won't that be romantic, Sandra?'

When Sandra made no reply, Steven turned most of his attention back to Sergeant Vanner, and reassured him, 'Don't worry, after they are dead, we can do battle on our own!'

'The cemetery is surrounded sir!' Vanner said with conviction.

'And I suppose someone is creeping up behind me right now?' Steven retorted.

'No sir, but it may not be long before you are surrounded too. Lay your weapons down before anyone else gets harmed.'

At that moment, Sandra, who had trying to recover some of her focus and energy in spite of the pain of her wound, half said half shouted.

'Lizzie is Ok, she's up in the catacomb ... so there is no need for anyone to get shot or die!'

Pressing the antique pistol further onto Sandra's head Steven said, 'You know ... you really shouldn't tell tales out of school.' Then looking to Andy he said, 'Any way time is pressing ...'

Steven's next words remained unfinished as Andy quickly took three steps backwards; stood beside a gravestone and statue, ducked down behind it, only to reappear again, like a cheeky child playing "Peek-a-boo!" Having repeated his actions, the grinning Andy then asked Steven, 'What's a matter diddums, didn't your mummy change your nappy enough? Did sitting in all that, shit, affect your mind ... shit brains?'

It was an obvious attempt to rile Steven and Steven knew it! Never the less, whilst still holding the pistol to Sandra's head; and in an instant of uncontrollable pride and rage, Steven raised his revolver and savagely fired off two shots at his tormentor – both of them missing!

Re-emerging from behind a grave stone, and looking up at the damaged stone angel, Andy gave Steven another smile, and said, 'Which would explain why you're also such a shit shot … me ol' China! Not to mention a shit planner! My guess is that you planned to leave no witnesses, so you can carry on regardless! But we've arrived, and now that makes another three people! Even if you wound two of us with your remaining three bullets, you're gonna have to be one fucking good shot … pal!'

The look on Steven's face told Andy and the remainder of the group, that Andy's point had more than a slither of truth. To emphasize his point Andy added 'Even if you try to reload, at least one of us will overpower you, or will get away and lead the SWAT team straight to you!'

The fact that Andy's point was true was bad enough to Steven, the fact that the revolver had only two bullets left, made him feel worse – but not defeated!

Then Bell, edging from behind the nearest tree, stepped forwards.

'Better to retreat Steven, whilst there's time left and wait for the right time, you'll find a better way, unless it all ends here!'

Steven looked at Bell but said nothing.

'You could take me as a hostage – no use taking her!' Bell said gesturing to Sandra, 'She'll likely faint if you try to move her further, then what will you do, carry her over the wall on your shoulder? Take me, and I'll promise I won't try anything to thwart you. After that, you're on your own. Even though I have offered you all this, they won't risk my life if I'm a hostage, and if all fails then at least you'll have the pleasure of shooting me as a second prize!'

The two men stared at each other, whist no one moved for what seemed a long time – except to Andy. To Andy, time was rushing by. The fact that Sandra could be killed was enough to stop him rushing in of course! But the fact that she would be murdered with his own pistol, stopped him thinking, let alone moving! The only remaining hope for Andy, that Sandra may yet live, lay in the antique barrel of the gun that may yet kill her!

At that moment, Steven shifted his weight, to get a better purchase behind the wheel chair! Tilting the antique pistol with his movements, the barrel ended up – at an even steeper angle!

Sandra was by now, acutely aware, of what was happening! With a soaring hope, she could feel the gentle vibration of the shot, dawdling, down what seemed to be the mile long, barrel! Never the less, the lower the shot descended, the higher Sandra's hope began to soar! Then a millisecond later, Sandra felt sheer ecstasy, as the cool touch of the undersized shot, came to a gentle rest against her perspiring forehead!

But, taking Steven's warning to heart, Sandra decided not to be a "tell-tale" anymore! However the look between herself and Andy, told all!

Keeping a challenging eye on Steven; Andy moved away from the safety of the gravestone and kept on moving to the side, so that Steven was obliged to follow him with the revolver. It wasn't until Steven had both weapons and his arms almost akimbo, that Steven called a halt.

'If you take one more step I will shoot your girl, you, and everybody else I can.'

Andy looked into the eyes of Sandra, who smiled, that, that is exactly what he should do! Looking at Steven as calmly as he could Andy replied, 'Ok! We're both reasonable men … 'ow about if I meet you 'alf way?' with that he raised his right leg and left it … dangling in mid-air!

Andy's movement was enough to tip the balance of Steven's body; so that the mouth of the antique pistol gun began to creep away from Sandra's head! It was also enough for the undersized shot to fall out; land on to Sandra's wounded shoulder, roll down her chest, onto her leg and then tumble onto the leaf-covered, earth!

Everybody present had seen the shot fall, except Sandra who had felt it, and Steven – who had been pushed too far!

'No!' Steven stated, smiling at Andy whose leg was still, half raised, 'With me it's all, or everything!' then he fired the revolver at Andy!

As soon as Steven opened fire, the other three men moved. Andy tumbled forwards into a roll; Sergeant Vanner moved from behind a gravestone, Bell hit the deck and Sandra felt utterly deafened!

However, Andy had not been quick enough – he had been hit in the side by Steven's shot – and there followed a moment of chaos!

Seeing Andy shot, and in spite of her damaged shoulder, Sandra immediately grabbed both wheels of the wheelchair, and with a cry of pain, she propelled herself and the wheelchair downhill – leaving a clear line of shot for Sergeant Vanner!

As Vanner's shot nicked Steven's neck, Steven fired his very last bullet back at Vanner, hitting him in his thigh and making the Sergeant drop like a stone!

Steven was wounded, in neck, but only slightly and he was still very alert!

Then, above everything, there came the sound of a siren; then several sirens, and the sight of several blue flashing lights reflecting in the sky; as the police vans travelled at speed along the road on other side of the outer wall – the cavalry were about to charge!

But before hardly anyone could tell exactly what was happening, Steven had departed! Before every one could even half recover their wits, he had run back around the bend in the path and back towards the catacomb – with only David Bell dashing up the hill after him!

Meanwhile Sergeant Vanner spoke calmly into his phone, 'He may try to escape over the cemetery walls or by a side exit! Put a grid around, I repeat the subject is Steven Chadwick, he is wearing a grey top; dark trousers, age early to mid-forties, he is armed! I repeat, subject is armed and has shot a member of the public and myself!'

But Steven had far from escaped! After David Bell had followed him to the entrance of the catacomb, Bell halted!

In the relative, if temporary, area of calm outside of the catacomb, Bell and Steven faced each other, whilst each tried to calm their breath. Bell stood outside the entrance and Steven stood a metre or so inside. Holding both revolver and pistol in his hands, Steven spoke first.

'Stay where you are David, or I will shoot you.'

Bell looked to see that no one else was coming, and then he replied.

'I know, but you still have the option of coming out, before you are forced or carried out, you deserve better than that.'

'Deserve! Do you really think they, deserve my meek surrender? Or perhaps you believe that, the good people should always win, because they deserve to! So everybody can the live happily ever after?'

'I believe that you should surrender because it is the, good thing, to do.' replied Bell.

'Really! Don't tell me that you think that I can be persuaded, by the promise of some goody-goody … or perhaps, Godly reward!' Looking Bell up and down, Steven sneered, 'If that's all you've come to negotiate with, then you'd better leave before I do become merciful,' with that Steven aimed his (empty) revolver at Bell's heart, 'by putting you out of your, insanity!'

'No,' Bell replied, 'I bring you a far more convincing reason, for choosing to do good.'

'Really, do tell!'

'Because, it works!'

At that moment Steven, stopped smiling.

'Not for me, it hasn't!'

At that moment, two pinpoint spots of laser light, skewed, across the outer wall of the catacomb, and then settled on Bell right temple! Another two beams settled on the right side of his chest!

'Stay exactly where you are! Do not move your hands or arms, or we *will* open fire!'

The command came from the SWAT team leader, as he knelt behind a skewed gravestone, no more than twenty metres to the right of Bell, but blindsided to the presence of Steven. As Bell stayed exactly where he was, Steven grinned at him, and then moved another step further back into the catacomb.

Bell then asked Steven, 'If it hasn't worked for you, then at least let it work for Lizzie.'

From within the shadows of the catacomb, Steven quietly replied, 'Don't worry about little Lizzie, I never intended to kill her, and I am not going to, you have my promise!'

At that moment the SWAT team leader shouted, 'Drop to your knees and put your arms out in front of you!'

Bell dropped to his knees and put his arms out, whilst Steven moved further into the shadows of the catacomb's interior. Just before he completely disappeared, he stepped forwards again, and quietly pronounced.

'By the way! What I told you about not killing Lizzie, I told you under the complete protection of the Anonymity Code. Is that agreed?'

Bell glanced to where the SWAT team waited, and then he turned back to Steven. He then raised one eyebrow, and replied in an almost whisper, 'Agreed!'

As Bell agreed, Steven felt that he was somehow, back in control, he then nodded once, and moved to his left and out of sight!

It took the back-up teams a further seven minutes to surround the cemetery – and the SWAT team five, to surround the catacomb!

After checking that all was ready, Rupert made his announcement.

'Steven Chadwick, this is Chief Inspector Rupert. Come out, unarmed, with your arms raised, and no one will be harmed!'

From inside the far end of the catacomb, Steven replied straight away by shouting out, 'Oh really! How fucking nice of you Chief Inspector Rupert!' Then he shouted, 'I have a hostage! Her name is Elizabeth. If you enter, I shall put a bullet in her head, and blow her brains out!' then he added 'This may harm her!'

Steven then knelt down besides Elizabeth the corpse (circa 1824), and reassured her, 'Don't worry my dear, you won't feel a thing!' then leaning in even closer he whispered, 'Besides my dearest, if it came to it . . . if it was you or me . . . I'd . . .!'

Whatever Steven was about to say to the late departed Elizabeth, it was interrupted, by Rupert's reply on the loud hailer.

'If you do not follow our instructions, we will be forced to enter the building! I repeat, come out with your arms raised, you will not be harmed! There is no need for anyone to be harmed, Steven.'

Holding a handkerchief to his wound, Steven stood upright once again and shouted, 'What do you think this is Chief Inspector, a fucking Peace Picnic! Of course people will get hurt! I'm already hurt! And unless all of . . . you . . . come in here. . . unarmed . . . with your arms raised above your heads, then I can assure you that more people are going to be harmed!' Sitting down besides Elizabeth once more, he shouted out, 'You and your piglets have exactly three full minutes to comply, Chief Inspector!'

Outside the catacomb Rupert turned to Sandra, who was back in the wheel chair, and also behind two SWAT officers, and an attentive medic, 'Are you sure Lizzie was alive before you left?' Rupert asked.

Sandra simply replied, 'Yes, she was drugged, but breathing?'

Back inside the catacomb Steven continued his conversation with Elizabeth (circa 1824). Sitting down beside her, and putting his arm around her shoulders, he noticed her crucifix, then he smiled and sat back, 'So they tried to fool you too, did they? But as you probably can't appreciate by now, my dear Elizabeth, death is no big deal at all. And I'm afraid that all their promises, about an afterlife, well … it was just a load of … leech-pooh really!'

Then looking about the catacomb Steven grew thoughtful then said, 'Mind you at least you will have been spared from . . .!'

At that moment the mega-phone interrupted Steven once again, as the police negotiator's tannoyed voice stated, 'Steven this Detective Sergeant Peter Macready speaking. Is Lizzie all right? We can end thi . . .!'

Steven, half lifted himself up, and shouted out! 'Do you fucking well mind . . . Macready? We are trying to have a serious conversation in here!'

After waiting a few seconds, Steven sat back down and turned back to Elizabeth then continued, 'Now where in the hell were. . .? Oh yes . . . leech-pooh!' Then shrugging his shoulders Steven continued, 'Of course you wouldn't have heard in here, but now days, science has uncovered just about all of the lies! In fact, many theorize that there isn't even a God! Or, if there was, then he died trying to make all of his love, ever-expanding, in the Big Bang!'

For a second or two Steven looked into the mid distance, and then coming out of his reminiscence, he continued, 'You see, the Big Bang was when an immense amount of matter, was held in an very, very tiny place, then instantly released. This in turn created life, which just sort of fell into place. Though in fact it was more pulled into place, by gravity . . . so I guess it sort of pull/fell into place. Though in fact they say, that the universe will eventually stop expanding and end up cold ... and unmoving!' At that point Steven frowned slightly, then continued.

'My point being is of course, as I expect you've already guessed my Dear, is that, if matter can turn into thought. For clearly we are thinking beings made of matter from the Big Bang, then is it also true, that an immense amount of thought, can create matter? Say, if all of our accumulated thinking, say a billion years' worth of knowledge, about Life, the universe and everything; were to be held in very tiny place; such as a tiny computer, then suddenly released at a convenient time and place; would we be able to then, re-boot the universe, Life and start everything again?'

Then looking down at Elizabeth's crucifix; and without even a hint of sarcasm, in his face, eyes or upon his lips, he added, 'Or should I say ... would God . . . do it all again?

Leaning back against the coolness of catacomb wall, Steven looked up at the surrounding tombs and said, 'I wonder, if God really did blow himself up, in an act of ever expanding love, would that make him the original and only truly . . . loving . . . suicide bomber?'

Shrugging his shoulders and kissing Elizabeth on her head, Steven smiled, questioningly. At that moment the conversation between Steven and Elizabeth was again interrupted, by the arrival of a remotely controlled, tractorized CCTV camera called 'Dog!'

As 'Dog!' entered the catacomb, it turned its head towards the unconscious form of Lizzie, hanging over the barrier, then it stopped.

'Hello!' Steven said, 'Oh dear! Have you lost your owner, have you been abandoned? If so, we know exactly how you feel!'

Dog then swivelled it "eyes," so that its operator and Rupert could focus more clearly. As Rupert watched the screen, he noticed that a young woman, who he presumed to be Lizzie, was indeed hung in a forwards position over the nearby barrier rail, as Sandra had previously informed him. Then the dog's operator moved the dog to the right and adjusted its zoom lens; so the he and Rupert could fully appreciate the clear and true situation, at the far end of the catacomb!

'Jesus H Christ!' Rupert exclaimed, 'He's cuddling a . . . *corpse*!'

'It's Elizabeth!' Sandra informed Rupert, 'He took her out of her coffin and swapped her for the real Elizabeth . . . I mean Lizzie! Lizzie was still hanging over the barrier when I saw her last. Elizabeth is the corpse . . . unless he's gone and got another one out!'

The 'Dog' turned its head to the right, then back again.

Turning to Sandra again, Rupert said, 'I can't see any army-type revolver, but he is holding your antique pistol! Are you sure it's not loaded?'

'I'm sure!' Sandra replied.

Crouching, a metre behind Sandra, Bell said nothing.

Having seen and heard more than enough, Rupert turned to the SWAT team leader crouching besides him. Rupert then nodded and said, 'Whenever you're ready?'

Back in the catacomb Steven had brought up the music app' up on his I-Pad, then he pressed play, for his best loved piece of music, the final chorus from "Bach's Mathew Passion!"

At that moment, a flash-bang-grenade, accompanied by a tear gas canister, clattered in though the catacomb's entrance, and exploded in a cacophony of noise and tear gas! If the duel explosions were supposed to distract and disorientate Steven, they failed miserably, for Steven was once again, in a complete and utter world of his own!

Moreover, believe it or not (dearest reader), in Steven's world of "milk and honey" there is no violence! Indeed as he wandered amongst his people (for he felt as essential to them as they were to he). Moreover, the idea of violence seemed so stupid, it was virtually unthinkable! On a flower-drenched hillside, a lion plays a (no biting or clawing) game of "catch me if you can," with some highly excited prancing lambs as they weave to and fro amongst groups of picnickers! Everyone is highly intelligent and good looking, and have been genetically programmed to beget no more than one child in a lifetime (and to profusely blush, grin and fart whenever they tell a lie!).

Then, on the very borders of his inner paradise, there appeared a … *smudge*! As Steven watched it, the smudge became both a vision and feeling – a sort of vision made of feelings. The vision, was one of an antique flint-lock-pistol; the feeling, was that the pistol was somehow pressing into his temple, and that all he had to do to remain here forever, was pull the trigger!

Only then, as the tear gas vapours spread towards him, did Steven gently lay Elizabeth's corpse aside; stand up, and take three steps forwards and halt, beneath the shaft of moonlight shining down on the far end catacomb floor. Looking down at the flintlock pistol, Steven then pulled the cock back into its 'fire' position! At which point; the SWAT team crashed through the doors, stopped and simultaneously swivelled to face both ends of the catacomb.

As the four laser points of lights flittered upon his chest, Steven swung the pistol in an elegant arc, until the pistol's mouth kissed his right temple, and with his eyes streaming with tears; that may have come from the tear gas, or from the moving ending of "The Passion" or from a place far … far … away … Steven concluded,

'Fuck this for a playtime … I'm going home!'

At which point, Steven gave a final grin and pulled the trigger; which released the hammer, which hit the firing plate with a soft and final … *"Thunk!"*

Final chapter

WHEN (AND BEYOND)

When you can reach above your moral vertigo, and fill your opening palm with a whole brave new, honest, world, which you alone can save or harm. Then say, 'This is my world because only I have the power to rule!' Then yours will be the hand that takes your once crumbling world, from the trembling grasp, of a once powerful fool!

ONE YEAR LATER

Coffee and shortcake

As Lizzie chooses to walk through the 623 year old, stone arched walkway, instead of across the town's rain swept Main square; she twiddles the round piece of antique pistol-shot, which hangs from the end of her necklace. The piece of shot was a gift from Sandra, when Sandra and Andy left, to live in America. As she twiddles away, Lizzie is hoping that the ancient walkway will come out in the vicinity of an "Olden style" teashop.

In the town's 266-year-old courthouse, half a mile from the arched walkway, the jury members are shuffling their way along the narrow corridor, which leads into the number 2 court. Two court guards are escorting the defendant (a career criminal called Arnold Preedy) up the sadly worn stone steps, leading from the holding cells, to the courts. Arnold is desperately hoping for a not guilty verdict (Derrr!) . . . or at least a light prison sentence!

Whilst Lizzie is listening to her footsteps echoing off the moss speckled, stone walls of the ancient walkway, a breeze carrying the aroma of freshly baked coffee, entices, her to think of freshly baked scones, jam and double cream!

In the well of number 2 court, a solicitor is quickly finishing the remainder of a muesli bar, before the judge returns to the bench.

Passing beneath the now, permanently raised and rusted, portcullis of the ancient walkway, Lizzie enters into an equally ancient cobble-stoned square. Brief hints, of freshly baked, butter shortcake mingle with the smell of roasted coffee, and Lizzie is beginning to change her mind about the scones.

In the dock, Preedy, the defendant chooses to stand, whilst waiting for the judge to arrive, but one of the escorts indicates for him to sit. The defendant continues to stand but his legs begin to shake, so he sits.

Having found her "Olden style" tea shop, Lizzie sits at one of the dark oak tables inside of the 218 year old coffee house. Whilst trying to choose from the menu, she notices how the re-appearing sunlight, glistens off the cut glass, sugar bowl, on the table besides the window. Lizzie chooses to move to the window table, so as get a clear yet casual view of the other tourists meandering past, in, and out of a bookshop selling new and second hand books.

In number 2 court, the jury are asked if they have reached a verdict.

In the coffee house, a waitress comes to the table and asks Lizzie, 'Is you ready to choose, my Dear?'

Lizzie spends the next three quarter of an hour; slowly eating two slices of slightly over sweet, yet, "Oh so, scrumptiously humbling," real butter short cake, in between tentative sips of dark, bitter, coffee, which the waitress regularly refreshes, without further charge.

In a room below the courts, the now convicted Arnold, talks earnestly with his defence counsel, about the chances of an appeal, against the length of the 3 year and 6 month prison sentence. The counsel points out, that without fresh evidence; such an appeal is so unlikely to succeed, that it would receive no funding through legal aid. Arnold then complains about there only being justice for the rich; whilst his counsel listens sympathetically.

Leaving the coffee house (with three slices of shortcake, nestling in a monogrammed paper bag) Lizzie enters the second hand bookshop.

In the underground garage of the courthouse, two sealed bags, containing Arnold Preedy's personal possessions, are loaded into a purring, white, prison van.

After leaving the bookshop, Lizzie hurries along the main street, as she heads towards the railway station, she is clutching a long-wanted, second hand book (a romance). Alongside the book, is the monogrammed paper bag, containing the three slices of short cake, which she hopes will last her for the two hour journey home!

As Lizzie steps out from a kerb dissecting the pavement, a white prison van pulls to a stop, about three metres away. The van driver lifts his hand, smiles and waves Lizzie on. Lizzie smiles back and raises her hand in return, crosses to the other side, and then hurries on towards the railway station.

On the train, she gets comfortable whilst waiting for the journey to begin. As she waits, she watches the returning rain trickle down the carriage window.

Fifty minutes later, as the rain-streaked-train dutifully speeds Lizzie safely homewards, she is half way through, the third chapter, of the book, whilst dipping into the monogrammed paper bag, for the third, but final, slice of shortcake!

And there, dear reader, is where we finally leave Lizzie! What is more, if she knew, that we were leaving her – then, Lizzie being Lizzie would depart with much regret – as I do, having to leave her! But, then again, dear reader, is it so wrong, not to be willing, to resist, such a … slightly over sweet, yet "Oh so, scrumptiously humbling …"

Trisha and the trashed tooth!

The mighty rock stands there, in the warm Aegean Sea, like some ancient, dark monolith, beyond decay, defiant of all that the wind, sea and nature could throw at it. The rock stands there, like a discarded tooth, spat out in parting disgust, by some long departed, but once feared ancient God, as he left this evolving world!

"Phewt! Ouch! Owwwww! Me tooth! Look God-mum, I lost me tooth!"

"There, there, my God son, don't you worry; let it stay there as a reminder to these ungrateful mortals – that you are beyond their fleeting vision! Let them stare in wonderment at the majesty of your discarded anger, we are beyond them now!"

As Trisha sits on the shore, her gaze momentary shifts, from the dark monolith and towards her two children, Nina and Harold, playing "Catch me if you can" with the surf, as it rhythmically strokes the sun-warmed sands.

The three of them, Trisha (who has been drug free for a whole year) Nina and Harold, are taking a long-weekend, trial-bonding, mini-holiday, on their own, but subject to the requirements of the children's welfare officer, and the agreement of their foster parents.

For a moment, Trisha's thoughts flow and ebb, between her own childhood memories of beach adventures, and her present need for parental vigilance. However, slowly her attention drifts back to the day that she nearly drowned!

It was a warm day, and it had been the first time Trisha had worn her father's snorkel and goggles. Her father, Larne, lay dozing on the beach, no more than 10 metres from the clear calm sea. Trisha knew in her mind, not to venture out more than the 100 or so meters beyond her swimming capabilities. The mind however, like the sea, also has deceptive under tides, as well as tantalizing treasures; like the fabulous arrays of fish that beckoned to the young Trisha's bedazzled vision!

For some time Trisha floated face down, seaweed like, on the sea surface. However, it was only when she eventually lifted her head that she suddenly realized – how far she had drifted from the shore! Now the once near beach, with its sprinkling of friendly holiday makers, had been replaced, by a thin, distant, and aloof line of warning!

At first, Trisha behaved with admirably sense, as she slowly and calmly front crawled her way back towards the shore. It was however, only when she paused, for breath, and to look up again, that she realized that she was now even further away from the shore – than when she first started!

As tentacles of panic wrapped themselves around her heart, the young Trisha felt as if she were being relentlessly, pulled down into uncaring depths, below her fast-failing legs! She began to desperately, shout out, but soon realized; that even if the people on the shore could understand her, they could not hear her! As she trod water, she couldn't even tell which part of the beach her father must be still sun-bathing!

Then as all of her tiring limbs, began to fail, Trisha suddenly thought, "This is it! This is where I'm going to die, right here, off the coast of some foreign land!"

As the young Trisha tried to focus through her salt and tear-stung eyes, each of her last "precious moments" appeared as if it were being fast-forwarded, by some disinterested, onlooker! Then, with a brief but angry, stab, from Trisha's young pride, the moments seemed to . . . slow . . . and then pause!

Without any conscious decision, the young Trisha found herself focusing on a nearby seagull, who was casually paddling on top of the water, no more than three metres from her face. For a few seconds more, the sea gull took a wary look at Trisha, and then it flapped its wings, and took off towards the shore.

It was then, that the indifference of everything, began to ebb into the young Trisha's being; until she just lay on her back, and looking up into the sky, she began to casually kick, her way towards the shore – come what may!

Whether her fears had stretched the distance to the shore, or her calmness had shortened it, Trisha never found out. Yet, in what seemed to her, to be no time at all, she found herself in no more than a metre of water!

When she reached her father, Trisha flopped down and told him all about her ordeal, and then apologized for losing his snorkel and goggles, "Out there somewhere!" but somehow her father didn't seem too concerned about their loss!

Suddenly, a piercing scream, from a seagull, overhead, jerks Trisha's thoughts back from the past! When she re-focuses on her two children, she sees . . . that all was well, and they are building a sand castle.

Two hours later, and now, dressed against the cool of the early evening, all three; Trisha, Nina and Harold, watch their sand castle dissolve in the encroaching tide, like some ever returning shared hope, being overwhelmed by an ever returning, shared fear!

Five minutes later, Trisha and her two children are running, line abreast, hand in hand, down, up and over the dune-hilled sands, as all three feel a shared pride, in their day's achievements!

One hour later, the shore itself disappears under the moonlit Aegean Sea; out from which a mighty rock stands, like some ancient dark monolith; beyond decay, defiant of all that the wind, the sea, nature and even history, could throw at it!

George

As we catch up to George, so to speak, he is enjoying a day out at the local park with Mary and Fern. Young Toby had to stay indoors, with Aunty Carol, because of his asthma. Unfortunately, although his attacks are less frequent, they are becoming more severe – that is Toby's asthma attacks, not his father's attacks on women!

In the time since attending the residential and co-related counselling, George has managed to build, a wall, around his urges. He contains his urge to rape or assault, behind a series of emotional "blocks" such as; "Wouldn't or would marry – wouldn't rape," "Good news – bad news," "What then . . . etc. . . . etc.?" and a variety of distraction techniques, such as "Surprises." All these blocks, and more are cemented, with his newly acquired, empathy, for any potential victim, whether they are real or imaginary! As far as his offending is concerned, the good news; is that the lower the stature of rape becomes, the higher, respectively, the "blocks," containing those urges become! The bad news is that he has re-offended!

George keeps in regular touch with the helpline and is not afraid or complacent about contacting them, particularly when his urges become too disturbing. However, he does not always call Crime Frontiers. Mostly he manages his urges, but there are occasions when he doesn't. In the last year, he has committed two attempted indecent assaults and one actual one! On two occasions, George went to grab at the woman, but stopped at the last moment, and then walked away! The last assault was when he put his hand up the woman's dress, before running away.

George was almost caught, the last time; he only managed to escape arrest, because the woman he assaulted, was too drunk to identify him from inside the back of the searching police car.

Relatively speaking, one could say that George has vastly improved his control – though the last woman he attacked would not necessarily agree with that.

As it happens, if you, dear reader, were to go to the homes of all the people George has, directly or indirectly victimized, and ask them what they thought of George, their answers would vary! Furthermore, if you were to then ask them; if it were better that he should continue with his crimes until he was caught and punished; or give up his crimes – yet go unpunished. Well, I'll leave it to you to imagine, as to what they might say!

Whether George, completely stops, or further reduces, or escalates his offending, is not part of this book. But for now, we will leave him in the park, with Mary and Fern, and the various people passing by. For the vast majority of time, George enjoys his freedom to walk in such places . . . unmolested, by his urges!

Why, who knows, if George returns to the park some time, one of the people he passes, might well be someone you know, or he or she may even be your good self . . . dearest reader!

Sandra and Andy

After the drama of England, Sandra decided to return to America. She was warmly welcomed by Uncle, Aunt Betsy and of course Debby! However, what pleased Sandra even more was the welcome all three of her loved ones gave to Andy!

Sandra and Andy have not married . . .yet! However, there is also another reason for Sandra's and Andy coming to the USA. They are part of a small team, aiming to open an American version of the Crime Frontiers advice line. The American version of the Anonymity Code, is to be put forwards under the, possible. protection of the statute allowing freedom of speech. The American version will not contain any adaption; by which any named potential victims will be informed of any threat to their life or safety!

However, as we catch up to them, Sandra is once again about to visit her father in prison! Since Sandra last visited her father in the high security lifer's prison in Utah, the season and place have changed. It is now high summer along the swamp-ridden banks of the Mississippi; and there is no mist to wipe away from the glass partitions in the prison visiting booths, a mile or so away!

Shortly after Steven was sentenced, to life in prison in England, Sandra told Andy all about her own abuse at the hands of her father – and about her, big lie, to her father. Andy did not condone or criticise Sandra for telling her father the lie; that she killed her mother. As far as Andy was concerned, in similar circumstances, he might have told the same lie, if he had thought of it!

Now both of them sit quietly, in their car, parked near a wooden bridge that spans the small river tributary. Over the other side of the bridge, and about one hundred and fifty metres along the dusty road, a group of visitors waits for the prison bus to arrive, which will take them directly to the visiting centre.

All around, the hot clammy air seems to slow life to a laboured crawl. In the slow moving, insect infested waters below, a toad relentlessly croaks its rhythmic warning to any other male toad that might happen to be around.

Amid the nervous tension in the car, Andy suddenly turns to Sandra and asks, 'You never did tell me. If Steven 'adn't of used Lizzie as a shield, inside the catacomb, would you 'ave shot 'im?'

Sandra turns, smiles, then replies, 'As sure as you would have … my sunshine!'

Andy then nods his confirmation in reply.

'But then ...' Sandra teased, whilst stroking Andy's face, 'I wouldn't have had my knight in shining armour to rescue me – even if he did do it by hiding behind gravestones!'

Andy gives her a challenging look, then a smile, and replies, 'Well … it worked didn't it?'

'It certainly did!' Sandra agrees, and then she kisses him on his cheek.

Andy kisses her in return, and then asks, 'You sure you don't want me to come with you – at least as far as the prison main gate?'

'No! This is one I'll do completely on my own,' Sandra replies, giving Andy another kiss. Then looking towards the waiting group of visitors, she opens the car door and steps out.

As he watches Sandra walk over the bridge and along the road, Andy switches the radio on, and is pleased to hear that they are playing classic blues numbers.

Five minutes later Sandra suddenly returns to the car, as the bus, leaving a dusty trail in its wake, drives away from the stop and up towards the prison!

As she gets in, Andy looks questioningly at Sandra, but says nothing.

Then Sandra looks at Andy, half smiles and says, 'I guess the secret will keep … for a year or so longer!' Then with a mischievous smile, she puts on and buckles up her safety belt.

Two minutes later Sandra and Andy drive off, with the sounds of the original version of Nina Simone's "Feeling good" filling the humid Mississippi air.

As the sounds of the car and the radio fade into the distance, the toad continues its rhythmic threats, oblivious to all about … it is even oblivious to the tiny ripples of water, that the approaching young crocodile makes … as it glides towards its prey. Then, with time-honoured and even prehistoric tradition, the crocodile snaps its jaws – *shut*!

David Bell

After his admission about, bending, the Anonymity Code, by texting

Steven, Bell finally, resigned from Crime Frontiers. After tying up loose ends, Bell eventually left England all together.

One of the loose ends was visiting Steven, at the high security lifer's wing of Parkhurst Prison. Steven had eventually been found guilty of Mary's murder; the kidnap of Dottie, the shooting of Sandra, Sergeant Vanner and Andy, and various related crimes such as firearms offences and animal cruelty. As he expected, the police could not prove he was the Body Part Murderer; and as no one from Crime Frontiers told them about his admission to being the killer, it being told under the protection of the Anonymity Code, the case remains open.

It is a fine day in Southern France, and the mid-morning sun shines with a promise of a very hot afternoon. David Bell sits in a restaurant, he is about to answer a question posed on the Crime Frontiers web site. Although he has officially resigned from Crime Frontiers, he still visits the web site on occasions. After reading a few of the emails, he came across one asking:

"What happened to the Nice Day bill?"

Bell's original purpose in the, Nice Day bill, was to create a new official daylong holiday! The day was to be called the "Nice-Day-day" and the holiday was in order to "Actively celebrate being nice to anyone who happened to be around!" The more controversial second part of the Nice-Day-day bill was, the proposal to introduce a legal statute that would: "Double the normal sentence or tariff, for any one committing, or having been found later to have committed a crime, during Nice Day-day!" Although the bill drew a lot of public support at the time, it was however eventually, rejected, by the European court of Human Rights.

After sending his reply to the website, Bell sits back and ponders the towering pinnacles of the cathedral, which in turn looks majestically over the tourist populated square below. Then his attention is, drawn, once again, to the glass fronted display in front of the restaurant, with its array of succulent cakes. As he sits and ponders, Bell has an over whelming feeling to rest; he wants to rest, and be done with crime!

Looking at the towers once more, Bell's attention glides downwards, until it settles upon the main entrance of the cathedral. On the marbled terrace, a group of parishioners flutter around a grateful priest. The priest is collecting their fears, hopes and compliments, so that he can re-spin them into silken promises of an after-life; to snare the dangling remains of their present one!

Although Bell appreciates the architecture of the cathedral, he loathes the way that all religions use their lies, "To kidnap our natural-pride in achieving good, and then have the insolence to demand a "rescuers" reward for its guilt-smeared return!" For a second or two, David Bell wonders about how such an esteemed set of lies, could be uncovered.

Suddenly David Bell sighs … as wants to do nothing more than … to merely enjoy watching this particular performance of life, as it criss-crosses its ways upon this theatre of life! Then, with a final sigh and a, peculiar smile, David Bell finally switches his mobile phone … *off*!

THE END.

Other works by the author:

Crimes 'n' rhymes:

A collection of light hearted and thought provoking poems; which also includes some of the themes used in 'Crime Frontiers'

……………………….

<u>The Crime Frontier's petition</u>

Crimefrontiers.com

A petition dedicated to creating; a legally protected, anonymous to call, independent advice line, for anyone who is thinking of committing a crime.

If you (or a family member/friend, neighbour etc.) have a problem with your/their current moral outlook, then who are you going to call for real-time, independent, trusted advice?

In so many respects, the availability such a crime-advice-line for potential criminals are, woefully disproportional, particularly when compared to tackling other potential personal disasters; such as our health, house, education or even our car.

In the same respects, if a nation is to refuse to allow such a confidential crime-line to its potential offenders (and by proxy to all intended victims), then it will be like; refusing a condemned criminal a last wish *before* he or she has irrevocably committed themselves (and the nation) to the "pervasive-cost of such post-crime parcels of purgatory!"

For any such service to succeed, all crime-line conversations must have a legally protected confidentiality. Any adviser/negotiator taking part in any advice session, must be legally protected; against any criminal or civil prosecution for refusing to disclose any details; about the caller or the crime, to any outside body, including the police or any past or intended victims of the crime.

However, such a service cannot be created or evolve without a government authorized, but independently run, properly organized body, that has well trained advisers and staff. To achieve all that, will take time and effort from your government's legislative body and you.

If you wish to let your government know how *you* feel Please sign our petition.

@ Crimefrontiers.com

Thank you for your time and effort so far!

Our aim is to get more than one million signatures

……………………………………………

7106628R00184

Printed in Great Britain
by Amazon.co.uk, Ltd.,
Marston Gate.